WHAT LIES INSIDE

BLOOD BOUND SERIES BOOK ONE

J.L. MYERS

A NEW ADULT PARANORMAL ROMANCE

MORE BOOKS BY J.L. MYERS

THE BLOOD BOUND SERIES

(New Adult Paranormal Romance)

What Lies Inside

Made By Design

Web Of Lies

Born To Die

~

OTHER BOOKS

Nerve Damage

(A Chilling Psychological Thriller)

~

FALLEN ANGEL SERIES

Ashes of Eden

Dawn of Reckoning

Breaking Lucifer

Cold-Blooded Fate

Falling Stars

BECOME A VIP AND GET A FREE BOOK!

J.L. Myers is giving away a free short prequel to the Blood Bound Series.
Use this link to get the your free copy.

http://bit.ly/JLFreePrequel

CHAPTER 1

My mind screamed for me to move. To fight the monster who trapped me with its arms. But my body remained paralyzed, a prisoner of flesh and bone. It wasn't fear. I knew that much. Inside I was striking out with limbs, nails, and teeth. But any connection to actual movement was lost. My whole body felt like it was filled with cement.

Parted lips closed in on my neck. My eyes darted around, desperate to find a way out of this. Darkness stretched beyond the waning light of a naked bulb. There was a single door, then nothing but damp stone and shadow. The stink of death and decay hung thick in the air. Horror seeped through my veins.

There was nothing I could do. No way to stop this. No way to save my life.

The sound of labored breath rasped. Not my own. Not this monster's. In the shadows it was impossible to see where it came from. Was someone watching? Fear snaked through my soul. The fear wasn't for my own life, not really. I was afraid for someone else. But who?

Any thoughts vanished as fangs punctured my flesh. A gasp escaped my lips.

Flames bloomed from the punctures, swarming across my skin. The monster clutched my body tighter and tighter with every sickening gulp.

As the flames began to dull, my internal screams and my drive to fight faded. Without the current of blood filling my veins, violent shivers took hold of my entire body.

My body was giving up.

With shallow contractions, my heart slowed. My mind wavered as my body began to fail. The crushing pain of imminent death faded. As my eyes fluttered shut, a memory of the boy I loved floated across the backs of my eyelids. I saw his dejected expression. I felt the moment he had crushed me against his body, covering my lips with his. Then I heard the words he had spoken for the very first time. "Amelia, I love you."

An icy tear escaped my eye. Now he would never know the truth. Never know that my feelings for him were still as irrefutable and irrevocable as ever. Never know that I would give anything just to be in his arms and feel the warmth of his kiss one last time. The realization was more agonizing than knowing my fate now, more agonizing than any lingering pain.

I love you too. The memory faded, dissipating like a cloud of smoke.

The room began to blur and spin. Unable to blink, my eyes stared up at the dusty light bulb. Blood loss pressed in on me. I was so deathly cold. The edge of my vision turned black, light being eaten away by a stain like blotted ink. Then empty darkness took hold.

This is it. I'm dying.

∼

MY HEAD ROCKED UPRIGHT, and my neck cried out in pain. Sweat beaded down my face and stuck my hair to the back of my neck. Panic tightened my chest, making it difficult to breathe. Had I been asleep?

I blinked against the glare of my laptop. I was in my bedroom, sitting in the dark at my desk. The website tour dates for my favorite band, Three Days Grace, were still coloring the screen. Dreaming? For the life of me, I couldn't remember. Now a new sensation was unfurling in my stomach, an unyielding hunger that tugged at me from the inside.

The time on the laptop screen was 9:33PM. I ate dinner two hours ago; I shouldn't be hungry. Yet I couldn't ignore the pain, the yearning that grew stronger by the second.

Pulling away from my desk, I tiptoed from my bedroom down the stairs and along the blacked-out hallway. Mom and Uncle Caius were sitting on the couch in the dark living room. The glow of the TV cast blue light across their serious faces. I snuck past the doorway just in time to hear…

Authorities are stumped over what appears to be the third vicious animal attack this month, leaving the most recent victim—a young man—dead, his body almost entirely drained of blood…

The television announcement faded as I entered the kitchen. The unlit space was just as it had been left, with the marble countertops spotlessly clean—no doubt thanks to Mom. I rummaged through the pantry, ripping into boxes of cookies, cake mix, and anything I deemed even remotely edible, which included a large bite of a raw onion. Still, nothing sated my wrenching hunger. In fact, everything I had unthinkingly shoved into my mouth, even the choc-covered mint slice cookies that were usually my favorites, seemed as tasteless as cardboard. Still, I couldn't ignore the grinding in my gut, the need to feed, so I backtracked to the fridge. The sight of vegetables, juice, milk, and cheese swelled a creeping nausea inside. Then I noticed a tray of raw and bloody steaks.

Saliva flooded my mouth as sharp pain prickled my gums. Entranced, I snatched the tray from the glass shelf and tore back the plastic film. The meat was cold and squishy in my hand, but that didn't put me off. I ripped into the cold flesh and my tongue cheered at the taste. It was better than anything I'd ever eaten, even better than chocolate. Its sweet, metallic flavor was hypnotizing. The world around me began to fade. I tore off another chunk as a moving shadow caught my eye.

"Amelia Athobry-Lamont," my mom's voice cut through the haze like an arrow. She was the only one who ever used my full name, and only when I was in deep trouble. It was a mash-up of hers and my dead father's last names. The lights beamed on. "What in the world are you doing?"

My limbs retracted, muscles tightening and shoulders hunching. The hunger that had come on so quickly and forcefully, dissipated. Startled confusion spun through my mind. The pounding of my heart was so fast, so persistent. I glanced down at the shredded steak hanging limply in my hands. What the hell *was* I doing?

"Amelia." Uncle Caius's strong voice approached from behind. His hand found my shoulder, forcing me to turn.

My eyes darted down to my feet, cocooned within my purple-laced black Vans. I couldn't look at him, the man who was so close to being the father I'd never had. He'd think I was crazy.

Uncle Caius lifted my chin, tilting my face upward as Mom stepped behind him. The age lines of his face deepened with worry.

4

Mom gasped and her pale complexion whitened. "You said this wouldn't happen," she directed at my uncle with a surprising tone drenched in accusation.

Uncle Caius shook his head, eyes saddened. "You knew there was a chance. Even after *all* we did." He released my chin and turned to Mom, his tone becoming sharp. "We should have told them sooner, prepared them for this."

Prepared? Wouldn't happen? Tremors caused my clenched hands to shake. "Should have told us what?"

"No, no, no!" Mom spun on the spot and paced toward the kitchen table, violently shaking her head. "It's their birthday in a week. I will not ruin their lives now. This *can* wait."

She was talking about my brother Dorian and me. She had to be. It was our 16th birthday in just over a week. But what could be so damning that it would ruin our lives?

Uncle Caius reached out and pried the bloody steak from my clenched fingers, then dropped it into the deep, round sink. He lifted his hand as if to ruffle his salt and pepper hair before lowering it, seeming to remember that it was sticky with animal blood. "Lamayli," he exhaled, pointedly looking at Mom. "This will not ruin their lives, and you know it cannot wait. It is far too dangerous."

Dangerous? My head swam and my mind screamed for me to run, to avoid whatever they were about to reveal. Would they tell me I was crazy? Say that this wasn't the first incident? Explain in calm tones that I was losing my rational mind? I fought the need to bolt. My voice escaped in a choke. "T-tell me."

Mom turned on her toes, somehow regaining her natural grace. Her head stopped shaking and tears were now falling from her electric-blue eyes. "Alright," she breathed. The word was so soft I barely heard it. Her eyes rose to my uncle. "Go get Dorian. If we're doing this, I only want to do it once."

Uncle Caius left with a nod, his quiet footsteps remaining audible as he went to retrieve my brother. My wide eyes turned on Mom, needing answers and unable to wait, but she wouldn't look at me. Instead, she clutched the edge of the table and kept her eyes downcast.

Moments later Uncle Caius re-emerged. Dorian tailed behind with chocolate colored bed head and bloodshot eyes, probably from online prowling for tail in the dark. Mom lowered herself into the seat heading the table and motioned for us all to follow. Dorian raised a questioning eyebrow at me. Guilt-ridden, I shrugged, not having any of the answers he needed just as much as I did. Blood roared through my ears as I glanced at Mom. She'd begun drumming her French-tipped nails against the hardwood of the dining table.

"So, what's with the family meeting?" Dorian questioned, curious but clearly unconcerned.

Uncle Caius cleared his throat. "I can tell them, Lamayli."

Mom's face shot up, lightning fast, causing me to jump. "No! Please. Let me. I want them to hear it from me."

Our uncle nodded and Mom sucked in a ragged breath. "I didn't want to tell you this way," she said, glancing from Dorian to me. "But Caius is right. After what we've witnessed tonight, it is clear I cannot shelter this from either of you any longer." Mom laid her head in her hands, rubbing slow circles over her temples.

"Have we done something wrong?" Dorian questioned.

I knew the answer would be no, of course we hadn't. But I had. I'd done something sick, something crazy. Perhaps she thought Dorian would too. But why?

"No," Mom replied. She lifted her head and looked at us through glazed eyes. "None of this is either of your faults. I need you both to remember that." Her words died then with a spluttering sob.

"Your mother and I never wanted to hurt either of you," Uncle Caius spoke for her. He placed a cold hand over mine. "We thought we could stave off the transformation, possibly forever. However, we can see that it has already begun in you, Amelia. It is only a matter of time before Dorian develops the thirst, too."

Dorian voiced the question I was too terrified to ask. "The thirst?"

"Yes, sweetheart." Mom lifted bloodshot eyes to my brother. "Your sister's body is developing a need for blood, blood that must be consumed. Soon yours will, too."

I felt my stomach turn at the word *consumed*, remembering the taste of the bloody steak. In the same instant, my mouth watered and a familiar sensation danced across my gums. Praying for a rational explanation, I went to talk, to ask if what we had was some form of rare blood disorder.

But my words choked back when Dorian's eyes widened in a look of sheer horror. He shot to his feet. "What the hell!"

Uncle Caius's hand tightened over mine. "Sit down, Dorian. Amelia would never harm you."

Harm him? The words caused my mind to boggle.

"But her teeth!" Dorian pointed while bouncing on the balls of his feet. I'd never even seen him look worried before, but right now he looked seriously scared, ready to bolt.

With all eyes on me, I fearfully raised a hand to my mouth. My fingers grazed over sharpened canines that protruded from my gums.

Oh my god, I was a freak! Hyperventilating, I freed my other hand from Caius's grip and jumped to my feet, kicking back my chair. Only vampires had fangs—and they weren't freaking real. "What's wrong with me?"

Dorian froze, still as a statue, his terrified eyes locked on me. Mom spluttered in desolation.

Yet Uncle Caius remained calm. He rose from his seat, turning slowly to face me. "Amelia, sit back down. We will explain everything."

I shook my head, taking a step back. "No. Tell me now!"

Mom wiped away her tears and sniffed. "You're both…" She paused, looking like she might be physically sick. "We're…"

"Vampires," Uncle Caius spoke gently. "We are all vampires."

Dorian let out a nervous laugh. "You're joking, right? This is a pre-birthday prank. And those," he said, pointing at my fangs, "are fake. Good one, you seriously had me going for a second there."

I stared across the table with vacant eyes. "This can't be. It's...impossible."

"C'mon Amelia," Dorian went on, the confidence in his voice fading. "The charade is up."

Tears stung my eyes as anger began to boil inside of me. "This isn't a charade!" The callousness in my hissed words startled us both.

Dorian's wavering smile finally vanished, replaced by an expression of total fear.

The way he, Mom, and Uncle Caius were staring enraged me further. Watching them I knew the truth; folklore and pop culture were right. Vampires did exist. And I was one of them. I was a monster. In blinding fury I launched myself across the kitchen and onto the counter, crouching like a wild animal. I ripped the bloody steak from the sink and tore into it with my fangs. "See!" I screamed, raising the shredded meat above my head. "Does this look like a joke?"

Dorian gagged and backed up, hitting the bay window. Mom simply stared, wide-eyed.

"Amelia, let us explain." Uncle Caius stepped toward me. "Just take a deep breath and try to calm down."

"Calm down? Calm down!" My breathing was fast and ragged. The room was beginning to spin. Whatever was happening to me was their fault. It had to be. My lungs began to ache. I couldn't breathe. I needed air. Even more than that, I needed to get out of here. I needed to be far away from them with their expressions of pitying fear. "You made me a monster. I hate you for this!"

I launched from the marble counter, shot through to the entryway and escaped out the front door. The cool night air hit me as my feet pounded the gravel driveway. A spray of white snow kicked up behind me. I could feel my muscles lengthening and retracting like tightly coiled springs, pushing me forward at an inhuman speed. Houses flew past in a monochrome blur. My eyes focused only in front of me. Freezing wind whipped past my face and into my eyes. In the T-shirt and jeans I had on, the wind chill should have bit into my skin. Should have, but didn't. I wasn't even cold. These changes inside me further confirmed my fears. They were telling the truth. I was a...*vampire.*

I shook the unbelievable word from my mind and focused on the pavement as the balls of my feet hit harder and faster. I knew my intended destination. The night club my best friend, Kendrick, visited every Friday when he wasn't off snowboarding. Right now I needed his support, and hoped for his undying loyalty. Seething fear surged adrenaline through my body and gripped me from within. What if he thought I was a monster too? Imagining his reaction terrified me. How could he accept this...this living nightmare I was becoming?

The passing houses fell behind me, replaced by commercial strips. I pushed myself faster still, keeping to the shadows and somehow passing with ease the moving cars on the streets. I pulled to an abrupt halt after taking a shortcut through an unlit alley. To the right was the club's entrance, with a bright flashing neon sign above the doorway. *Pulse.*

A solid-built bouncer manning the door caught sight of me as I neared. "ID?" It was clear from his smirk that he knew I was underage.

I gulped, shrugging my shoulders. "Please, I just need to find my friend."

The bouncer's smirk thinned into a humorless line. "No ID, no entry."

Like an irritating itch you can't quite reach, his radiating aura of authority angered me. I squared my shoulders and clenched my jaw, staring him down. "Let me in."

The bouncer's superior expression faltered. He blinked once, then slowly pulled back the velvet robe and stood aside. I darted through the entry, so relieved to be inside that I didn't stop to question his split-second change in attitude.

The pulsing music hit me first, sending shockwave vibrations through my body and painfully through my ears. The smell, like walking straight into a brick wall, hit me second. Salt, body odor, alcohol, and a scent I'd never experienced before tonight: *blood.* My mouth watered while the other scents made me want to gag. Trying to ignore the draw of that new scent, I pushed myself away from the gyrating bodies on the strobe-lit dance floor and over to the bar. The scents dulled as my distance grew.

With a ragged breath, I slid onto one of the barstools, scanning the busy crowd for Kendrick. Please be here.

A guy's strong cologne hit me even before he spoke. But it wasn't Kendrick. It was Joel Nickel, a senior and, as star quarterback, the king of our school. "Hey, hot stuff," he began with slurred speech, and then paused. "Hey, I know you. You're a sophomore,

Amily or something?" He smiled and winked. "Fake ID huh? Planning to get messy and have some fun tonight?"

Part of me was thrilled that the superstar of our school was even acknowledging my existence. The other part just wanted him to leave so I could scope out Kendrick. "Amelia," I said, and turned to the bar, hoping he'd get a clue and leave me the hell alone. He didn't.

Instead, he took a step closer. "Come on babe, how's about a drink?"

He was too close, standing only an inch from me. I could smell his blood under the astringent cologne, and worse than that, I could hear his quickening pulse.

"No!" I snapped, muscles twitching, aching with thirst. "Go away."

Joel chuckled, amused. "Playing hard to get?" He inclined his lips to graze my ear. "I like a challenge."

His alcohol-drenched breath beat against my neck, sending a ripple down my spine. I could hear the blood pumping faster and louder through his body. Too close. Too freaking close!

That already-too-familiar tingle danced across my gums. My mouth salivated. I went to move, to force myself away from him before I became the monster from my favorite Skillet song. His hand caught my shoulder, and it was more than I could take. His scent was now stronger, moving with arousal through his veins.

No longer in control—no longer even myself—I spun on the spot and whispered, "Dark and secluded..."

A victorious smile tugged at Joel's lips. He curled an arm around my waist, pulling me from the bar. We passed the partygoers and slipped out the back door and into the dark alley. Urine and the wafting smell of garbage from a nearby dumpster coupled the scent of his blood.

Joel turned to face me. But I was faster. My hands shot up to his shoulders, nails digging in as I drove him back against the brick wall.

He chuckled, amused. "A fiery one... I knew it."

His complete lack of awareness to the threat before him angered and excited me. The option to stop, to walk away, was long gone. The thirst had taken over. His hands found my waist and traveled up, forcing their way beneath the fabric of my T-shirt.

Disgusted by his touch, I jerked his back off the wall then slammed him back against the bricks. "Don't move!"

Joel's hands dropped obediently and he smiled. "You're the boss."

His words evoked a broad smile across my face. Too broad, I realized, as his own smile fell. His eyes widened in shocked disbelief. "What the fuck?"

Moving at lightning speed, I clamped a hand over his mouth and forced his face to the side. I pressed my other hand against his chest, pinning him to the wall. His arms flailed, but it was no use. I was stronger. My eyes zeroed in on a fat vein pulsing along his neck. Then instinct took over. My teeth plunged into his flesh. The warm, metallic taste of his blood filled my mouth. It was an entrancing flavor coupled by the sound of his racing pulse.

A moan of pleasure escaped his lips and his muscles relaxed. His resistance had ceased. That's when I noticed it. His heart was slowing. The blood loss... *I'm killing him.* Part of me cried out to release him, to not be the monster my uncle and mom had claimed me to be. But I couldn't stop. I didn't want to.

When his body slumped against me, my strength somehow kept him pinned. Death was close. Still, I couldn't stop. Not now. Not yet. Not when something buried so deep within me was awakening.

The smells of the alley soared, muddling together in their intensity to become indiscernible. And I could hear...*everything:* stray drops of rain hitting puddles, rats gnawing on discarded rubbish. Then something else reached my ears, something quieter. Footsteps?

A blur shot from the shadows. Something as hard as concrete connected with my arm, ripping me from my victim. Then I was flying backward through the air as Joel crumpled to the ground. I connected with a *thud* against the adjacent wall before falling in a heap on the uneven asphalt. Instantly, the spell of Joel's blood was broken. The reality of what I had just done spun like a maelstrom through my mind. I'd killed him!

Tears plagued my eyes, spilling down my face and tinting my sight rose-colored. I swiped at them, but stalled. Blood was smeared across the back of my hands. Crying blood?

I barely had time to wonder how that was possible when the intruder's towering shadow closed in on me. He clutched something in his hand that glinted silver with the escaping moonlight. A weapon? I blinked up through tear-filled eyes, knowing my life was about to end. With heavy clouds blocking the moonlight again, and through my distorted vision, I could barely make out his dark features. "Kill me," I sniffed, letting my bloody tears stream down my face like a waterfall. "I'm a fucking monster!"

The boy with hair black as night faltered, pausing right before me. The hand holding the weapon stalled. "You *want* to die?"

CHAPTER 2

The alley door to the club burst open and suddenly Kendrick was standing there, his face stricken, golden-brown hair damp with sweat and plastered to his forehead. I felt relieved and mortified all at the same time. He'd never accept me now.

My eyes shot back to the boy who had torn me from my victim, the boy who had faltered in killing me. The damp and stained asphalt in front of me was empty. The boy had vanished without a sound.

Kendrick's eyes darted around. Yet he somehow missed poor dead Joel crumpled in the shadows. He knelt to cup my face with his hands. "Are you okay? Tell me what happened."

Certain that blood stained my cheeks, lips, and chin, I struggled to force my tear-stung eyes up to meet his. Fear swooned beneath my ribs and my heart fluttered. My victim, the unknown attacker, and Kendrick seeing the disgusting creature I had become; it was all too much. Sobbing, I lifted a shaking hand in the direction of Joel. "I killed him!"

Kendrick's eyes didn't reveal the fear I so dreadfully expected. Instead, they softened as he got to his feet. He crossed the alley and crouched before Joel, raising a finger to his throat. "He's not dead."

A wave of relief washed down my entire body, as cool as the water of a breaking wave. I began to stand. But before I could make my way to Kendrick, he raked tense fingers down Joel's chest. His nails cut like knives through Joel's shirt, leaving scarlet ribbons across his skin.

"Kendrick, stop!"

Joel stirred, his eyes darting past Kendrick to settle on me. Mortal fear contorted his face. "Keep that psycho bitch away from me!"

Kendrick shook the guy aggressively, forcing his attention away from me. He spoke in a low and commanding voice. "You were attacked by a rabid dog. *We* saved your life."

Joel's face dropped before his eyes rolled back in his head. Then as quickly as he'd come to, his body slumped, unconscious.

"What happened?" I cried, panic threatening to drown me. "What'd you do to him?"

Ignoring me, Kendrick took Joel by the ankle and swung him over his shoulder, as if he weighed no more than a rag doll. "Amelia, I need you to stay here. I'll be right back."

Swaying with body-draining confusion, I stared after Kendrick as he walked up toward the street. Cars flashed by, and his footsteps were audible even as he rounded the corner. What the hell was going on? Kendrick was lean muscled, not a body builder. How had he lifted Joel like that? With my eyes frozen on the street, I began pacing, needing to move to keep upright. Why wasn't he scared of me? How could he be so freaking calm? And what the hell did he do to Joel?

Kendrick bounded back down the alley, shoving his iPhone into the pocket of his checkered shirt. Remembering the blood staining my face, I frantically tried to wipe away the evidence.

Unmoved by my appearance, Kendrick collected my hand and pulled me in the opposite direction of the street. "Your mother is frantic. I need to get you home."

"What? How do you…"

"Caius called," Kendrick said, cutting me off. "They guessed you were coming to find me."

I planted my feet, and almost tripped on a crack in the sidewalk before yanking Kendrick to an abrupt halt. "Wait," I demanded. "What's going on? What happened back there? And why aren't you terrified of me? I attacked the freaking *quarterback*. I tried to kill him!"

Kendrick turned to face me, hand squeezing mine. "I could *never* be afraid of you, Amelia. None of this is your fault."

A shocking revelation hit me like a cold hard slap to the face. "You knew?"

Kendrick smiled and pulled me into a hug. "Yes. I've always known."

"But how?" I pulled away. "How can you know that I'm a…"

"A vampire?" He clasped my hand and pulled me forward, continuing to walk. "Because," he said in a soft and gravelly voice. "I can pick my own."

A sickening shiver ran down the length of my body, chilling me to the bone. Kendrick was a vampire? My initial instinct was to pull away from him. To run screaming, back up the sidewalk to the busy street of partygoers and music-pumping cars. But this is Kendrick, a reasoning voice inside my head whispered. He would never hurt me. Trying to hide my fear, I asked, "You kill people?"

"No," he replied, almost looking offended by my question. "And you don't have to, either."

With Kendrick forcing me along at a ridiculous speed, we covered most of the way home in silence. Betrayal clouded my emotions. Mom and Uncle Caius had lied to me all these years. Even worse than that was Kendrick's betrayal. He was my best friend. The same boy I'd known since grade school, the only person to befriend me when we moved to Anchorage, Alaska. When he'd left for private school, our friendship had grown stronger, with every weekend spent together. He'd taken me hiking and snowboarding. He'd even taught me how to ride a motorbike—because one day I *would* have my own. We'd ironically watched supernatural movies in my room until the break of dawn on countless frosty mornings. I'd always felt drawn to those types of movies and shows. I'd always felt different, like I didn't really belong, except when I was around Kendrick. But I'd never fantasized about actually being any type of monster. Normal would have been just fine. And Kendrick had known this entire time that I would one day become what he already was…a vampire?

My mind spun with everything that had happened tonight, flooded by endless questions. How did this happen? *Why* did this happen? My thoughts shifted to the boy who had interrupted my kill. Who was he? And where did he disappear to? In the end, I settled for what I hoped would be the simplest question. "Kendrick," I said, receiving a questioning look from him. "How did this all happen? How did we become…" It felt ridiculous to say the word out loud, "*vampires?*"

Kendrick's silvery-blue eyes stared ahead as we passed under draping maples, their leaves littering the sidewalk. "I was born this way, a Pure Blood like your uncle, as was my mother and grandfather and so on. We're considered royalty, the only ones among vampires able to procreate. The truth was never hidden from me. I knew what to expect."

After a long nervous pause, I dared to ask, "So, I was born this way, too?"

Kendrick shook his head and slowed his pace. We had just rounded a familiar corner lined with parked cars, and were closing in on my house. "No. Well, not exactly. I think I should let your mother explain. She's waiting inside with your uncle and Dorian." We crunched over the snow-littered driveway and mounted the front steps. "Are you ready?"

Instinct dared me to bolt. But I couldn't. It was time to learn the truth of how this all began. "I think so." I paused and pleaded with my eyes. Kendrick had always taken my overreactions with a light heart. He could diffuse my volatile temper, usually with just a single word or look. Right now I needed him, his support and undying loyalty. "Will you stay, please?"

Kendrick slung his arm around my shoulder and pulled me close. "There's nowhere else I'd rather be."

Once inside and within the comforting curve of Kendrick's arm, we entered the living room. A few glowing lamps and a crackling open fire spread a warm hue over the space. Any other time, the setting would have been inviting. But the brooding tension of everyone inside was palpable. I sucked in a nervous breath and followed Kendrick to the couch.

Mom sat across the room in her usual spot, a green armchair. Her back was straight and her shoulders were drawn back. Uncle Caius was at her side with one hand resting on her shoulder. She had been crying, even more than before. Her eyes were puffy and bloodshot, the delicate skin of her face blotchy.

Dorian was perched on the arm of a matching couch. It bordered the wall closest to the entry and sat squared before a black-painted coffee table. The muscles along his bare arms and neck were taut, and his hands were curled into fists. His wary blue eyes shifted to me. They were rimmed with dark lashes, matching his hair. "I'm sorry," he whispered. "I shouldn't have reacted that way. Your fangs, they ugh, just…surprised me."

I forced a smile and dropped down beside him, reaching over to squeeze his knee. His muscles twitched. I pulled my hand away, as fast as if I'd reached into the naked flames of the open fire. No matter what he said, it was clear he still feared me. "It's okay," I said, trying without success not to feel wounded by his reaction. "I would have flipped out, too."

Uncle Caius cleared his throat from across the room. "It's time, Lamayli," he directed to our mom. The shadows of the room emphasized his grave expression while darkening his salt and pepper hair.

Mom took a deep, chest-raising breath then exhaled, clutching her hands together. "What I am about to say isn't easy. Nevertheless, the time for sheltering you both has come and gone. Do you remember the story I told you of how your father died?"

I nodded, and beside me, Dorian did too. From a young age, Mom had explained our father's death as a break-in that went horribly wrong. She had described him as a heroic man who had challenged the intruder to protect his family. The tragic result was his death.

"Well," she went on. Her hands were clutched so tight that her French tip nails dug into the backs of her hands. "The details of that story are not entirely correct."

Kendrick's hand found mine. Dorian slid off the arm of the couch to sit beside me. Apparently, he was more consumed by Mom's words than his need to keep at a safe distance.

"There *was* an intruder," Uncle Caius spoke firmly while squeezing Mom's shoulder. "Though he was not a man committing a break-in. He was not even human."

Gaining visible strength from Uncle Caius's touch, Mom sat up even straighter. "I was pregnant with you both at the time. Your father fought heroically, but the creature's strength was too great."

Hearing our mom talk about our father and seeing the sparkle of tears in the corner of her eyes tugged at my heart. She never mentioned him. Over the years she'd always refused to answer any of our questions. We had never even seen a photograph. The only sliver of information we had was that his surname was Athobry. Now I knew why. The memory of the man she had loved so deeply, and lost so horrifically, was just too agonizing to relive.

"He died protecting us?" Dorian's strained voice emerged beside me.

"Yes, sweetheart." Mom nodded. "But it wasn't enough to save us. The creature was a rogue vampire consumed by bloodlust. Not unlike the thirst you experienced tonight," she said, eyes shifting to me in a way that turned my stomach. "He turned on me next. I was left for dead and bleeding out. If not for Caius, we would have all died there." She glanced up at our uncle with a look of adoration. "He gave us new life when the only alternative was death."

Mom's words spun through my head, painting bloody images of that night. I saw the fanged monster. His chin was covered in blood, his burning red eyes prowling for more. The thing nightmares were made of. I could see my mom with a ballooning belly. She was screaming over a lifeless body. The father I'd never known. I imagined him as an older replica of Dorian, with dark hair and chiseled features. Tacky, dark blood coated him. Yet something more than the visualization bothered me. How could Uncle Caius have saved us? A conflicting theory edged its way into my mind. It was the only explanation that could work in with everything Mom was claiming.

"You're not really our uncle?" I searched Uncle Caius's dull, silvery eyes for confirmation.

He shook his head, pursing his lips. "No, Amelia. I am not your biological uncle. Though I have always cared for and loved you both," he said, glancing from me to Dorian, "as I would my own flesh and blood."

"But how could you save us?" Dorian questioned.

Uncle Caius clasped his hands in front of him. He walked forward, casting a long shadow as he perched on the edge of the coffee table. "In the vampire community, murder is against the law."

Bile spiked my throat at the word *murder*. I had almost killed Joel to fulfill the thirst raging inside of me, the bloodlust.

Caius caught my worried expression and took my free hand in his. "Breaks in our laws are closely monitored. I had been hunting the assailant and caught up to his scent. I forced my way inside, but it was already too late. Your father was dead, and your mother was hanging between life and death. I had only moments to act, to make a decision."

"A decision?" Disbelief colored my tone. "You considered letting us die?"

Uncle Caius's expression rippled with guilt. But his voice wasn't the one to offer insight.

"He went against The Council," Kendrick explained. "Turning children into vampires has long been outlawed. They are much too difficult to control through the initial bloodlust."

Kendrick's knowledge and words shook me. I wanted to blame someone for the monster I was becoming, to seek vengeance for this curse. But I couldn't. We were all still alive and breathing because of Caius. He had gone against their laws to give us new life. He was our savior and our creator. And he had been there since that first day, catering to our wants, doting on us like any wealthy and caring uncle would. He was family. The only living family we had.

"It was a risk to disrespect The Council," Uncle Caius added. His eyes glazed with a look of distant memory. "But I couldn't leave your mother to die like that. So with only moments to spare, I tore you from her womb and infected you all with my blood. Even then, death could have claimed each of you. Only half of those infected live, while the others reject the change and die." Pride stole the glaze from his eyes. "But you were both fighters, so strong, so determined to live."

"But why is this *bloodlust*," Dorian's voice caught over the word, "only occurring now?"

I remembered Mom and Caius speaking cryptically, after discovering me gnawing into the bloody steak. *You knew there was a chance even after all we did,* Caius had said. "You did something to us," I stated accusingly.

"I begged him to," Mom cried, wrapping her arms tight around her waist. "I was eternally grateful for our second chance at life, of course I was. Still, I would never have chosen this life for either of you."

"Up until now," Uncle Caius said, releasing my hand to move back to Mom's side. He patted her shoulder in an effort to calm her down. "The ancient remedy I gave you and Dorian staved off the transformation, culled your thirst. We hoped it would halt the turning process completely. Though we have all witnessed it tonight. The effects are diminishing. You should expect your thirst to become stronger, and your strength and speed to increase."

"You may also develop an allergy to the sun, like me," Mom interrupted.

Caius cleared his throat and Mom looked up. There seemed to be a warning in his eyes. "We do not know that yet, Lamayli." With a sigh, he looked back to Dorian and me. "In the end, you will both become full-fledged vampires. It is only a matter of time."

A wave of dread washed down my body. This is only the beginning? I had already lost control once. I thought of the disappearing boy again. If not for him, I would have killed Joel. It was only a matter of time before I did it again.

Kendrick cleared his throat and squeezed my hand. "Ms. Lamont, Lord Bathory," he said, looking at my mom and uncle, "there's something we need to tell you."

Instantly my stomach lurched. The metallic taste of Joel's blood reared up my throat. I knew what Kendrick wanted to say. He was going to tell them. Tell them I'd attacked and almost killed a guy from school. Shallow breath caused my lungs to ache. I couldn't bear for them to know. Couldn't bear to see their staring expressions at seeing the monster I was fast becoming. "Kendrick, don't!"

He squeezed my hand again, which did little to calm the nerves searing through my body. "It's okay," he whispered. "They'll understand."

Throwing Kendrick's hand aside, I jumped to my feet. "Understand!" I shrieked. With a single bound, I cleared the coffee table, smacking my knee before backing up to the wall. My body threw a menacing shadow. It grew so large that it covered Dorian and the framed, family portrait above his head. "How will they understand that I almost killed the freaking quarterback!"

Floored by my own lips' betrayal, my hands shot up to cover my mouth. My eyes scoured the room. Dorian sat as still as a statue, eyes wide and face a sickly shade of green. Kendrick looked ready to step in and restrain me, with one arm braced against the coffee table.

Within my chest my heart was leaping. My hands curled into

fists at my sides. The need to bolt was drowning me, but I couldn't move. Fear kept me frozen stiff.

Mom rose to her feet and walked slowly toward me. With shaky arms outstretched, she looked like she was attempting to soothe a wild animal. Uncle Caius stood watching, not quite on edge, but in quiet preparation. It was clear nobody was about to let me flee.

The feel of being caged like an animal shattered my fear. Mobility flooded back to my limbs. I went to run, but Mom's arms, so gentle and yet so strong, curled around me. "It's alright, Amelia. It wasn't your fault. All these things you're feeling are normal. Being a vampire does that. Everything's heightened."

Screaming and grunting, I thrashed against her. Mom's grip held tight, never giving an inch. Long minutes passed and still I was trapped. With exhaustion smothering my need to escape, the weight and conviction of her words began to sink in. I suddenly stopped struggling and hung my head. "Mom, I'm sorry. I didn't hear…"

"Shh," Mom soothed, loosening her grip around me. She ran a hand down my back, smoothing my long, blond hair. "It's alright." When she released me, I saw her face. It wasn't filled with the sorrow and fear of earlier, but the strength and resolution of a woman now in control. "Amelia, I promise you can learn to control this." She turned to face the others. "You will experience this, too, Dorian. And we will all get through this, together. But not here." Radiating control with her shoulders drawn back, Mom moved back to her seat beside Caius. "We need time and seclusion, and the removal of temptation until you are both in control. We leave for the cabin, tomorrow."

CHAPTER 3

"*J*ust a minute, Amelia," Mom's voice jarred me to a standstill on the porch.

Sheltered by the roofline's shadow she produced a small cylindrical tube from the pocket of her designer sweats. After waiting up all night so she could see us off on our first day of school, she was ready to sleep through her first day. It was preparation for her new position at the Portsmouth Vampire Council, which began each weekday after twilight.

I snatched the tube from between her fingers and lifted it to eye level. "Nasal decongestant?" I questioned incredulously. "I just want to be invisible. But everyone is already going to be looking at the weird new girl. Now you want them to think I'm a dweeb too?"

"It's menthol." Mom shrugged. "I thought it might help distract your sense of smell."

With a groan, I let Mom hug me. Then I retreated to the car, shoving the nasal tube into the glove box. There was no way in hell anyone was going to see me using that thing. Dorian was already in the driver's seat, warming up the engine, as he always did.

"We're not ready." I glared at the opulent French mansion—our new home—shrinking in the rear-view mirror. Apparently, Uncle Caius had a lot more money than I'd realized.

It was a double-story, with a mixture of stone and beige-rendered walls, soaring windows, and high ceilings inside. Acres of green land surround its walls, back-bordered by a thick shelter of oaks. There was a stone-bordered gate that fronted the property, offering a scenic view of the rolling swells of Rye Beach. Just watching the mansion shrink as we drove away made me long for the cabin. There I had felt safe, from myself. This mansion was too big, too cold. It could never feel like home. It could never feel safe.

The move had been inevitable. Kendrick had brainwashed Joel into believing he'd been attacked by a rabid dog. Being a Pure Blood, his ability to compel was stronger than any turned vamp's. Still, Mom and Uncle Caius were worried that me being anywhere near Joel would break the compulsion and endanger our secret lives. So they weren't about to take any chances. Our destination had been decided with a job offer. Uncle Caius wanted Mom on the Vampire Council in Portsmouth. With a little encouragement, she'd agreed. It was one of many sub-councils that operated around the world in service to The Armaya, the epicenter of vampire legislation and politics. As the only surviving Pure Blood of his lineage, our uncle held a seat there on The Armaya's Royal Vampire Council. After that our move had been arranged to the small, sleepy town of Rye, bordering Portsmouth, New Hampshire.

More than six months had passed at the cabin. It was hundreds of miles from our old home in Anchorage and hidden amongst the wilderness of the Alaska Range. As Caius had predicted, Dorian began the transformation soon after our retreat. I couldn't hide my relief at his fading fear of me. We were one and the same, cut from the same cloth, and now we shared a secret. The thing we had become.

"We are ready," Dorian countered. "And you heard Mom. We passed all the tests successfully."

With an irritated breath, I turned and stared out the window as manicured trees fronting oversized, gated properties passed by. Yesterday Mom admitted to the tests she had planned to assess our self-control. I had been beyond pissed. Still, no amount of arguing could change her mind. Now Dorian's laid-back attitude was beginning to grate on my nerves. I clenched and unclenched my hands. "So we didn't attack and kill a few delivery men. So what? How does that compare to a classroom full of blood-pumping human bodies?"

"Amelia," Dorian said, glancing in the vanity mirror backing the sun visor. He ran a hand through his thick, dark hair to re-shape it. "We'll be fine." He looked at me sideways and smiled. "You know, you're stronger than you give yourself credit for."

I crossed my arms over my chest, doubting Dorian's faith in me. How could he truly believe that after everything that happened?

When we first relocated to the cabin, Mom and Kendrick had taught us to hunt. We started with herds of Caribou, graduating to more challenging prey like packs of wolves, and even the elusive mountain lion. Kendrick, between frequent snowboarding breaks, had come hunting too. But I had detested the whole process. How could honing our predatory instincts make us safer around humans? But as my natural desires took over, I became thrilled by the chase, my muscles snapping into action and my fangs ready and waiting. After each hunt, each kill, the thrill would dissipate, replaced by a body-shaking guilt. My speed, strength, and lust for blood proved beyond any and all doubt that I truly was a monster, and I always would be.

I took reprieve from one fact alone. Vampires weren't immortal. Our lifespans were extended, but I wouldn't forever be this blood-thirsty creature, a killer. One day I *would* die.

I pulled my New Student packet out of my bag and began memorizing my three-week class rotation and the school map. The last thing I wanted was to have to ask for directions.

A moment later, Dorian turned off Ocean Boulevard onto the private, gated entrance of our new school, St. Volaras. It was the best private school in the area, holding over five hundred students. The size of the student body alone only unnerved me further. Today would be an assault of temptation from unknowing victims. And, if I did lose it, there would be countless witnesses that no amount of compulsion could cover up.

Dorian revved the engine of our turbocharged Audi Cabriolet. He dropped back to second gear, following the line of high-end cars through the student parking lot. The A5 was a joint birthday present from our uncle Caius. It was a reward for coming so far in our ability to restrain.

Every part of me hated the car and everything it represented, everything it reminded me of. I glared at Dorian, knowing he'd revved the engine to draw attention. I hated that he was so confi-dent and self-assured, when all I wanted to do was remain invisible.

Dorian ignored my glare and pulled into a spot rearing the lot, before jumping out of the car.

I sat without moving, wishing I could just disappear. Then Dorian poked his head back through the driver's side door. "You can't stay here all day."

I bit the inside of my cheek. "Wanna bet?"

"C'mon," Dorian said, rolling his eyes. "Don't make me drag you to class kicking and screaming."

Although his tone was joking, I didn't doubt his threat. He was set on the idea of a normal life and wasn't about to let me mess that up for him. Cursing him under my breath, I snatched my bag from the back seat. Outside I yanked my zip-up hoodie on. It was my favorite jacket, black cotton with a detachable hood. If it had been made of leather it would have been perfect for riding a motorbike.

I got out of the car and froze. Students littered the parking lot. To me they resembled herding bovine, blissfully unaware and ripe for the picking. I groaned, picking up a scent that was all too familiar these days. Human blood. In the cool morning air, it was faint but still distinct.

"If I were you, I'd wipe that look off your face." Dorian stepped in front of me, blocking my view of a group of preppy-looking girls. "People are beginning to stare."

I looked away from the clustering students, refocusing on Dorian's piercing silver-blue irises. They were now the same color as mine, and from what we'd been told, a consistent vampire trait. "What look?"

Dorian smiled, lips parting to reveal the points of his fangs. "That crazed, I'm so starving I could eat you, look."

My jaw dropped then quickly clamped shut. I couldn't even control my expression? There was no way I could do this!

"Yes you can." Dorian clearly knew me too well. "Look, Amelia," he said more seriously. "We can have a normal life. You can. This is just the first step. Will you just try, for me? You know I can't do this without you."

With a deep breath, I planted my hands on my hips. I knew Dorian was using emotional blackmail, but I caved anyway. "Okay. But if I kill anyone, I'm blaming you."

Dorian roped his arm through mine and yanked me forward to walk alongside him. "Your murder is my condemnation. Got it."

As we headed to the main building, I held my breath. My sight rose above the heads of surrounding students. The building was three levels of brick, with rectangular windows and tall glass doors. Dorian was already checking out the surrounding female members of the student body. I wasn't beyond counting bricks for a distraction. Before I could begin, someone darted in front of us.

The boy's scent—if you could call him a boy, with his over-developed muscle mass—reached my nostrils instantly. It was fiery and sweet, and somehow different from any human's I had ever picked up on. The urge to extend my fangs pulled at me from within. I swallowed, struggling to push the sensation back.

The guy edged forward. His tan face was frozen with a threatening scowl, and his hands curled into fists. "Go back to where you came from," he snarled through tight lips. "You're not welcome here."

Dorian instinctively tensed and released my arm, ready to take action. But before he could even utter a word, he turned and stalked away.

Dorian shrugged his shoulders "What was that about?"

A startling realization struck me. "He could tell. He knows what we are."

Dorian laughed, pulling me aside to let passing students through the main doors. "You take paranoia to a whole new level, Sis."

Certain belting him would draw attention I held back the urge. Instead, I settled for a piercing look that I wished could kill, or at least inflict torturous pain. "I'm paranoid?"

Dorian waved his hands in a half-assed surrender. "C'mon, you know I didn't mean it like that. That jerk is probably just a dumb jock, pumped up on steroids."

I wasn't convinced, but Dorian was already past the incident and busy catching the eye of a pretty girl. He glanced down at his watch. "Classes start in five. So go, get settled. I'll see you at lunch." He pushed me through the glass doors with a wink, before backing away in the opposite direction. "You'll be fine. I promise."

I sucked in a quick, deep breath and held it. My lungs ached in protest. Students swarmed the foyer. I pushed past them, bounding up the stairs to the second floor. Psychology was first up. I shot through the door to room 2.6, taking a vacant desk. It was by one of a handful of windows that lined the far wall. With my lungs contracting and on the verge of forcing me to breathe, I dumped my bag on the desk and threw open the glass barrier. Poking my head out into the seasonally cool fall air, I sucked in a much-needed ragged breath.

Whispers about the 'new girl' were hot on every student's lips. Vampire hearing, lucky me! This day just kept getting better. They thought I was strange, a total weirdo. And who could blame them? I was acting like a freak!

Shrinking back into my seat, I kept my head down with my hoodie sheltering my face. My long hair hung as a solid barrier between me and them. The scent of fresh blood intensified as more and more students filled the classroom. There was nothing I could do in this setting to dull it. But I could drown out their chatter.

I pulled my iPod from my backpack, plugging the earbuds into my ears. It was jam-packed with music from all my favorite bands: Red, Skillet, Three Days Grace and Lifehouse, just to name a few. It used to have pop music too, but since discovering my darker side my taste in music had followed suit, and the urge to dance wildly in the privacy of my room no longer felt uplifting. In spite of that, I smiled. The cover was new, glossy purple—my favorite color, which in the right dark shade was nowhere near being girly pink, ick! It had been a parting gift from Kendrick who'd uploaded the new Three Days Grace album. My heart squeezed, wishing he were here.

Still able to scent the students, I stifled a groan. My arms coiled around my waist, nails pricking my sides and breaking the skin. The distraction helped, just enough to keep me cemented in my seat, until the classroom door opened again.

In an instant, the energy in the small room shifted. I removed my earbuds. The gossip on everyone's lips had faltered.

Then it hit me. The same unique, fiery, sweet scent of blood I had encountered not five minutes earlier. No...not him again.

Against my better judgment, I brushed my hair behind my ears and dared to glance up. My world froze. Any remaining chatter became irrelevant as I stared on. Standing in the doorway was not the guy who had threatened Dorian and me. This boy had similarly colored satin-black hair, styled into messy, loose spikes. His charcoal V-neck shirt acted like a second skin, clinging to reveal a sculpted torso. The light from fluorescents bolted to the grated ceiling bounced off his bronzed arms, offering shadowed definition to his protruding biceps and numerous...*scars?* Nudging recognition tickled at the back of my subconscious. I couldn't rip my eyes away. *I've seen him before.*

The boy caught sight of me as he entered the room, and stalled. His honey-glazed eyes, rimmed with iridescent green, widened.

Somehow able to move again, I averted my eyes. But it was already too late. I could hear the heavy steps of hunting boots closing in on me. A hard lump crawled up my throat and my heart-rate increased. The potency of his fiery scent soared. It invaded my lungs and made my mouth water. He was close, way too close. With a throat-constricting gulp, I tried and failed to force my lust for his blood back down. Then I blinked up to meet his curious gaze.

"Hi. You're new." His tone was steady, maybe even friendly. Yet there was visible conflict in his eyes.

"Uh-huh," I replied, as a telltale tingle ran along my gums. *No, please. Not now.* I could practically taste the hot sweetness of his blood on my tongue and hear the irregular beat of his strong pulse. A sequence of events flashed manically through my mind. I saw myself leaping over the desk in one swift move and sinking my now fully extended fangs into his neck. *Control yourself!* I pinned my lips together, concealing my fangs. My nails dug into the cushioned seat, acting as an anchor to stop me from acting out the deadly fantasy still reeling through my mind. For a second I longed for the nasal tube stashed back in the car.

"I'm Ty Malau," he said, iridescent eyes narrowing at me.

Uncomfortable silence thickened the air as he watched me, waiting for a polite introduction. It was clear he had no plan to let me be until I spoke. So I looked away, covering my fanged mouth with one hand. Through my barricading fingers, I managed to croak out, "Amelia Athobry-Lamont."

"It's nice to finally meet you, Amelia," Ty said.

My eyes shot back to his smiling face. Finally? There hadn't been any kind of emphasis on the word, but something about it, or maybe even the sentence he'd used it in, bothered me. Was I reading too much into this? Something about him seemed so inexplicably familiar. But for the life of me, I couldn't place him.

Ty motioned to the spare seat beside me with a scarred hand. "Mind if I sit?"

My tongue floated in a pool of expectant saliva and my hands began to tremble. They were still clutching the cushioned chair for dear life. The threat of release was growing. Please, just leave me alone. I knew if he didn't walk away soon, I would lose all control. Ty shifted his weight from one leg to the other. I could almost feel the growth of anxiety rippling in waves off his body. Shit! I mentally slapped myself. I'm staring at him like he's something to eat. Look away, dammit! With great strain, I forced my eyes away from his perfectly symmetrical features, and down onto my iPod, wishing again for Kendrick.

A quiet grunt emerged from Ty's throat. "Never mind..."

His retreat to the other side of the classroom dulled the overwhelming punch of his blood. With his scent around me fading and my fangs retracting, I allowed my lungs to breathe again. The short, testing breaths relieved some of the involuntary reactions to his proximity. I could still smell his blood, as well as the other students. But I took a sliver of comfort from the fact that I *had* managed to control myself, just enough not to turn this room into a bloody massacre...*yet.*

The classroom chatter had resumed. It seemed almost everyone had been watching Ty and me with bated breath, and now it was all they could talk about.

I plugged my earbuds back in and dropped my head against my bag. My eyes squeezed shut. *"You'll be fine,"* Dorian had promised. A silent laugh vibrated my chest. Yeah right!

THE REMAINDER OF THE MORNING, with constant and at times agonizing restraint, had so far passed without any bloodshed. Every moment around humans, I felt on the precipice of crumbling. Always, the sinister plotting of how to take one of them down without repercussion played at my thoughts. Reprieve seemed unattainable, until my first double art class before lunch.

The art center was a separate and small building. It was located down a quiet path shrouded by a thicket of sassafras trees and isolated from the main building. Its seclusion and smaller class headcount disturbed me. There'd be fewer witnesses if I lost it, less mess to clean up. It would take more control than I thought I could muster to keep my mind from planning someone's bloody demise.

Preparing for a doubled forty-five minute game of 'ignore and don't kill,' I walked stiffly through the open door into class. A girl with pixie-like features and sleek fiery-red hair jumped in front of me. My mouth clamped shut, holding my breath.

The girl's face beamed as she swayed on her much-too-high-for-school stiletto heels. "Hi, you must be Amelia. I'm Vanessa."

Her bubbly personality floored me. So far she was the only person—apart from the mysterious and tempting Ty—to introduce herself to me. The memory of him tugged at me from within, our entire interaction imprinted on my mind. I could remember every detail of his appearance and the few words he'd said to me. Still, I was no closer to placing him.

Now this girl was watching me, waiting for a reply while I stood reminiscing. "Uh, hi," I said with caution.

Vanessa motioned to the back of the classroom, where two vacant easels waited. They were the only two left available. "Come on, I saved you a seat."

With a smile, she turned and led the way past the other students already seated. A broad beam of warm sunlight streamed through the wall, made entirely of glass panels. The light encompassed the two vacant easels and a single paint rack positioned between them. Not nearly a good enough barrier to separate her from me.

The sun's rays cast a distinct line across the polished cement floor. I paused at its edge, staring blankly past Vanessa and into the lush fernery beyond the glass. Sunlight was supposed to burn vampires. Well, all turned vampires, from what I had been told.

Yesterday I even witnessed it. I let my mind drift back. I had been in the front passenger seat of Mom's Mercedes SUV, bewildered by the huge mansion before us. The day was overcast, wind-blown clouds sheltering what should have been a pastel-blue sky. Mom slid from the car while Dorian and I stared. Was this monstrous structure really our new home?

Then the clouds shifted. A sizzling and gag-worthy stink of burning flesh reached us. Mom swore—something she rarely did—and dove into the back seat. Tugging the door shut behind her, the UV resistant tint provided refuge from the sun's escaping rays.

"Mom!" I cried, twisting in my seat. "Are you okay?"

Dorian's arm shot out, collecting her hand and pulling it forward. "Shit!"

A bubbling welt of scorched flesh covered her forearm. "Language Dorian," Mom chastised. "And I'll be fine." She pulled her hand from Dorian's. Instantly the redness began to soothe, the bubbled skin smoothing until her arm was totally unblemished.

I turned back to the dashboard, dropping my head into my hands. "Tell me again," I said, hating the quake of my voice. "Tell me how you're affected by the sun, when we're not?"

Mom had gone over this subject many times at the cabin, but I was still unsettled by her explanation. The story just didn't add up.

Mom flattened her blouse and sighed. "I was turned as an adult. However, it seems the circumstances in which you were both infected has provided immunity." She edged forward, her posture straight as she rested a firm hand on each of our shoulders. "Now, this *is* the last time I will repeat myself."

Back in the classroom, Vanessa had taken her spot and was waiting, watching me with a mixture of what looked like impatience and anticipation.

Shaking the memory from my mind, I stepped into the light. The curve in Vanessa's smile twitched, her piercing blue eyes blinking.

"Welcome Amelia." The sudden voice caused Vanessa to jump,

knocking her knee against the paint rack. A thin woman, in paint-spattered overalls and a paintbrush holding her hair back in a bun, stood at the front of the classroom. "I'm Mrs. Ruby." She looked to Vanessa. "Vanessa, would you please explain the project options to Amelia?"

Vanessa nodded, shifting her eyes back to me. Her face was painted with a perfect and what I thought was a faked smile. There goes my paranoia, again.

"So, we have two options," she said. "Create a portrait of what we see ourselves becoming in ten years, or reveal our hidden selves. The side we keep secret from the world."

The image of me devouring a blood-baggie that morning, with greedy drops of crimson escaping the corner of my mouth, intruded on my thoughts. Not pretty. Bile threatened to rise up at the back of my throat. I swallowed in an attempt to push it back down. Then I grasped a tube of paint from the rack to mask my discomfort. "Sounds interesting…"

Vanessa leaned closer, eyes sparkling. "So, what *do* you see yourself becoming in ten years?"

I clung tighter to the paint tube. The lid popped and a squirt of green shot at the ground. A murderer, I thought. Though I doubted ten years would pass before I did finally lose control. "Um…" Needing to evade her watching eyes, I snatched paper towel from the rack to clean up the mess. I searched my mind for a normal response, before hesitating and coming up blank. "I really don't know."

Vanessa crossed her arms over her chest. "Well, what about the second option? Got any deep dark secrets I should know about?"

Yes. I'm a vampire and drink blood, I thought, but had the better sense to respond with, "Nope. What about you?"

I attempted to keep my voice level, even though I was lying

through my teeth. Teeth? I did a double take, running my tongue over my teeth. They were completely level and *human*. My fangs aren't extended? And that's when it hit me, or should I say, didn't hit me. I couldn't scent her blood.

My eyes shot up to Vanessa, who shrugged. "Well, I am kinda a fashion Nazi, which sucks for me. Unlike almost every kid at this school, I'm on a scholarship. Even with a part-time job, I'm reduced to shopping online."

"Where do you work?" I looked her over while sniffing the air. Diamanté-studded stretch jeans and a fitted, red leather jacket. No scent.

"Nowhere, really. It's more of an errand-based gig." As I kept staring, a frown pinched Vanessa's brow. "What?" A look of horror transformed her expression. "Oh my God, don't tell me I have body odor!"

Wiping the primal look from my face, I shook my head. "No. Sorry." I held up my hand that still clung to the paper towel smeared with green paint. "It's the paints," I said, drilling my brain for a normal excuse. "They, uh…smell the same as the ones from our old school. Kind of like toe-jams and toothpaste."

"Oh, good," she said, voice hesitant, "as long as *you* can't smell me."

Forcing a smile, I began squeezing different paints onto a pallet. I should have been figuring out what I planned on painting. I should have been doing anything and everything to appear normal. But my mind was elsewhere. Yes, I felt relieved to have met someone I didn't want to drain, to drink from until they were lifeless in my arms. Still, I couldn't get my head around her lack of scent. Who was this girl?

"Hey," Vanessa said, breaking my train of thought. "What's your cell number?" When I frowned, wondering why on earth she'd want my number, she said, "You do have one, don't you? I mean next to lip gloss, it's the one accessory a girl can't live without."

Puzzled, and trying not to stare at her heavily glossed lips, I pulled my iPhone from my jeans and handed it over. It was personalized with a Three Days Grace case.

Vanessa snatched the phone and dialed from it. Then she pulled her own phone, sporting a cover speckled with diamantes, from her jacket pocket. It chimed and her fingers glided over the glass screen. "All done," she said, handing mine back. "I texted you my number too."

"Oh, thanks." The phone chimed and I stuffed it back into my pocket. The interaction left me feeling even more confused. She's just being friendly, I tried to convince myself. But my suspicion didn't agree.

After that, I stared at my blank canvas for what felt like forever. I was trying to force myself to think about the project, but my mind kept wondering about the unusual girl sitting beside me. When the bell rang, I realized my efforts had been useless. I had spent the entire class staring at my canvas and tapping a dry paintbrush against my thigh.

Vanessa rose to her feet and looked down at me. "Got any plans for lunch?"

"Uh, no," I replied. Where was she going with this?

"Great! You can sit with us."

Eat in a cafeteria full of humans? Yeah, that'll end well. "I can't," I said quickly, thinking up a lie. "Math quiz tomorrow. I need to study."

"Study can wait." Vanessa strung her arm through mine and yanked me forward. "Besides, I'm not taking no for an answer. Oh and don't worry, my friends don't bite," she said, flashing me a wicked grin, "unless provoked."

CHAPTER 4

"This is a bad idea," I mumbled, low enough that no one would hear.

The cafeteria was packed with warm-blooded students, totally unaware of the living monster walking amongst them. They smelled so damn delicious. I thought of the opaque bottle filled with blood and hidden inside my locker and groaned. Vanessa led the way to the buffet line. As we neared I almost sighed. The smells of hot and cold food muddied their human blood.

Once our trays were filled, I followed after Vanessa. The scent of food declined while the punch of their blood soared. My hands clung to the flimsy plastic for dear life. She headed for the back wall of the long hall, which was entirely made of glass panels. The transparent barrier offered a scenic view of the almost empty courtyard. Frosty wind brewed beyond the glass, billowing through the barrier of greenery. The space was decked out with a few park benches. They were all unoccupied, except for one. Dorian sat in jeans and a hooded sweater. He was waiting for me after my pleas in Math that morning for a human-free lunch zone. But he wasn't alone. Cindy—at least I think that was her name—from Math class was standing by the bench, tugging her cardigan tighter around her. She was smiling that *I'm so into you, please ask me out,* smile. Clearly Dorian hadn't wasted any time.

Despite his company, I desperately wanted to go to him, or to at least motion him inside for backup. Except his head was turned to Cindy, resting against his hand with his fingers raked through his hair. Turn around, dammit! In a matter of seconds, I'd be introduced to Vanessa's friends and be expected to eat with them. I needed him here, not out there chatting up his first soon-to-be ex-girlfriend. With his quick reflexes, only he could restrain me if I did turn from Jekyll to Hyde.

Dorian's attention remained unwavering, and too soon we were closing in on a table where a lone guy in a black leather jacket waited. The guy's head was dropped, satin-black hair obscuring his features. For a second, I almost felt relieved that I would only have to contend with one other human. Vanessa, though I didn't understand it, wasn't a temptation. So refraining from killing just one of them didn't seem completely impossible.

As we neared, my relief vanished, faster than a vacuum sucking up smoke. The potent smell of his blood hit me like a semi. The scent, so fiery, was one I could not ignore or confuse. My breath caught in my throat and my heart began beating wildly beneath my ribs.

Ty cocked his head to the side. His eyebrows rose as Vanessa dumped her tray beside him. "You brought company?" He didn't sound impressed by any means, though he didn't sound entirely displeased, either.

Vanessa flicked her red tresses over her shoulder and dropped into the seat beside him. "You're welcome." Without further word or gesture, she began digging into her risotto.

Ty's eyes traveled from her to me, where I stood frozen in shock by the smell of his mouth-watering blood. "So," he said, a calculated smile curving his full lips. "Are you going to sit, or do you prefer to eat...standing?"

His piercing gaze churned up butterflies within my stomach. I envisioned myself, hunched over my prey in the forest, fangs buried in fur-covered flesh while I fed. Blood drained from my porcelain cheeks. *Don't just stand there, move!*

Feeling as though my body was thawing from the inside out, I slowly lowered my tray to the table opposite Vanessa. Ty's green and honey-glazed eyes were fixed on me with intense, gauging focus. My hands began to tremble. Was he trying to figure me out?

The tremble of my hands cascaded down to my legs as I slid the cushioned chair back. Its legs offered up a screech of iron across blue-checkered tiles. I cringed and rushed to sit, hairs across my arms lifting in anticipation of stares all around. But in my hasty movement, my foot connected with the leg of the chair, and then I was falling.

A clumsy vampire? Go figure.

Due to Caius's concoction that held off our vampirism, my agility was still more human than vampire, and my new reflexes took a second to kick in. I caught myself, butt slamming into the seat and face burning with mortification. I had to pull myself together. A few deep breaths through my mouth aired some of Ty's scent from my nostrils. The rate of my pounding heart began to decrease. Though nothing, it seemed, could cull the sickening butterflies that still churned up my stomach. When I finally dared to look up, I caught Ty's gaze fixed on me. An amused smile lit his angular face.

"So, Amelia," Vanessa interrupted, breaking the silent tension.

The sudden sound of her voice caused my body to jerk. I had been so consumed by Ty and the way he was watching me that I had completely forgotten she was sitting right in front of me. "Uh, yeah?"

Vanessa arched back in her seat, shrugging out of her red leather jacket. "Ty mentioned that you're in his psychology class. Though," she added, looking like the cat that caught the canary, "he was quite disappointed when you shunned him."

My jaw hit the ground and my eyes darted to Ty. In the same millisecond, he jutted out an elbow to collect Vanessa's side. The reflex was so fast it almost seemed to blur. "Damn, you've got a big mouth."

Ty was *disappointed*? As my head spun, wondering if Vanessa was talking trash, or just trying to bait me, a figure sauntered up to our table.

"Thanks for the invite," Dorian said in a tone more amused than annoyed. "I thought we were having lunch...*outside*."

Instantly I felt terrible. I had been so consumed by Ty's presence that I had totally forgotten about my brother waiting for me in the cold. "Sorry," I said, pulling out the chair beside me. "I meant to come out and get you, but you looked busy."

"You do know it's freezing out there," Ty mocked, throwing a glance over his shoulder at the glass door to the courtyard.

"Thick skin," Dorian replied, shrugging as he sat down. The way he seemed so calm, so normal and so in control, irritated me. "When you've spent your life growing up in Alaska, I guess you become somewhat immune to the cold." He glanced up at Ty, then across at Vanessa with a broadening smile. "By the way, I'm Dorian. Amelia's brother."

"We know," Vanessa spoke up. "That's Ty and I'm Vanessa. I'm pretty sure we have chem together."

They got onto the topic of teachers after that. Ty occasionally threw in a comment or question here and there while I sat in complete silence. It was all I could do to ignore his scent that flooded my mouth with saliva. My eyes burned to make eye contact or check out those unusual scars, speculating how he'd gotten them. So I forced my gaze away, coasting over the yellow-walled cafeteria. White rectangular tables ran in rows, fully packed with bodies. For a second, I almost felt relieved. Among the groups of herding teens, the one guy who had threatened Dorian and me this morning was nowhere in sight. In the situation I had gotten us into, we didn't need any more conflict. Dealing with Ty and Vanessa and my growing urges was enough.

Beside me, Dorian was still talking with animation. He appeared totally unaffected by Ty's proximity. My irritation grew to resentment. Why was this so easy for him? As an extra precaution, I had my feet curved around the chair's legs. Still, the physical restraint was not enough to deter my thoughts. Not enough to stop my mind from wondering how I could taste Ty's blood and get away with it. Feeling my gums prickle in anticipation, I tore the wrapper off my bought chocolate bar and took a bite. If anything could distract me, it was chocolate. Though even with my thirst ebbing, nothing could remove the pressing weight of Ty's eyes bearing down on me.

Shifting my attention to Vanessa wasn't any better. She appeared completely relaxed, now throwing questions like live grenades at Dorian. She wanted to know everything, a quest to discover our whole life story. I couldn't control my growing suspicion. Just friendly, or maybe too friendly?

Dorian, on the other hand, knew the drill. He answered every question without flinching, keeping our secrets hidden with his nonchalant attitude while lying and flirting like a pro.

I was still eyeing Vanessa with suspicion when Ty's voice cut through my thoughts. "So, Amelia, what do you think?"

Under the table my free hand spasmed, hitting the metal frame. I fought the urge to wince, not from pain but for having been so distracted that Ty's voice had startled me. "Sorry, think about what?" Ty met my eye and I did a double take. But the flicker of gold I thought I'd seen across his irises wasn't there. Now I'm imagining things?

"Dorian wants to join the swim team," Ty said. "So we're planning a swim off."

Dorian leaned into me with his shoulder. "Geez, where have you been? We've been hashing out the race details for the past five minutes."

"Swim off?" Oh God, don't tell me.

"With Dorian's not-so-humble boasting on how good he is at *all* sports," Ty said, clear sarcasm tinting his tone. "I just couldn't resist."

Ty and Dorian were planning to race each other? My stomach dropped with a sudden swell of nausea. "I don't think…"

"So, we're thinking Friday," Dorian said, cutting me off. "Ty needs to tee it up with the coach and get permission slips."

I squeezed, fingernails slicing my forgotten chocolate bar in two. He couldn't be serious! We needed to keep a low profile. Remain off the radar. Not draw attention. Uncurling one foot from the chair's leg, I struck out, connecting with Dorian's shin.

He twitched in his seat, a grimace hijacking his pale face. "What?"

The genuine confusion in his expression enraged me. "You know what," I hissed under my breath.

"We don't," Ty said, causing the rate of my heartbeat to spike. "What's the problem?"

I cringed at his expectant tone. My whispered words to Dorian over the noisy lunch crowd shouldn't have been audible to anyone else. Still, whether I had expected Ty to hear it or not, he had. I tried to speak, to somehow explain, but any possible explanation died on my tongue. There were no words, no excuses.

"Oh, Amelia's just worried I'll show you up." Dorian's casual tone surprised me, yet again. He was so bloody calm. "It would be pretty embarrassing for the *head of the swim team* to lose against the *new guy*."

Smugness curved Ty's lips. "Oh, I'll beat you, *new guy*, don't you worry. I'm pretty fast."

There was no doubt that Dorian would kick Ty's butt. Vampire against human... With our incredible speed it was hardly fair. Though Dorian winning wasn't the real issue; using our superior abilities around humans was. It was far too risky.

"I'm sure Ty can organize the whole swim team to watch too," Vanessa chimed in.

"Of course," Ty nodded, goading eyes shifting from her to Dorian. "What's the use in racing if no one's there to see me win?"

My insides began to ache at all the stress these two were causing me. I didn't know how much more of this I could take. Dorian scoffed beside me, finding comedy in Ty's words, while I fought the urge to dry-retch. Pleading with my eyes, I placed a firm hand over Dorian's. "Please don't."

He waved me off. "You worry too much."

It was clear that nothing I could say or do now was going to afford me the outcome I wanted. Dorian never shied away from a challenge. I bit my tongue hard. The pain and taste of my own blood distracted me from the nausea still curdling my stomach. This wasn't over. Later and without spectators, I would make him change his mind.

As I began preparing a solid argument to sway Dorian, a dark figure moved at the corner of my vision. In the same instant, the intensity of Ty's blood flared. I'd almost forgotten it throughout the stressful discussion. Now it was so strong that it filled my lungs and caused my head to swell. Tingles danced across my gums and without enough warning to hold them back, my fangs sprang free. Then I felt his presence; the dark figure stood directly behind me.

"What the hell is going on?" His voice cut through the air, disgruntled and familiar.

The screech of chair legs and numerous gasps reached my ears as action-hungry students turned in their seats.

My head whirled to find a tall, buff guy. His bare arms, scarred like Ty's, were stiff at his sides. It was the very same guy I'd been scanning the cafeteria for minutes ago. With wide eyes, I stared at him then down at his hunting boots that matched Ty's. How had I not heard his footsteps?

"Troy," Ty said in a deep, even voice. "This is Dorian and Amelia."

Troy stalked around the table, squaring up before Ty who remained seated, looking almost bored with the situation. Troy glared down, eyes skewering Ty with a cold and deathly stare. "They shouldn't be here. *You* should have dealt with this when you had the chance."

With the physical tension between them and the matching scars, I wondered suddenly if they brawled on a regular basis. Then panic over his cryptic words overrode my curiosity. The same fear that had plagued me earlier twisted my insides. I was right. He must know.

"Please excuse Troy," Vanessa said, carelessly curling a lock of hair around her index finger. "Like a dog, he's a bit *territorial*."

Troy's eyes whipped past Ty to her. Insult darkened his expression. "Did you just call me a dog?"

"Just calling it as I see it," Vanessa shrugged.

Troy crossed his arms defiantly over his broad chest and turned his glare back to Ty. "I refuse to put up with this shit!"

"You're out of line." Ty's voice was sharp as a blade. He rose to his feet, sliding his leather jacket off in the same movement. He wasn't quite as tall as Troy. Still, the power emanating from every inch of his taut, bronzed muscles made one thing strikingly clear: he was not about to back down. "You have two choices. Behave, or leave."

Troy's arms dropped with tension to his sides. Was he backing down?

Regardless, I jumped to my feet, forcing Dorian up by the sleeve of his sweater. In this moment, I couldn't contemplate their matched and overpowering scent. Or if Troy's cryptic words actually meant what I suspected. It was time to leave. And really, I shouldn't have let this happen in the first place. Agreeing to have lunch with humans... What was I thinking?

My voice emerged in a rush, lips covering my still extended fangs. "No. Stay." Besides not wanting to be the cause for anyone to fight, I couldn't stick around with their intense, coupled scent. "We're leaving."

Clutching Dorian's arm, I spun and began walking, away from drama, away from temptation, and away from Ty.

AFTER SCHOOL, Dorian peeled out of the student parking lot and onto Ocean Boulevard. I slung my arms over my chest and clutched my sides. Because if I didn't, the resent-clouded anger billowing within me would win, and I'd belt him across the face.

"I can't believe you!" Too angry to look at him, I glared out the window at the miserable rain pelting down all around us. It sheeted everything in monotones, from the prestigious estates and their lavish grounds to the expensive cars parked with surfboards along the shoreline. "We're supposed to blend in, appear normal. Not challenge the head of the swim team to a swim off, with the intent of using your inhuman speed to win. Mom will never allow this."

Dorian threw an arm over the seat to rifle through his backpack. A second later he'd pulled free two sheets of paper. They were permission slips for parental consent. One was to take part in a swimming race. The other was to observe from the stands. Their letterhead paper matched the permission slips hidden in my bag. They were for a geography excursion to the White Mountains later this week. "Mom wants us to do human stuff, and this is as human as it gets. And if you recall," he added, keeping his eyes on the rain-slicked road ahead, "Ty challenged me to race. You know I can't back down from a challenge."

Wishing that the look alone could inflict torturous pain, I propelled my icy glare onto him. The earlier irritation I felt toward Dorian took over. My lips spat with venom. "So he challenged you, who cares? And why is everything so freaking easy for you! Couldn't you smell them? How could you not have wanted to bite them then and there, to drain every drop of blood from their bodies?" I was screaming, voice shrill and unrelenting. But I didn't care. After fighting every instinct that seemed so natural to me now, the tether of my control was wearing so thin, it was on the verge of snapping.

Unshaken by my outburst, Dorian's lips parted with a half smile. "So, are you angry about the race, or because I didn't kill Ty and Troy? 'Cause I'm getting a mixed signal here. Don't draw attention by doing something normal, like competing in a sport, or draw attention by murdering in plain sight."

Ouch! That hit a note. I hung my head, letting my blond locks fall around my face. I was being a total hypocrite, expecting Dorian to hide away like I felt I had to while hating him for his lack of obvious struggle when it came to predatory instinct.

Dorian grasped a drink bottle from the cars cup holder and handed it to me. "Here, this'll help."

I eyed the black sports bottle in my hands, wishing the blood inside didn't taste better than chocolate. This was the usual way we consumed blood these days, cold and dead. It was a daily necessity that quelled some of the rampant thirst. Our stock was provided by one of the Armaya owned blood banks and kept chilled like most human beverages. Though the only thing human about drinking blood was that the blood *was* human. My fangs extended while my body shuddered. The level to which I'd enjoyed hunting, it was so primal, so embedded in this creature I was. But after each kill, the crushing guilt set in. It gnawed away at my insides like poison melting through my organs. The black eyes of terrified deer and golden eyes of startled wolves forever lingered on the back of my eyelids. *This way is better*, I thought, lifting the bottle to my lips and wishing the words held conviction rather than uncertainty. Wishing the thought of fresh blood, and the memory of the one human's blood I had tasted, didn't instill in me a crippling sense of starvation.

Deflecting my thoughts I asked, "So, you and what's-her-name? You didn't waste any time."

"Cindy," Dorian said while slicking his dark hair back with his hands. "Pretty, huh? And why wait. I've been girl-less for six months. That's like a lifetime in teen years." A playful smile crept across his face. "So, what's going on between you and Ty?"

The dead blood I had just downed spiked my throat, and I fought not to cough. "W-what do you mean?"

Dorian's eyes gleamed with perception, an expression that made me want to slap it from his face. "You two couldn't keep your eyes off each other."

Without wanting to, I thought back. Ty's calculating gaze had plagued me with nerves. On top of that, the sight and smell of him had invoked involuntary reactions in my body. I shook my head, grimacing. "It's his scent. It's just so—overwhelming."

"Yeah, I picked up on that too," Dorian said. "They've probably got a rare blood type or something."

"I guess." Tears at feeling so out of control, of finding adaption so difficult when Dorian was breezing through, pricked at my eyes. "How is it so easy for you?"

"It's not," Dorian said absolutely, resting a cold, supportive hand on mine. "It's a struggle. But I know I can keep it together, just as I know you can, too. You give yourself far too little credit." His gentle expression transformed with a mischievous grin. "Now, back to you and Ty, what's really going on?"

I jerked my hand from his. Inside I could feel my heartbeat elevating. "I told you." My tone was icy and sharp. "It's his blood. I literally want to kill him!"

Dorian gazed thoughtfully through the windscreen, barely slowing as he turned a sharp bend on the rain-slicked road. The Audi screeched in protest, sliding. Then its four wheels reclaimed the road. "If that were true," he said, raising an eyebrow, "you'd look at Troy the same way. But you don't." His mouth gaped as though he were rearranging the pieces of a puzzle. "Ah, I see," he said, looking back at me with gleaming eyes. "You're into Ty. You're attracted to him."

Fire seared up my neck and across my cheeks. The notion of wanting to kill someone while being attracted to them was utterly ridiculous. He was wrong. The urge to lash out seized me and I clenched my fists, narrowing my eyes at Dorian. "I am only going to say this once. Troy is a steroid-pumped jerk. Ty isn't. That's the *only* reason I look at them differently."

Dorian raised a doubtful brow as we drove through the stone barrier fronting our house. "Whatever you reckon, Sis." But the look on his face said, *I'll get to Mom before you do.*

Knowing he'd lock me out of Mom's office if he had the chance, I jumped out of the car before it rolled to a stop and raced into the house, failing to slam the office door before he leaped inside.

Mom smiled. "You just missed your uncle on the phone. He was calling to see how you're both settling in. Unfortunately, he's swamped with work at the Armaya. However, he said he might be able to visit in a couple of weeks." Mom was already dressed in a blazer and A-line skirt for her first meeting at the Portsmouth Vampire Council. "Now tell me, how was your first day at school?"

I threw my backpack down at the side of her desk. "Mom, please, you have to say no."

"What is going on?" she demanded, nodding at the two chairs across from her for us to sit. "Did something happen?"

"What?" I suddenly realized the worry on her face came from fear that we'd failed to control ourselves today. Before I had a chance to voice my *how could you send us to school if you thought we'd kill someone* rant, Dorian spoke.

"No," he said, "nothing like that. Amelia is just overreacting, as usual."

"Now, Dorian," Mom spoke sternly. "You know being a vampire heightens your emotions. So far you have found most of the transition quite routine. Amelia, on the other hand, has always been more emotionally charged. So her ability to control her influx of feelings will take more time and patience."

"Whatever." Dorian rolled his eyes and thrust the two forms into her hands. "I want to join the swim team, and to qualify I have to race their captain."

"A race?" Mom pursed her lips in thought. "Well, I don't see the harm."

"You don't see the harm!" I shot up and kicked my bag. Everything spilled out: textbooks, pencil case, iPhone, and the damn excursion slips. It had an extended deadline of tomorrow morning, seeing as it was already well into the new school year. Every other student's had been returned last week.

Mom snatched the permission slips up from the ground, scanning it over with narrowed eyes. "And I suppose you don't want to go on this geography excursion either?"

"Mom, you don't understand." I threw clasped hands across her tidy desk, pleading. "Today was hard, really hard. I don't think I…"

"Amelia," she said, cutting me off. Her eyes were gentle but set with determination. "I don't want to force you to do anything. But I will not let you hide away, believing you're some despicable creature. You are not. You are a good person." With a steady breath she pulled a pen from her blazer pocket and signed all three forms. "Learning to co-exist with humans is a process. And you and Dorian are doing so well. I am so extremely proud of you both."

I cringed. The race was bad enough. Now I had to stress about the cons of being trapped on a human-packed bus ride to the White Mountains. Not enough clean air, too many bodies, and no escape… unless I dive out one of the windows. I knelt to stuff the spilled items into my backpack. Then knowing nothing I could say would change her mind, I snatched my two forms from Mom's desk and stomped from her office.

Upstairs in my room, I dumped my bag on the carpet before flopping onto my bed. Today sucked! And I still had algebra homework and a paper on Freud's Theory of the Unconscious to get started on.

With another sigh I pulled my iPod from my bag, playing the Three Days Grace song *Let you down*. I peered past the mauve tapestry draped around the corner post of my bed. Through the high-arched window the cloudy sky was darkening. Ty flitted to mind and I wondered again how I could know him. But I couldn't. Before this move, we'd never even left Alaska. Maybe I just wished I knew him. Still, something about him kept me speculating and totally uneasy. I wondered how long it'd take before I let everyone down and tried, maybe even succeeded, in killing him. There was only one solution. Stay away. Better never to know him than to kill him.

I rolled off the bed and glanced around the room, my room. It was so big, with walls and a high ceiling all in varying shades of purple. There was a hint of paint fumes, and I wondered if Caius or Mom had organized it to be painted before we arrived. A white antique dresser sat across the room with an oval mirror spanning its length. Two side tables flanked the disarray of my oversized, purple bed. Above a lavish chandelier with glittering, crystal teardrops filled the room with twinkling light. Their design mirrored the others that marked almost every room in this expansive house. Even with my Lifehouse, Three Days Grace, and Skillet posters splashed across the walls, the room still felt bare. Nothing else in this room was really mine. It was all new, compliments of our wealthy vampire uncle. I hadn't kept anything else from my old life in Anchorage, bar a few comfortable clothes. At the time I had wanted to be punished for the *thing* I was becoming. Now, seeing this big empty space, I wish I had kept something more that reminded me of a time when I thought of myself as almost normal, just a human.

I turned back to the window and yanked the dark-purple drapes closed. Then, with the weight of the day bringing me down, I dropped back onto the bed and flicked off the black-velvet lamp. The song *Animal I have become* came on and my iPhone beeped. Instantly my mood lifted, expecting the text to be from Kendrick. Then it sank. It wasn't him.

'Wanna grab a bite after I kick your brother's butt?'

It was Ty. How had he gotten my number? Then I remembered art class when Vanessa had requested my number. She gave it to Ty?

My pulse quickened and I sighed, throwing my head back against the pillows. So much for keeping my distance... Pursing my lips, I read the text again and frowned. Grab a bite? That phrasing made my paranoia kick in.

Hold up. My eyes bugged. Was he actually asking me out? Or was this just some kind of ploy to figure out why I was such a freak? Or was it even worse, a cruel prank on the strange 'new girl?' In truth, I couldn't imagine Ty actually wanting to go anywhere with me. Not after how moronically I had behaved at lunch. I shrugged. No matter what his motivations were, I knew my answer and keyed in a response. *'Can't. Busy.'*

Anxious he'd reply I stared at the screen. My free hand rifled through my bedside table's drawer for my hidden after dinner mints. Chocolate always helped calm my nerves. After a few minutes without reply and four chocolates later, I breathed a sigh of relief, turning the music back on.

When the phone unexpectedly beeped again, I almost jumped out of my skin. But the text wasn't from Ty. *'What's new? How's school?'*

Warmth coated my heart like warm honey. It was Kendrick, my best friend, the one whose help and guidance had been the only thing to get me through the long months at the cabin. I keyed a response, *'School sucks! WYWH.'* Wish you were here. I clutched the phone to my heart.

Salty tears blurred my vision, and I blinked them back. Before this moment I hadn't allowed myself to dwell on it. But without Kendrick's support, I truly felt alone, like I was drowning in my own blood. I knew I had Mom and Dorian, and that they would do anything for me. But it just wasn't the same.

A final text came through. *'Maybe I can visit. But I GTG. Miss U 2.'*

*a*t the first opportunity, I vaulted off the bus and darted behind it. My hands braced against my knees while I sucked crisp, untainted air into my lungs.

It was Thursday; only three days since Mom had signed the bloody permission slips, which any and all arguing hadn't gotten me out of. The bus ride to the White Mountains in a stuffy, packed-to-the-brim bus had been long, way too long. I had been seated up front, blockaded by Dorian against a window. Still, the urge to turn on everyone trapped within the slow-moving vessel was overwhelming. Not even my supposed reprieve, the menthol nasal tube that I hid in a clenched fist fearing anyone might catch sight of it, could deter my wicked thoughts. The collective scent of blood, heightened by not only Ty but Troy too, was far too pungent.

Now at our destination, the beautiful and dense green forests of the White Mountains, everyone poured off the bus. Groups of twelve were being arranged as Dorian sidled up behind the bus, finding me still curled in on myself. He patted a supportive hand across my back while the geography teacher announced his name into group one with Mrs. Ruby. When I finally got placed into group three with Mr. McKenna from psychology, I groaned.

Dorian hauled me upright. "It's outside, fresh air. Just tail behind your group," he said with a squeeze on my arms. "You can do this."

I felt tempted to chuck a pink fit. But I knew Dorian wasn't about to demand the teacher move me, not when his eyes were already wandering to a group of pretty girls. Besides, there was no way in hell I could argue the point myself, surrounded by blood-scented teens, without the possibility of letting my fangs loose. "I hate this."

Dorian sighed, then half smiled, lowering his voice so that only I could hear him. "Think of it this way. If you lose it, you only have to kill everyone in your group. That's only twelve people. And I'm sure there are plenty of good places to stash bodies out here." He brushed his hands together. "No witnesses, no crime."

"That's not funny!" I swung my fist to connect with Dorian's stomach, but he jerked back just in time.

"Call me if you need," he said, lifting his phone from his pocket as he backed up to his group. "I'll *always* back you up."

Left with no escape, I sighed. My assigned group had already taken off up the winding gravel path. Now Mr. McKenna was calling for me to hurry up. Trailing far behind, I sucked in a deep breath of fresh air. Then instantly wished I hadn't. A much too familiar scent intruded as the crunch of gravel reached my ears. The sound was approaching from behind. No, please no.

My heart jumped into my throat and I whirled. Ty and Troy were bounding straight for me. Troy passed by, face stormy as he caught up with the front of the group. Instead of following, Ty slowed, falling into step beside me. The smell of his blood mingled with a touch of chlorine in the air. Picking up my pace, I groaned internally.

There must have been swim practice before school. I forced my view from him and onto the dense surrounding scrub, which breathed life with a spectrum of colored, wild flora. If only the raw beauty were enough to distract me from him.

"So," Ty said with clear hesitation. "What about coffee, as friends?"

His proximity made my mouth water, and I knew he had spoken. But above the irregular beating of his heart, I hadn't been able to concentrate enough to hear the words. Instead, I dug into my jeans pocket with shaky hands and retrieved the nasal tube. Before I could think twice, I lifted it to my nose. Then I cringed. Now Ty had seen me use a nasal decongestant. Great!

"Sorry, what?" Hiding the tube back in my pocket, I glanced at Ty. I fully expected to find his expression guarded with a look that said *you're a nerd!* Only Ty wasn't staring at me like I was a nerd. He was smiling, a curious and confident smile that brought warmth to my cheeks.

"Coffee, as friends…"

I hated coffee with a passion. Give me hot chocolate any day. Wait, was Ty asking me out? Not that it mattered. What did matter was that I not give in to my primal instincts. And I could only do that if I eliminated my biggest temptation.

"Look, Ty," I said, keeping my eyes ahead. My fingers itched to raise the decongestant to my nose again. "You need to stay away from me."

"And why is that?" Ty's voice sounded amused and light, devoid of the confusion I had expected given my words.

Because I'm a monster, and every moment I'm near you I contemplate ripping your throat out to drain every last drop of your sweet-smelling blood. I glanced back at him, studying him head to toe. His black hair shimmered in the broken sunlight that filtered through the thick canopy above. The black shirt that clung to his body emphasized his defined arms and abs. His casual, black jeans were torn across one knee. In so many ways he appeared like a regular teenage boy. Yet in others he was distinctly different. Ty's eyes were watching me, the green of his irises sparkling.

Knowing he was waiting for me to respond, I drew in a deep breath. "Because, I'm not someone you want to know."

Ty's smile didn't waver, nor did his forehead crease with misunderstanding. It was like my response hadn't confused him, almost like he had expected it. "Why don't you let me be the judge of that?"

My stomach churned. What did he want from me? The notion that Dorian could have been right crossed my mind. That Ty was, for some unconscionable reason, attracted to me. Just as fast as the thought flooded my mind, I shook it away, laughing internally. No, I told myself. He can't be. Dorian was wrong. Because if Ty *did* watch me the same way I watched him, then that would mean that *I* would have to be attracted to Ty, too. Me, a monster, drawn to my prey for more than just its flesh and blood.

I shook my head. "Please, Ty." I hated having to say the words. But I had to. It was the only way. My arms clamped over my chest, almost bracing as I glared through the trees and into the surrounding mountainside. It was so beautiful and peaceful, a stark contrast to how I felt. "Just leave me alone."

"Fine." Ty picked up his pace. That one word as he stalked away from me stung like pins poking through my flesh and into my stomach. I stumbled, pulling to a stop, coiled arms lowering to tighten around my gut. *You don't like him. You want to kill him. This is best for everyone.* The words did little to reassure me, or to lift the discomfort I felt. I took a ragged breath and forced my body to straighten, arms dropping to my sides. Non-tainted air swirled through my lungs, washing away some of the sting from my insides.

It was just his blood, I assured myself. Still a little voice inside my head that I couldn't quite dislodge whispered that I was deluding myself, believing only what I wanted to believe.

Needing a distraction to quell the contradicting voices in my head, I pulled my purple-cased iPod from my pocket. I sighed, missing Kendrick. Then I plugged in my earbuds and blasted the words to Red's song *Fight Inside*. The sting of their words reflected my constant struggle to hide the monster inside of me. The monster I would always be.

Slowing my pace helped dull the scent of the group's blood, including his. After walking for almost an hour, I began to relax, began to believe that maybe Dorian had been right. Maybe I could do this.

When the group neared the summit, the taste of salt in the air intensified from their perspiring bodies. The group had paused for a break at the lookout, and everyone was peering out over the timber railing. I paused further down the track, keeping my distance while watching the group. Ty stood to one side of the students before a damaged piece of railing. There was bright yellow 'caution' tape cordoning off the hazard. Troy stood by his side. As usual, his face was strained as he spoke to Ty with clear agitation. I felt tempted to remove my earbuds. Picking up their conversation even from this distance, a good sixty feet away, would be easy. But I decided I really didn't want to hear what Troy was bitching about. Even if I did suspect it had everything to do with me.

When the group resumed their course, following the now rocky path back into the depths of the forest, I ambled up to the same spot Ty and Troy had been standing. I pulled my earbuds from my ears, peering out into the plunging valley. Splashes of green, gold and deep-russet covered the treetops with the progression of fall. Above, a single Falcon soared through the air. Its repetitive call was like a fire alarm on overdrive as it dipped and dived beneath a cloudless, pastel-blue sky.

The air around me was crisp and perfectly clear. Time to move on. I craned my head. The other students were making ground down the path. Ty was tailing a few feet behind. I was about to take after them when I stalled. The fiery and sweet smell of blood, *his blood*, reached me.

Before I could speak or move, Troy appeared before me. His expression was dark and his scent wrapped around me. "Don't even think about it."

Had he seen me looking at Ty? Folding barricading arms over my chest, I took a much-needed step back. "Think about what?"

"Trying your luck with Ty," he practically snarled. His hand hovered over the pocket of his jacket as if about to pull something free.

I stole a glance down the long pathway, but it was empty. The group and Ty were already gone.

"It's not like he actually likes you," Troy went on, hatred poisoning his words. "Anything nice he says to you is purely pity. You're a freak of nature. He regrets not having dealt with you when he had the chance."

Freak of nature? Dealt with me? Irritated confusion brought fire to my face. And the smell of him so close had my fangs peeking through the top of my gums. Sick of this guy's cryptic bullshit, I unfolded my arms and clenched my hands. "Look, you steroid-jacked jerk. I don't know what your problem is or what the hell you're talking about..."

"I'm warning you," he grated, stepping close enough to poke me in the chest.

My fangs broke free and I darted back, knowing I'd lunge and bite him if I didn't. Wrong choice. My Vans slipped on the loose stones at the edge of the cliff. Then my back hit the 'caution' tape, snapping it on impact. Instantly my mind and body came alive. Everything was happening in slow motion. A good thirty feet down was a small outcropping. Not enough to kill a vampire, but a human? Definitely. I could leap forward, clearing Troy and saving my skin. But at what cost? My cover would be blown. No, the only human option was to fall.

Suddenly a hand shot out of nowhere, collecting my wrist in a heated vice-grip. I blinked, bewildered as Ty hauled me to safety. My body flew forward through the air until my feet hit solid ground. "Are you okay?"

No, I'm not okay. I almost had to fall off a cliff because your so-called friend got in my face, I thought, struggling to retract my fangs with the double-up of their scent. Instead I said, "Where the hell did you come from?"

Ty narrowed his eyes over his shoulder at Troy. "Leave us."

Troy shrugged. "Whatever." He turned without a word or even a glance at me to jog down the beaten track.

Ty threw a glance down the path. "I heard arguing, and when I came back around the corner I saw you and Troy. I'd almost reached you when you stepped back into the caution tape."

I remembered looking down the empty path before the fall. Could Ty have gotten to us that quickly? Doubt weighed against my mind. He was apparently a good swimmer, but was he a fast runner too? Or was he something else entirely. Something more than what he appeared to be?

Ty's lips parted with a broadening smile. "So, how are you going to repay me?"

Wrinkling my nose, I frowned. I had to figure him out. "Repay you for what?"

Ty arched one eyebrow. The honey of his irises appeared brighter, reflecting a pale shadow of my face. "For saving your life."

"Oh," I said, trying to ignore the still lingering cloud of his scent. "Thanks." I looked up as Ty brushed the tousled hair from his eyes. "I guess I owe you my life."

Ty smiled but shook his head. "No. Just a date…"

CHAPTER 6

*L*ate on Friday afternoon, I stood outside the double doors to the indoor pool. My forehead pressed against the small, square window. The time between the excursion yesterday and this very moment had flown by in the blink of an eye. My paranoia over Troy's words, *You're a freak of nature,* and something about Ty dealing with me, pressed on my mind. Everything he said was cryptic. But could he really know our terrible secret? Who were these guys?

Overshadowing that mind mess was the fact that I had, with much reluctance, agreed to Ty's date, as long as my mom approved. And surprise, surprise, she had, stating that at sixteen most girls had already been on their first dates. Thanks to that, I hadn't been able to sleep last night. Now I was stuck with a problem and it was all catching up with me. Ty and Dorian were about to race. Then straight after, I'd be expected to go on a date with Ty.

With a deep, preparatory breath, I pushed through the double doors and almost fell back against them. The thick, chlorine-soaked air hit me like a face full of boiling water. It was so lung-burningly pungent, that it almost drowned out the scent of human blood. Almost. Worried my weird behavior was drawing attention, my eyes darted around the room. The swim team with their matching Speedos took up the three bottom right rows of bleachers. A few held black and gold banners. They matched the ones strung around the metal-clad walls, with *'Go Sharks'* and *'Ty is Number One!'* printed across them. Vanessa sat on the other side of the bleachers with Troy, holding a fashion magazine and whispering. Ty, thank God, was nowhere in sight.

I rushed up to Dorian who was at the starting blocks and revving himself up for the race. A fresh wave of trepidation flooded my chest. It was a long shot, but I had to try one last time to get him to reconsider. "Dorian," I whispered, confident the swim team's chatter would keep my words from being overheard.

"Wow," he said, looking a little surprised. "I thought you were just tired this morning. Now it's the end of the day and you still look like shit."

I frowned at the insult, but I knew his words held truth. I couldn't stop worrying about my date with Ty. I'd barely slept at all last night. And with the swim-off fast approaching, even when awake my mind had been racing. "Thanks, just what I needed to hear." The weight of Troy's sneering eyes tunneled into me, and I turned away. "Dorian, please," I whispered, eyes pleading. "Pull out of the race. I have a terrible feeling."

Dorian stretched out his swimming cap and molded it over his head. "Step out of the spotlight?" he asked, tucking in a few escaping locks of chocolate-brown hair. "Never. But I will do you one thing."

I planted my hands on my hips, skeptical. "And what's that?"

Dorian's lips curved up at the sides into a cheeky smile. "I promise to win by only a hand's length." His eyes softened as he ran his hand up and down my arm. "Have some faith. I can do this. You know I would never expose us."

"Come to wish your brother luck?" Ty's distinct voice startled me, echoing from behind. "'Coz he'll need it."

Ty's scent bloomed, poisoning the air. It almost brought me to my knees. Then he was standing right beside me, scarcely dressed in his black Speedo and smiling. At the sheer sight of him, my breath caught in the back of my throat. I swallowed hard, trying to force the sensation back down while spear-winged butterflies flooded my stomach. Like his arms, his sculpted chest was also marked by small irregular scars. I frowned, eyes traveling down to his abs then gliding further down. Indents ran diagonally from his hips, dipping below the low-lying fabric of his Speedo. Warmth flashed across my face. My eyes shot up to find Ty's expression lit by amusement. I mentally shook myself. Stop freaking staring!

As my eyes darted away, Dorian stepped beside me. He was looking at Ty with a cocky smile tugging at his lips. "You wish, Malau. I'm gonna wipe the floor with you!"

"We'll see," Ty said, raising an eyebrow. "Though you should know…" He pointed to a maple trophy cabinet. It was positioned between the door to the male and female locker rooms at the other end of the pool. I narrowed my superior sight. The cabinet was packed with polished, gleaming trophies. Most were awarded for state championship, and every single one had 'Ty Malau' etched into the metal plate. "I never lose."

I gulped. This was not gonna go down well. Dorian refused to bow out of the race. And Ty, evidently, had never lost. Feeling defeated, and tempted to ogle Ty's naked flesh again, I turned away. "Good luck," I mumbled, retreating to a spare seat centered evenly between Troy and Vanessa and the swim team. It was on the top row, leaving a good forty feet between me and them. It also gave me a clear view of Troy, just in case he decided to get in my face again.

In the seconds of my retreat, an overweight man had appeared at the sidelines. With a whistle in hand, he must have been the coach. "One lap, up and back, freestyle all the way. Come close to beating our shark and you're in."

My sight shifted to Ty, who watched me with a mesmerizing smile. I took a ragged sigh of relief. The distance separating us somewhat pacified the frenzy of volatile butterflies still swarming my stomach.

Without any hesitation, the coach put the whistle to his lips. The shrill sound gained everyone's attention. There were eight starting blocks heading each side of the four, twenty-five-meter lanes. Ty and Dorian stepped onto the first two. They froze in perfect suspense, then the whistle chirped, shrill and ear-piercing.

Both boys exploded off the blocks in flawless freestyle form. At first, Ty led by two feet. But I knew that wouldn't last. Dorian was biding his time, keeping just behind Ty until they flipped to finish the fifty-meter sprint. Dorian burst off with wall. He shot past Ty and took lead position.

With my gaze locked on the two of them, I felt somewhat surprised. For a human, Ty was doing a remarkable job of keeping pace with Dorian, who was so close to pushing his speed past an acceptable level that it made my heart race.

Now they were closing in on the finish line. My sight locked on Ty. Water erupted around him, glassy droplets reflecting light from the domed fluorescents above. The sight obscured my view of his body, which blurred, almost seeming to darken.

I blinked then zeroed back in on Ty. He was rising for his last breath. His eyes were open, and looking at me. The honey of his irises glowed brighter, turning gold and iridescent. His body beneath the rippling water quivered. Then he shot into lead position, hand collecting the wall just an inch before Dorian's.

Cheers boomed from the swim team, while the two guys emerged from the pool. Above their deafening cheers, the persistent and loud echo of my heart pulsed through my ears like crashing waves. My jaw hung open in shocked horror. Ty won?

For a split second, I wondered if Dorian had taken my plight seriously and let Ty win. Only that couldn't be the case. The total shock encompassing my brother's face was a mirror reflection of my own. My breath was coming in short, sharp bursts. My lungs began to ache. What the hell!

With trembling legs that felt as heavy and rigid as concrete pillars, I struggled to stand. Sharp pain shot from my feet and up through my entire body as I slowly forced my way down the stands. Fear-fed confusion clouded my mind. I needed to make sense of what had just happened. But no normal, rational explanation could make sense of how a human could have beaten my brother. He was a vampire, with speed that could outdo even a shark's. Which left me with one conclusion, one so disturbing that it made my blood run cold. With his speed, unusual eyes, sharp hearing, potent scent, warm touch, and numerous scars…Ty was something else, something dangerous and inhuman. A monster, like me… We needed to get out of there, and fast.

With Ty distracted by the congratulations of his swimming peers and the coach, I forced my way through the crowd. My legs wobbled like jelly, but my eyes found Dorian with a look that said, *see what you've done*. His stricken face ignored me, so clearly trying to hide the shock of losing.

For a brief moment, smugness tempted me. Dorian had lost the composure he always held so easily, his flawless facade finally cracking. But I couldn't enjoy the moment of his downfall. Not when this harmless situation had turned so volatile so fast. The desperation to flee was coursing adrenaline through my veins. My whole body began to jitter. We needed to get the hell out of here, and far away from Ty.

I snatched Dorian's bag from the sidelines and thrust the towel into his chest. "Let's go."

Dorian threw the towel around his waist then waved in Ty's direction. His facade had been reclaimed. "Sorry man, gotta go. C'ya tomorrow!"

A part of me ached to look at Ty, to read his expression. But I didn't. I couldn't. Instead, I clutched Dorian's arm and turned away, marching. I could sense the weight of Ty's intense eyes boring into the back of my head as we flew through the double doors.

A blur of beige and redwood from double-stacked lockers and classroom doors rushed past as we sped through the empty corridors. We burst out the main doors. In seconds we'd crossed the rain-drenched parking lot to jump into our car.

Dorian fired up the engine, his chest rising with labored breath, mirroring my own. He glared out the windshield, chlorine water soaking through his towel and onto the leather upholstery. He seemed frozen, the set of his jaw tight. Was he seriously waiting for the car's turbo to warm up? Or was he just too shocked to move?

Anxiety grew within me by the second. I wished I had my own ride so I could tear us from this place. A speedy Ducati, my favorite motorbike, would do. My eyes darted to the rear-view mirror, expecting to see Ty. The space was clear. No one had followed us.

Dorian finally came to life. His hardened expression hit me like a physical blow. The silver of his eyes raged. "What the hell was that!" He slammed his foot onto the clutch, plunging the gearshift into reverse. The tires skidded as the car launched backward, barely clearing the vehicles beside us. "How the hell did he beat me?"

Dorian located first gear in a flash and gunned the engine. The car responded with a roar and the whistle of turbo, fish-tailing from the parking lot and out onto Ocean Boulevard. The tide was calm under the setting of a cloud-covered sun. "I didn't even see him pass me on the last stroke!"

I shook my head. My tongue felt dry and unresponsive, refusing to move as my head spun. The image of Ty's bright eyes haunted my memory. Had that really happened? I turned in my seat, forcing words from my mouth. "You didn't see it?"

Dorian's hands tightened around the steering wheel. "See what? I was blinded by those bloody fluorescent lights."

Dorian didn't notice. I thought again of what I had witnessed in the pool. There had been so much water splashing and swirling. Even with my predatory sight, the view hadn't been crystal clear. A rational explanation lit up like a light bulb in my mind. The fluorescents could have emphasized the already luminous color of Ty's eyes, and reflected through the splashing water, blurring his body beneath the surface. Still none of that explained how he'd won. I turned over every detail of the race until my brain began to throb. Nothing I came up with could explain away the win. Dorian kept glancing at me like he was waiting for an answer, needing to know what I had seen.

"It was... I just..." Why was I hesitating? Why wasn't I airing my thoughts and suspicions to Dorian? Even if it were a trick of the light, he'd want to know. He'd want to draw his own conclusions. But I couldn't tell him what I'd seen. Maybe I was worried he'd laugh at me. Maybe it was something entirely different. "It was nothing. I saw nothing."

Dorian's brow creased. He slowed the car and pulled into our paved driveway. A set of headlights caught the car's side mirror, reflecting blinding light into my eyes. I blinked, cocking my head to the side and caught sight of my reflection. My eyes were bloodshot and lined with dark puffy circles. Dorian had been right. I did still look like shit. The car rolled to a stop at our front steps and I leaned back. A flash of bright blue through the mirror caught my eye. I whirled in my seat to find a WRX parked right behind us. The car was fully kitted out and dropped with nineteen-inch white-painted rims. Ty was waiting inside.

"What the hell is *he* doing here?" Dorian was scowling at him through the rear-view mirror.

I mentally slapped myself while my stomach swelled with nausea. Shit! Shit! Shit! I had totally forgotten about the date, and now Ty was here. Helpless desperation clung to me. Dorian had been out with Cindy when I'd told Mom about the date, so I quickly explained the situation: the excursion and Troy's part, and Ty's subsequent heroism that saved my skin, and our secret. "I have to go," I said. Our sudden departure would have stirred enough suspicion already.

Dorian was shaking his head, his hair falling into his eyes. "No way in hell. We still don't know what happened back there."

In truth, I really didn't want to go, to have to act like everything was normal, like Ty winning wasn't anything but ordinary. But I had to. There was no other choice. "Look," I said, trying to keep my voice level, even though inside I was screaming against my own resolve. "Ty doesn't know that he shouldn't have won. But after running off, and especially if I refuse to go with him now, he might begin to wonder."

Dorian struck out, clutching my wrist with tense fingers. "I don't like this."

"Me neither." I wriggled my wrist free and crossed my arms over my chest. "But we have no other choice."

With a loud sigh, Dorian slumped back against the seat. "Alright. But I'm tailing you."

I didn't bother to argue, and actually felt less nervous knowing Dorian would be close by to keep an eye on things. Apart from having to get through this date without adding to Ty's suspicion, I had to get through it without killing him. "Fine, but don't follow too closely."

Dorian hitched his brow in a James Bond kind of way. How he found the humor in this situation was beyond me. "Don't worry about me. I'm stealth."

IN A SUDDEN MOVEMENT Ty's hand broke from the steering wheel. My entire body stiffened. But Ty didn't touch me. He simply reached out to spin the volume dial on the stereo face. A song I knew well vibrated through the speakers. It filled the car with the rock words of Skillet's song *Monster*. Seeing as I was, in this very moment, imagining all the ways I could sink my fangs into Ty's flesh without causing an accident, it fit the situation all too well.

I shook off the dark thoughts. Then I noticed what I had been too apprehensive to see when Ty had picked me up. Skillet was printed in bold white letters across the front of his black T-shirt.

Ty caught my lingering gaze. "It's the band that's playing."

I looked to Ty, surprised he knew the band. They were awesome, but nowhere near mainstream. "I know. I love their albums *Awake* and *Comatose*. The music just…"

"Speaks to you," Ty said, finishing my sentence word for word. "Yeah, me too."

Following Ty's unexpected arrival I had made up the lamest excuse for disappearing, saying '*I thought you'd pick me up here.*'

Problem was, Ty had no idea where I lived. Ty had also been fully dry and clothed. At human speed, getting dried and dressed fast enough to follow us home, was virtually impossible. My paranoid fears surrounding Ty resurfaced—the speed of being inhuman.

Now with my window down, the scent of menthol from the nasal tube shielded in my hand and the surrounding dense plant life filled my nostrils. The combination made me want to cough. Still it was better than the alternative, which involved closing the window and being swarmed by the scent of Ty's blood. So far only minutes had passed. Each felt like painful lifetimes. We were still on Ocean Boulevard, taking the scenic route that would deliver us to Portsmouth and the *little Italian restaurant* Ty had arranged for our supposed date.

As I had been doing every consecutive minute, I pretended to check my reflection. Our car tailed way behind. Dorian was barely visible within the driver's seat. Its headlights just peeked around the single car that separated us. The smallest sliver of relief eased my swelling apprehension. Good, at least he was keeping his distance. The last thing we needed was to add to Ty's suspicion. Already, I could sense growing tension thickening the air. Ty's hands were continually releasing the steering wheel, fingers flexing before curling tightly back around the leather. And my own tension? Though it eased at times, it never faded. The elevated beat of Ty's heart pumping delicious-smelling blood throughout his body kept me on edge. Sucking fresh air from the open window while keeping the nasal tube hidden in my hand was only doing so much.

When the car separating us disappeared, I threw another glance in the rear-view mirror. Curving, tree-dense roads had replaced the flashes of ocean between the trees. Dorian was tailing further back than before, his headlights only just appearing as we rounded another unlit bend.

I knew I shouldn't. But I couldn't stop myself. I stole a quick glance in Ty's direction. The jugular vein along the side of his neck was pulsing. Blistering heat flared across my face. I went to force my sight away when a sickening *thwack* sounded.

Ty's scarred arm shot across my chest so incredibly fast, it left me no time to react. He slammed on the brakes and swerved off the road. The tires skidded across gravel and his training bag slid off the back seat, clanking with the sound of colliding metal.

What the hell? My heart jumped into my throat. Shit, he'd seen Dorian!

Readying to fight, my body went rigid. My hands clenched into fists. The grip was so tight my nails sliced through the flesh of my palms.

But Ty didn't advance. Instead, he glanced over at his bag and dropped his arm from my chest. "Are you okay?"

My lips seemed cemented shut. Unable to respond, I nodded.

Ty pursed his lips and threw open the driver's side door, exiting the car.

I jumped out behind him, finally finding my voice. "What happened?" My eyes darted around, scanning for Dorian. Through the darkness of the winding, tree-lined road, he along with the white headlights of our car, was nowhere in sight. He must have killed the lights and pulled to the side of the road just before the last bend up the road.

Ty was now behind the car, his back to me as he knelt down to the gravel, before rising to his feet again. He turned toward me, cradling a hand-sized bird with kid gloves. "It flew into the windshield."

He hadn't seen Dorian. Thank God. I stepped closer to Ty. The motionless, black bird was lying on its back across his palms. Its wings were extended and hanging limply over his fingers. My voice escaped in a whisper. "Is it okay?"

Ty pressed a finger to the bird's chest. Then he retracted and extended each of its wings. A look of sheer relief spread across his face, lifting his lips at the sides. "It's just stunned."

The bird stirred then, twitching with life. Ty's arms dropped then flung upwards in a gentle motion, his hands opening at the highest point. The bird lifted into the sky. Its flapping wings pulled it higher and higher until it disappeared beyond the thicket of trees lining the road.

I turned to Ty, awestruck. "How did you... I mean, how could you tell it could still fly?"

Ty's smile deepened. "Instinct."

THE WAFTING SMELLS of hot food filled the small Italian restaurant, a variety of cream and tomato blended pasta and mozzarella-topped pizzas. Finally I was able to think past my thirst for blood.

Grazing humans occupied almost every purple-clothed table littering the restaurant. I turned my sight from them to look at Ty. "Um, I forgot to congratulate you on winning."

After the bird incident, we had completed the drive here in relative silence. Ty's unexpected gentleness had surprised me, and now I felt a shift in my feelings. Not that I was exactly sure what that shift meant. The only thing I did know was that I wanted to figure Ty out. I needed to know what his motivation in inviting me on this so-called 'date' was. Even more than that, I needed to uncover the secrets he was hiding, the thing that made him distinctly different from regular humans.

"So, congratulations."

A broad smile snaked across Ty's lips. "Thanks. Though your brother didn't make winning easy." He studied me for a moment before looking back to the laminated menu in his hands. "He had me on the stretch back. But I guess I got a burst of energy right before the finish."

A plausible reason to explain Ty winning popped into my head. "Do you do steroids?" Unfortunately tact had never been one of my strong points.

Ty brushed the hair back from his widened eyes. "Do I look like someone who takes enhancing drugs?"

With a slow shrug, my eyes raked over Ty. His muscle density and definition exceeded that of any regular teenager. My initial instinct was to reply 'yes,' though the offense Ty had taken in my question pinned my lips shut. If it wasn't drugs…then what? I shook my head. "Sorry, that was a lame joke. I didn't mean to imply anything."

Outside, the cloud-sheathed sky shifted with a brewing icy wind. The full moon above broke through. Its ghostly reflection shone down to catch on something dark across the road. Ty was saying something about Dorian having a spot on the swim team while I squinted over his shoulder to the parking lot. A black Cabriolet was parked with Dorian watching from inside. Somehow it had completely slipped my mind that he'd been tailing us. A sudden feeling of guilt pressed against my chest. Not for forgetting about Dorian, or even for leaving him out there waiting and wondering, but for letting Dorian follow us in the first place. The swelling guilt was fed by a realization, a true belief that I should never have doubted. Ty wasn't dangerous. Sure he was different, and I was certain he was more than he was pretending to be. Still, even through my own suspicion, I couldn't believe he was a threat. His reaction to hitting the bird displayed that, as did his actions in saving me from falling to my supposed death at the White Mountains. A growing part of me felt compelled to figure Ty out, to try to uncover what he was hiding. But if he discovered Dorian spying, I'd never unveil the truth.

"Uh, Ty?" He looked up from the menu that obscured half his face. "I'm just going to use the ladies. Could you order me the lasagna?"

Ty nodded with a smile as I rose to my feet. His back was facing the restaurant's entry. It remained that way as I slipped past him and out the glass door. I darted across the road through slowing traffic, and mounted the curb to the lamp-brightened parking lot.

Dorian was still wrapped in his wet towel, but had managed to pull a hoodie on from the back seat. "What's the story?" he whispered through the open window. There was concern in his tone, but it was obvious in his lighter expression that he was actually having fun with this spy mission.

"Not much to report," I lied, bending down to rest my arms along the sill. "He seems completely normal. Except I think he takes steroids."

Dorian almost spat his next words which had climbed an entire octave. "You asked if he took drugs!"

Guilt pressed harder against my chest, this time for lying so blatantly to my own brother. "Yeah… Of course he said no. But it's the only thing that makes any sense."

Dorian's face hardened, doubtful. "He still shouldn't have beaten me, drugs or not."

I racked my brain for a believable lie. Then recalled the bright fluorescents Dorian had mentioned after the race. "You were only planning to win by a hand. And you did say you were blinded by the lights. What if you lost focus?"

Dorian went quiet for a moment, tapping his chin with his index finger. I could practically see the wheels spinning behind his narrowed eyes. "I guess I was a bit distracted. But I still think something more is going on."

With irritation beginning to fray away my nerves, I rose from my crouched position. "Well, your suspicion doesn't mean he's dangerous. You saw what happened with the bird, didn't you?" Dorian hitched his eyebrows, confirming. I made a conscious effort to lower my rising voice. "He's not a threat. But I do want to get to know him." It wasn't a total lie, just a twisting of motives. I'd let Dorian believe my wanting to get to know Ty meant I was admitting feelings for him rather than it being to figure him out. Feeling a bout of uncertainty, I reaffirmed, *I'm doing this to figure Ty out. That's the only reason.*

Shaking off the confusion, I looked to Dorian whose hardened expression had given way to surprise. "Alright," he said. "But call me if you need to." A devilish smile danced across his face as he flashed his fangs. "Oh, and do try not to drain him. There's no point wasting your time 'getting to know him' if he ends up dead."

"That's not funny." Agitated, I turned with flared nostrils. A line of stationary cars waited on a red light, and I bounded through them and back through the glass door to the restaurant.

The waitress who had just brought out our food occupied Ty. She flashed him an obviously flirtatious smile before retreating to the kitchen. Flames flared up my neck, blazing coals within my chest. *Jealousy?* I almost laughed. No, that's impossible. I'm pissed because she's toying with my…prey. I shuddered, not sure which was worse.

Ty glanced up as though he'd sensed me lingering across the room.

With a mental shake, I ambled over to our table. "Sorry," I said, taking my seat. "Bit of a line for the ladies."

A genuine smile warmed his face. "Yeah, guys don't get that problem." He leaned forward, forking a piece of tortellini. "So, tell me more about yourself."

Although the request was acceptably normal, tension-fueled suspicion drew my brows. I tried to hide my discomfort. "Um, okay." I started with the normal existence I'd led prior to discovering our dark family secret. Then I added in Mom's current charity work while keeping the council stuff to myself. Explaining my mom held a spot on the Portsmouth Vampire Council? Yeah, that'd be a good idea. Plus I imagined any slip on that matter leading to an all-out townsfolk-with-pitchforks scene. While everything I did reveal seemed quite boring and totally mundane, Ty seemed genuinely interested. He even threw in a question now and then between mouthfuls.

"What about you?" I asked, desperate to deflect the spotlight back onto him. I dug into my lasagna, wishing it was chocolate. At least the taste distracted me from collective blood in the air. "What's your story?"

"I live with my father, he's a senator. My younger brother is away at boarding school."

"And your mom?"

Ty glanced down at his almost finished plate of food, his expression pained. "My mom died when I was a kid."

My heart contracted, and without thinking I reached out to touch his hand. Ty recoiled as though my extending hand had been a striking snake. "Sorry," I said, jerking my hand back. "I didn't mean to bring up painful memories."

Ty's strained eyes peered up to meet mine, a weak smile pulling at his lips. "Let's talk about something else."

"Okay." I bit my lip in thought. "How long have you been into swimming?"

The lines on Ty's face softened, a lighter expression spreading across his face. "I began competing when I started at St. Volaras. But I've been into swimming ever since I can remember." His eyes became distant like he was remembering another time and place. "It's calming, just my body gliding through the water. All the crap of the world seems to wash away."

Ty continued talking in dreamy animation. Lost between the sparkle of his eyes and trying to concentrate past his scent, I missed most of what he was saying. He arched back in his seat, his signature smile painted across his full lips. "So, is your brother driving you home? Or can I have that pleasure?"

I choked on a chunk of lasagna, feeling as though I had swallowed a dozen razor blades. The fork fell from my hand and clanged against my plate as I clutched at my throat. Eyes of surrounding patrons diverted, surprised and staring before swiftly looking away. I tried to breathe, my lungs aching while my hand moved absentmindedly to pull at the buttons on my black shirt. "W-what do you mean?"

"I saw you go out to the parking lot," Ty said, keeping his tone light. "Did Dorian follow us?"

I frowned, utterly confused. Ty didn't seem annoyed or angry. He actually sounded...amused? Stop staring and speak! "Um...he's kind of overprotective." I studied Ty's expression, trying to gauge whether he was buying my lies, and felt somewhat relieved. His face was lit with the same amusement received in his tone. "I told him to leave, though."

Ty's warm-honey eyes sparkled, looking deep into mine. "I can understand his concern. I would be protective over you too."

My cheeks blushed at his words. I was certain surprise was etched across my face. Protective—*of me?*

Ty smiled, flashing his pearly white, perfectly straight teeth. "I have something I'd like to show you, a detour on the way home."

"What is it?" The skepticism was evident in my tone. Could I trust him?

"It's a surprise." Ty's eyes broke from mine, looking away. Was he disappointed? "But if you'd rather just go home, that's fine."

"I don't know." Uncertainty clouded my words while the prior events of the night sped through my mind. Ty wasn't dangerous. He would never hurt anyone. And after his expression of protectiveness, let alone the act of saving my skin on the mountain, I believed without question that he would never hurt me.

As I was about to reply, Ty spoke up. "You don't trust me?"

Without me meaning to, my head was shaking back and forth. And I understood why. I did trust Ty. Raising my eyes to his, I gulped. Would my own self-control hold? Or would I end up regretting my next words? "Okay, let's go."

CHAPTER 7

*M*inutes after leaving the restaurant, we were out of the city and leaving its warm lights behind. Ty turned his turbo-charged WRX onto a pitch-black gravel road shrouded with overhanging trees. I squinted and held my breath, trying to glimpse what lay ahead. My stomach clenched with nerves. Where on earth was Ty taking me?

After a few long seconds, the gravel road gave way to an open clearing, a lookout. Ty rolled up alongside a log railing. I shot through the passenger door, folding over the barrier to suck in fresh mouthfuls of air. A steady breeze blew, clearing his scent and filling my lungs. Now able to think again, my eyes roamed. Below the hillside the city sparkled, alive with nightlife. Everything was awash with the warm glow of streetlamps, from the moving cars to the illuminated advertisements. The sight was a stark comparison to where I stood, with black shadows carved by billowing oaks.

When warmth settled behind my back, I turned and almost jumped out of my skin. Ty was standing right behind me. A perplexed expression encompassed his symmetrical features. I hadn't even heard him exit the car. I glanced down at his black hunting boots. How had I not heard those crossing the gravel? He towered over me, at least six-foot-one to my five-six. His warm-honey eyes watched me. The breeze suddenly died down. The heat of his body so close swelled his fragrant blood through the minimal space between us. Fear of my fangs extending had my hands curling into fists, nails digging into my palms. The rest of my body became suddenly rigid.

Oblivious to my strain, Ty reached up to touch my cheek with heated fingers. Then he brushed the hair back from my face. His hand lingered there, his fingers just grazing my neck. Goosebumps rose like a rippling wave over my skin. His face was barely inches from mine. Too close. My pulse elevated. *Move away*, my mind screamed. My body ignored me, remaining frozen stiff. Then before I could grasp what was actually happening, Ty dipped his head and pressed his full lips gently to mine. My eyes snapped shut as my fangs broke from their sheaths. But something more than wanting to bite into Ty was terribly wrong. Against my colder than human flesh, Ty's lips were hot, far hotter than any human's should be. Blistering compared to a vampire's.

With my lips still locked to his, my eyelids flung open. His intense gold eyes were staring into mine. Without thinking, I jerked away, forcing my hands into his chest. I backed up until I hit the railing, raising a hand to my still-burning lips. A loud thumping echoed through my ears. It was my heart, I realized, drumming faster than I imagined was even possible.

Ty's face held a mixture of confusion and hurt, but something was different about him. I knew I wasn't imagining it this time. His still glowing eyes shone with brilliance under his hurt expression.

They looked like golden jewels, somehow catching the light of the glittering stars above.

Ty shoved his hands into the pockets of his jeans. "Sorry. I didn't mean to, I just…I thought you wanted me to kiss you."

The shock of what had just happened retracted my fangs. With my heart drumming beneath my ribs, I took a hesitant step forward. Did I want Ty to kiss me? Before it had happened, I would have said with total conviction, no. But now…I wasn't so sure. "It's just, your lips." I could feel my cheeks warming at the memory, hot on cold, skin on skin. My first ever kiss. "They were on fire. And your eyes…" I trailed off, needing a moment to decide. No, after all the strange things I'd seen, head-on *was* the best course of action to figuring Ty out. "They changed color!"

Ty immediately spun away from me, blocking his face from view. With caution, I closed the space between us to rest a shaking hand along his shoulder. "Ty, what are you hiding?" Ty turned around almost reluctantly, blinking. His eyes were back to their usual warm-honey and iridescent green coloring. But he wouldn't look at me. "Ty," I said, reaching out to touch his arm. "You can trust me."

"Can I?" Ty's calculating eyes rose, searching mine for a brief moment before his expression hardened. "Sometimes they change color, depending on my mood." He took a step back and shrugged. "That's all."

His warmth faded as he moved back to his car. I couldn't help feeling loss at his distance. There was a tiny part of me that wanted to back down, to let this interrogation go. Yet there was no doubt in my mind that there was more to Ty's unusual eye color than he was letting on. I had never seen eyes of that vibrant shade in my life. Well, at least not on a human, I thought. During our transition at the cabin I had hunted packs of gray wolves. Many had golden eyes, though none had been as luminous as his. Everything fed my suspicions and a growing hope that I was right. But I wanted proof. On top of that, Ty had brought me here for a reason. It had to be more than just wanting to kiss me. With a surge of agitation at his closed-off attitude, I planted my hands on my hips. "I'm not buying it."

Ty spun back so fast he blurred, his jaw clenched and his open hands were stiff at his sides. "Well then, why don't *you* tell me what happened."

His aggravated words hissed through clenched teeth, burned like hot coals against my flesh. Hurt, I dropped my eyes to the gravel. "I don't know," I whispered. "But I do know there's something different about you."

Peering up slowly I saw that Ty was still glaring at me. "You're imagining things," he spat through tight lips.

Fresh agitation swirled within my chest, and my hands curled into fists. I knew I should let the subject lie, but my mouth refused to obey. "I saw you before you won the race, and I know you saw me too. You can't convince me that *that* didn't happen as well." Ty shook his head but didn't respond. My voice lowered. "You're not human, are you?"

Ty staggered as though my words had literally hit him. He closed his eyes and shook his head. "I *am* human. At least in all the ways that count…" His lips snapped shut with a start, and he turned back to his car. He arched his head up to the night sky. It was lit by a full moon and surrounded by a galaxy of glittering stars. His jaw clenched again as he yanked the driver's side door open. "I'm taking you home."

I slumped into the passenger seat. Ty dropped into the driver's side, firing up the engine. His jaw remained tense as he curled tight fingers around the steering wheel. The strain caused his knuckles to whiten. A moment later, he flexed his fingers with a deep sigh. His hardened eyes shifted to me then back to the windshield as he planted his foot. A spray of gravel shot out from all four wheels. The WRX came to life, peeling away from the lookout. In seconds we had cleared the dark gravel road.

I sat in silence with my hair whipping from the fresh air pouring through the open window. My mind was spinning. Ty had inadvertently admitted to being something more than human. His chameleon eye color, ridiculous speed, over-developed muscle build and inhumanly heated flesh were proof enough. All of this filled my head with questions but gave me no definitive answers.

The saltiness of ocean swells filled the air as Ty veered onto Ocean Boulevard. He cleared his throat and glanced in my direction. "There's a party next Saturday. Come with me."

I stared at him, stunned. Was he actually asking me out again? After all the friction of tonight, the request wasn't just crazy, it was absurd. *Use it*, a little voice in my head spoke simply as an idea came to mind. "Fine, I'll go with you *if* you answer me one question."

A curious smile, etched with mischief, pulled at his lips. "And what might that be?"

Certain he wouldn't reveal why or how he was different, I settled on what I hoped would be a simpler question. "Why is your skin so warm?"

Ty's smile hardened but his tone remained relatively light, almost goading. "Well, you're not so normal yourself. Are you?"

A lump began to rise up my throat. If Ty *didn't* know of the monster I struggled to hold at bay, he was damn good at messing with me. With a painful gulp I forced the lump back down. "No answer, no party."

Ty shrugged. "If you say so."

"I do."

"Then why don't we just agree," Ty suggested, tone level and controlled. "That we're both *different* compared to most people, and leave it at that for now."

Different? A graphic image of Ty's horrified face at discovering the kind of monster I really was flooded my mind. In spite of my curiosity, I decided to let it go. Any line of questioning would no doubt lead to returned questions, questions I absolutely wasn't in any position to answer. I couldn't let him know the real me. No one ever would. "Fine," I said. "I can live with that, for now."

Ty turned off Ocean Boulevard and through the stone-hedged gates of my driveway to pull up behind the Cabriolet. Normally the car would be stored in one of the four lockable garage spaces. *Safe from the elements*, as Dorian liked to say. Except now it wasn't. He'd left it parked in the exact same position it had been when Ty had picked me up. Which meant Dorian was still suspicious and covering all tracks. When I sighed, dreading a suspected onslaught of questions from my brother, Ty leaned across the center console. My eyes snapped shut and I clutched my sides with force. After what had happened at the lookout, I knew I couldn't control my lust for Ty's blood *if* his flesh connected with mine again. *Please don't kiss me.*

Click.

A strong flow a cool air brushed over me and my eyes fluttered open. Ty was repositioned in his seat and watching me with one arched brow. The passenger door stood wide open. I mentally slapped myself. He wants me to get out so he can leave and get away from me. And I just sat there like a moron. I clambered out of the car with shaky legs and forged a weak smile. "Thanks, I guess. Tonight was, um…different."

When Ty remained silent, his curious eyes watching me, I swung the door shut. Feeling like a total idiot, I went toward the house.

Ty called out through the open window and I stalled. "See you at school."

With that, the window rose and the car reversed. It rumbled from the driveway, leaving me alone and standing in a band of porch light.

After a few long minutes of dumb staring, I went inside. My mind was rolling over everything, from the race to the uncomfortable end of our date. Is that what a normal date was usually like? Or was that just normal for one with Ty?

"Amelia," Mom's quiet voice sounded from the living room, her hearing sharper than a fox's. "Can you please come in here?"

Her expectant tone made me cringe. I dragged my feet across polished marble to stand in the tall archway. Everything in this room was pristine, from the mink-white carpet and four crystal chandeliers to the mixture of plush and wooden furniture. Mom was sitting in her usual spot, the same green armchair she'd had shipped from Anchorage. It was the only thing that looked out of place.

Mom was dressed in blue designer sweats and had been painting her acrylic nails ruby-red. She pushed the bottle aside, her expression eager yet restrained. "Hi, sweetheart. How was it?"

"It was…nice." I absentmindedly cracked my knuckles, almost wishing I could forget the entire night.

Mom raised her eyebrows, and for a moment I thought I saw a shift in her expression. Then it was gone, and she was fiddling with the zipper of her sweat top. "And?" she prompted.

With an impatient breath I said, "We had dinner at a little Italian restaurant in Portsmouth." There was no way in hell I was about to mention Ty's detour. I was still way too twisted in knots about it. I swear I could still feel the smoldering heat of his lips pressed to mine. The glow of his golden eyes was imprinted on my brain.

Mom tucked her loose blond hair behind her ears. Her ice-blue eyes narrowed and subtle frown lines scored her face. "So there weren't any *problems*?"

She was asking if I'd slipped and lost control. Disappointment and self-doubt weighed against my chest. If Mom doesn't trust me, how can I trust myself? "No, there weren't any *problems*." I clutched my hands stiff at my sides, sensing a growing anger welling within. "You're the one who's been pushing us to live normal lives!" For the second time today my nails dug into my palms. Except this time I squeezed harder, breaking the flesh with a sting. "Why, when you never believed we could?"

Mom's face dropped, riddled with guilt. "That's not true." Rising to her bare, manicured feet she glided forward. Her steps were so light she almost looked to be floating. She grasped my shoulders with firm hands. "I have all the faith in the world in you *and* your brother. Although I do understand that all of this has been terribly difficult, especially for you. I won't deny I was concerned. But you're doing so well." Her arms circled around me, locking me in a tender embrace. "Amelia, I am so proud of you."

Feeling my anger diffuse but with growing exhaustion kicking in, I pulled away. "It's late, and I'm really tired. Where's Dorian?" I had half expected him to be waiting in the living room with Mom when I returned home.

Mom moved back to her seat. "In bed, I think. Why?"

A weight that I hadn't even realized was there, lifted from my shoulders. "No reason."

I turned with a yawn and tiptoed up the broad, curving stairs. Making a sound wasn't an option. If Dorian heard me, I'd be screwed. When I closed my bedroom door behind me, standing in blackness, I breathed a sigh of relief.

"Trying to avoid me?"

The familiar voice spoken from the darkness caused my entire body to convulse. Dammit! I flicked on the chandelier. Dorian stood out against a sea of varying purples on the foot of my bed. He was dressed only in a pair of pajama bottoms. An expectant look was scrawled across his face. I attempted to cover my shock. "What are you doing in here? I thought you were already in bed."

Dorian flashed a devilish smile before hurtling a bottle of blood through the air at my head. "I'm guessing you need this."

My swift reflexes kicked in and I caught the glass bottle just in time. With my body needing the boost, I gulped down the contents. Then I raised my eyebrows in question.

"Unless you were lying to Mom about controlling yourself," Dorian said, flashing his fangs. "But, seeing as I heard his car come and go, I am going to assume you didn't go dental on him."

My face dropped, and I imagined what little color there was draining from my cheeks. The candid memory of Ty's hot lips against mine, and my fangs breaking forth in animal instinct, flooded my mind.

"Anyway," he said, reclining back on his elbows while watching me intently. "What happened after I left?"

With a shrug, I walked over to my bathroom and turned on the fluorescents. They flickered before gleaming against the white marble counter. I placed the empty bottle down. Then I snuck a piece of chocolate from the vanity's top drawer, shoving it into my mouth. "We had dinner. Then Ty drove me home." The air suddenly felt humid, which was impossible given how cool the fall nights in Rye were. Sweat began to coalesce across my brow, a physical tell that hinted at my deception. I splashed water up over my face before turning back to Dorian.

"So," he said, skepticism painting his tone. "Nothing else unusual happened?"

Feeling like a criminal on trial, I crossed the room to rummage through my walk-in. For the minimal amount of clothing I owned it was oversized and much too extravagant, with unending shelves and roller-fed drawers. I kept my face turned. "No, nothing. He seems completely normal." As I turned back to Dorian, I racked my brain. There had to be something I could say to redirect his train of thought. Bingo. "Though, he did notice you followed us."

The shock that jumped across Dorian's face was palpable. He lurched upright, his shoulder colliding with one of the solid, mauve-wrapped pillars of my bed. "Shit! Was he angry?"

Recalling Ty's unexpected reaction, I shook my head. "No. I spun some bull about you being overprotective, and he bought it." I pulled a pair of black satin pajamas from the only filled drawer in my walk-in and glanced back to Dorian's unsatisfied expression. The blood had given me a little boost, but I was still exhausted. The last thing I wanted was to continue this discussion. Keeping Dorian in the dark was already hard enough. "I'm going to bed." When Dorian didn't move, I crossed my arms over my chest. "Go away so I can change!"

Dorian rose to his feet, his eyes narrowing. "Okay. But I'll be keeping an eye on him." He crossed the room, and with one last glance he shut the door behind him.

"KILL ME," I sniffed, swiping away the tears that streamed down my face. "I'm a fucking monster!"

I glanced up to the person who had ripped me from my prey. The blurry haze of my rose-colored tears seemed to wash away with a blink of my eyes. Standing before me was a tan guy wearing hunting boots. A guy I recognized all too well. His iridescent, gold eyes gleamed down on me. They were brighter than the full moon escaping the angry, rolling clouds above. My breath caught in my throat and my eyes widened in utter disbelief. It couldn't be him.

But it was. The same guy who had captured my curiosity from the first moment I'd laid eyes on him. The same guy who sparked involuntary reactions within me like no other person ever had before.

His corded muscles twitched beneath the skin-tight, black shirt covering his chest. His scarred hand was clutching a pointed, silver weapon at his side. Silver, the one element that could burn a vampire's skin on contact—and kill them, if it pierced the heart. The sound of his voice reverberated through the air, as unmistakable as his face. "You *want* to die?"

His lips split to reveal sharp-pointed canines as he lunged, muscles taut with power. The weapon in his hand was aimed at my heart.

I bolted upright, my chest heaving with crushing ragged breath. My eyes darted around. Silhouetted shadows surrounded me. The familiar and unmoving shapes told me one thing: I was no longer trapped in the darkened alley backing the nightclub in Anchorage. Instead, I sat amongst a tangle of purple linens on my own bed. The satin pajamas I had thrown on earlier were plastered to my body by sweat. I struggled to control my breathing. It was just a dream.

Knowing that didn't slow the slamming of my heart against my ribs, or make the images any less disturbing. Because this wasn't the first time I'd had this dream. Since that fateful night back in Anchorage, I'd woken from the same nightmare almost every night, always with a sudden jolt. But tonight had been different. Before tonight, I had never been able to identify the mysterious boy who had interrupted my kill. He had always appeared faceless. Now the reality of that night seemed so vivid, so unforgettably clear. The features that made up his face, the deep, unwavering tone of his voice, and the infinite power he exuded. A body-jarring shudder ran from the crown of my head down to the tips of my fingers and toes.

Was it him all along? Was the boy from the alley Ty?

DURING A WEEKEND of text wars with Kendrick, I'd made only passing mention of my first ever date. Kendrick seemed uninterested in talking about it, which was good. I didn't want to have to answer questions when I still had so many of my own. Following that we set up Skype so we could watch a marathon of The Vampire Diaries together. It had been my pick, as Kendrick preferred boring snow-boarding documentaries.

Now it was finally Monday. Feeling down, I headed for my last class of the day, art. A desperate need to see Ty had pulled at me since waking from my dream the other night. If only I could see his face to discount entirely the conjured recollection.

It's impossible, I kept telling myself. It was just a merging of the real and the imagined, a distortion of reality. But I couldn't forget the clarity of his features, voice, and eyes, the way he'd looked at me. Then there was the way I'd felt when seeing him on my first day at St. Volaras. He'd seemed so familiar then. It was too coincidental, wasn't it? Or was it really just a cruel trick of my mind?

But Ty had been absent from our shared psychology class. He hadn't been present in the cafeteria for lunch, either. In fact, no one bar Dorian had made an appearance during lunch hour. So where were they all? And what were they doing?

I stepped through the open doorway to my art class. The sound of gossiping students filled the air. I hurried past them toward the sanctuary of my easel at the other end of the room. Mrs. Ruby— unperturbed by the growing chatter—assisted students near the entry. The glass panels along the back wall were slightly open. A light breeze blew, cleansing away the collected scent of blood tainting the air.

With a deep clearing breath, I settled at my easel and began squeezing paints onto a pallet. Then I stared at my developing portrait, as if staring would will inspiration my way. The portrait was coming along, slowly. A decent portrayal, I thought, of how I saw myself in ten years. My skin was still porcelain white, and my lips were the chalky shade of a wilting rose. Golden-blond hair billowed down my back, even longer that its current waist length. Not a single blemish or wrinkle marked my ageless face.

I will *never* live a normal life.

The depressing statement couldn't have been truer. Turned vampires could live for around half a millennium. And according to our mom, born vampires, Pure Bloods, could easily double that. After what she and Caius had done to Dorian and me, our lifespans could be closer to a Pure Blood's than a turned vampire's. So as the humans around me aged at a regular pace, I would not. Eventually those who knew me would notice. So an existence of constant moving and new faces, of pretending to be normal when I was anything but, was what lay ahead for me. For all of us.

"Ugh," I sighed. Without the distraction of Vanessa's incessant chatter on all things fashion, my mind wandered back to the unbelievable and still crystal clear dream of Ty.

The familiar sound of heeled stilettos clinking against the polished concrete floor cut through the muddled mess in my mind. I looked up to catch Vanessa strolling into class, late. She was dressed in a short tartan skirt and ankle boots. Her long red hair hung in loose, bouncing curls over her shoulders. She stepped around me, eyeing my portrait. "New direction?"

Wondering what was encouraging her critical expression, I

turned back. My eyes widened. In place of my own silvery-flecked, blue eyes, I had painted iridescent gold ones. They were the same eyes I had dreamed of and seen in the flesh as his lips connected with mine. They were the same unusual and changeable eyes that belonged to Ty. I snatched a moist sponge from the paint rack and wiped away the evidence, smearing gold across my painted face. "Just experimenting," I said, turning my sights back to Vanessa. "You weren't at lunch."

Vanessa shrugged with a look of indifference and took her seat. She began organizing paints onto a pallet. "I was studying in the library. God, I hate being so perfect." She turned her sapphire eyes onto me. There was a disapproving edge to her tone. "So, your date with Ty... How was it?"

Tightness constricted my chest and my fingers rose to my mouth. I could still remember the heat of Ty's burning lips pressed to mine. Just recalling my thirst for his blood had my gums tingling. "It was, um...different."

Vanessa's lips twitched as though she were about to respond but then thought better of it.

"By the way," I said, trying to keep my tone light to mask the anticipation that dyed my throat. "Where is Ty today?"

Vanessa's eyes narrowed at her own canvas. "Camping in the White Mountains. He and Troy take off school with their fathers sometimes, to experience *the wilderness*."

Was she lying? I frowned, uncertain. With the constant power-struggle between Ty and Troy, I doubted they could stand any amount of time camping together. So if he wasn't with Troy and their fathers, was he even camping at all? "When do they get back?"

Vanessa waved a dismissive hand. "Oh, they should be back in a few days."

Unconvinced, I resettled into painting, fixing the gold that was now smeared across my canvas. Conflicting thoughts ran through my head. There was Ty's absence, our date, the dream, Vanessa's excuse for Ty being away, and the mysterious boy from the alley. What did it all mean?

By the end of class my head was throbbing from my racing thoughts. I retreated back to the main building, stomping through the packed corridor to my locker. I retrieved my iPhone—thinking of Kendrick at seeing its Three Days Grace case—and dialed Ty's number. The progressing ring in my ear caused an uncontrollable flutter of my heart. I knew calling him like this after our strange date was rash. But I had to know where he was, and with who, and *if* Vanessa was covering for him, why.

"Amelia?" Ty's surprised voice echoed through the speaker.

"Where are you?" I demanded, tone impetuous but kept low to avoid attention from passing students.

"No, 'hey how's it going?'" God, I could hear the mocking in Ty's voice.

I slammed my locker shut and slumped against it. A few kids turned to stare before swiftly averting their eyes at the venomous look plastered across my face. "Just tell me where you are."

"Okay," Ty said with audible hesitation. "I'm visiting my brother at boarding school, in New Hampton. Why?"

Liar! The voice inside my head held no uncertainty this time. I wasn't sure how I knew, but there had been something in Ty's hesitant voice that was a clear tell. Ty was the one lying, not Vanessa. Agitation grew like flames up my neck, enveloping my face. I hung up and shoved the phone into my pocket before I could crush it in my hand. Secrets, lies… What was he hiding?

CHAPTER 8

*B*y Wednesday, Ty still hadn't returned to school. But when I stepped into my psych class after lunch, I froze. The scent of chlorine and *his* blood filled the air around me.

My eyes raked over the classroom. Posters of psychological jargon covered the walls, and each of the desks—set in twos—were occupied by other students. Ty usually sat up the back. He wasn't there. Then I found him, sitting at the desk beside my regular spot. His training bag was on the floor at his feet. The sight of him, looking so casual and so freaking laid-back, boiled my blood. I yanked my earbuds from my ears, cutting off Red's song *Mystery of you*. How could he act so normal, when he was so full of it?

Sucking air I stalked across the room, passing the desks of whispering students, to stand before Ty. I could sense the critical sneer from a few girls around the room. Our names were on their hushed, flapping lips. They're jealous? Ty was hot, seriously hot. But with the hostility my body language was currently propelling at him, their jealousy was laughable.

Ty glanced up, face lit by a confident smile. "You're mad?"

I dumped my textbooks and iPod on the desk and planted my hands on my hips. "Shouldn't I be?"

Footsteps reached my ears as the classroom door swung closed. "Seats please everyone. Let's get started," Mr. McKenna instructed, pushing his glasses up on his nose. When I didn't move he pointed to the desk beside Ty. "Sit down, Miss Lamont." He turned to the blackboard and began writing up a list of read-through chapters.

With a groan, I begrudgingly stepped around Ty. I shoved open the windowpane, breathing through my mouth in an effort to clear the aroma of his blood from my nostrils. A slight, icy breeze floated through the crack. The effectiveness was fractional. Tingles still cascaded across my gums, prickling with the threat of fangs.

"You have every right to be mad," Ty whispered beside me.

My hands were shaking with anger and restraint. I couldn't bring myself to look at him. "So glad I have your permission," I spat, sarcasm dripping from my words. "So, where were you, really?"

"It's complicated."

Blowing out an exacerbated breath, I glared out the window at the gloomy, ashen sky. If I were lucky, the impending storm would hurry up and bring with it a gale force of fresh air. "Whatever. I don't care." But I did. For some unfathomable reason I needed to figure Ty out. I needed to know where he had been and what dark secrets he was keeping. I needed to know who or what he really was, and if he was anything like me.

"Yes you do." Ty sounded so sure of himself. He flicked through his textbook to the instructed reading. Then he paused, cocking his head sideways. "How about this? Go to the party this Saturday with me."

Was he kidding? I turned my narrowed gaze to Ty. He was watching me with anticipation. "And why the hell would I do that?"

Ty didn't even flinch at the edge in my whispered tone. Instead, his bright hazel eyes gleamed intently. "To have *some* of your questions answered."

"Now?"

"No." Ty shook his head. "At the party, *after* we arrive."

I contemplated the pros and cons. Uncover the mystery of Ty, versus lunging at him with bared fangs. I slumped back in my seat, noticing what I swore were new thin, whitish scars across his arms. Unable to suppress my curiosity, I decided that figuring Ty out was worth the risk of attacking him. "So, all I have to do is go to this party with you, nothing else?"

Ty's lips lifted at the sides. "I can add conditions *if* you'd like me to." I narrowed my eyes, causing him to chuckle. "No," he said more seriously. "I wouldn't do that. Just come to the party and I'll tell you whatever you want to know."

I bit my lip. This is a bad idea. But my inner voice couldn't change my mind. "Fine, I'll go."

"Give me a sec, gotta tidy up."

I darted inside my room and yanked the door shut behind me. With my heart pounding, I flew to my bedside table. I snatched up the empty glass that was tinged with dried blood and shoved it sideways into the top drawer.

After a few, quick, calming breaths, I let Vanessa in. "Sorry about that, come on in."

Vanessa shimmied out of her Gucci button coat, handing it to me as she strutted across my room. In calf-high boots, shorts and an eye-catching top, she looked like a model. A second later she disappeared into the long rectangular space of my walk-in. She had followed Dorian and me home in her dinged-up Corolla after school this Friday. It'd been her idea to help me figure out my wardrobe for the party tomorrow night. According to her, my style lacked enthusiasm and finish, something she seemed more than willing to assist me with when she invited herself over. Not that I minded. Ty had promised to offer answers to my many questions at the party. Still, prying *some* info about him from Vanessa in preparation couldn't hurt.

"Seriously?" Vanessa's voice drifted from the walk-in even though I couldn't see her. "This closet is huge and you're taking up —what, one freaking drawer?" She muttered under her breath at how dismal my clothing selection was.

I leaned against the wall in wait, dread searing through me. What outfit would she inflict on me?

A progression of clothes flew from my walk-in, hitting me in the face before falling to the carpet. Finally Vanessa emerged with a much-too-short, black ruffled skirt, and a red and white silk top sporting a plunging neckline. It was the only daring outfit I owned. Mom had given it to me as a gift. "With your pitiful resources, *this* is the best I can do."

I mumbled, "More like a curse." Then, unable to entertain the thought of ever wearing such girly, revealing clothes, I began to argue but froze mid-sentence. Beside the white-painted, antique dresser across my room was a waste-paper basket. Just poking out of the top along with a chocolate wrapper was an empty blood baggie. It was the same one I had squeezed out this morning.

"What's wrong?" Vanessa began to turn, following my line of sight.

I clutched her shoulders, trying not to inflict pain. "Nothing, the clothes are great! I was just wondering, um…will my Vans match?"

"God no!" Looking mortified Vanessa rushed past me. She flung the skirt and top onto my bed before disappearing back inside my walk-in. "Purple-laced shoes with a red top aside, those shoes are hideous."

With Vanessa out of sight, I abandoned her coat and shot across the room. In less than a second I snatched the blood baggie from the basket and shoved it into the dresser's top drawer. That was close, too close.

Struggling to control my breathing, I turned to catch Vanessa re-emerging from my walk-in. She was carrying a set of black suede, over-the-knee boots which she thrust into my face. Another Mom *present*. "You have to wear these. They're perfect!" she almost shrieked. "Man, Ty's going to have a heart attack when he sees you. Oh, and you'll want to bring a bikini, there's a heated pool."

With a silent groan, I took the boots from Vanessa's hands and hurled them onto my bed. My opportunity to probe her for info on Ty was limited. "So, Ty's um…different." I coiled my arms around my waist and pinched my sides. I sounded like a moron. Vanessa's eyes narrowed. "I mean, he just doesn't seem like a regular teenage guy."

"He's not," Vanessa confessed. She moved to the tall, arched window and plopped down on the ledge.

"Oh?" I couldn't hide the eagerness my voice betrayed. Was Vanessa actually about to offer a revelation?

"He's a private person." Vanessa eyed me up and down. The speculation in her expression was clear as day. "Well, he was until you came along." She turned her head, causing her hair to fall over her shoulders as she gazed out the window. Heavy rain pelted down. It sheeted everything it touched in glimmering monotones. "He's different around you, less restricted, less *controlled*."

"And that's a bad thing?"

Vanessa blew out a long breath, head twisting back to me. "When he's around you, his guard is down. It defies his...*religion*."

The way her voice grated over the word *religion* only confused me further. It almost seemed like she had opted for that word in place of another. "So, Ty's not allowed to date or something?"

A chime sounded and Vanessa pulled her diamante-studded phone from her boots, looking at the screen. "This should be interesting," she said under her breath. Then she slid the phone back into her boot. "I've gotta bounce. Cash job. But what were we, oh right. *Dating...*" Her voice turned sharp while her sapphire eyes pierced through me. "Is *that* what you and Ty are doing?"

Feeling my stomach turn, I shook my head and dropped onto the foot of my bed. My arm curled around one of the tapestry-wrapped posts for support. "No, of course not, it's just..." Unsure of how I felt or what I wanted to say, I broke off. I couldn't very well tell her that my agreeing to attend this party with Ty was solely to interrogate him. And that was the only reason. Wasn't it?

"Look." Vanessa rose from the window ledge and almost stomped in her boots to my bedroom door, swooping up her jacket before clutching the handle. "I'm saying this as Ty's friend, for both of your sakes. Stay away from him. This can only end badly."

"Is that why you insisted on coming here?" My accusation stopped her in her tracks.

Vanessa shrugged. "I love fashion, and you need help. Dressing like a guy is *not* okay." She frowned at my casual jeans and tank top. "But Ty is like a brother to me, and I know him. You two can't work."

I POPPED a fifth consecutive piece of chocolate into my mouth as I paced back and forth. Then I glanced through my bedroom window again. The clouded sky was darkening with night. The driveway was still empty. *He's late.* Just as I thought the words, Ty's WRX veered into sight, catching the house's exterior lights against its freshly washed panels. Anxiety seeped through to my bones like acid as I bolted from my room. Tonight I'd learn the truth.

Stepping out of his car, Ty was dressed in black denim jeans and a hooded V-neck, just visible beneath a black leather bomber jacket. He was heading for the door as I flew out onto the rain-slicked steps. I slid and almost landed on my butt before awkwardly righting the fall. My face burned. Stupid freaking boots!

But Ty didn't seem to notice, a broad smile lighting his perfect features. "Wow!" His eyes widened, sparkling as though they were drinking me in. "You look delicious."

My face grew hotter and I tugged at the too-short hem of my skirt, feeling self-conscious. "Vanessa picked it out."

Ty's smile faltered. "I know."

She told him? My heart sank at recalling Vanessa's cryptic words. *Stay away from him. This can only end badly.* Having mulled the words over again and again since she left yesterday, I had jumped from one conclusion to another. But now, knowing she'd told Ty, I wondered what his reaction had been. Standing before me he seemed unsettled, like he was being pulled from different angles.

Ty's voice cut through my mental turmoil, his smile returning. "Just ignore Vanessa. She likes to meddle." He pulled open the passenger door, standing aside. "Shall we?"

With uncertainty, I lowered myself into Ty's car. Then knowing his scent would soon curl around me and assault my nostrils, I retrieved the nasal tube from my right boot. Concealed in my palm, I raised it to my nose while jabbing the button to lower my window.

When Ty resumed the driver's seat I asked, "Whose party is it, anyway?" Please don't be Vanessa's.

Ty's shoulders stiffened and a flash of gold rippled across his irises. He shrugged, directing the car through the front gates. "Does it matter?"

Distracted by the sight, I shook my head. The flicker of that unmistakable color sparked a memory of the dream I wished I could forget, as Ty had lunged at me, weapon raised. Shaking off a dark chill, I found my voice. The time was now or never. "Ty, have you ever been to Alaska?"

Ty frowned, eyes set on the dark road ahead of us. "No. Why do you ask?"

Tension released from my body, soothing like a receding tide. It wasn't him. Of course it wasn't. I cracked my knuckles. "No reason."

After a few minutes of uneasy silence, Ty pulled into the long gravel driveway of what appeared to be a country club. It was an elaborate double story of extending gray stone and balcony-laced walls. A cone-pitched roof made up the domed entrance. Half of the foregrounds were taken up by a gravel parking lot. The rest was decorated with manicured hedges and rose bushes, all illuminated by yellow-hued garden lights.

As we stepped out of the car, I said, "People live here?"

Ty walked up beside me. With clear hesitation written across his face, he took my hand. His skin was rough and calloused, the hand of someone who worked with them on a daily basis. The warmth of his touch radiated up my arm, causing my heart to skip a beat. But I didn't resist. Instead, I allowed Ty to pull me forward, around the side of the house and into darkness. The seclusion raised my pulse, while my mind conjured up unspeakable images. I imagined forcing Ty to a standstill and slamming him against the brick wall, then plunging my fangs into the soft-looking flesh at the base of his neck. Gritting my teeth, I tried not to hum the chorus of *Monster*. Then I consciously loosened my grip on Ty's hand. In my resistance to playing out my sick fantasy, it had tightened to almost bone-breaking severity. I snuck a shooting glance at Ty. He didn't seem uncomfortable in the slightest, or even to have noticed.

After a few more tension-filled steps, we emerged out of the darkness. I sucked in a quick cleansing breath and glanced around. The largest outdoor entertaining area I had ever seen surrounded us. A resort-style pool encompassed most of the space, with a rocky island in its center. It was surrounded on three sides by the U-shape of the house. I did a double take on noticing a slope curving down the island. The raised and rocky structure was actually a water slide. Teens dotted the courtyard and pool, and a steady beat of music filled the crisp night air.

Ty's hand released mine, bringing me back to reality. "What's your poison?" He inclined his head toward the bar and motioned to the bartender.

I paused, surprised and a little uncomfortable. Then I glanced around, sniffing the air. There wasn't a single visible adult, and almost everyone, even the teens in the pool, had alcohol-scented drinks. I shrugged. Alcohol had very little effect on vampires, so I didn't see the harm. Besides, I needed a distraction. "Uh, sure. Vodka lemonade."

Ty called out our drink order to the bartender, requesting a bourbon and cola for himself. Once served, he grabbed the glasses from the tabletop and handed mine over.

A loud, repetitive pulse of music radiated through my body with force. My sight redirected across the pool as I sipped my drink. The space had been transformed into a club atmosphere. A growing sea of bodies danced provocatively under an array of flashing strobe lights. I sniffed the air and was surprised. Even from the other end of the courtyard, I could detect salt, blood, and chlorine mixing on the air.

As I continued sipping my drink, a mixed group made their way over from the dance floor. A slight breeze had picked up, delivering a waft of nose-assaulting perfume. Ty stiffened beside me. The muscles along his neck corded with strain as a girl's flirtatious laughter rang through the air. Then Ty's scent deepened. It grew with intensity and clouded my mind. Desperate for a distraction, I downed the remainder of my drink. I leaned into the bar and away from Ty.

"Shots of Tequila or Vodka?" a guy I recognized from chem questioned. He slumped onto one of the leather cubes that surrounded a cane-weaved coffee table.

"Gotta be Tequila!" another answered, following suit.

One guy shouted their eight, double-shot order to the bartender, while the crowd made themselves comfortable around the table.

"And keep 'em coming!" yelled a girl wearing a mini skirt that molded to her curvy hips. A seriously tight tank top flaunted her generous bust. She didn't ooze the smell of blood and alcohol from her pores like the other kids. Instead, she reeked of the vanilla perfume I had detected moments ago.

Just looking at her made me feel flat as a board in comparison and, if I was being totally honest, a little jealous. I'd never been daring enough to dress with such confidence.

The girl staggered with intoxication and caught sight of us. She flicked her black abyss of hair over her shoulders and straightened to attention. "*Ty,*" she said in a voice that was both alluring and intimate. "It's been a while."

Ty downed his drink then slammed the empty glass down on the counter. It exploded in a rain of splinters, and Ty huffed, brushing the shards from his unharmed hand. A few of the kids had gasped, but Ty took no notice. Instead, he turned abruptly from the girl and grasped my elbow, pulling me away.

Throwing a glance over my shoulder, I caught the girl watching after us. Her eyes were narrowed into a death stare. "Who was that?" I demanded, instantly disliking the girl. Everyone else I had recognized from various classes at school. I was certain I had never seen this girl before.

"No one you need to know."

Pulling my elbow free from Ty's powerful grasp, I crossed my arms over my chest. I had played along with his conditions and now it was his turn. "Time for answers..."

"Alright," Ty said with a sigh. With his back turned, he stripped down to a pair of blue board shorts, revealing more scars across his back. Even with his scars, his perfect body sent dizzying warmth through me. I fought to keep my jaw from dropping. He threw a backward glance over his shoulder, eyes seductive and inviting. "Coming?" Without waiting for an answer, he dove into the crystalline water of the pool, breaking the surface like an arrow before emerging ten feet away.

Recovering, I glanced around, worried. Dorian had already known about the party when I told him I was going with Ty. His invite had come from a new girl at school. Apparently Cindy was already old news. Though him seeing and following us was the last thing I needed. Since the swim-off last week and my poor explanation for Ty winning, he hadn't even brought the subject up, much to my relief. He was generally a carefree guy. Still, whether he appeared concerned or not, I was certain he hadn't forgotten. It would only take something small to re-ignite his suspicion.

I scanned right to left. The group at the bar was engrossed in an exuberant drinking game, and the dance floor across the courtyard was still crammed with gyrating bodies. A few kids bobbed in the water on the other side of the pool, which must have been heated considering the chill in the air. Dorian was nowhere in sight.

I reluctantly kicked off my boots and shed my clothes. Thank God I'd decided to wear my bikini underneath. The green of Ty's eyes gleamed as they raked over my body and vibrant purple bikini. The stupid thing covered far too little flesh and emphasized the tiny peaks on my chest. Scalding heat crept across my cheeks. Why didn't I wear a one-piece? Or, come to think of it, a full-bodied chastity suit? Hoping the water would provide *some* reprieve from his eager expression, I lowered myself down into the pool. I waded closer to him, but not too close. "So tell me…"

"Wait," Ty demanded, raising a hand to cut me off. "Not here. It's too…public." He pointed to the rocky island, acting as a water slide in the center of the pool. "There."

My fingers curled into fists beneath the water. "You're stalling."

Ty edged closer, his face inches from mine. "Amelia," his warm breath washed over me like a soft caress. "I made a promise, and I intend to keep it. Just *try* to trust me."

I nodded dumbly, the power of his scent totally clouding my judgment. Ty shot me a captivating smile, then dove beneath the surface and swam over to the island. And I followed. This was a bad idea and my mind screamed for me to stay away. But my body wouldn't obey.

We pulled from the water and Ty stepped forward, grasping my hand. The sight of beaded water running down his scarred and muscled chest raised my pulse. He turned with a wink and pulled me after him through an entrance I had only just caught sight of. It was in the side of the island and camouflaged by green ferns.

Inside, the cave was lit by the licking flames of kerosene torches that sent moving shadows of our bodies skulking across the rocky walls. Thick humidity hung in the air. As we rounded the corner, I realized it was due to an oversized hot tub, steaming with bubbling water.

Without even a second's warning, Ty spun on the spot. His body was so close. Too close. His skin was almost touching mine. His intoxicating scent whirled around me, its potency spiked from the claustrophobic heat. His audible heartbeat raced in time with mine.

Too freaking close! My mind screamed, over and over.

But I couldn't move. My body was paralyzed by fear. Fear that I would lose control.

Ty's hands moved, blurring with speed to connect with my hips. I gasped as he forced me hard-up against his smoldering body. His hot lips, slightly parted and scorching, connected with mine.

I tried to pull away.

But his grip on my hips tightened. His lips trapped mine, deepening the kiss. Breath evaded my lungs.

And every inch of me melted. All the fight in me to pull away and run was gone. A deeper yearning had taken over, a primal need for every part of him. His touch. His mouth. But predominately his blood.

Our lips moved in rhythmic motion, tongues—fire and ice—dancing in our mouths. My arms flung around Ty's neck, preventing him from escape.

Encouraged, his hands clutched my thighs. They lifted my weight with ease and my legs curled around his back, tight and trapping. Ty took a rushed step, lowering our entwined bodies into the hot tub's scorching water. Steam rose from the surface. Its coiling tendrils set my skin alight and strengthened the scent of his blood. The reckless abandon of our kissing deepened, getting hotter and harder.

A familiar tingle rippled across my gums. But I didn't care. Thoughts of stopping evaporated.

Instead, my body pressed harder against his. I clung viciously to his neck, nails breaking flesh.

Ty seemed not to notice, pressing hands gliding down my back. The electric touch forced my fangs to split from my gums.

Releasing his lower lip, my mouth trailed down his face and neck with nipping kisses. A fleeting memory of my victim back in the alley flashed through my mind. The look of Joel's terrified expression as the monster within me took over was unforgettable.

It's happening again.

But the crippling fear was quashed as Ty's pulse hammered beneath my wet, cold lips. It raced faster with each frenzied kiss. Faster than I thought was humanly possible.

"It's okay. Do it," Ty whispered, voice gravelly through hard breath. "I want you to."

Saliva flooded my mouth, and a merciless desire to taste him seized me. Ty couldn't know what he was inviting me to do. Or could he?

Either way, I couldn't stop.

The terrifying thought only encouraged my inner monster. All thought was suddenly abandoned and my body took over. My tongue traced the pulsing vein along his neck, tasting, toying. Then unable to hold back for another second, I bit down hard.

The skin punctured with more effort than I had anticipated. A dissipating concern as his sweet, fiery blood spilled into my mouth. It was unlike anything I had ever tasted, better than animal blood, better than Joel's. If heaven had a taste, this would be it.

I was hypnotized.

Ty groaned with pleasure—a venom-induced reaction to the bite of a vampire. His hands glided intimately over every inch of my tingling skin. I clutched him tighter. I couldn't stop.

"I knew what you were," Ty exhaled, barely audible. "From the very first moment I laid eyes on you."

His words cut through the bloodlust with an electric jolt. I jerked away in one swift movement, feeling as though I'd been electrocuted. My body cowered against the far end of the hot tub. Oh my God. What had I done?

With my face turned, I struggled for breath. My heart hammered. I couldn't stand for Ty to see me, the monster I really was, what such a horrific creature really looked like. I knew what I must look like right now: there would be bloodstains covering my fanged mouth and my eyes would be red-rimmed with startlingly silver irises. It was the face of a living, breathing monster.

As I crouched frozen in shock, Ty cautiously moved closer. His hot hand rested against my shoulder in a clear effort to turn me toward him. I resisted, hands shooting up to cover my horrific features. But Ty was stronger and managed to twist me to face him. "Amelia, don't." His tone was level and strong but held a twinge of desperation. "Don't hide from me."

Crimson tears blurred my vision, turning everything to a rose-colored haze. I struggled to hold them back and blinked up at Ty. His expression appeared gentle under a mask of vulnerability. He's not scared of me?

"It's okay," Ty said, voice as soft as velvet. He released my shoulder to curl his fingers around my wrists. With a strong tug, he forced my barricading hands down.

"I'm sorry!" I screamed while blood-tainted tears streamed down my face.

Ty didn't leap away from me in horrified disgust or scream about how vile I was. Instead, he reached up, resting a gentle hand against my bloodied jaw. His thumb brushed away a stream of tears. "Amelia, I know what you are, and I don't care."

My eyes squeezed shut. Part of me needed so badly to believe his words. But I couldn't. No one would ever truly accept me. Anger spiked like venom in my veins and my eyes flung open. I belted Ty's hand away, and with clawed fingers frantically tried to scratch his blood from my face. "How can you say that?" I snapped. "What I just did to you… I'm a fucking monster!"

"Then so am I." A shockwave rippled through me like an earthquake, freezing me as still as a statue. Ty smiled and collected my hands. "Amelia, don't you know how much you mean to me?"

My voice caught, feeling like a dagger had pierced my windpipe. I tried to swallow. "Mean to you?"

Ty looked away, catching the flicker of torch flames against his neck. Their light highlighted the puncture wounds I had inflicted. The blood-flow, which had forged a thick, red torrent down his neck and over his collarbone, had almost stopped. The skin was closing over right before my eyes. How was that possible? My brow knitted in confusion, eyes lifting to study Ty. "What—are—you?"

Ty's lips parted. Then a piercing scream cut through the air.

CHAPTER 9

We leaped from the hot tub simultaneously and raced back through the shadowy cave toward the source of the screaming. To my surprise as I ran—not restraining my vampire speed—Ty kept pace. We burst from the cave's entrance. My eyes darted across the now empty pool, finding the cause of the commotion. I sucked in my breath.

Dorian stood head to head with Troy, who towered over him. The same intoxicated girl who had clearly known Ty, cried, "*It didn't mean anything!*"

The leather cubes around the cane table had been vacated. Being barely six feet from the challenging guys, it was no surprise. The drunken group now took up refuge behind the bar, all watching wide-eyed and pale-faced. It was clear none of them wanted to break up *this* volatile standoff. Body-jarring music no longer pumped from the dance floor across the courtyard. All that remained was a deafeningly silent array of flashing lights. The dance crowd was still, edging forward with mirrored gape-jawed stares.

Waves of tension rolled from Dorian and Troy as they stood locked in a death stare. It was so thick I had to force back the urge to gag in horror. Damn Dorian! What the hell was going on?

Troy's face burned red as he broke the stare, clenching his fists. "You were taking a body shot from my girlfriend's cleavage!" He rushed forward to shove Dorian with unrestrained force.

Dorian staggered back. His hands shot up in defense. His eyes narrowed as he hissed through gritted teeth. "I didn't know she was anyone's girlfriend."

Troy remained still, nostrils flared and chest rising with fuming breath. Dorian shrugged and began to turn away. Troy instantly launched forward, hands wrapping around my brother's neck. "BULLSHIT!"

Gasps escaped the lips of onlookers, including my own.

Looking scared out of being drunk, the girl jumped at Troy, clutching his shoulder. *"Stop, please stop!"*

Troy flung her off and she stumbled back, slamming into the bar. The force would have floored most people. Yet somehow she remained standing.

With the distraction, Dorian pushed against Troy's chest, breaking the vice-grip hold around his neck. Angry welts were left painted across his skin. "Back off!"

Dorian turned to leave again, but Troy kicked out at his ankles. Astonishment contorted my brother's face. He fell, barely catching himself before his face collected the pavement. He rolled instantly, but Troy was already lunging. In a split second he had my brother pinned to the ground. Dorian thrashed under Troy's weight, unable to free himself.

Who the hell was this guy? Troy's strength and speed seemed to outdo Dorian's. What in this world could be as strong and as fast as a vampire? I knew the answer. I had known it all along... *Ty.* Now

Dorian would, too. I couldn't explain away what was happening. I couldn't excuse it with rational-sounding lies. Everything was about to come crashing down. Still pinning Dorian to the ground with his knees, Troy delivered a vicious blow to the face. A crack sounded and a spray of scarlet spurted from Dorian's lip.

"Stop!" the hysterical girl screamed. "You'll kill him!"

Dorian spat red, face hardening with fury. "You are beginning to piss–me–off." With a grunt he forced his back off the pavement, swinging a violent blow to Troy's face. Shock sealed the other guy's features as Dorian threw another punch before kicking him off. Both guys scrambled to their feet, facing each other in ready stances.

"This has gone on long enough," Ty murmured. The fight was already way out of hand. There were too many spectators, witnesses. This needed to be dealt with, and fast.

With a nod of agreement, Ty and I dove into the pool. Aware that he was swimming as fast as humanly acceptable, I kept pace. My eyes jumped from Ty and back to the guys as we neared. Troy lunged forward again, landing a left to Dorian's cheek. Then he countered instantly with a right to his stomach.

The movement had been so fast it had almost blurred. Caught off guard, Dorian doubled over, wincing as he stumbled to the ground. His eyes blazed as though suddenly alive with flames. Plump drops of fresh blood dripped from his lip. "You *shouldn't* have done that."

A threatening smile split his lips, revealing extended fangs. Panic rose from my gut. His back faced the crowd by the bar, but it would only take a slight turn of his head for the still gap-jawed kids to catch sight. Shit!

Dorian leaped from the pavement and the two collided, while the panic-stricken girl—who seemed oblivious to Dorian's fangs with tear-filled eyes—screamed for them to stop. Her desperate pleas fell on deaf ears while sledgehammer punches continued to fly.

Finally out of the water, I flew at Dorian as Ty closed in on Troy. I knew I was only wearing my bikini before an entire audience, which horrified me. But I had no choice. In this second, the two had broken from their struggle. Troy stepped forward to deliver another pain-inflicting punch. Just before they connected, Ty intervened. He grasped Troy's arm with brutal force and wrenched it down behind Troy's back. Ty's free arm slammed tight over the other guy's chest.

Dorian went to move forward, ready to continue the onslaught. I leaped in front of him, shoving him hard. "Retract your freaking fangs," I hissed.

Dorian's mouth dropped open. "I didn't mean to. I…"

Agitation had built up inside of me and was preparing to explode. I shoved him back and kept on shoving, pausing just long enough to swipe my clothes from the pavement before I pushed him through a door marked as a bathroom on the side of the house.

A quick glance over my shoulder showed Ty forcing Troy back. With his face hard up against Troy's, it was hidden from the gaping crowd. But I could see him clearly. His jaw was set, lips curling back with ferocity and eyes blazing. A flash of sharpened canines appeared as he snarled into Troy's ear, "Back down, Beta."

Troy's expression remained hardened, but his resisting arms dropped, face cocking sideways and chin elevating slightly. His body, although physically taller than Ty's, slouched, making him appear smaller. A submissive gesture… Confusion narrowed my eyes. In our solitary months at the cabin, I had witnessed similar displays of superiority when stalking packs of gray wolves. They're… Apprehension tightened my chest.

I slammed the door behind me and turned the lock. The square room illuminated, wall-mounted lights gleaming against glossy tiles and porcelain fixtures. I blinked away the glare. Then with Ty's hot blood coursing through my veins, I fought the temptation to physically belt some sense into Dorian. "Are you epically insane!"

Dorian shrugged while I pulled my clothes on over my wet bikini then tugged on my boots. Even in front of him I still felt exposed and way too naked. His breath turned from ragged to level with a sigh. He dropped onto the wooden bench between a glass-framed shower and granite vanity. A raised pink line surrounded by smudged and drying blood was all that was left of his split lip. His black polo shirt and cargo pants hung ripped and stained with his blood.

His lack of concern caused bubbling frustration to rise within me. I threw my hands in the air. "What you did was beyond stupid. Everyone was watching." Although my voice emerged harsh and shrill, Dorian didn't even flinch. He simply crossed his arms over his chest while cocking one eyebrow. "And your freaking fangs! Were you planning to rip Troy to shreds in plain sight?"

Dorian's jaw tightened and he shot to his feet. "Look," he said, meeting my prosecuting gaze with a scowl that could kill. "Troy started it. And somehow he held his own. I mean, he was incredibly strong. That last hit really freaking hurt!"

"Well," I said, matching his scowl with one of my own. "From the sound of things, you deserved every blow. Body shots off his girlfriend?"

"It wasn't like that," Dorian said, his tone back to being level and controlled. Then his eyes flickered with sudden realization, brows lifting. "But that's not the real issue. Is it?"

A jolt ran through my body. I couldn't control the guilt that rippled across my face.

Dorian's eyes widened with realization. "You lied to me?" His voice was filled with disbelief. "You knew all along." He stepped forward, coiling tense fingers around my biceps. "Tell me what the hell they are."

My eyes averted, head dropping in regret. "Dorian, I'm sorry. I downplayed the incidents with Ty. I was certain something was different about him. But…" I hesitated. My suspicions on Ty were strong, but could I believe them? Was there some other rational explanation? "I don't know exactly what they are."

Dorian looked as though I had literally punched him in the gut. My heart ached while his grip on my arms tightened. "Why?" he asked on a breath of a whisper. "Why did you keep this from me?"

"I…I…"

A pitying smile thinned his healing lip. "You're falling for him."

With a jolt I stepped backward, freeing my arms and hitting the door. "No," I whispered, shaking my head. The taste of Ty's blood spiked the back of my throat. "I hardly know him. I couldn't possibly."

I met Dorian's watching eyes. His expression had shifted to determination. "So, you know what we have to do now?"

I swallowed, trying to clear the acidic blood from my mouth. "I know." My likeness reflected in the floor-length mirror behind Dorian. At least Ty's blood no longer stained my face. Having to explain what I had done to Ty in the hot tub? No thanks. Confronting him was enough to deal with. "Okay. Let's get some answers."

Leaving the bathroom, we crossed the courtyard. I scanned around in search of Ty. The bar was abuzz again with drunken teens, already past the excitement of the fight and throwing back a line of shots. Vanessa sat amongst them. She caught my eye with a disapproving frown. Then her gaze shifted purposefully to a set of glass sliding doors that led into the house. Just beyond the glass and standing in darkness, were Troy and the girl responsible for the fight. From the tense expressions on both their faces, it was clear the incident was far from resolved. I focused past the chatting group at the bar and the pumping music radiating from the dance floor. My hearing turned sharp, zeroing in on their intense argument.

"I don't like this," Troy was saying.

The girl propped her hands on her hips. "You think I do?" She laughed. "You know I would rather set my own skin on fire. But this is the only way, and you know it."

With a frown, my eyes glided up. There was a large picture frame taking up the wall behind them. Three people made up the portrait, a middle-aged man and woman with black hair and tan complexions. The third person sitting between the two was a boy who looked more like a man. He had oversized bulging muscles, the same tan skin, black hair and mirroring hazel eyes. Ty's reluctance to reveal whose party we were attending suddenly made perfect sense. This was Troy's house, the guy who hated me without explanation. Unsettled, I shuddered. We were on *his* turf.

"Are you coming?" Dorian's voice almost startled me.

Turning my head from the couple, I pushed back the unease within me. Then I sniffed the air. Ty was here, somewhere. I could scent him. "He's over there."

Dorian followed my lead to the dance floor. We waded through clusters of sweaty teens gyrating to the music under a blinding array of multicolored lights. When we broke free on the other side, we found yet another bar. This one was longer than the first and entirely made of thick, frosted glass.

Ty sat at the end, throwing back a shot of bourbon. His expression was apprehensive. In the seasonally cool fall night air, steam lifted from his dripping-wet board shorts, though I noticed his bare chest and arms appeared completely dry.

Seemingly aware of our presence, he peered up. His gaze fell on Dorian. "Hey man, you alright?"

Dorian slung his arms over his chest. There was not a single scratch or bruise on him. "Enough with the small talk."

To create a barricade between him and Ty, I slid past Dorian. Then I motioned to the bartender for a drink. "Vodka, straight up." With Ty and Dorian watching me, I threw down the shot then requested another. Ty looked amused. "The t-truth," my voice shook with nerves. "We want the truth."

Ty leaned forward, causing Dorian to tense behind me. In a hushed voice he spoke directly to me. "I'll only speak to you." He raised his hazel eyes to Dorian. "Alone…"

"Not on your life," Dorian snarled, fingers readying into fists.

My arm shot across Dorian's chest, my eyes pleading. At least the thumping music kept our discussion from being overheard. Not a single person had turned at my brother's challenging words. "Dorian, please…"

"I don't trust him," Dorian rebutted, standing his ground.

I collected his hands and squeezed. "Then trust me."

Dorian's shoulders slumped with a sigh. "Alright, but make it quick. Or I *will* come looking for you." With a last warning glare directed at Ty, he turned and stalked back through the close-knit dancers, disappearing from sight.

Ty rose to his feet, holding out a hand. "I guess it's time."

I quickly downed my second shot. Not even a full bottle would've calmed the growing butterflies churning up my stomach. "Damn vampire metabolism," I muttered. Instantly I froze. No one was looking at me, thank God. But Ty was. He even looked kind of amused. That was different.

Feeling slightly more at ease, I laced my fingers through his. Ty pulled me in the opposite direction of the dance floor, around the side of the house. We passed through beautifully manicured gardens of hedged bushes and paved paths, and then climbed a spiraled staircase to a secluded balcony. Vines twisted around the carved stone balustrade. They rose up to the ceiling and darkened the space with shadows. The scent of Ty's blood was there with total clarity. Its intensity made me think of Skillet's song *Better than Drugs*. Now I personally understood the depth of those very words. Yet right now it seemed less irresistible. Had my stolen taste quelled my rampant thirst for him? And if so, how long would it last? With my luck, not long enough.

Ty moved, dropping onto a stone bench that ended the balcony, and pulled me down beside him. His head dropped, strained eyes staring down at our entwined fingers. "We're different to regular human beings."

"You and Troy," I assumed.

Ty peered up with a nod, meeting my steady gaze. "Troy isn't happy about any of this. He used to be different, less angry, and less on edge before *it* happened." His explanation trailed off as he turned his head from mine. I reached out and touched his cheek, crooking his head back to face me. "Ty, before what happened?" Within my chest, my heart was jumping. There was no turning back now. I had to know the truth. Was he really what I thought he was? "*What are you?*"

A look I couldn't decipher hijacked Ty's expression. "Many would call us monsters, *if* they ever caught a glimpse. We're..." Pausing, he peered up with pleading eyes. "Promise me something?" I took a deep breath and nodded. "Promise me that what I'm about to tell you won't turn you against me. Promise that it won't change the way you feel about me."

Nerves bubbled up my throat, making me want to cough. The way *I* feel? Within my chest my heart was racing. Sweat made my palms wet in his. More volatile butterflies violently turned my stomach. They were all reactions that seemed to occur every time Ty was near. Had Dorian been right all along? Is this what falling for someone felt like? I couldn't deny the magnetic pull I felt toward him, the fascination with everything that made Ty unique. I had tried so hard to steer clear of him, to hide the monster within me, fearing his reaction. Yet nothing I had said or done had worked to keep him at arm's length. Not even my actions in the cave could deter him. He accepted me, accepted the monster inside of me, the blood-hungry creature dwelling within a deceptive human shell.

With a start that shook my entire being, a profound realization washed over me. I had been lying to myself this entire time, pretending that all that drew me to Ty was the lure of his blood and the mystery of what made him different. But it was so, so much more. It was in the way he looked at me, the acceptance that sparked within his changeable eyes. And it was embedded in every fiber of my being that reacted so involuntarily—and at times embarrassingly —to every part of him. He could reach me with a single look, or any harsh or softly spoken word, with the slightest graze or roughest touch of his flesh against mine. The feel was dizzyingly breathtaking and irreversibly consuming. From this moment on, I knew I couldn't deny it.

I pulled my hands free and wiped my sweating palms across my skirt. Then I raised my eyes to Ty's. Frozen fear encompassed his expression. "I would *never* turn against you, Ty. I don't care what you are. Nothing could change the way being near you makes me feel. This part of me," I said, collecting Ty's hand and pressing it over my racing heart. Against my chilled skin, his heated touch rippled goosebumps over my arms. The wave continued in a chain reaction down the entire length of my body. "That you ignite."

The tension in Ty's face dissolved. His shoulders dropped as he let out a breath of relief. Then, with a squeeze of my hands, a low rumble emerged from his throat. "I'm a lycanthrope, a werewolf."

The nerves that had plagued me earlier at uncovering the truth subsided. All the pieces had gelled together. The glimpses I'd seen in Ty and Troy, reminiscent of a forest-dwelling wolf, now made perfect sense. I was right.

A disarming realization rippled through my mind. I couldn't hurt him. It felt like a crushing weight had been lifted from my shoulders. Ty was stronger than me and just as fast. I had witnessed it on numerous occasions. Now I felt a surge of renewed hope. If I ever did lose control with him, his unnatural abilities would be there to stop me. "So *that's* why you're not afraid of me," I spoke more to myself, than to him.

Ty's eyes widened. "That's why you've been avoiding me?"

Feeling ashamed, my gaze dropped. I pulled my hands free from Ty's. "It's your blood," I confessed. "It just smells so…*good*." Heat careened up my neck and across my face. "Every moment I'm around you, I fight the urge to…" *Sink my fangs into your flesh*, I finished in my head, unable to say the words out loud. Raising my eyes, I saw Ty's expression darken. My chest constricted. I'd said too much.

"You're meant to feel that way." Ty's voice held none of the revulsion I had expected. "Vampires are our only mortal threat. We're raised to be enemies. It's unnatural for us to feel anything but hatred for each other."

Pressure tightened my chest while anger welled in my throat. Unnatural? I had only moments ago accepted and confessed my feelings for Ty. Now I was meant to believe that those feelings were wrong? That they went against everything that defined us as inhuman beings? Throwing my hands in the air, I shot to my feet. "The hell with natural, I don't care what anyone says or thinks!" I realized I was shouting, and dropped back beside Ty. "The way I feel about you," I said more quietly. "I won't let *anyone* tell me it's wrong."

Ty slung an arm over my shoulder and hauled me against his bare, heated chest. "I think our families may hold different views, when they find out."

I jerked away from Ty's comforting arm, facing him with pleading eyes. "Then we won't tell them!"

"We don't have to," Ty replied. "Lycans are taught to spot vampires from an early age. We're raised to detest everything about your kind, and to recognize you for the killers you pretend not to be."

"But we don't…" I broke off having wanted to say, we don't kill. Only the memory of Joel crumpled in the alley, stilled my rebuttal. I shook the memory from my mind and chose my words carefully. "My family drinks packaged blood. We don't want to kill anyone."

Ty's hand grazed my cheek. "I know. I could tell you were different from the first moment I laid eyes on you." He stared over the stone railing and out into night sky. A quarter moon, now free of clouds, shone down on us. The wistful expression on his face appeared to be remembering a distant time. He refocused moments later, steady eyes peering into mine. "I know you struggle with what you are. But I also know you are *not* a killer."

A pang of guilt shot through my heart. I may not have killed yet, but I had come so close. He wouldn't understand. How could he?

"My family has never known of a family like yours." Ty tipped my head to wipe away a fallen tear. "It will be difficult for my father to accept. But we'll cross that bridge when the time comes, *together*."

Ty squeezed my hand with reassurance, which did little to shake the heavy boulder sitting in the pit of my stomach; a sickening feeling conjured by crippling guilt. I knew what I had to do. It was the only thing that could ease this burdening pressure that was building inside of me. I had to tell Ty…everything. The night I had discovered I was a vampire. What I had done in a rage of blinding bloodlust. "Okay, but I need to…"

Shadows darted through the garden below, choking the words from my throat. It was Dorian and that damn girl again. *What the hell is he doing?*

"You need to what?" Ty questioned.

"Huh?" I shook my head, looking back to Ty. The way he was watching me with total acceptance, tugged at my heart. I couldn't bear for that to change. So I bit my tongue and allowed the new problem at hand to overshadow the discomfort I felt. "I um, need to do something. About that." I pointed as Dorian and the girl disappeared behind a wall of square-trimmed hedges. "And I won't be able to keep what you've told me from my brother. He's beyond suspicious."

Ty sat in thought for a brief moment then smiled. "Amelia, I trust you completely. Tell him anything you want."

CHAPTER 10

I climbed down the spiral staircase to the garden. It was peacefully quiet down here, bar the low thrum radiating once more from the dance floor. If only peacefulness and beauty could relieve the turmoil tearing through my weighted stomach. Rose bushes lined a small, paved path leading away from the courtyard's flashing lights and into the darkness of the grounds. The only light came from the cloud-swept quarter moon that gleamed ghostly shadows around me. Apart from the shadows, the garden appeared abandoned. But I knew they were out here. The smell of that girl's sickly perfume lingered on the faint, icy breeze, making my nose wrinkle.

When I reached a wall of six-foot trimmed hedges with a single arched walk-through in the center, I paused. There were two distinct voices, Dorian's and hers. I peeked through the gap. Just beyond a concrete birdbath was a stone bench with the same girl perched on its edge. She was pressed hard-up against Dorian, thrusting her bulging breasts into his chest. I couldn't believe she wasn't freezing to death in that tank top and mini skirt. Even with my vampire skin, I could feel how seriously cold it was. Not that Dorian was dressed any better. He was wearing the same bloodstained cargo pants, but his black polo shirt was gone, leaving his pale chest bare. Irritation frayed my nerves. The fight had been bad enough. As if we needed any more attention.

Eavesdropping from behind the barricading wall, I tried to gauge my next move. The girl leaned forward, slowly slinging one leg over the other. She whispered into Dorian's ear. "It's a shame Troy interrupted our body shots. Though I'm glad I broke up with him, gives me plenty of time to get closer to you."

Dorian smiled a seductive, *I want to get in your pants*, smile. It was one I had witnessed on numerous occasions, his trademark for picking up girls. Casually draping one arm around her shoulder, he ran his fingers through her black, wavy hair. Through the movement, I noticed a gold symbol across the back of her neck. I stared as the clouds shifted. Moonlight flickered across her tan skin, making the symbol glitter. Three parallel wavy lines crossed diagonally through the center.

That's weird, I thought. She couldn't be more than sixteen or seventeen. How had she gotten a tattoo? And how could it glitter?

"So Marika," Dorian purred. "What are you doing in Rye?" He continued running his fingers through her long hair. "You don't go to our school, do you?"

"I grew up here and moved away almost a year ago. But I missed my friends and the animal shelter so much, that I begged the 'rents to move back." With a sultry smile, her palm floated above his chest, index finger tracing his lightly defined pecs. "So, you managed to hold your own against Troy. I was pretty impressed." She pressed her body against his.

128

Dorian cocked one eyebrow and lifted his free arm to flex his bicep. "Thanks. I do try to keep in shape."

Marika let out a playful giggle, before leaning her face closer to his. Her brown eyes beckoned while her lips parted.

With my stomach in knots, I leaped from the shadows. Knowing how Dorian usually operated, I definitely didn't want to see how far *this* situation would go. "Dorian, I've been looking for you every-where. Can we talk for a minute?" With a venomous glare propelled at Marika, I dodged around the birdbath. *"Alone..."*

"Sorry, I was going to come and find you, but as you can see I got caught up." Dorian shrugged innocently while looking slightly irritated at my interruption. "This is my sister, Amelia." The smile returned to his face as he looked back to Marika. "And Amelia, this is Marika."

I glared past her to Dorian. "I need to talk to you, *now*."

Marika stood up, tan face flushed with annoyance and hands planted on her hips. "Well, I was going to hit the dance floor, anyway." She looked to Dorian. Her next words were spoken in such a fakely sweet voice and so thickly laced with seduction that they made me want to hurl. "Coming to join me, stud?"

Dorian smiled encouragingly. "Sure. I'll just be a minute."

With a *'humph'* Marika turned abruptly, brushing past my shoulder and slinking away. The pungency of her perfume went with her.

I stormed over to Dorian and hauled him to his feet. "What the hell are you doing? Do you have the memory of a goldfish? I mean you were just at blows a half hour ago because of that girl. Now you're getting all *friendly*?"

Dorian shrugged, a smug expression painting his face. "We were just talking."

"Don't treat me like I'm stupid," I said, narrowing my eyes at him. "You know as well as I do that you weren't *just talking*."

Dorian folded his arms over his chest. "Why do you care, anyway?"

"Because that girl is trouble." After tonight's fight, and how quickly she'd ditched Troy for my brother, that was more than clear. The fact that she knew Ty didn't help, either. Plus after hearing her argument with Troy, I didn't trust her. "I just don't want to see you get hurt."

"Hah," Dorian laughed, throwing his head back. "You've gotta be joking."

Dorian, as a rule, grew tired of any girl he dated in at most a couple of weeks. He never got attached. Yet even with the facts, something inside me screamed that this time would be different.

"Fine," I said. "Just don't come running to me when your heart finally gets broken."

With a wave, Dorian brushed my concerns aside and pulled me down onto the stone bench. "So, what did Ty say? Did he explain?"

"Yes, he did." Letting my worries about Marika get replaced by the nerves I had felt earlier, I sighed. "And I'll tell you everything. But you have to promise to keep your mouth shut." Dorian nodded in agreement. "I mean it, Dorian. No one can know, especially not Mom."

Dorian crossed his hand over his heart and winked. "I promise. Now spill."

"Okay, here goes." I took a deep breath before looking up at Dorian's suspense-filled eyes. "That guy you took on *is* as strong and as fast as we are. You could have been seriously hurt." Dorian raised an eyebrow but remained silent, waiting. "They're different from humans. Kind of like us."

Dorian's brow crinkled, suspense replaced by confusion. "Just tell me what they are, already."

"Okay, okay. Ty and Troy are…" Clutching my hands together, I sucked in another deep breath. Please don't flip out. "They're lycans, werewolves."

I sat in frozen silence watching my brother take in the heavy news. His eyes had grown wide. Then they narrowed like he was contemplating the possibility. "You're being serious? They actually exist?"

I nodded, feeling numb, my body tingling in wait for him to blow up.

"Wow," Dorian exhaled on a long breath. His body was relaxed. His face revealed not a single ounce of tension.

A wave of relief washed down my tingling body. I had expected Dorian to blow up at the news, especially after his run-in with Troy. But he was taking the revelation surprisingly well. Maybe too well.

Dorian's face brightened into a cheeky smile. "So, my sister is dating a werewolf." He chuckled, entertained. "I plan on having a front-row seat when you tell Mom."

I punched him in the arm, hard. "Don't tease, and don't forget. You promised!"

"I know, I know. My goldfish memory does tend to last longer than five minutes." Dorian rubbed his hands together, looking devilish as he got to his feet. "Now, I'm off to catch up with the minx on the dance floor, before she gets *cold* waiting for me." He took off in a light jog, disappearing back through the hedge's arched entry.

After a few minutes of my mind reeling, I ambled back through the garden. Weight pulled at my insides. What I wouldn't do for a piece of chocolate. But right now I had to find out more about this new girl. Who was she? How well did she know Ty? And what did she want with my brother? Just thinking about the commotion she had already caused filled me with anxiety. There was just something off about her. But what? I headed for the one person I suspected could enlighten me and hopefully diffuse my suspicion.

Ty was across the courtyard, propped atop a cube around the cane coffee table. He no longer sat in his dripping wet board shorts, now dressed in his jeans and thin hoodie. His bomber jacket was draped over one knee. I frowned. I had hoped to find him alone. Not luck there. Vanessa sat alongside in a stunning white dress, her blaze of hair like a warning beacon. They appeared to be playing a casual game of poker.

Ty—in the way he always did—sensed my approach and glanced up with a forced smile. Vanessa however, busy studying the cards in her hands, seemed unaware of my advance. Knowing now what Ty was, I detected an obvious air around him. He was strong and capable—a force to be reckoned with.

"How was Dorian?" The concern in Ty's voice mirrored his apprehensive expression.

Vanessa was now aware of my presence and regarding me with clear speculation. I decided to keep my response short. "We had a good *chat*, and he seems fine." I tugged my skirt down to keep from flashing anyone my wet bikini bottoms, then dropped onto the cube beside him and scanned for Dorian. There. Through the close-knit bodies that swarmed the dance floor, I could just make him out. Ick! He was all hands as he groped Marika's sultry dancing body. With such a blatant sexual display, I almost expected Troy to come lunging from the shadows with murder painted in his eyes. I glanced around at the alcohol-sweating dancers. Not there. Then at the few kids playing what looked like 'spin the blow-up dolphin' within the pool's crystalline water. Not there either. Thank God. I looked back to Ty. "Though, I did kind of catch him getting friendly with that new girl, Marika."

Ty's face dropped and his darkening eyes stared down at the cards in his hands.

The sinking sensation swelling up my stomach increased. The taste of his blood rose to the back of my throat. "She told Dorian she used to live here. Do you know her?"

"We all grew up together," Vanessa offered. Her sapphire eyes sparkled with interest.

Ty's forearms tensed and he glared at her. His hands clenched into fists, crumpling the cards scissored between his fingers.

"What Ty doesn't want to say," she continued, ignoring his hostile warning, "is that he used to date her. Well, before she dumped him for Troy."

I sucked in a startled breath, eyes darting to Ty. A flurry of questions flooded my mind. Why didn't he tell me? Had he loved her? Did he miss her? Did he want her back?

"Can't you ever just butt out?" Ty growled at Vanessa, who shrugged with indifference. He collected the unharmed cards from the table and packed them into a square cardboard box. "How about I get you home," he suggested, glancing up at me. "We can *talk* on the way. And besides, you do look beat."

Wanting to be alone with Ty to get answers, I nodded. Besides, I could feel the brunt of the night's events catching up with me. If Dorian got himself into trouble again, he'd have to get out of it on his own. "Okay."

With a stiff nod from Ty to Vanessa, we retraced the path back around the house and out to Ty's car. For the first time tonight, I noticed how truly cold it was. Frost had settled on every car and every blade of green grass. A thick fog hung in the air. Even with my superior eyesight, I could barely see the outline of the front gates bordering the property.

Ty opened the passenger door to his car. I awkwardly slid into seat, tugging again on my skirt. A second later Ty was in the driver's seat. He threw his jacket into the back and it landed on his training bag with a *clank*. That didn't sound like goggles. Before I could ask what hard object he needed for swim practice, the engine roared to life. The radio murmured quietly. *Now the fifth vicious murder in under a fortnight...*

Ty reached out with a frown and clicked the stereo off. Then he clasped my hand, the warmth of his touch radiating up my arm. "I know a lot has happened tonight. Not just between us, but also with Dorian and *Marika*." His tongue scraped with unrestrained hatred over her name. "Are we okay? Did Dorian accept what I am?"

"Dorian took the news about you *surprisingly* well." I studied Ty's expression as I continued. "He seemed more consumed with getting to know Marika."

Ty snatched his hand free to plunge the gearshift into first. The car chirped, gliding through the fog and out the front gates. His hand found mine with a squeeze. "I'm sorry I didn't mention her earlier." He threw a quick glance my way. "I guess with everything else it just didn't seem important."

A sharp bend appeared through the swirling fog at the last second. Ty pulled his hand from mine—quick as a flash—and dropped back to second gear. The car made a squealing protest but clung to the road like a magnet.

Unperturbed and forcing the car back to top speed, Ty collected my hand and raised it to his heart. "Amelia, I want you to know that I want you, only you."

The unusual beat of his heart soothed my worries, dissolving the clatter of questions clogging up my mind. I smiled, my muscles releasing all the tension of the night. Sleepiness weighed on my eyes. "Me too."

I STOOD SURROUNDED by ivory-tinted limestone and reaching cabinetry. The space was awash with brilliant white chandelier light. It took only a second for me to realize that I was standing in our home's kitchen. The limestone island, big enough it could double as a sacrificial altar, was proof enough. Yet knowing where I was didn't dislodge the disorientation I felt.

Everything appeared to be in its rightful place, with dirty plates and blood-tinged glasses collecting on the marble counter next to the deep, round sink. But something was wrong. The persistent pounding of my heart made that crystal clear.

"How did you expect me to react?" My eyes shot to my mom, whose strained voice had startled me. Natural poise abandoned, her hands clenched into fists and belted down against the countertop. The force sent a burst of hairline fractures straight through the limestone. "When you're seeing that...that filthy mongrel?"

Acid spiked the back of my throat. *She knows*. I felt like vomiting. But an uncontrollable fury at her insult of Ty ignited within me. "Don't speak about Ty like that. You know nothing of what he is."

Mom shook her head almost regrettably. She stepped around the island to lay a gentle hand on my shoulder. "Amelia, sweetheart, you know this must end."

Violently, I threw my hands in the air, batting her arm away. I opened my mouth to scream in protest. Nothing came out.

Panic seeped through my core as everything faded to blackness. Restricting arms tightened around me. "Let me go!" I tried to scream, thrashing to get free.

"It's okay," a deep and familiar voice spoke. "It's just me."

My eyes blinked open as my back connected with something soft. The constricting arms around me released. I couldn't see. Pins shot through my eyes while my lids fluttered. The room slowly lightened. Through blurred and spotted vision, varying shades of purple grew more and more prominent as my senses awakened. Warmth bloomed beside me, along with the sound of an irregular heartbeat. *Ty.* I struggled to focus. "What happened? Where are we?"

Ty's hands found mine. "You fell asleep on the way home. I didn't want to wake you, so I carried you up to your room."

It was just a dream. I frowned, my eyes finally clearing. Ty was sitting before me, framed by the mauve-swathed posts of my princess-style bed. His brows arched in surprise. "What's wrong?" I asked.

"It's your eyes," Ty said, covering his expression. "Your whites, they're completely red."

I flung my legs over the edge of the bed and rummaged through my nightstand. In a second I'd passed my stashed chocolate and recovered a palm-sized mirror. My reflection shocked me. The blue of my irises looked similar to when I drank blood, completely silver. Though right now there was a stark difference. The whites of my eyes when I drank blood usually became rimmed with red. I had seen the reaction when drinking packaged blood at the cabin. But now, without having consumed anything since the party, *since Ty*, they appeared completely stained with the crimson of fresh blood. Confused, I shook my head. "It must be a latent reaction to your blood." As I stared at my reflection, the red slowly faded back to white. Thank God. Yet I was far from feeling relieved. Something was still nagging at me, filling me with unquenchable dread. "Wait! How did you get inside, I mean, when you brought me home?"

"Your mom let me in," Ty replied, his tone level and devoid of concern.

The air suddenly tasted stale. I coughed, gagging, and began to hyperventilate. "You met my mom!" Oh my God, it's happening. My dream is coming true.

"Hey." Ty leaned in, rubbing his warm hands vigorously up and down my shaking arms. "What's wrong?"

"You met her, and now she knows." I struggled not to scream. "She knows what you are."

Ty shook my arms, forcing me to look at him. "No, she doesn't. When you fell asleep I took something to mask my scent. I'm certain she had no idea."

I sniffed the air. Ty was right. His scent was gone. Still, his words did little to shake the memory of my dream and the disappointment hedging Mom's expression. "How can you be so sure?"

He smiled, taking a deep breath. "Because, I could hear her heart beat."

I frowned. How could Ty's detection of her beating heart prove anything?

"It didn't elevate," he explained. "If she were suspicious, lying, or in any way trying to hide something, her heart would tell."

I slumped back against the many fluffy pillows adorning my bed. "It was just a dream?"

Ty's rough hand grazed my cheek. "Sounds more like a nightmare."

Suddenly I became aware of his proximity. Not to mention that we were alone in my bedroom, on my bed. He sat facing me, one knee folded with his free hand resting against it. There was only an inch separating his fingers from the bare flesh between my hiked-up short skirt and knee-high boots. Memory rushed of those very hands clutching my thighs and lifting me off the ground with such easy strength.

Blood heated my cheek under the warmth of Ty's palm. He edged forward, brushing his sweltering lips against mine. "I'm going away tomorrow. I won't be back till sometime next week."

I jerked away for him. "What? Where are you going?"

"My father called earlier." Ty's eyes shifted to the bedroom door. "It's a family thing. I really can't elaborate, not yet."

He was still keeping secrets? Irritated, I folded my arms over my chest. "Can't, or won't?"

Ty blew out a long, slow breath. "Both." He collected my hands and looked into my eyes, his own rippling with a glint of gold. "It's for the best. Just trust me on this one."

The last thing I wanted to do was let the subject lie. But a deepening thirst was rolling through my stomach. Even though I couldn't detect Ty's blood, I could still hear his heartbeat and see the pulsing vein along his neck. "Okay. I'll let it go," I said, feeling my fangs peeking through, "*for now*. But don't think I'll forget."

Ty's smiled and he dipped his head, lips meeting mine with restrained force. "I wouldn't dream of it."

CHAPTER 11

*W*ith Ty suddenly absent—a fact that irritated me to no end—I expected the remainder of the weekend to be slow and boring. I couldn't have been more wrong.

Dorian and I sprawled across the soft grass of our backyard under the canopy of a cherry tree with my iPod running through the Lifehouse album *Smoke and Mirrors*. Now that fall was in full swing, its leaves ranged from burned russet to browning gold. Mom's first charity event, a fundraising auction, was to take place here next Saturday. Ironically, the proceeds would go to the Department of Hematological Medicine in support of research into rare blood diseases. The event would require a lot of preparation. Decorations and flowers needed to be ordered. Waiters and other staff needed to be booked. Auction items also needed to be sought. Mom took on the brunt of the laundry list. Dorian and I were left to picking out—from the many catalogs she had collected—lighting, a stage, and a podium. There would also be a marquee to accommodate Mom's extensive guest list of colleagues from the Portsmouth Vampire Council, and local bored-housewife charity volunteers.

A number of vampires were expected to attend—extended royalty *and* turned vampires who weren't immune to the sunlight. Because of that, the event would commence at twilight.

We spent the afternoon flicking through catalogs with Dorian continually taking breaks to text Marika. Now the sun was diving for the horizon. The late afternoon temperature began to plummet. Around us, fog began to rise. A thin film of frost began to form on everything in sight, growing like cracked crystal. With the grass beneath us becoming damp and sticking our clothes to our bodies, we got to our feet. I snatched up my iPod and the completed order forms.

In that same second, Mom exited the terrace doors. She was making straight for us with light and ethereal steps. To me she had always been delicate-looking and graceful. Dorian with his drawing charisma was more like her than I had ever been. "How's it all coming along?"

I narrowed my eyes dubiously. The question hadn't been out of the ordinary, but her lit face made me curious. What was she up to?

Dorian, oblivious, thrust the order forms into her hands. "All done."

Mom skimmed the forms then turned her giddy expression back to us. "Well, after all your hard work, I have a surprise." Her red-painted lips parted with a delighted smile. "We have a visitor."

She peered over her shoulder towards the terrace doors. A dark figure emerged, partially shrouded by a row of young cherry trees. The guy sauntered our way in a zipped-up hoodie. The hood was pulled over his head, obscuring his features, and his hands were shoved deep into the pockets of his black cargo pants. Even without the hoodie, which he always wore under his boarding jacket, I would have known who it was.

"Kendrick!" I squealed, bounding across the frosty grass and flinging my arms around his neck.

Kendrick lifted me up and twirled me around on the spot. "Told you I'd visit," he whispered in my ear, before lowering me back to the ground. He glanced to Dorian and Mom, smiling. "Thought I should come and see how you're all living here in *sunny* New Hampshire."

"Kendrick," Dorian said, tipping his head in greeting. "Where are you staying?"

"Here!" I blurted. "You have to stay here."

My eyes shot to Mom for approval, who nodded. "Of course Kendrick will stay with us. And now that he's here, Amelia, will you show him up to one of our spare rooms?"

"Definitely!" I collected Kendrick's hand, and began a rushed tour around the house, flying at vampire speed and talking at a barely intelligible babble. In minutes we were outside the spare room. It was on the second floor and just down the hall from my own bedroom. I flicked on the light switch and the chandelier illuminated. The space housed hardwood furnishings and had a walk-in closet and adjoining bathroom. Two arched windows were positioned on either side of a king-size bed, shielded by thick indigo drapes.

I bounded inside and flung my body onto the satin-sheeted bed, pulling Kendrick down with me. We landed with a bounce, laughing. "I can't believe you're really here."

Kendrick rolled onto his side, propping up on one arm. "I've missed you, too."

"How long are you staying?" I asked, hating to even think of him leaving anytime soon. "Wait, what about school?"

Kendrick bent into a sitting position and ruffled his golden-brown hair. "Weeks, maybe longer. It depends."

I bit my lip, sensing a hesitation and tenseness from him that moments ago had not been there. "Depends on what?"

"On you," he confessed, glancing sideways at me and drawing his shoulders back. "Your mom's concerned that you're not adapting as easily as Dorian. She thought me being here might help."

"So that's why you're here?" I couldn't hide my disappointment.

"Of course not," Kendrick said, drawing me up off the bed and into his arms. "I've missed you so much. The Armaya is so bloody boring, and without you nearby to escape to, I feel like I'm contracting cabin fever. I just needed to see you." His arms loosened around me but didn't let go, his fingers entwined at my waist. "So when your mom asked mine, I begged her to let me come. She agreed, so long as I attend school with you."

With my disappointment waived, I smiled. "What's it like there?"

Although Kendrick had grown up around our family, I had never been to the place he called home. He had always been reluctant to speak about his family and had always made excuses not to hang out at his place. Now I understood the reason, the secret he had kept of being a vampire before I knew I was one too. He lived at the Armaya with his mom—a beautiful woman I had only ever met when she'd dropped Kendrick off for the weekend. She, alongside our adopted Uncle Caius, held a spot on the Royal Vampire Council.

Kendrick sighed. "It's monotonous, and structured, everything that sucks the fun out of life."

"Then don't go back," I pleaded, unlocking Kendrick's hands and clutching them with my own. I couldn't deny how normal I felt whenever I was around him. He'd always accepted everything about me, even my mood swings. "Stay here…with me."

"Amelia, I can't ignore my obligations, my birth-right." He shook his head regrettably then painted a cheeky smile back across his lips. "But I've escaped for now!" His arms spread out wide in dramatization that made me giggle. "Tell me about you. How have *you* been? What's new?"

My breath caught and my throat felt suddenly dry. In all the excitement and shock of Kendrick's arrival, I had totally forgotten about Ty. How could I tell Kendrick that I was involved with a were-wolf? He was my best friend, but he was also a royal heir and bound by their laws. In his eyes, Ty was our mortal enemy.

"Amelia, what's wrong?" Kendrick's hand found my jaw, tilting my face up. "Your mom was right, wasn't she? You're still having trouble settling in, in accepting being a vampire?"

Unable to hold his gaze, I averted my eyes with a nod. What would he do if I told him? What would he have to do? The fear of retaliation or condemnation sent shockwaves through my body. I couldn't force my lips to move, to say what I knew I should and to see the shock and disappointment across his face. I couldn't tell him. Kendrick could never know.

Kendrick curled his arm around me, pulling me against his chest. "It's okay," he said, stroking the length of my hair down my back. "I'm here now, and I'm not leaving anytime soon. I promise."

As I took up position at my easel beside Vanessa, she peered up through narrowed eyes. "So, you and Ty…"

She didn't appear at all thrilled at the idea. Not that I had expected any different. Before the party she had made it abundantly clear that she didn't approve of us getting to know each other in any way. Although besides her cryptic warning, I didn't understand why. Did she know what Ty was? A growing coldness invaded my stomach. Or what I was? Not wanting to meet her icy eyes, I glanced away. Other students stole glances around their own easels at me, but I tried to ignore them. They were babbling over the details of the party, and the jaw-dropping fight they had all witnessed. "Yeah, and?"

"Oh nothing," she said, flinging her hair over her shoulders. As she did, a glint of gold caught my sight. The broad beams of sunlight that streamed through the glass-paneled fernery had caught on something.

My eyes darted to Vanessa and the supple exposed flesh of her neck. Apart from the gold hoop earrings dangling from her small ears, there was nothing. *I'm imagining things.*

"Though aren't you at all curious of where Ty keeps disappearing to?" Vanessa's goading expression said more than her words. She knew exactly where Ty was, and why. And I didn't.

Fed up with her self-righteous attitude, I crossed my arms over my chest. "I don't suppose you're in the mood to enlighten me?"

Vanessa smiled a not-so-friendly but devious smile. *"Hunting..."*

I frowned, thinking of the hunting boots Ty and Troy always wore and their erratic and increasing scars. Did werewolves survive by hunting prey, on the flesh or blood of wild animals? The thought was somehow settling, to think that Ty could be more like me than I had ever imagined. But what if I'm wrong? Since learning the truth just two days ago, I hadn't had the opportunity to discover anything about werewolves. Ty being absent again didn't help, and neither did Kendrick's arrival. But I wanted—no, needed—to know who Ty was, how he lived, and what made him so unique. *And*, I thought to myself, *why he wanted me.*

"Hunting?" I questioned.

With a sweeping gesture, Vanessa waved me off. "Yes. But if

you want to know *what* Ty's hunting, you'll have to ask him yourself." She turned back to her canvas and resumed painting.

For the remainder of class I stared at my artwork. It was developing much slower than the other students' pieces in the class. My continued distraction with Ty was the usual culprit for keeping my mind wandering and unfocused.

When the shrill clanging of the bell sounded, I leaped from my easel and shot through the door and across the courtyard of puddled paths and oak-accompanied gazebos. Once inside the main building, I stopped short in front of my locker. I swung the door open and knocked my elbow. Dammit! I snatched my iPhone from the shelf, speed-dialing Ty's number. With students hurrying past, the action reminded me of the last time I had called him from this exact location. This time, again, my question for him would be related to his absence.

"Amelia," Ty's surprised voice echoed through the speaker. His breath sounded fast and ragged. "Is everything okay?"

"Yeah, I guess. It's just…" I closed my eyes and hung my head inside my locker. "What are you hunting?"

"Who told you to ask that?" His incensed tone struck me, sending a jolt through my body. "It was Vanessa, wasn't it?"

"It doesn't matter who told me." Right now, outing Vanessa wasn't my concern. Figuring Ty out was. "I'm not angry," I added. "I just need an answer." When Ty remained silent I continued in a hushed voice. "It's wild animals, isn't it? You hunt them to feed? Kind of like," I lowered my voice further, "like vampires hunt animals for blood?"

Ty sighed. "I'm sorry. I didn't mean to react that way. Vanessa's tactlessness seriously grates on my nerves." He paused, taking a deep breath in before blowing it out. "And you're right. We do hunt wild game. Now," Ty said, tone lifting. "Who's Kendrick, and should I be worried?"

Damn Vanessa!

During lunch she had made a quick appearance, catching sight of Kendrick and demanding an introduction. Then Marika had arrived glued to Dorian's side. Troy hadn't been there, which I gathered was due to the secret *wolf expedition*. Vanessa though, after only a few minutes, had politely excused herself. At the time I'd assumed the sight of Dorian and Marika together had offended her. Now I knew better. Her sudden departure had been an excuse to run and tell Ty about Kendrick.

I fought the impulse to bash my fist through the locker door beside mine. That would only direct attention my way. Instead, I took a deep breath. Then I explained who Kendrick was and why he was here. I expressed my concern with telling Kendrick who Ty was. Ty agreed. There was no need to create drama. After that, we quickly covered the charity auction Mom was hosting.

"I can drop past Saturday morning and help with the setting up," Ty offered.

"I'd like that," I replied. "But just remember—"

"Your mom and Kendrick don't know I'm a werewolf," he interrupted. "And we're going to keep it that way."

ALL HOPE of holding down my lunch on Thursday faded as I entered the cafeteria. Past the tables of animated teens, laughing, chatting and eating, I could see the scene at our table. Marika sat in Dorian's lap, thrusting her bust against his chest while twirling her curly, black hair flirtatiously around one finger. This disgusting, physical display had been escalating all week. At least Troy had been absent

WHAT LIES INSIDE

with Ty. I couldn't begin to imagine the bloodshed that would have resulted when he glimpsed his ex-girlfriend pressed against another guy. But soon enough I wouldn't have to.

Unsurprisingly, Marika was dressed in a skin-tight, lime-colored boob tube sporting what looked like traces of dog hair from the animal shelter. The shortest denim skirt I had ever seen covered her round butt. Knee-high, black leather lace-up boots topped it all off. Any trace of chlorine lingering on Dorian from his morning swim practice was overwhelmed by the dousing of vanilla perfume coating Marika's entire body. Any jealousy I'd had because of her confident dressing had dissolved since her recognition of Ty at Troy's party. Now all I felt was unrelenting irritation at her and Dorian's flaunted physical interactions.

As I took my seat between Kendrick and Vanessa, I tucked my iPod into my jeans. I'd just been listening to a new band Kendrick had suggested, *Kutless*. Dorian turned to whisper something into Marika's ear.

"You are so bad," Marika giggled. "But *I* have an even naughtier idea." She stroked his chest suggestively. Then at a level that all enhanced beings such as Kendrick and I could detect, she whispered the vomit-inducing details into his ear. They began making out in plain sight, hands groping and the sound of wet lips smacking.

With a groan, I pushed my lunch tray away and forced back the sensation to gag. "*Great*, they've kicked it up a notch," I moaned. Kendrick chuckled beside me, unaffected by the scene before us. My elbow shot out, collecting his ribs. "It's not funny."

"It's disgusting," Vanessa spat from my other side. She crossed her arms over her chest. For once it seemed we were in agreement on something. Though I knew it wouldn't last.

Dorian and Marika finally ceased kissing, needing to come up for air. Thank God.

"I can't wait for the charity auction," Marika announced, shifting her brown eyes onto me.

Dorian invited her! I glared at Marika as irritation scratched under my skin. "Oh, I didn't know *you* were coming." Dorian had grown accustomed to my not-so-latent dislike of Marika. He'd even stopped telling me off when I was being insolent.

Marika raised her lip in a half-snarl. "Your *brother* invited me, and I just couldn't say no."

"Hey since we're all *friends*," Dorian piped up, forcing my angry glare from Marika. "I reckon we could talk Mom into letting everyone sleep over after the auction."

"Are you insane?" I spat. Spend more time watching his sexcapades? I twitched in my seat, suddenly feeling as though I were sitting on a sharp bed of spikes. "I don't think…"

"Oooo, sleep over," Marika cut in. "I'm in. My 'rents let me do *whatever* I want."

I jumped up, kicking back my chair harder than I had meant to. It skidded across the blue-checkered tiles, thudding against the glass wall behind me. The abrupt movement caused Vanessa to jump in her seat. Now a sea of widened eyes from surrounding students was bearing down on me. Too irritated to care, I ignored them. "Dorian, a word…"

Feeling my gums tingle, I stormed from our table and through the glass doors outside. The courtyard was a quaint clearing of paved squares and aluminum picnic benches. It was surrounded on three sides by a splash of green from bordering fernery. I stomped up onto the bench seat, dropping with an intentional *thud* onto the tabletop.

"Don't do this," I hissed through extended fangs. In this moment I was so pissed that I couldn't control my predatory reactions.

"Don't force me to endure this shit. I *won't* be responsible for my actions when she pushes me past breaking."

Dorian scooted beside me with a sigh. "Why do you hate her so much?"

His lack of defensiveness to my insults and hostility caught me off guard. Trying to remember how irate I was, I tensed my fingers, nails scraping indents along the aluminum with a hair-raising screech. "I just have a terrible feeling about her. She's not *good* for you."

Dorian reclined on his arms, cocking his head to face me. "And if I warned you against Ty, would *you* listen?"

My jaw dropped, fangs retracting. For a split second I thought of Ty. The only thing that had joined us all week since the party was that one short phone call. I'd tried to call him since, but he hadn't answered. Just as fast, my thoughts shifted to the party. Dorian had barely reacted to finding out what Ty and Troy were. "But you accepted him. You never said…"

"Of course I didn't." Dorian straightened to rest a palm across my knee. "You are your own person, Amelia. I may not agree with your choices, but they are yours to make." When I remained frozen and silent, guilt tugging at my heart, he continued. "Look, I don't expect you to like her. Just give me the same respect I show you. Allow me to make my own choices in life, *without ridicule.*"

I'm a hypocrite. I drew in a long breath then blew it back out through tightened lips. I couldn't expect Dorian to fold to my opinions. And I couldn't protect his heart from being broken any more than I could my own. "Fine, but could you at least tone it down on the PDAs?"

"For you?" Dorian's smile was full of mischief. "I'll try."

I pulled up from the bench and we walked back inside.

"All good," Dorian stated, resuming his spot beside Marika. "We'll clear it with the 'rents tonight."

Kendrick's questioning gaze narrowed at me. With a shrug of defeat, I retrieved my toppled chair and slumped into it. I may have lost this round, but I'd argue like hell when we got home.

"You found it!" Mom was exclaiming into the phone as Dorian and I passed through the frosted-glass door to her office.

She sat behind a flurry of what would have been mess on anyone else's desk, but not hers. The glass top was neatly stacked with catalogs and Post-it tabbed order forms. There were so many piles of swatches we could have been in a showroom. Her golden hair hung wavy around her shoulders, released from its usual French knot. There was a maroon blazer draped over the back of her white leather chair. Being daylight outside, thick blackout drapes—an inoffensive shade of cream—covered the tall, arched window. The only light in the room was the yellow glow from a bright desk lamp.

"Wonderful. I will come by personally to pick it up." Mom held up a hand, motioning for us to wait. "Yes, one hour. I will see you then."

"That sounded important," I mused as she hung up the phone.

Mom waved off my curiosity with a dismissive hand. "Oh, just another item for the auction," she said, before eyeing us with speculation. "So what can I do for you both?"

Dorian dropped into the seat across from Mom and clasped his hands in front of him. "We'd like to have our friends stay over after the auction. In return we'll offer free labor on Sunday to help tidy up."

"Ahem," I cleared my throat intentionally.

"Okay. Okay," Dorian said, eyes flashing over his shoulder to me. "*I'll* offer free labor."

Mom reached across the desk to pick up a gold-framed photo. "You've both grown up so quickly," she said, gazing distantly at our family portrait.

It was an old photograph, faded by time. Mom was lounging back on her armchair and cradling two infants. She was smiling, her face a proud motherly beam. Her blond locks were short, a halo around her head that mirrored mine. Dorian's almost-black mop was a stark contrast.

Mom's focus returned and she looked up pointedly. "Okay, but this is how it's going to work. You will all sleep in the rec room, door open. And don't think I won't be listening. No funny business."

My jaw dropped for the second time today. "You can't be serious. Sleeping in the same room as...*humans?*" I faltered over the word, knowing that if Ty stayed here there wouldn't be *just* humans.

Mom replaced the photo frame beside the lamp. Then she crossed her arms over her chest, wrinkling her white, silk blouse. I groaned. I knew that move all too well. Her mind was already made up. "Having friends over is part of having a normal life. I know you want that, Amelia. Besides, if anything goes astray, I'll be here to..." She froze, lips snapping shut.

"Be here to what?" I questioned. Then realized what she had been about to say. Utter surprise contorted my expression and painted my words black. "Clean up our mess?"

Mom averted her eyes and began flicking through swatches. "No. Of course not. I shouldn't have said that. I have complete faith in both of you." Her eyes rose to look from me to Dorian. "I wouldn't allow this otherwise. And I know I don't need to worry about you," she said, glancing behind us.

My head twisted. Kendrick was loitering in the doorway, casually leaning against the frame. With his sneaky vampire stealth, I hadn't even heard him.

"Of course, Ms. Lamont." He tipped his head formally, seeming so much older and wiser than seventeen. "I'll keep an eye on everything, too."

My eyes formed an incredulous glare. *Traitor!* But Kendrick ignored the piercing gaze.

"That would be much appreciated, Kendrick." Mom smiled and clapped her hands together. "Now, I have much to finalize for the auction before heading to The Council tonight."

"Hint taken." Dorian shot to his feet and bounded around the desk to hug Mom. "Thanks, Mom." He looked at me with an expression that said, *let's go before she changes her mind.* He grabbed my arm and pulled me from the office with Kendrick tailing behind.

WHEN WE ARRIVED at school the next morning, the parking lot was a haze of frosty air. Graying clouds littered everything in sight with a mist of fine rain. Dorian skipped across the parking lot, having caught sight of Marika emerging from her red Jeep. He took her into his arms, planting a wet kiss against her pouty lips.

I groaned. "*Great,* another day of this…"

"It doesn't have to be," Kendrick voiced beside me. In the rain his golden-brown hair was darkening to a rich caramel. "Let's skip."

Skipping school wasn't something I usually did. But the alternative was another lunch watching Dorian and Marika practically doing it. "What'd you have in mind?"

"I'm sick of dead blood." Around the parking lot, students were scurrying to get out of the rain. Kendrick watched them as though they were herding cattle. "But your mom was quite clear on the conditions pertaining to my visit. No human victims."

My stomach dropped, churning with predatory instinct and seething disgust all at the same time. "You feed on humans? You kill them?"

At the cabin *he* had been the one to introduce us to packaged 'dead blood,' as he had called it. Back then I'd never questioned it. As far as I knew, Kendrick only drank packaged blood and the fresh blood of wild animals.

Kendrick draped an arm around my stiffened shoulders. "No, not kill them, just...*feed*. We erase their memories with compulsion. They have no recollection."

A flash of memory scorched across my brain, of Kendrick raking tense fingers down Joel's chest in the alley.

"You were attacked by a rabid dog," Kendrick had said. *"We saved your life."*

Kendrick had altered Joel's memory in that moment by compelling him, which I sucked at. No amount of practice had helped at the cabin. Apparently, Caius's ancient remedy to prolong our vampire traits while being a turned vamp had affected more than my need for blood and vampire agility. So far there hadn't been a single success, excluding my unplanned compulsion on the bouncer outside *Pulse*.

I wanted to question him for probably the hundredth time on my lack of ability. But my mind was elsewhere. The memory of what I'd done to Joel and my uncontrollable lust for Ty's blood stole my thoughts. "But, how can you stop? How can you make yourself pull back *before* it's too late?"

"With practice," Kendrick said simply, as though that explained everything. When I frowned, his arm dropped from my shoulder. He pointed past the school's square brick buildings and cropped fields.

"Come on. I'll show you," he said, tilting his head to flash his fangs, "on something less appetizing than humans."

We walked from the parking lot with purpose. "Got your music?" Kendrick asked.

I pulled my iPod from my jeans and smiled. "Never leave home without it. What are you in the mood for?"

"Red's great for snowboarding, running too."

Now out of sight, I put my iPod on speaker to play *End of Silence.* We took off, sprinting. At blurred vampire speed we were faster than the moving cars around us. *Even faster than a red Ducati,* I thought, which didn't make me want one any less. I tried to spark conversation over the music as we ran. "How's your mom? What's my uncle been so busy with?" After that I moved on to questions about the Armaya and its workings. Kendrick didn't seem open to discussing any of it, tersely answering my questions with vague indifference.

Within thirty minutes, and after barely raising a sweat, the cars and houses of the residential community thinned. Winding roads that rose through a thicket of browning trees replaced them.

"Well, who do you hang out with, then?" I asked as the song *Wasting time* ironically came on.

The asphalt under our pounding feet gave way to loose gravel, then to a hardened dirt path.

"My friend Marcus," Kendrick replied to my surprise. "He's pretty cool, easy going, and all. You'd probably like him."

When the path disappeared we pulled to a stop. I shut off my iPod. All that surrounded us was a tall barricade of trees. Their auburn, gold, and brown leaves littered the damp forest floor.

The lack of heaving in my chest surprised me. "Where are we?"

"Mount Major," Kendrick answered. "The reserve's packed with game."

"So what…"

"Shh…" Kendrick silenced me, raising a finger to my lips. "Listen."

I tuned into the sounds of the forest. Leaves rustled in the faint breeze and small creatures scurried unseen within the dense scrub. There was a distant sound of a gushing stream, and something else. The soft beat of cloven hooves against marshy ground.

Kendrick laced his fingers through mine, pulling me forward to dart through the trees. My Vans skidded on decomposing leaves. Still, even with Kendrick running full pelt, I somehow managed to keep up. How could I be as fast as him?

My thoughts evaporated as Kendrick came to an abrupt halt at the edge of a grassy ridge. His arm flung out to restrain me. "Look," he whispered. "Down there."

Past the fallen, moss-covered tree that lined the descent was a grassed clearing. A herd of white-tailed deer were grazing unaware. The herd's large stag had its head raised with nostrils flared, testing the air for danger. The scent of their gamey blood found me then, swirling on the faint breeze. The light patter of their hearts reached my ears in the same instant. I glanced to Kendrick for instruction.

"Follow my lead," he said, smiling before leaping over the fallen tree.

I trailed after, keeping right on his heels. Kendrick's speeding steps were soundless, but leaves crunched under my Vans. The buck's head twisted. Its black-marble eyes widened with fear and a high-pitched warning escaped its throat. The herd tensed, springing into flight and darting in every direction. Kendrick lunged, flying through the air to land on the back of the stag. It squealed in panic as his weight and strength brought it to the ground. Its hooves kicked erratically as I closed in, connecting with my chest before my hands restrained them. My heart was pounding, adrenaline surging through my core. The stag's heart was fluttering wildly. The sound and feel under my palms stirred memories of Kendrick's hunting lessons back in the forests bordering Anchorage. Except back then we'd hunted to kill. Restraint had never been the objective.

Using all my strength to resist, I spoke around fully extended fangs. "Now what?"

Kendrick's lips parted, fangs protruding. "Drink."

Without any further invitation, I plunged my fangs into the stag's thigh. It squealed as its hot, gamey living blood spilled into my mouth. Kendrick watched, still restraining the animal while I fed. After a minute the buck became still. Its legs turned limp *almost* as though it were faking death.

A firm hand found my shoulder and squeezed. "Now stop."

It was Kendrick, instructing me to do what we had come here to do. The song *Animal I have become* was playing in my mind. I didn't want to be that blood-crazed creature. But each gamey drop made my body scream for more. Pulling away wasn't an option. The taste of the buck's blood wasn't as tempting as Ty's, or even a living human's. But it was still live blood. And right now, I wanted—no needed—every single drop. I growled and clutched the buck's thigh tighter, drinking deeply.

Kendrick's hand tightened, nails piercing my flesh. "If you can't stop yourself from killing a meaningless animal, how can you ever be certain you won't kill a human?"

Ty. A flickering image of his trusting eyes dyed with acceptance flashed across my mind. If I can't stop, I'll never be able to trust myself with him. Ty's strength would always be there to restrain me. That I knew. Though would he really want to stay with me if I kept trying to kill him by draining his lifeblood?

Although my body trembled in negation to my inner resolve, renewed determination flared through me. I released my clenched fingers that were embedded in the buck's flesh and tore my fangs from its thigh. The deer startled, surprised by his sudden release and scrambled to its feet. It took off, pelting through the trees, white tail bobbing as it disappeared from sight.

Kendrick smiled down at me as I crumpled to the ground. My chest rattled with ragged breath. "I did it. I freaking did it!"

CHAPTER 12

"I guess you should get going," I said to Ty the following morning. My hands were pressed against his bare, defined chest, feeling the new scars that marked him there. Scars he'd already refused to explain.

We stood within the lush greenery of the garden backing my house. Beside us was the huge marquee that had been delivered and erected this morning. People buzzed everywhere around us, from delivery men to laborers and wait staff. All were dressed in uniform and busy carting boxes to and from the marquee. Ty had arrived, as promised, early this Saturday morning to assist with the finishing touches for this evening's auction. Mom had been pleasantly surprised to see Ty again, and to my total relief—given that he'd taken something again that he explained was an elixir that masked his wolfy scent—she hadn't seemed aware of the subtle differences that marked him as a lycan. Maybe she won't freak when we tell her, I had thought. Still, crippling fear had gripped my heart. It was an intense coldness like a hand squeezing the organ tight. The memory of my vivid dream was too terrifying to forget.

Ty's hands found my hips and he pulled me against his hot flesh. "Trying to get rid of me?" His hazel eyes sparkled, brighter than the smile that stole his lips.

Able to feel the irregular beat of his heart, I removed my hands from his chest. I began nervously fiddling with my iPod, turning off Skillet. Knowing Ty was into their music, I'd played their songs on speaker all morning. "Of course not..." I said. But I was lying.

Apart from the beat of his heart, the memory of his scent was making my mouth water. Still, his proximity wasn't the only reason I needed him to leave. Kendrick was out in town picking up supplies since his stay here appeared to be ongoing. And I was thankful, because I still hadn't told him about Ty, or even the fact that I was seeing someone. Now my time was running out. The last thing I wanted was for him to find out this way. I needed Ty to leave.

I glanced down at his black shorts and boots. They were dotted with sawdust from our assembly of the stage. "I just figured you'd want to wash up before the auction begins."

Ty's head dipped, his hot lips finding mine. The gentle touch sent an electric wave throughout my entire body. "Okay," he said as he pulled away, and I almost regretted making him leave.

But just as he turned to go, Kendrick materialized, bounding through the terrace doors to the kitchen. He caught sight of us and looked Ty over with clear disdain. "Hey, who's the help?"

My stomach clenched, and my eyes darted back to Ty who was watching me questioningly. I tried to speak, but my throat was suddenly as dry as hot sand.

"Ty Malau." He extended a hand. "Amelia's boyfriend. You must be Kendrick."

Ty's candid words caused my eyes to widen. *Boyfriend?* Since admitting my feelings for Ty at the party and learning the truths he was hiding, I knew we had begun something strong and compelling. A relationship like none I had ever experienced before. Though I hadn't for a second dreamed of putting a label to what we were. Tempting fate was never a good idea. I looked back to Kendrick whose face had paled to the whiteness of parchment paper.

Ty cleared his throat beside me, hand finding my waist. "I'll leave you two, alone." He kissed me on the lips quickly but hotly. Then he disappeared, jogging back through the doors Kendrick had materialized through.

Swallowing the dryness that felt like sand clogging up my throat, I dared to look at Kendrick. His eyes were glassy, his arms locked stiff at his sides and hands clenched into fists. I went to speak, to try to explain, but he turned abruptly and stalked back into the house.

He was angry beyond words. That was painfully clear. Of course he would feel hurt. I'd kept this from him. It was something I had never done before. Kendrick had always been my confidant, my best friend. He was the one person I could turn to no matter what. But why was he this upset? A spine-chilling suspicion etched its way into my mind. Oh my God. He knows Ty's a werewolf.

I had to diffuse this situation before anything else could go wrong. And by anything, I meant him telling my mom. I darted into the house. The hired workers were busily checking through boxes of crystal and china. They barely took notice as I flew up the arcing stairs and into Kendrick's room.

Music and snowboarding posters now colored the walls. A new boarding mag lay on the bedside table. Kendrick stood staring out the arched window to the left of his bed. Beyond the glass, half the sun peaked through fluffy, white clouds. "Have I done something for you to doubt my friendship?" he questioned incredulously. "My loyalty to you?"

I sped across the room to grip his forearms. "No, of course not…" My sight turned hazy. "I wanted to tell you. I just…" My voice caught as I choked back a sob. I was scared.

Kendrick sighed, his broad shoulders dropping. "You feared my reaction. The way I'm acting now." He cupped my face with open palms, wiping away my tears with his thumbs. "Amelia." He blinked slowly. "I know you don't trust yourself. But know this. *I* trust you. So if you want to date a human, you should."

My head jerked back out of his hands. "What'd you just say?"

Kendrick shrugged, frowning. "That you should be with whoever you want to, human or not." He smiled—a not entirely thrilled but somewhat resolved smile. "I just want you to be happy, Amelia." He drew me into his arms, chin resting against the crown of my head. "I just didn't think you'd be into a muscle-bound pretty boy."

Of course he couldn't tell. Ty's scent was still blocked by the elixir. With my stomach turning with lie-induced knots, I pulled from his arms and faked a smile. "*Jealous?*"

Kendrick laughed at that, throwing his head back. "Are you saying I'm not cut like him?" He puffed out his chest while flexing his biceps.

At the sight of his put-on, strained expression, the weight of my worries instantly washed away. I couldn't help but laugh. "What would I do without you, Kendrick?"

He smiled, silver-flecked irises shining. "You'll never have to find out."

"YOU LOOK AMAZING," a deep voice spoke, approaching from behind.

Even with his unmistakable scent absent from the breeze, I knew who it was. Smiling, I turned from the early arriving guests I had just directed down the lit stone path to the marquee. Ty was approaching from the terrace doors. He no longer had on shorts and hunting boots. Instead, he wore a black, single-breasted suit and white shirt that covered his new and old scars. A pearl-white tie hung around his neck, and his hair was slicked back. My heart skipped.

Ty's sparkling eyes ran from my face slowly down my body to my strappy heels—expensive and brand name, according to Mom. His pupils were enlarged and focused, drinking in every inch of me.

Self-conscious, I glanced down at my black chiffon cocktail dress. My cheeks warmed at the sight of its low, V-cut neckline. Way too much of my non-existent bust was on display. I tugged at the hem that sat well above the knee. Why were Mom's *"presents"* always so damn short? "My mom got it especially for tonight."

Ty wrapped his arms around my waist and lifted me off the ground. Something hard pressed against me from the inside pocket of his suit. "Well, you look beautiful."

The warmth of his skin through his suit and my dresses fine fabric made me forget the object hidden in his jacket. Involuntary ripples of goosebumps cascaded down my body. Ty lowered me back to the ground, his hands finding the slight curve of my hips. A perfect fit. He dipped his head to join our lips with a soft, yet fiery kiss. My knees went weak and my heart fluttered. If not for his strong hands holding me up, I would have crumbled to the grass.

"Is there time for me to steal you away?" Ty breathed against my lips, unaware of the involuntary effects he had on me.

With a mesmerized nod, I pulled from his grasp and took his hand. "Of course…"

While drawing steadying breaths, I led the way down a

branched-off, stone path. Past the marquee was a secluding wall of beech hedges that had turned a wonderful shade of copper with the full onset of fall. A quaint alcove opened up before us, with a single stone bench in its center. The sun was a glowing sphere that loomed behind wind-blown clouds. As it dipped toward the horizon, birds chirped their final calls.

Ty pulled me down onto the bench and took my hands in his. "I'm sorry I took off earlier. I wanted to stay, but I figured you'd want to talk to Kendrick alone." I studied his face, expecting to find masked jealousy in his expression. But there was only genuine concern.

"Did you tell him about me?" Ty asked, breaking my stare. "Did he already know?"

I shook my head, causing my long hair to fall over my shoulders. "He didn't know." A peculiar feeling gripped me then. It was the weight of someone's eyes watching me, watching us. Unable to see anyone past the bordering hedges surrounding us, I looked up. My eyes settled on the left then the right of Kendrick's bedroom windows. Even with the diminishing light, I could see that the curtains were drawn. No one was standing there. A piercing pain seized my heart then. I had lied to my best friend and had no intention of revealing the truth to him. Looking back to Ty, I raised a reassuring hand to his face. "And I didn't tell him. I won't."

Ty smiled and took my hand, bringing it down to rest over the steady, yet irregular beat of his heart. "I wasn't worried. If you had told him, I would have understood. I trust you with my life, Amelia, with my blood."

The recollection of Ty's blood spilling into my mouth and coursing through my veins brought rapid warmth to my cheeks. I looked up, eyes fluttering. "Ty, I want to know who you are," I said, my heart skipping with nerves. "I want to know who it is I'm falling for."

Ty's hands dropped to my knees. He stared down at them, his brow knitted. "Are you sure?"

I collected his hands and curled my fingers through his. "I've never been more sure about anything in my life."

Ty nodded, eyes rising to meet mine. "Each born male inherits the *lycan* gene. Females can too, but the dominance seems more closely linked to males. It only bonds with females through some form of mutation. Anyway, once we reach adolescence, the transformations begin. That's when our eye color changes, too. At first we go through uncontrollable shifts over a number of days." His eyes strained and his expression turned stormy. "It's the most agony I've ever lived through. Though it does get easier, less painful," he added, face lifting a fraction. "After that, we remain human until the next full moon. With age we're able to transform on demand, though the full moon will always induce an uncontrollable shift." Ty studied my face. It looked like he was waiting for any sign of shock or repulsion. He found none.

"Will you ever show me?" I asked.

Ty frowned down at our entwined fingers, angular jaw clenching then unclenching. "I don't know. I'm still getting a hold on the transformations, and I would never want to put you in any danger."

Freeing one hand I reached for Ty's jaw, tilting his head up to meet my eyes. "Ty, I know you would never hurt me." I smiled. "I'm a vampire, remember? I'm stronger than you give me credit for." A question I had never thought of asking until this very second popped into my head like a live telegram. My lips spoke without permission. "How long do werewolves live?"

Ty leaned back against the rail of the stone bench, looking guarded. "We generally live an expected human lifespan."

My heart sank. I would outlive him at least five to one. Ty knew quite a bit about vampires, so he had to know I would live for centuries. What he didn't know was that Dorian and I were different. After what Mom and Uncle Caius had done to prolong the transformation, we could live for ten centuries.

"You'll outlive me ten-fold," Ty said, as though hearing my thoughts.

"How can you know that?" I asked, startled.

Ty's calloused hand found my cheek, fingertips grazing my neck. The sound of his pulse drummed through my ears. "Because you're a royal, aren't you? Only they can endure sunlight."

Needing to dull the sound of his pulse, I pulled back and shook my head. "No. We're not." I didn't really want to cover the bloody tale of our creation, but Ty waited in silence, brow furrowed in confusion. So I quickly covered the story Mom and Uncle Caius had revealed to us, skimming over the part about my father dying in our defense.

When I had finished talking, Ty blew out a long breath. His arm came around my shoulder to draw me against him. Around us, the sky had darkened to indigo, the breeze disappearing with the light. "Your father was a hero."

A pang of grief tugged at my heart as the breeze dwindled around us. The sound of the hedges' rustling died down. For the first time ever, I was experiencing emotion for the father I had never known, for his sacrifice and his love.

But that wasn't all that gripped me in this moment, wasn't what caused my body to turn as rigid as solid steel. I could hear Ty's steady pulse. It was louder than before. And even though I couldn't smell it, I could imagine the taste of his rich blood on my tongue. Involuntary tingles swarmed my gums, threatening to extend my fangs. I shot to my feet. "I have to greet guests. I'll see you inside."

Darting back up the stone path, I paused just outside the marquee's curtained entrance. I doubled over, breathing hard.

"You wanted to bite him. Didn't you?" Kendrick's strained voice caused me to jump.

I stared up at him in disbelief. "You were watching?"

Kendrick shrugged. "No. I mean, yes. I was just looking out for you." His eyes dropped with a sigh. I couldn't be angry with him. He looked so defeated, jaw set and shoulders slouched. "Just be careful."

I watched him as he walked past me and into the marquee. People buzzed with excitement inside, all dressed to the nines and sipping champagne from crystal flutes. White candles were suspended in glass holders from the pitched roof, which was woven with black silk and taffeta. With the sunlight now gone, the warm glimmer of flickering flames made the room feel like it was illuminated by thousands of fireflies under a black-as-night sky. Kendrick wove through the excitement without notice and dropped into a white cane chair at our table. Polished, gold-plated cutlery, white china, and lily centerpieces surrounded by more tealight candles filled the table. A plastic bidding paddle also sat beside each place setting. All our hard work had paid off. But I really didn't care. Kendrick was hurting, and I didn't understand why. Was he just worried that I couldn't control my instinctual urges with Ty? Or was it something more?

Feeling powerless, I slid through the transparent glittering curtains, picking a path through the groups of rich locals, who were unknowingly conversing with vampires. At the front wall, I paused before the stage Dorian, Ty, and I had built that morning.

Desperate for a distraction to erase Kendrick's defeated expression from my mind, I glanced around the stage. There were so many auction items. Most were perched on columned pedestals. There were antique vases and clocks, stone-carved statues, and a multitude of expensive-looking jewelry, new and old. An array of large and small paintings also lined the walls. Each was strung between the silk and taffeta that had been draped from the pitched roof to fall delicately down the walls.

With my head clearing, I began to turn away. It was time to bite the bullet and endure an evening of uncomfortable tension between Kendrick and Ty. But before I could take one step, a single piece caught my eye. It was a gold jewelry box. Amethyst stones encrusted the intricate rose design and sparkled with the flicker of candlelight. I couldn't look away. Or move. An invisible force had taken hold of me. It was like the gravitational pull of the sun that forced my body forward. The auction would be called to attention soon. I should be getting to my seat. Still, I couldn't break the invisible and gripping hold. My fingers grazed the cool metal, curling around the jewelry box to pick it up. As I did, something clinked. There was something inside. I lowered the piece back to the pedestal and tried to lift the lid. It wouldn't budge. Then I noticed a keyhole carved into the front. Was it locked?

"Amelia, sweetheart." My mom's voice echoed behind me, snapping me out of my hypnotized state with a body-jarring jolt. "Look who's here."

I turned to see Mom gliding toward me, bringing an invisible cloud of lavender with her. A pleased smile lit her face. With her blond hair pinned back, and ivory layered gown flowing in ethereal waves after her, she looked like a goddess, a creature too beautiful to be of this world.

A vampire stepped out from behind her. In his hand was a single black calla lily that held the deepest hint of purple. He was dressed in black Armani. The surrounding candlelight emphasized his shadowed face of dark-circled eyes and gaunt cheeks. He looked terribly tired and old.

"Uncle Caius!" I squealed, darting past Mom with outstretched arms. Caius enveloped with firm open arms. "I can't believe you're here. Mom didn't mention you were coming." I shot a mock glare at Mom who smiled with pure delight.

With a chuckle, Uncle Caius released me from his affectionate embrace and handed me the vibrant flower. They were my absolute favorites, the same flowers Caius used to bring for me during his weekend visits in Anchorage. "It is wonderful to see you too, my dear Amelia. I have missed you greatly. And please forgive your mother. It was my idea to surprise you."

"You're staying, aren't you?" I swayed back and forth on my heels like an excited child and almost lost my balance. Why had I agreed to wear these stupid things?

"I would love to," Caius said. He leaned his weight against a white cane chair at the hostess's table, being front and center of the stage. Small place cards scrawled with calligraphy sat before each china place setting. My uncle's name was printed in the spot next to Mom's. "Unfortunately, I can only stay for the auction. I have pressing council matters to tend to," he went on. To which I pouted, a move that usually worked in getting my way. Not this time though. Caius's staid expression refused to falter. "Now, now, I promise we will see each other again, very soon."

"Alright," I said, sounding like a stubborn child and reluctant to give in that easily.

The parting of the curtained entrance evaporated my ability to argue further. Over the heads of formally dressed attendees, two people had just entered, Ty and Vanessa. Mom and Caius had begun talking beside me. Without a scent to alert them, they seemed unaware of Ty's presence as he sat with Vanessa at our table across the marquee. Kendrick half glanced up, acknowledging their arrival with disinterest.

"Who are *they*?" Caius's sharp voice stabbed through me, causing my heart to jump.

I didn't need to follow his outstretched arm to know he was pointing at Ty and Vanessa. I tried to speak but couldn't. My tongue was suddenly dry and sticking to the roof of my mouth. Even without a scent, if anyone could tell what Ty was, he could.

"Oh," Mom spoke, now following Caius's line of sight. Puzzlement scrawled across her unlined face. "They're Amelia's friends. Why?"

Caius shrugged and buried his hands in the pockets of his black pants. "No reason."

"How about we introduce you?" Mom suggested.

Panic bolted through my bones and my eyes darted from her to Uncle Caius. I couldn't risk the possibility of Ty's eyes flashing gold. "But the auction," I said, voice quaking and words rushed. "It'll be starting any minute. You two should settle, get seated."

"Amelia is right, Lamayli." Caius's voice was level and devoid of concern. "We should get seated." My sudden relief was quickly overshadowed. Caius tilted his head toward me, his expression turning grim. "Amelia, I am glad you have made friends." His eyes shifted back to our table. For a second I thought I saw a flash of contempt mixed with fear stealing across his disheveled features. Then it was gone, and he just looked incredibly tired. "But don't forget what happened back in Anchorage. You almost killed a boy there."

Images of that night flashed through my mind like the turning pages of a picture book. In the background of my mind the song *Let you down* began to play. The monster was still inside of me. It always would be. And I would always struggle to control its predatory instinct, the primal thirst for blood. Uncle Caius was right to be concerned, right to fear me screwing up again.

"It would be wise to refrain from forming any *close* relationships," Caius went on. "At least until you can trust in your restraint."

Feeling empty inside, and discounting any progress I had convinced myself I had made, I nodded obediently. "Thank you for your concern, Uncle Caius. I will not let you down."

Caius smiled. It was a strained, lip-thinning smile.

Mom held out a hand to him. "Let's get settled," she suggested. "And Amelia," she said as they took their seats. "Please send Dorian over to say hello once he arrives."

"Of course," I said with a stiff nod. Mom and Caius began greeting guests already seated at their table. The conflict was already forgotten. But I couldn't forget my uncle's warning words. Am I kidding myself? Will I ever be able to fully trust myself with Ty, or anyone with a pulse?

I took my seat between Kendrick and Ty. Kendrick totally ignored my arrival by beginning a snowboarding game on his iPhone. *Fan-freaking-tastic!* Ty smiled from my other side and placed a warm hand over my knee. I dropped the black calla lily across my plate. But before I could sort through the four-sided conflict of Caius, Mom, Kendrick, and Ty, a new one surfaced. Dorian and Marika had just ducked through the curtains. Dorian raised his eyes with a nod, greeting us all as they took their seats across the table. I couldn't help the sneer that crossed my face on glimpsing Marika. Her black, wavy hair hung loosely around her dark-olive shoulders, bouncing in time with her generous bust. The red dress was something else, low at the top and short below. It fit so snugly it could have been a mistaken for a second skin.

"Or painted on," I muttered under my breath.

The auctioneer up front cleared his throat at the podium,

distracting me from my sneer. "Welcome all. This promises to be a wonderful evening."

I subconsciously tuned him out when Marika laughed flirtatiously. The sound drew not only my eye but also numerous disapproving looks from surrounding attendees. She began nipping at Dorian's neck, her eyes set across the table at Ty. Fire flared up my throat and my stomach knitted.

Ty, however, appeared unaware of her antics, inclining his head in my direction. "Who's that with your mom?" he asked, lifting his chin in their direction.

Stifling my animosity for Marika, I turned in my seat to view Caius. His back was facing us with his head raised to the still babbling auctioneer. "My uncle…" I leaned into Ty, my lips brushing his ear. "I don't think he could tell. But we need to steer clear, just in case."

Ty nodded with understanding. "If you want me to leave…"

"No," I cut in with a whisper, collecting and squeezing Ty's hand. "The elixir's working." This morning was the first time I'd seen him since the party a week ago. And I'd missed him. "It's fine. It'll be fine."

Vanessa leaned her head forward to glance past Ty to me. "Is there a problem?"

"Mind your own business," Ty grumbled, shooting her a dirty look. "Not everything has to do with you."

Vanessa, with an expression of contempt, pulled her head back in. She mumbled under her breath something that sounded like, "not yours to order around."

The auctioneer had finally begun describing the first item in detail. It was a portrait of a young girl. Black-and-white clad waiters discreetly moved about the room. They delivered gold-plated platters topped with delicately displayed canapés to each table. The marquee was a quiet hum of chatter and mouths chewing. Our table sat in relative silence, apart from Marika whispering something nauseating into Dorian's ear. To my right, Ty and Vanessa had their heads twisted, their eyes focused on the item up front. Kendrick was still playing his game and blatantly ignoring me. I sighed, craving chocolate. Even though it wouldn't enlighten me to Kendrick's mood, it would make me feel better. I sighed again, frustrated. We'd never really had an argument before that had resulted in silent treatment. This tension was new, and I wasn't going to let it go on. After the auction I would *force* him to talk.

"Oh, Dorian," I voiced across the table, just remembering what I still hadn't told him. "Uncle Caius is here, up front with Mom. You should go and say hello."

Dorian's eyes lit up like the naked flames of the burning candles between us, and he sprang to his feet. For a split second he hesitated, expression turning blank. "I'll be back soon." He squeezed Marika's shoulder and skirted around the tables to Caius.

After the auctioneer's long-winded description, bidders began raising their paddles. The price hiked rapidly until it slowed and settled at thirty-four thousand.

I realized then that I hadn't been bothered by Marika's tactless, over-the-top flirting since her whispers across the table. Usually it was all I could do to keep my eyes off her disgusting flaunted sexuality. Except right now she sat quiet and poised. What's she up to?

Marika twitched, seeming to feel my sneering eyes. She flashed me a wicked smile before turning her parted, fully red lips to Ty. "You're staying tonight," she whined in a sugary-sweet voice. "Aren't you, Ty?"

"Staying where?" Ty asked, twisting his head from the stage to meet Marika's batting brown eyes.

"Didn't Amelia invite you?" she questioned, flashing me a mock frown while clicking her tongue against her teeth.

I bit my lip. It had completely slipped my mind to invite Ty to tonight's sleepover. After Caius's surprise arrival, it was the last thing I wanted to deal with. A night enduring Marika and her ability to make me want to hurl would be bad enough. To top it off, I still had to decipher Kendrick's mood. And just to make it fun, there would be Vanessa, making her little comments and butting in. Even worse than all of that was the possibility of being left alone with Ty, of losing control and biting him, again. No, tonight would not be fun. But as Ty looked to me, eyebrows raised, I couldn't explain all of that to him. I couldn't say no. Pursing my lips, I nodded.

"Well then," Ty spoke quietly, rising to his feet. He dug into his pocket to retrieve his phone. "I have to make a quick call. Let my father know I won't be home tonight."

"Use my room," I said, catching his free hand, "left at the top of the stairs, last door."

"I know," he said with a wink as he stood.

I blushed and looked away as Kendrick cleared his throat, remembering the time he'd carried me up there after Troy's party.

More and more auction items passed after that. Each piece was nice and unique in its own way; hand-carved this and hundred-year-old that. Though none caught my eye until the sixth item was moved with its pedestal beside the podium and auctioneer. It was the delicate jewelry box that had drawn me in with a magnetized pull. Even from the other side of the marquee, the undeniable draw was evident.

"This gold-plated, antique jewelry box is from the seventeen hundreds. It's encrusted with polished, amethyst…" the auctioneer was rattling on.

But I wasn't listening. My free hand was clutched around the twisted cane of my chair. It was all I could do to keep my body from vacating my seat, from moving closer to the item that beckoned me to its raw beauty.

"…needs re-hinging," I managed to hear the auctioneer say as he replaced the floral-footed item on its pedestal.

Instantly bids began to fly, paddles shooting up in an erratic wave. Most of the bidders, with their pale complexions and silvery-blue eyes, were attending vampires. They rapidly spiked the price to fifty thousand dollars.

"One hundred thousand!" a man's distinct voice bellowed up front.

I raked over the jaw-dropped crowd to find my uncle with his paddle raised. "What would he want with a jewelry box?" I mumbled to myself.

"One fifty," shouted a female vampire across the room. She appeared to be in her thirties, with skin so pale it was almost translucent beneath a veil of crimson-red hair.

I barely had time to wonder who this elegant vampire was, or why she seemed so intent on winning, when another bid rang through the air.

"Two hundred," Caius returned, shooting the bidding vampire a warning scowl.

The bids continued to fly, batting back and forth between Caius and the female vampire. Finally the price slowed at six hundred thousand.

The female vampire raised her nose indignantly and lifted her paddle again. "Six hundred and twenty."

The whole room sat in hushed suspense. Everyone was perched on the edge of their seats in wait for another bid. Caius leaned back in his seat. His arms were crossed over his chest and his face set with frown lines.

"Well," the auctioneer's voice emerged shaky, rattled. He was clutching to the wooden podium like it was greatly assisting his ability to stand upright. "I have six hundred and twenty thousand dollars. Will anyone give me six forty?" He glanced from Caius to the crowd, scanning for the next bid. "I have six hundred and twenty, going once...twice..."

"Seven hundred!" Caius bellowed.

A succession of gasps erupted. The boom of Caius's voice and jump in the bid had caught not only me but also everyone within the marquee by total surprise. With eyes of wide Os, the auctioneer belted the hammer down then directed it at Caius. "SOLD...for seven hundred thousand dollars!"

Much like everyone else in the room, I sat in quiet shock, my face mirroring everyone's astonished expressions. I couldn't believe it. What could Caius possibly want with a jewelry box? It just didn't make any sense. I swiveled to ask Kendrick's opinion and realized that Ty's seat was still empty. He still hadn't returned from his call.

While the auctioneer continued with the next item, I silently rose to my feet. Only Kendrick and Vanessa still occupied our table. My eyes shot back to Uncle Caius. Dorian was still crouched beside him, talking in congratulatory animation. Marika and Ty were nowhere to be seen. "Where's Marika?" I whispered.

Vanessa shrugged. "Probably getting another drink."

But I wasn't convinced. My gut, now clenching like a vice, told me she was up to something, something bad. "I'm gonna go see what's keeping Ty," I said to no one in particular.

Kendrick's hand caught my wrist as I began to move away. "Want help finding him?"

"No," I replied bluntly while thinking, *now you're talking to me?* I yanked my wrist free. "I'll be back in a minute."

CHAPTER 13

The kitchen was a mess of discarded platters and champagne flutes. Waiters rushed around preparing more food and drinks for the distinguished guests. Ty, and more disturbingly Marika, were nowhere to be seen. Ty must still be up in my room, I tried to reassure myself. Still clearing tonight with his father... But no amount of reassurance could shut down the clenching of my gut. The nagging sensation of something not being right just wouldn't budge.

I vaulted past the occupied wait staff, through to the marble-clad foyer and up the stairs. Once on the landing, I continued in the direction of my room and its closed door. A quiet noise, a sort of shuffling, caught my attention. I froze briefly before walking on. As I closed in on my bedroom door, muffled voices reached my ears. There were people inside my room. The clenching of my gut squeezed tighter as I reached out, pushing down the door handle. A hushed giggle erupted, ringing through my ears. The sound was so eerily familiar that it shot a pang of unexplainable fear through my body. My hand shot back lightning fast, and I peered through the crack of the door. The beat of my heart drummed wildly beneath my ribs, sending throbbing jolts down my frozen body.

Inside, the chandelier was extinguished and the purple drapes were pulled shut. All the darkness revealed were the dark outlines of shadows. After a few seconds my vision focused. Two figures were moving together within the darkness. Ty must have found my room occupied—*yuck*—and gone elsewhere to make the call to his father. So who the hell were these people? Wait staff or auction attendees?

Squinting into the darkness, I could see the silhouette of a couple. They were in an intimate position on my bed, the guy's hair blending in against the darkness of my room. It stood out in complete contrast against the woman's long blond tresses. Their firm, caressing hands moved erratically. Over and over their lips connected with ragged breath. The guy's shirt had been discarded, revealing a tight, muscular physique. A light-colored tie hung loosely around his neck. His pants had also been abandoned, leaving scarcely a pair of boxer briefs concealing his manhood. The girl beneath him was only wearing lace panties and a bra. The black stood out against her oddly pale complexion. She gripped his tie and pulled him closer. Their breathing emerged louder and faster as the intensity increased. The guy trailed frenzied kisses from her pale lips down to her neck.

Sudden rage welled within me. The shock of finding two strangers in my bed subsided. I drove the door wide open, flicking on the chandelier. "What the hell are you two doing in here?"

In the lit room I could see *everything*. Crumpled clothes and discarded shoes littered the mink-white carpet. A strangely familiar blond woman was lying sheltered by the lilac sheets on my bed. Embracing her was…

All the blood drained from my face. My breath caught in my

throat. It felt like someone's hands were clutched around my neck, squeezing with intent, strangling to kill. Tears muddied up my sight, turning the room and *him* to a distorted smudge.

Ty had torn his lips from the girl in his arms. Now he was blinking at me with a look of bewilderment as if trying to clear the sudden light from his eyes. His face dropped suddenly. An expression of shock-horror contorted his features. "Amelia, how can you be—" His voice caught and he physically gagged. His face drained of all color.

Disgusted, I tore my stinging eyes from his almost naked body. I glared at the girl who had buried her face beneath my sheets. Seething rage gripped me, flushing my cheeks with torrid blood. *"How dare you!"* I screamed. Sharp pain struck my chest. It felt like a knife was literally piercing my pounding heart. I choked back the tears. "You fucking asshole!"

Ty jumped from the bed as if to cross the room to me. My hands shot out in negation with blurred movement, bringing him to an abrupt halt. I hissed through gritted teeth. "Don't you dare come anywhere near me." Nausea rolled my stomach. I was going to be sick. "Not ever again!"

Icy tears streamed down my face and I spun on my heels, launching my body at the stairs. It felt like I couldn't breathe, like noxious fumes suddenly tainted the air. I needed to get the hell outta here. But as I began my hasty decent, my body collided with a force that hit me like a brick wall. My eyes blinked rapidly, clearing my vision as a strong hand caught my arm.

"Amelia, what's wrong?" It was Dorian, his voice panicked and eyes darting past me. "What happened?"

Kendrick loomed right behind him, stance as still as a lion preparing to attack a gazelle. "What'd he do?"

Fighting back the tears, I threw a backward glance at my room. I half expected to find Ty coming after me. But no one was there. "Why don't you ask Ty and the girl he was about to screw in my bed!"

I broke Dorian's firm hold on my arm and vaulted down the stairs. Ty's surprised voice stuttered, *"w-wait, let me explain."* Then a sharp crack sounded as I made my escape through the front door. An uninvited pang of fear for Ty's safety tugged at my aching heart. Still I didn't turn back. I couldn't. All I could do was run. So that's exactly what I did.

WHEN I FINALLY RETURNED HOME WELL AFTER midnight, the house was dark and dead quiet. Only a dim glow emanated from my bedroom window.

Kendrick was sitting on the front steps in a band of porch light. "Damn you're fast," he said. "I couldn't catch up to you."

Letting the anger I still felt for Ty cloud my mood, I threw my arms over my chest. "Since when have you been a sexist pig?"

Unaffected by my insulting outburst, Kendrick laughed. "You know I didn't mean it like that. I just…" He paused, brow creasing. "You're a turned vamp, different yes, but still turned. Royals—and I say this without any malice—are faster and stronger. We hold greater abilities in comparison to turned vampires. Or at least we're supposed to."

Allowing the subject to distract me, I pursed my lips. Except my brain felt like it was packed with disgusting, green sludge, making comprehensive thought impossible. My legs began to tremble from the thrashing run I'd forced them to take through Mount Major. "What do you think it means?" I asked finally.

"I don't know. It could be nothing." Kendrick shrugged. "Or it could be a belated side effect from what Caius did to prolong the transformation."

"I guess so," I breathed, mounting the front steps and taking his outstretched hand to pull him up.

"What he did was really shitty," Kendrick said, his tone filled with unrestrained revulsion.

I tensed and my stomach turned, desperate to avoid any discussion on Ty and what I had seen.

Kendrick squeezed my hand. "Sorry, I won't mention him again. But I want you to know." He turned to meet my hazy, and I'm sure puffy, red eyes. "I will always be here for you." He wrapped his arms around me and pressed his lips to my forehead. "You mean everything to me."

I pushed the front door open and was about to trudge up the stairs when Kendrick swooped me up into his arms.

"What are you doing?" I squeaked, trying to keep my voice from waking Mom and Dorian.

"You look wrecked," he said, mounting the arching stairs.

"I'm fine, really," I replied. "So you can put me down now."

Kendrick looked at me, doubtful, still climbing the stairs. "We're almost there." He jumped the last few steps, carrying me down the dark hallway to my bedroom. A single crack of light shone from underneath the closed door.

After Kendrick lowered me to the ground, I felt awkward, unsure of what to say. "Um, thanks I guess. I'll see you tomorrow."

"Are you sure you want to be alone?"

Alone was the last thing I wanted. In the past, Kendrick had spent many nights sleeping over in my bed after all-night movie marathons. Now the thought of having him in my bed just increased that awkward feeling. "I-I'll be fine."

"Okay. But if you change your mind…" He clutched my hand,

drawing it up and pressing it to his heart. "…promise you'll come to me."

I nodded, already regretting making him leave as he turned away to disappear into the blackness of the hall. A sigh escaped my lips and I slumped back against my bedroom door. Entering my room and seeing the crumpled sheets of my bed, the bed *it* had happened in, would be torture. Sleeping in that same bed would be even worse. But I had to. I couldn't hide from this. Avoidance, no matter how hard I wished, wouldn't extinguish the pain that tugged at my heart. With closed eyes I began to turn, my fingers curling around the brass door handle. As I went to push down, a firm hand connected with my shoulder. The shock of unexpected touch caused my body to jerk. I spun on the spot. Paranoia had me expecting to find Ty, believing he'd forced his way inside just to inflict more emotional torture. But it wasn't him.

"Dorian!" I couldn't hide the relief in my voice. "You scared me half to death."

"Sorry," Dorian said with a sheepish look. He held out his hand, offering a full bottle of blood. "I heard you come in, and I was pretty sure you'd need this."

I snatched the bottle and turned the cap before chugging down the contents. After my run, my body felt like it had been hit by a Mac truck. Though with the instant boost the blood provided, some of the aching in my limbs began to subside. "Thanks," I said, swiping the back of my hand across my mouth.

"So, are you going in?" Dorian asked, visibly chewing the inside of his cheek. "Or do you plan to stand out here all night?"

Determined not to let this break me, I drew my body to full height, feigning stability. "No time like the present."

I sucked in a deep breath and pushed the door open, eyes scanning around the room. Everything appeared to be in its rightful place, but there was one distinct difference. Earlier the bed's covers had been a mess of purple-crumpled swirls. Now they were turned down with crisp and untainted linens of indigo and ultramarine.

With my heart squeezing, I swiveled back to Dorian. "*You* did this?"

"I didn't want you to be reminded of what happened." He shrugged and forced a smile. "I know this is really hard for you. And, Amelia…I know you don't want to talk about it, and I hate to bring it up. But you need to know." I braced against the doorframe and nodded. Dorian took in a sharp breath and exhaled with his next words. "Earlier when I stormed your room, I only found Ty. There wasn't anyone else in here."

My gaze slid sideways to my bed. The gut-wrenching events replayed in my mind. I could see her blond hair, hear the eerily familiar giggle, and remember the unusual pallor of her complexion. I had no idea who the girl was. But I did know *what* she was. My wide eyes skittered across the room, settling on my arched window. The dark purple drapes were half drawn and the glass panel sat wide open. That's why Dorian didn't find her in here. I turned back to Dorian, my eyes pleading. "Dorian, please, I need to be alone."

Dorian, his jaw set and clearly not wanting to leave, simply nodded. "I'll come see you in the morning."

I watched him walk away, left with my thoughts, memories, and a realization that shook me to my core. One I had already known but refused to acknowledge before this very moment. *Ty betrayed me for another vampire.*

After standing in shell-shocked stillness for so long that I lost track of time, I shook myself back to consciousness. I closed the window and began to strip. First I kicked off my heel-snapped shoes. Mom was not going to be pleased. Then I peeled back the torn fabric of my chiffon dress, which clung to my body with sweat and melted snow. Then I stood before the full-length mirror backing my bathroom door. Patchy dirt marked my ivory skin. Snaking up my arms, legs, and even up my neck to cross my face were webbed, blackish-blue veins. It was a physical sign that my body was still greatly deprived of blood. Leaf litter tangled my hair like a nest. My face was a pasty shade of gray, with my irises surrounded by harsh red veins. Thinking of the many supernatural movies I'd watched over the years, I thought, this is what real monsters look like.

I sighed and my body tensed all over. The pain inside my chest still plagued me, like a tightening line of barbed wire with inch-long spikes. I sighed again and forced my body into the bathroom. The fluorescents were much too bright. Glare reflected off the white marble tiles and floor, shooting pain into my eyes. I blinked away the discomfort. Then I turned on the hot tap inside the open-walled shower and stepped onto the cobblestone tiles. If only the scalding water could burn away the image of Ty almost naked and rearing to enter that *slut*. Soap and hard scrubbing easily removed the debris from my skin, but nothing could rid me of the filthy aura that was draped over my mind and body. It weighed me down like a soggy, moldy towel. What made things even worse was that the burning water reminded me of Ty, of his heated touch, his smoldering lips pressed to mine, and the taste of his fiery sweet blood.

In the end I gave up, and after a quick dry, I slipped into satin shorts and a cotton tank top. If only I could fall asleep quickly. I hesitated in pulling back the vibrant covers and blinked, seeing the disgusting scene playing again. My stomach lurched with a twist. Then something caught my eye. In front of the glowing steel lamp on my side table was the jewelry box Uncle Caius had won at the auction. As I stared at the amethyst-encrusted box, my brow creased. Something about it was different. It was still as beautiful as I remembered. Except something was definitely missing. Then I knew. The magnetized draw I had experienced before the auction was gone. And the lid which had been jammed shut now sat open with a flat card propped up inside. I gingerly retrieved the card, glimpsing the distinguishable scrawl of my uncle's handwriting.

MY DEAREST AMELIA,

I realize this gift does not make up for my recent absence, but after noting your admiration of this piece, I knew you would appreciate the sentiment. I do hope you will accept my gift as an apology, and a promise that soon we will have much time to share.

Love Always,
Uncle Caius.

P.S. The hinges were rather stiff, they will require oiling.

Feeling foolish over my earlier skepticism at Caius's motives, I pressed the card to my heart. As I did, a gleam of light across metal flashed from inside the jewelry box. Within its mirrored lid and padded silk walls, was a small gold key. I plucked it out and twirled it between my fingers, eyeing the looped effect of its handle.

A remembered clang rose to the forefront of my mind. It was the moment before the auction when I had picked up the item and distinctly heard the movement of something within.

So that's what was hidden inside. For some reason I felt disappointed. I replaced the card and closed the lid in a stiff motion that creaked and groaned, locking the jewelry box. *It was just the key.*

CHAPTER 14

*A*fter gorging on half a block of chocolate from my bedside drawer, I forced my body under the soft, ultramarine quilt. An animated replay of every gut-wrenching detail plagued my mind. I saw their hands unrestrained and exploring, their lips connecting with labored breath. Worst was the way their bodies had screamed for one another. Each detail tightened the barbed wire around my heart and knotted my stomach.

Squeezing my eyes shut—so tight I that saw stars—I curled my body in on itself. I wished that alone could slow my mind and clear the sickening images. In actuality, it did the opposite. Their sexual display brightened like a raunchy movie scene. Every muscle in my body tensed harder, aching to strip my mind clear. But I knew my efforts were futile. I couldn't sleep here.

Pulling myself up from my bed, I rushed through my bedroom door and down the dark hallway. Gentle light filtered through the double-story windows of the foyer and past the marble balustrade. Sinister shadows slinked around me.

Ignoring the sliver of paranoia that was quickly creeping in, I stopped in front of the door to Kendrick's room. My head dropped against the white-glossed wood. Inside, I felt disgusted with myself. How could I be so broken over someone I hardly even knew? But most of all, I hated that I needed Kendrick's undying friendship, almost more than I needed air to breathe. My shoulders slumped with a sigh and I began to turn away.

"Amelia?" A crackled voice emerged through the closed door, causing my head to jerk up. The soft rustle of bedding reached my ears and a brighter glow of light shone from beneath the door. Quiet footsteps followed. The door opened and Kendrick rubbed his eyes. The glow of lamplight surrounded him like a full-bodied halo. "Hey, are you okay?"

Without meaning to, my eyes glided from the lean and toned muscles of his chest. Further down, cut lines dipped from his hips. I gulped. All he wore was a pair of black cotton boxer shorts. Warmth radiated across my cheeks. I had never seen him so, well...naked, before.

"I'm sorry," I croaked, shaking off the image of his bare chest, eyes darting away. "I didn't mean to wake you. It's just...I can't sleep there." I threw a glance back down the hall to my room. Tears were building in the corners of my eyes, and I hated it. I hated being so weak and so freaking vulnerable.

Kendrick's hands found my shoulders and pulled me into his arms, hugging me tightly. "Come on. You can sleep in my bed."

Kendrick released me and I nodded with a sniffle. He took my hand and led the way. Past the white leather couch draped with crumpled clothes, stood his oversized king bed. He shoved a snow-boarding magazine out of the way and pulled back the covers. I clambered onto the mattress. Still holding tight to Kendrick's hand I pulled him in behind me.

Kendrick resisted, freeing his hand from mine. "It's okay," he said, strained eyes shifting to the two-seater couch. "I'll sleep there."

Puzzled by his resistance, I frowned. Kendrick's bed here was huge. While the couch would struggle to offer a comfortable sleep for me, let alone his over-inflated six-foot-two. Yet his comfort was not the only thing that encouraged my next words or contorted my expression. "I'm afraid to be alone with my thoughts," I confessed. "*Please* stay with me."

Kendrick bit his lower lip. His face relaxed as he turned off his reading and bedside lights. "Amelia, I would do anything for you." He lowered himself down into the bed, reclining sideways against the dark, satin pillows to face me. "Now get some sleep," he ordered, leaning close to press his lips to my forehead.

"Thank you," I breathed. With a forced smile, I clasped his hand and pulled it over my shoulder, turning to face the other way. Kendrick's arm tightened around me, drawing me against his bare chest. His heart fluttered against my back. It felt strange to be this close to his almost naked body. It was new, I realized, this intimacy. We had always been close and unrestrained around each other. Yet somehow this was distinctly different. It was like our relationship had somehow graduated to a new level, a deeper level. And for everything in the world, I wouldn't have changed this moment or our friendship. Kendrick was a true friend, my best friend, and I loved him.

In the security of Kendrick's comforting arms, sleep finally claimed my exhausted body. Though not even unconscious slumber could steal my mind and memory.

Frozen in wide-eyed horror, I stood in my room at the foot of my four-poster bed. Ty was before me, touching and caressing the pale girl in his arms. His head of glossy black hair—with lips connected to hers—blocked her face from view.

It's a dream, I told myself. My arms coiled around my body, nails digging into my sides hard enough to cut flesh. *Please wake up. Please wake up.* It didn't work. Before me, my worst nightmare had come to life, and I couldn't escape.

Desperate not to see them, I tried to look away. My body ignored my internal command, my head refusing to move. My eyelids were fixed open as if held by grotesque clamps. I tried to scream, to cry out for them to stop. Instantly my tongue felt swollen, my throat clogged up.

As ice-cold tears streamed down my immobile face, Ty's lips moved, trailing down her neck and exposing her face. Vomit spiked my throat, burning with acidity. My eyes, now able to move again, fixed on hers. They were the same silvery-blue eyes of a vampire, of my own. The face I had expected to be alien was not. She had identical thin, pale lips, ivory skin, high cheekbones, and long, golden-blond hair.

Totally mystified, I stared at the now smiling and fanged reanimation of my own reflection. *The girl was...me.*

AFTER A NIGHT of repetitive nightmares that locked me inside my own living hell, I awoke with a start. Kendrick's comforting arms had just been ripped from around my body.

"How dare you take advantage of her," Dorian's irate voice sliced through the air.

I lurched upright, heart hammering. Broad daylight poured from the open doorway and into Kendrick's room. It coated every darkened shade of varying indigo, white, and stained hardwood in shimmering, rich tones. The unexpected brightness stabbed at my eyes, and I blinked rapidly. Darkened shapes coalesced, taking form right before me. Dorian, his face ablaze with indignation, was clutching Kendrick's bicep. His grip was so tight that fat drops of blood escaped from cuts his fingernails had created. His free hand was balled into such a tight fist that his knuckles whitened. He looked seconds from belting Kendrick square in the face.

"It's not what you think," Kendrick said. His hands rose, palms facing forward in a clearly defensive gesture. "Nothing happened!"

Dorian's eyes burned liquid silver as he raked Kendrick over with a look of disgusted disbelief. My best friend was still scarcely dressed in his boxers. Dorian's fist rose, muscles twitching to life.

"It's the truth!" I scrambled from the bed, tangled sheets catching around my limbs and tripping me. It took only a split second for me to right the fall. In the past, such clumsiness would have sent me face first into the corner of the square-edged side table. But as my feet hit the mink-soft carpet, I instantly regretted the hasty movement. Lack of blood made my head light and I staggered with dizziness.

Kendrick tore his arm out of Dorian's grasp, catching me before I crumpled to the floor.

"Get your hands off her," Dorian snarled, voice piercing like road spikes through soft tire-tread. He jerked me back and out of Kendrick's supporting hand.

"Cut it out, Dorian!" I tried to pry my arm from Dorian's grasp. His grip tightened, hand squeezing like it was an extension of his hardened face. "Look, I couldn't stay in my room. Not after what happened. Kendrick was being a friend. That's all!"

Dorian released me so suddenly that I staggered back. He ran a tense hand over his face, which seemed to instantly disarm him. "Sorry man," he said, glancing up at Kendrick. "I just thought...and after, well, yesterday...I guess I just lost it."

The air around us diffused like the ash of a bomb blast settling. It seemed only I was left wide-eyed and somewhat confused by Dorian's aggressive and out of character display.

"She's your sister." Kendrick moved forward to clasp Dorian's hand. They bumped shoulders in a guy-like display of granted understanding. "I get it."

The LMFAO song *Party Rock Anthem* sounded unexpectedly and I flinched. Dorian fished into the pocket of his jeans and retrieved his phone, glancing at the screen. "It's Marika." He frowned then turned his back to answer the call.

"Dorian, I need to see you," Marika's rushed voice was just audible to my ears.

"What's wrong?" Dorian whispered, striding to the open door as if the few feet would afford him privacy. "Where are you?"

"Just meet me at the animal shelter. My shift starts in thirty minutes." And with that, the line went dead.

Dorian shrugged and turned back to us, sliding the phone back into his pocket. His face was set with confusion, his eyes distant. "I gotta go," he said, the levelness of his voice a clear strain as he looked to me. "Will you be alright?"

"Of course," I lied. Even though I felt raw to the bone, I straightened my back to fake stability. "Go."

Once Dorian had slipped out of the room, I turned to Kendrick. "You too," I said, slinging my arms over my chest and dropping back onto his bed.

Kendrick's brows rose with surprise. "You're kicking me out of my own room?"

Guilt prickled my skin. After everything Kendrick had done for me, he didn't deserve to be sent off. But there was still so much mess clouding my mind. The drain from broken, nightmare-plagued sleep was increasing by the minute. Still, the thought of returning to my own room struck an almost prickly, tight feeling through my heart. It was too soon. I couldn't do it. "I just need to be alone for a while. Kendrick, please."

With a deep sigh, Kendrick pulled on his T-shirt and jeans that had been draped over the back of the couch. He came to stand beside me and bent, pulling his satin sheets over my legs. Then gingerly—with a touch I almost didn't feel—he kissed the crown of my hair. "Stay here as long as you want." He picked up his boarding mag and strode to the door. "I'll check in on you later."

MUCH OF THE day passed in slow motion. Each hour, minute, and second somehow seemed longer than the last. Sleep was patchy, offering some reprieve from the physical pain that gripped my heart. Although the physical pain subsided with sleep, the emotional and mental strain did not. With every moment of sleep came the re-enactment of my nightmare. It seemed so eerily real, mimicking in closer proximity the disgusting detail of what Ty had done.

The waking hours weren't any easier. The memory of seeing my likeness wrapped in Ty's muscle-bound embrace haunted my thoughts, forcing comparison between nightmare and reality. The pale skin I had glimpsed from the door and the long blond hair was so like my own. Was my subconscious simply playing a cruel joke on me? Still, no matter how hard I tried I couldn't shake the image of her, of my own face staring back at me and the parted lips revealing sharpened fangs which were my own. It was just a dream, I kept telling myself. Though no matter how many times I said it, I couldn't bring myself to actually believe the words.

The sound of my iPhone blaring Skillet's song *Never Surrender* drew me upright. It was a personalized text alert. I sighed and threw my legs over the edge of the bed. Beyond the arched windows bordering Kendrick's bed, the sun had just dipped past the mountainous horizon. The waning light cast dark shadows about the room. Dorian had ducked back in after Kendrick's departure with my iPhone. He was off to meet Marika but still wanted to be able to check up on me. Annoyingly, he had drawn open the drapes, insisting the sunlight would help lift my mood. Being too thought-consumed at the time, I hadn't bothered to close them.

I went to grasp my phone and paused. There was a full block of mint-centered chocolate with a Post-it attached. *Kendrick told me you and Ty broke up. I'm so sorry, sweetheart. Come see me when you're awake. Love Mom.*

Certain Kendrick wouldn't have told Mom the reason Ty and I broke up, I ripped into the chocolate. *Yay mint!* It was my all-time favorite flavor. A split second later two blocks were in my mouth. I sighed and took hold of my phone from the bedside table. The text was probably another one from Dorian. A full list of texts took up the entire screen. I slept through that? Five of the six visible texts were from either Dorian or Kendrick. Each held varying questions on how I was feeling.

The sixth text almost made me choke. It was from Ty. His arrogance sickened me while bubbling rage forced my vision into a blur. Blinking and unable to stop myself, I opened the text. The words glared up at me, black on white. *'Amelia, I need 2T2U.'* I need to talk to you.

I was tempted to crush the phone, but as I began to squeeze it blared again. My damning curiosity got the better of me. I braced myself, nails of my free hand slicing through satin to puncture the mattress's padded top. *'Let me explain. It's not what U think.'*

My curiosity vanished. I squeezed the mattress harder, rage

turning every muscle along my arms rigid. I almost felt the urge to laugh, just to stop the waterworks I felt looming behind my eyes. It's not what I think?

When the phone went off again, my face was boiling. My entire body was trembling, ready to explode. Incredulity burned from my eyes. Against my better judgment, I dared to read the last text. *'Plz tlk 2 me. I'm sorry.'*

"Sorry? You're SORRY!"

I struck out with shaking hands to snatch the ceramic lamp from the bedside. Then with a roar of pain that tightened my chest, I hurled the lamp at the door. The power cord flung out, whipping past my cheek. A sting of cut flesh bloomed across my face and the door swung open just as the lamp connected. A shower of ceramic erupted around my best friend, just barely missing his head.

Recovering from the initial shock, Kendrick rushed to my side, dropping to his knees. His hands gripped my thighs with needled fingers. "What happened?" He scanned the room, his body taut and ready to defend any threat. "Amelia, talk to me. Are you okay?"

I cupped his face with my hands and forced his still-darting eyes to meet mine. "He's not here," I said, glancing sidelong at my phone.

Kendrick slumped, dropping his head into my lap while whistling through his lips. "You scared the crap outta me. I didn't know what to think."

"You worry too much," I said softly. My fingers raked gently through his thick, golden hair. "But I think I'm ready."

Kendrick raised his head, eyes that looked almost hopeful searching mine. "For what?"

"To go back to my room…" I paused, biting my lip. "Will you stay with me tonight?"

Kendrick smiled, though tightness was still visible across his face. "Wherever you want me, I'll be there." He cupped my face with one hand. His thumb ran over the cut that I could already feel healing, smearing away the spilled blood. "Always."

CHAPTER 15

With Kendrick's guarding arm around me, we hesitated just outside the open classroom door, each with an armful of textbooks. Dorian—with wet hair from before-school swim practice—tipped an apparently directive nod at my best friend.

It was Monday morning and first up was Psychology. The class I shared with both Kendrick and Ty. *Fan-freaking-tastic!*

Dorian's brows rose and his set teeth parted. "I'll see you *both* at lunch."

With a nod from Kendrick, Dorian turned away and we entered the classroom. My best friend's free arm tightened around me. A girl at the front of the class glanced up from her perch atop a desk. She slapped the girl next to her. The movement sparked a chain reaction throughout the entire room. Now every set of eyes was flickering from us to Ty. I groaned internally as their flapping lips moved with audible whispers.

"Ignore them," Kendrick whispered into my ear.

But ignoring their incessant whispering, I found, was the least of my struggles. Already my eyes had crossed the room to settle on Ty. He occupied the desk we had shared beside a long window with a view down to the courtyard, his training bag at his feet. I could smell the chlorine in his damp, messy hair from this morning's training session. And I could feel the pain in his sad lingering eyes. Against my will my heart contracted. The barbed wire tightened its hold around the organ with a piercing sting. I winced at the pain. How can he still have this effect on me?

Pain or not, I wasn't about to give Ty the satisfaction of knowing he was getting under my skin. So I decided to fake it and walked on, forging a careless smile. My left arm hugged the books to my chest, while my right clung tighter to Kendrick's waist. With relative success, I sidled into the seat next to my best friend, right up at the back of the class. *Where Ty used to sit.* Ty's guilt-stricken eyes were still locked on me, his jaw set with lips pinned shut. I hoped he felt like dying.

Ty turned away, shoulders hunched with a show of defeat, almost as though he'd heard my thoughts. My heart sank. The last thing I wanted was for him to look away, to give up, to get over me and not feel the pain that had been so clearly etched across his face. Instead, I wanted him to yearn for me. To suffer knowing I would never be his again. To think I had moved on with someone else.

"Hey," Kendrick said, nudging me. "I thought I broke his nose. He doesn't even look injured."

I choked on the air. "You did what?"

Instantly my surprise paled to guilt. I was a sucky best friend. Kendrick still had no idea that Ty was a lycanthrope. Even if he'd broken Ty's nose, it would have healed by now. Yet I still couldn't bring myself to tell Kendrick the truth. For some unexplainable reason, I didn't want to cause Ty trouble or see anything bad happen to him. Because… I gulped, feeling as though I had just swallowed a brick. Because even after everything he'd done to me, I didn't and couldn't hate him. Realization hit me like a face of icy water. *Because I still loved him.*

Kendrick waved off my worried expression. "Obviously I didn't hit him hard enough."

Mr. McKenna strolled into the room then. He dumped an armful of texts and his tweed jacket on his desk up front. Then he scribbled today's lesson outline in white chalk on the blackboard. "Let's get started," he said, clapping his hands together.

The class fell in line as the teacher began rambling on. I opened my textbook with a sigh. A vibration against my chest caused me to stiffen. It was my iPhone, set on silent and buzzing with a new text. I pulled it from the inside pocket of my zip-up hoodie. The words shone like a taunting threat. 'FWIW.' For what it's worth. *'I'm not giving up on us.'*

I shoved the phone back into my pocket and snatched out my hidden chocolate bar. Without pause I ripped the wrapper back and took a huge bite.

Kendrick nudged me. "Who was that?"

I took another big bite, shrugging. "No one," I lied. The words made the chocolate taste like acid in my mouth. But I didn't want him to worry about me any more than I wanted to be the cause of a scene. "It's nothing."

"You only ever eat candy like that when you're freaking out," Kendrick growled. He belted his fist against the wooden desk and shot to his feet. The chair's legs squealed against wooden floorboards. "I know it was him. I oughta…"

Mr. McKenna turned with raised brows at Kendrick along with every student in the class. "Is there a problem, Mr. Baldassare?"

I gripped Kendrick's forearm, nails biting flesh and eyes pleading. "Don't, please. It will only make things worse."

With hardened eyes like chips of glass, Kendrick shook his head at our teacher. "No, no problem." He resumed his seat, murmuring under his breath. "But next time, there will be."

I ENTERED my art class later that morning. Anxious energy streamed through my body. The thought of having to endure Vanessa, and what I expected to be a big, smirk-riddled *I told you so*, fueled coiling dread within me.

Vanessa was positioned at her easel before the glass-paneled window. Her red hair stood out against her vibrant green top that matched the fernery outside. To my utter relief, she appeared totally engrossed, vigorously running the golden tip of a thin paintbrush in a circular motion over her canvas. I turned my iPod up, letting the words of Three Days Grace distract me. If I'm lucky she'll ignore me.

As if to spite my wish, she glanced up. And I was surprised. Her sapphire eyes were *not* sparkling with gloating as I had expected. Instead, they were open and kind. "Amelia. It's good to see you."

Having heard her through the music, I removed my earbuds. I sank down before my easel and crossed my arms over my chest. "It is?"

My eyes wandered over her portrait, which was almost completed. It was a beautiful mirroring of her thin and pale physique, pixie-like features, and blazing hair. Though unlike the designer clothing she usually wore, she had painted herself in what looked like body-fitted leather and wicked-heeled boots. Her hair was painted up in a high ponytail, and swirls of gold took up the background of the canvas.

"I've been meaning to talk to you." Vanessa twisted to face me, drawing my eyes from her portrait. "Away from prying eyes…"

Cynicism stole into my tone. "*Oh?*"

Vanessa smiled and clasped her hands in her lap. "You don't understand what really happened Saturday night. You only know what you saw."

Anger sent a flash of heat across my cheeks. "What I saw was enough." My retort was barely above a whisper and was imprinted with ice. I narrowed glaring eyes at her. "Why do you care, anyway? It's not like you ever actually liked me. You made it clear you didn't approve of me and…*Ty*." Just saying his name tore into my heart, and I clutched at my shirt. Would physically tearing out the organ be less agonizing? "You told me to stay away from him."

"I know," she replied, dunking her paintbrush into a pot of water. "And you're right. I didn't like you in the beginning. I only befriended you to gauge your intentions. Ty is my friend and I thought I was looking out for him, protecting him."

A dry, mirthless laugh cackled up my throat. "He's wasn't the one who needed protecting, now was he?"

Vanessa's strained eyes found mine. "Yes, he was. You both were." She bit her lip, appearing as though what she was about to say pained her. "But I *can* admit when I'm wrong. I shouldn't have interfered."

"Why are you telling me this?" The level of my voice had risen with frustration. Lingering glances from around the classroom turned on me.

Vanessa smiled, her eyes woeful and almost happy at the same time. "Because I can see it now, the agony he's in." She drew in a long, slow breath before exhaling. "Ty loves you, you know."

An involuntary spasm shook my entire body, and my knee connected with the tray of paints. I swore. Still, I couldn't strip the shock from my face or slow the now pounding of my aching heart. Loves me? Squeezing my eyes shut, I shook my head. Damn mutinous eyes. Don't cry. "None of what you are saying," I said slowly, voice shaking, "excuses what he did." Uncontrollable tears escaped my blinking eyes, streaking my cheeks. At least they weren't tinted red. That only happened right after drinking blood. "I will *never* forget what I saw. *Never...*"

"But it wasn't his fault. He didn't know…" Vanessa's lips sealed shut with a start, eyes diverting.

Using the sleeve of my hoodie I wiped away the tears. Her words had stolen my curiosity. "Didn't know what?"

"Look," Vanessa said, eyeing me pointedly. "You two are dumb for each other. It's quite *nauseating*. But it isn't my place to have this discussion. If you want to know what really happened, you'll have to hear Ty out. And believe me when I say that I would rather *not* be encouraging this. But I know when I'm rooting for a lost cause. Whether you believe me or not, hear this: Ty wasn't at fault." She turned back to her canvas and resumed the flowing strokes of gold-lined symbols.

I was left stunned and—yet again—unable to do anything but think about Ty. *Ah hell!*

DORIAN APPEARED OUT OF NOWHERE, head poking over my locker door. My body jarred and my elbow collected the metal frame. "Dammit!"

"Edgy much?" Dorian smirked, earning a glare from me. He

wiped the expression from his face, pursing his lips. "Coming to lunch?"

I groaned and hung my head. Being subjected to another hour of heartache would be torture. The option to flee and hide away was tempting. Though doing that would only show Ty how badly I was hung up on him. And there was no way in hell that I was about to give him the satisfaction. *Bad idea*, my inner voice whispered, but my mind was already made up. "*O-kay*," I replied in a less than convincing tone. "Let's get this over with."

"That's the spirit." Dorian slung his arm through mine and had to almost pull me down the student-swamped corridor and through the cafeteria's doors.

Kendrick sat waiting at a table near the doorway. Beside him were two spare trays brimming with food. Two chocolate bars were perched on the edge of the tray that was obviously mine. He glanced up with a smile as we took our seats. "You made it."

So he'd expected me to hide out too. With a forced smile, I pushed the tray and the candy bars away. Even chocolate couldn't tempt me to eat. Not now, when my eyes were already scanning the busy lunch crowd for *him*. My heart seized as I glimpsed Ty across the room. He sat at our old table opposite Vanessa, their lips moving in quiet conversation. Vanessa peered up with a sigh, catching my eye. She waved a little awkwardly then turned as Marika strolled over to them.

Ty glared up as she dropped into the seat beside him, shooting daggers from his eyes. "What do *you* want?"

With the noise of the packed cafeteria, I barely heard him. I focused my vampire hearing and stared. Bitter hatred radiated from every inch of his body, corded muscles twitching in visible irritation through the thin fabric of his T-shirt. His venomous tone had attracted attention from a number of students in their vicinity.

Marika's body almost trembled as she replied in a frantic whisper. I could just make out her words over the mindless babbling crowd. "Ty, please…" She clasped her hands in front of her, pleading. "I was doing you a favor."

Ty twisted his head sideways with a look of pure disgust. "You have no idea what you've done."

Marika sniffed, clutching at his bicep. Her eyes, which seemed brighter than their usual deep brown, appeared glassy, verging on the point of tears. "You're not meant to be with her."

I frowned, shaking my head. Was she referring to me? My stomach dropped, turning in caustic acid. Or the *other girl*? Just thinking of the mystery girl spiked an eruption of bile to the back of my throat. I swallow hard, trying to relieve the burning sensation, my eyes still set on Ty.

Scarlet color had cascaded up his neck and across his face. He clutched Marika's wrist. She grimaced before he thrust her hand away from his arm. "If you *ever* touch me again, I will tear your hand clean off the bone."

"What's up with that?" Kendrick asked, his sudden words causing my body to stiffen. He was sneering across the room at Ty and Marika.

I frowned, and then realized something. Dorian hadn't spoken or even moved since Marika had walked in. He sat, statue-stiff with glazed eyes trained on the two. "Dorian," I said, reaching out to shake his arm. "Are you okay?"

Dorian tore his eyes away. He exchanged a pained frown with me before glancing over at Kendrick. "What do I care?" he said, answering Kendrick's question instead of mine.

His sharp tone surprised me at first. And then I knew. The phone call he'd received on Sunday from Marika had resulted in their break-up. I felt disgusted with myself, an unworthy sister. As usual,

I had been totally self-obsessed. I hadn't even noticed the shift in his carefree demeanor.

"Oh, Dorian…" I collected his hand and squeezed. "I'm so sorry."

"Don't be." He slid his eyes from Marika to settle on a table full of cheerleaders. "She's just a stupid skank." He winked and smiled at the girls, who instantly began to gossip and giggle. They were clearly thrilled, but I could tell it was an act on Dorian's part, a ploy to mask his pain.

Anger strained my face. I glared at the bitch that had pummeled my brother's heart. She still sat beside Ty, her hands clasped in front of her. Not daring to touch him, she pleaded. "Ty, forgive me. You have to forgive me."

Troy approached their table then, taking up a position opposite the others. "Quit groveling, Marika," he said, his expression smug. "It's a serious turn-off." He patted his thigh and Marika pursed her lips, giving Ty one last look. Then she slinked around the table and onto Troy's lap.

My mouth dropped as she curled her arms around him and nibbled at his ear. "That bitch!" Dorian's hand, still folded in mine, tensed. I cursed myself internally. "Sorry."

Dorian shook his hand free. "I'm fine."

"We did what we had too." Troy's low voice across the room regained my attention.

We? I remembered Troy and Marika talking heatedly inside the house at his party. They had been arguing, Marika declaring that it was the only way. A sinking feeling weighed down my stomach. The only way to what? Had they somehow arranged some vamp girl to come on to Ty?

"And I will not apologize for looking out…" Troy dipped his head and whispered, "For the pack."

Until now, Vanessa had been uninterested in any of the drama taking place, sitting in silence with her head dropped. Now it shot up, sending her blazing hair over her shoulders. "That's enough!" She jumped to her feet, slamming her hand against the table. Her eyes skewered them with a look that could kill. "You were both out of line, and you know it."

Ty raised his hand, silencing Vanessa's reprimand. His face was still red with anger, eyes flashing gold. "*I* pull rank here, and you will both stand in line." He directed a pointed finger at Troy then Marika. "I will not tolerate any further bullshit from either of you. And I couldn't give a shit about what either of you thinks is justified. One more stunt and you will *both* incur my wrath."

Troy grunted and Marika's eyes widened, though neither of them dared to speak.

I was about to look away, when Ty glanced up, blazing eyes catching mine. The anger drained from his face in an instant, replaced by clear longing. My heartstrings tugged under the draw of his eyes, and I couldn't look away. He rose to his feet and began walking forward.

A warning growl rumbled from Kendrick's chest. My heart jumped into my throat. *Stop! Turn around*, my eyes pleaded. But Ty kept on walking. Kendrick flipped his half-full tray of food over and snapped it across the edge of the table. My stomach turned like a crashing wave. With a jagged piece of tray clutched in one hand, he leaped over our table. An eruption of gasps sounded all around as he landed before Ty.

I moved to rush after Kendrick and pull him back. Instantly Dorian's hand gripped my forearm, restraining me. "Let's just see where this goes."

Fear of exposure pulsed through my body. Kendrick stood with aggression pouring out of him, feet planted and shoulders hunched.

Ty's hands rose in surrender. Every set of eyes, even the kitchen hands behind the buffet line, were focused on the hostile display.

And then something registered. I couldn't scent Ty or Troy. I remembered psych class this morning. Apart from the chlorine, he hadn't had a scent then, either. Was he still protecting my lies to Kendrick by masking his werewolf identity? Had he even ordered Troy to do the same?

"You better turn around, Malau." Unblemished hatred emanated from Kendrick's hissed words.

"Kendrick, please," I pleaded, thoughts melting as nausea crawled up my throat. "Don't do this."

Kendrick threw a quick glance over his shoulder, cutting me with narrowed eyes. "No, Amelia. I won't back down this time." He turned back to Ty, fist clenched. *You*," he spat with venom, "*disgust me*."

All remaining chatter had ceased. The cafeteria echoed deathly silence.

I sank down in my chair, wanting to disappear. Where was a sinkhole when you needed one? The other option was to take off. But running from the cafeteria wouldn't stop this standoff. There was no escaping this.

"You don't understand," Ty said. He ran tense hands through his hair, which looked like it hadn't been brushed in days. "Just let me explain."

Kendrick took a further step forward, gritting his teeth. "She doesn't want to hear it," he snarled, loud enough for the entire room to hear. "So, if you know what's good for you, you'll turn around and scurry back to your seat with your tail between your legs. Just like the *dog* you are."

The crowd's reaction was a mixture of tense laughter and gasps. A number of closer kids scooted their chairs away, out of the line of fire. You couldn't blame them. I'd never witnessed this side of Kendrick before: the challenge, the arrogance, the pure hostility. His stance reminded me of Stefan from The Vampire Diaries when he went all Ripper. It was savage and wild, a shutdown of emotions that was animalistic in the way he glared down Ty. He was ready to attack without warning.

Ignoring his challenger, Ty looked to me. "Please, Amelia. Just one minute."

Kendrick closed the gap separating them, fingers grasping Ty's shirt in a white-knuckled fist. His other hand lifted the dangerous piece of tray, pointing it at Ty's heart.

In a flash, Troy and Marika sprang up to flank Ty. Low rumbles vibrated from their chests.

"Back off," Troy growled. He pushed back the edge of his leather jacket, hand hovering over something silvery sheathed to his side.

This was bad. Kendrick didn't afford him or Marika any attention, even though it was clear Troy was carrying a weapon. A start of realization sent a hand of cold fingers up my spine. He didn't figure any of them to be a physical threat against him. Because he didn't know he was challenging a pair of werewolves.

I tore free of Dorian's grasp and darted to my best friend, clutching his arm. "That's enough, Kendrick. Stop this!"

A dangerous smile parted my best friend's lips. He threw down the jagged piece of tray, curling his fingers into deadly looking weapons. His head cocked to the side and away from the gaping crowd. With his fangs threatening to protrude, he hissed his final threat through clenched teeth, low and inaudible to every watching human. "If you don't back off now, I will rip out your beating heart with my bare hands."

Troy and Marika stiffened. Before anything could happen, Ty raised his hand for them to wait.

"Break it up, break it up!" Mr. McKenna's voice rang out. He'd just caught sight of the confrontation from the hall and was bounding our way.

Ty's face hardened. There wasn't even a sliver of weakness as he tore his shirt from Kendrick's hold. "Fine," he mouthed. "But this isn't finished. I *won't* give up on her." With a grunt, he turned and stalked away.

After a second, Troy and Marika followed with backward looks of loathing.

"Next time it'll be detention for all of you," Mr. McKenna said, looking relieved at the outcome.

Kendrick's shoulders slumped with a sigh and he looked me in the eye. "Sorry."

Within my chest, my heart was smashing against my ribs. My blood raced. It felt like my head was about to explode with anger. I was furious with my best friend for his reckless actions and blatant disregard of me begging him to stop. "I don't want to hear it." I whirled on the spot, face fuming, and stormed away. *Told you this was a bad idea.*

AFTER FALLING into a restless sleep that night, I awoke abruptly. Rather than being within the safety of my room and bed, I was lying on a throw of soft ferns.

Following the cafeteria incident, the day had passed without any further run-ins. Ty had kept his distance, and Vanessa hadn't tried to sway me further into hearing him out. Marika and Troy had also restrained themselves enough to only shoot glares our way. And

Kendrick had made it impossible to stay mad at him, apologizing with a box of chocolates that he'd skipped class to buy. How could I stay mad when chocolate was involved?

The day's tension had dissipated. Still, I couldn't shake my unease over everything that had happened or relieve the pain that still gripped my aching heart. Mental exhaustion weighed me down like rocks accumulating over my chest, and I had fallen into a fitful sleep.

Now I felt the panic of disorientation setting in. I rubbed at my eyes with balled hands and propped myself upright, forcing my rising breath to slow. The surroundings slowly cleaved into focus. A small clearing, bordered by a thicket of pine and oak trees surrounded me. They thinned on one side, letting the moon's three-quarter light through.

I rose from the dew-dampened ferns, following the ghostly shine of moonlight through the clearing. On the far side, I found the edge of a sheer cliff that plunged into indistinguishable darkness. Above, not a single cloud blemished the night sky. Instead, a million stars glittered like someone had thrown a fistful of diamonds across its dark surface. Their shine along with the moonlight illuminated not only the space around me, but the jagged mountain terrain layered with snow that rose up before me. I sucked in a breath of awe as confusion set in. My conscious mind had just caught up with me. How in the world did I get here?

With a sidestep I leaned against the rough bark of a large oak tree. A light breeze brushed past me, carrying with it the strong scent of pine. There was another scent too. It was so diluted that I almost thought I was imagining it. *I'm dreaming,* I realized suddenly.

"It's beautiful, isn't it?" breathed a familiar and yet not entirely unexpected voice.

Rearing off the solid tree, I spun. A guy stood at the bordering tree line, dressed in nothing but a pair of cut-off jeans. His hair hung over his forehead and his eyes glowed with intensity. *Ty.*

My breath caught in my throat and my heart ached with its rapid beat. The sight of him instilled a deep longing within me, tainted by irrefutable anger. "*You* brought me here?" Disbelief edged my sharp words. "How…" Ty stepped forward and my hand rose in repudiation. "No! I don't care. I don't want to hear anything you have to say."

I stormed past him, making for the tree line. I still had no idea how he'd brought me here. And there was no way in hell I was about to stick around to find out.

Ty reached out to grasp my arm, but I darted away. "Wait!" he called out, a crackle evident in his voice. "You can't go. You have to listen to me."

I whirled on the spot and glared at him with skewering eyes. "No, I don't!" I turned back, continuing on my intended path. "I'm leaving."

"Amelia, stop! You can't…"

His words died as my forehead connected with something. Caught off guard, I stumbled back. Shock and embarrassment hammered my pulse, bringing a warm buzz to my ears. With a shake I recovered. Then I raised my hands until they connected with an invisible barrier. What had looked like a living tree line was not. It was a flat surface, somewhat like a looking glass that peered into a place I couldn't quite touch. I pushed against its flat, hard surface. It rippled beneath my palms, so rigidly stiff that involuntary twitches crawled up my arms. I pushed again, harder this time. An electric shock bolted through my hands and I repelled back. With my jaw set and arms dropped, I turned. Tension fixed my fingers into clawed weapons that strained every muscle along my arms and up to my neck. "What have you done?"

Ty clasped his hands in front of him. "Amelia, I'm sorry. I didn't want to do this. But it's the only way I could get you to listen to me." He shook his head, looking almost regretful. "Please understand. You left me no other choice."

A warning hiss blew through my lips and they parted, revealing fully extended fangs. In Ty's silent hesitation, I scanned the clearing for a possible escape. Would his conjured force field extend past the cliff? I decided I wasn't past hurtling myself from the edge to find out.

"I wouldn't do that," Ty said, seeming to have read my mind, or to have at least interpreted my searching expression. "Look," he rushed on, lines of frustration pinching his brow. "This is a dream. You're dreaming. It's the only way…"

"Well then," I scoffed, cutting him off. Dreaming? What a joke. "If what you're saying it true, and I highly doubt it, then I'll just wake up."

Ty shook his head, looking rueful. "I am afraid I can't let you do that. I brought you here. See," his voice dropped to a whisper and he spread his arms out wide, "I created this place."

In an instant shift, the moon and stars began to disappear. The sun rose swiftly over the adjacent mountain. Captivation held my widened eyes, as the burning globe crept higher and higher. Its growing beams of light stretched down to the valley below. Warmth and a golden hue spread over everything it touched. Wakened by the dawn, the sounds of chirping birds rose from the treetops.

The tension stiffening my clawed hands released. I cocked my head to the side, wide eyes shifting to Ty. I believed he was telling the truth. Still, there was no way in hell I wanted to stay here and listen to his version of events. My own memories of that night were enough. But I was trapped and out of options. "If I listen to you, you'll let me go?" At Ty's nod, I walked back over to the oak tree edging the cliff and dropped to the ground. My arms and legs crossed in defiance. "Hurry up. I'm already bored with this."

Ty edged closer, hands clasped under his chin. "I know you don't want to hear anything I have to say. But I need you to know the truth."

I ignored him, irritated and unwilling to give him any satisfaction.

Ty blew out a breath of exasperation. "Fine, if you won't respond at all, I'll just do the talking." Angst radiated from his tightly coiled body as he began pacing. "What happened that night, it's not what you think. See, I thought I was in bed with you. I was mortified when you appeared at the door."

My head came up with eyes throwing poison. "Liar! You are so full of shit!" His words infuriated me, tearing fresh, jagged strips from my heart. It took every ounce of my self-control not to lunge at him with bared fangs. The idea of tearing into him was so tempting. "Why don't you do us both a favor and stop talking? You're just insulting my intelligence and embarrassing yourself with your ridiculous lies."

Ty raked his fingers through his hair in frustration. I glared away, struggling to hold at bay the boiling anger that was cascading up my neck and across my face, verging on an uncontainable explosion. What a jerk!

"Amelia, please," he pleaded. "It's true. Didn't you notice that the girl looked like you?"

A jolt of pain-filled memories rose to the surface; her pale vampire skin and long, blond hair. Then I saw the eerie dream that shockingly revealed my own likeness as the girl beneath him. The overwhelming sensation to gag curdled my stomach. It *was* just a dream, wasn't it? My brain pulsed against my skull. He's lying, he has to be. "So what," I hissed. My eyes closed while I struggled to slow my elevating breath. "We looked slightly alike, and…and that was good enough for you? I can't believe—"

"No!" Ty shouted, cutting off my rant. "Not slightly, exactly!"

The conviction that radiated from Ty's voice forced my eyelids to fly open. For the first time since this so-called 'dream' had started, I actually wanted to hear what Ty had to say. "What the hell does that mean?"

Ty stepped toward me, realizing the slight shift in my temper. Though his words rushed as if he feared I'd shut off at any moment. "After I went up to your room to call my father, you came in. Well, at least I thought you did. She looked like you in every single way. She even sounded and smelled like you. You—I mean, she—coaxed me into the bed, and I followed. I never thought for a second…" His expression strained, hands curling into fists. "Amelia, I honestly thought she was you. I would *never* jeopardize what we share. Never betray you in any way. You mean *everything* to me."

Tuning my senses, I studied his face. There were no hints of deception. His eyes were glassy and despairing, unwavering as he held my gaze. On top of that, there was no flutter to his heart, which he'd taught me was an indication of deceit. *I believe him.* The realization shook me like the aftershock of an earthquake. "How is that possible?" I whispered. "And who was she?"

Ty's expression darkened. "The girl was…Marika."

I slapped my forehead. So freaking gullible! The girl I had glimpsed had been a stark contrast to Marika and her black abyss of hair, deep-brown eyes, and dark-tan complexion. "Well done." I clapped with mock applause, masking the fresh sting of barbs that pierced my heart. "I almost believed you." The anger was rearing within me again, like a deep and sickening inferno. It engulfed my stomach, sending scorching waves snaking outward. I had to get out of here. I wouldn't endure this revolting torture and longer. Beyond contemplation, I dug my heels into the dirt. My muscles tightened, ready to leap off the cliff.

"She's a werewolf!" Ty's desperate shouted words brought me to an abrupt halt at the edge of the cliff. He continued in a breathless rush. "I didn't know it then. Female-born lycanthropes are so rare. I never suspected."

Shaking my head I turned, lips pinned to look at Ty. My head was pulsing with the rapid beat of my heart, fueling a confusion-driven migraine. Where was he going with this? Marika being a werewolf made her wanting to get between Ty and me understandable. Their kind was raised to despise ours. I recalled her intense argument with Troy at his party and her plea for Ty's forgiveness in the cafeteria. At the auction I had even directed Ty to my room after she'd brought up the sleepover. She knew where to find him. All of this provided a valid motive. Still, it was not enough to explain all the evidence away, the fact that the girl resembled me and not her. "Tell me how."

Ty's lips parted, but no sound came out. He was vanishing right before my eyes. As he did, mouthing "*sorry,*" my surroundings darkened. Empty blackness enveloped my body as everything became quiet and still.

CHAPTER 16

*J*ambled from English class, our last subject for the day, feeling totally disheartened.

After last night's dream, I had woken disorientated and utterly confused. Had any of it been real? I'd waited all day to see Ty, to catch a glimpse of him. His expression alone would give me the answer. But he had been glaringly absent from the cafeteria at lunch. I sighed. I'm seriously losing it. Losing my grip on reality...

"What's wrong?"

The sudden voice caused my body to stiffen. Kendrick had been walking beside me this whole time. Crap. As usual, I'd been wrapped up in my own jumbled thoughts. Who I was with or what surrounded me hadn't even been a second thought.

I shook my head and ambled down the aluminum-treaded stairs. "It's nothing."

Kendrick looked doubtful. His eyes slid sideways, watching me. "You didn't sleep well."

Surprise stole my face and my pulse jumped. "What?"

We had reached the bottom of the stairs. Students rushed left and right, wanting to escape the end of a school day as fast as possible.

Kendrick smiled. "I came in to check on you last night. You were tossing and turning and I tried to wake you. But nothing I did worked. You just mumbled incoherently and struggled harder against me. It was like you were locked in your dreams. So I just waited until you settled." He raised his hand, thumb grazing my cheek to hook a loose strand of hair behind my ear. "The nightmare, what was it about?"

My heart skipped a beat and I looked away. How could I tell him what I'd dreamed? And that I wanted to believe that the dream itself and Ty's ability had been real? I barely believed it myself. Hell, I was wondering if I was losing my mind. He would only think the same. I shook my head, forcing my eyes back up to his. "Nothing worth worrying about…"

Soft lines creased Kendrick's face. "You don't have to tell me. I know he still haunts you."

Kendrick's clear perception turned my stomach. He had spent the night in my room and bed the night after Ty's texts, his arms holding my shaking body through every waking nightmare. He was well aware of how much what Ty had done still affected me. And he was forever devoted. He'd only returned to his own room and bed last night after I claimed I'd be okay. I blinked back the tears that were threatening my eyes. I had to tell him. Tell him everything, about Ty, the wolves…

"Let's go bowling," Kendrick suggested suddenly, face brightening.

Caught off-guard I frowned as my inner thoughts of confession crumbled. "What?"

"Take your mind off everything." Kendrick smiled. "Have fun. You do remember fun, don't you?"

I slapped his arm, the corners of my mouth lifting in an unre- strained smile. "Okay." I motioned to the books cradled in my arm. "Let me dump these and I'll meet you at the car."

Kendrick nodded and fell in step with the throng of students heading out the building's main doors.

I sighed again and weaved through the remaining students down the hall. Passing the procession of double-stacked lockers spanning between each classroom door, I made for my own. I felt torn apart inside. Continuing to keep secrets from Kendrick was taking its toll. A deepening pit was weighing down my stomach. Eventually I'd have to come clean, about everything.

When I reached my locker, my head was beginning to ache with a rhythmic throb. A fluorescent-pink flyer was taped to the door, announcing that there was a Creative Arts and Psychic Fair coming to town. I yanked it down, turned the combination, then swung the door open. A folded piece of paper slipped from behind the Vampire Diaries poster I'd taped to the door and flitted to the ground. My eyes scanned the faces of preoccupied students moving up and down the hall, but no one was watching me. I bent to retrieve the paper and unfolded it. Inside was a note, handwritten in neat cursive.

Sorry I couldn't explain everything last night.
Lost without you, Ty.

My heart clenched, tight in the hands of a vice-grip. The dream *was* real. Even now, I could remember every scent, every detail, and every word Ty had said. Not crazy. The relief that washed over my entire body tingled all the way down to my toes. The throbbing within my skull ceased. I ached to believe everything Ty had told me, but all the pieces weren't in place. I needed the whole story. I needed to talk to Ty. But Kendrick was waiting for me. Calling Ty would have to wait.

THE PORTSMOUTH BOWL-O-RAMA was raging tonight. With heating and a licensed bar, many adolescents had taken to it as their impending winter hang. Some kids I even recognized from St. Volaras.

I shrugged out of my wannabe motorbike jacket, shaking off the dusting of freshly fallen snow. We crossed the stained, brightly swirled carpet to stand before the front desk. It was a plywood counter that housed a computer monitor and keyboard. Its glass front revealed glossy bowling balls on individual stands.

The manager—as stated on his striped bowling shirt—looked up. "Booking?"

Kendrick shook his head, folding his arms over his favorite *Three Days Grace* T-shirt. "No."

"Well, we're packed tonight," the manager informed. "Everything's booked out."

I scoured through the multicolored lights that flashed casting beams over eighteen lanes. There were only two unoccupied lanes, one and twelve.

"No," Kendrick retorted. He pointed toward lane one without shifting his gaze from the manager. "It's not."

The manager followed his extended hand then looked back to him, frowning. "Already book…"

"*We* booked lane one," Kendrick cut in. He leaned forward,

holding the man's eyes with his. "Kendrick Baldassare. Check your screen and you *will* see my name."

Kendrick's commanding tone drew my attention. The silver of his eyes sparked as his pupils grew, almost extinguishing his irises entirely. I jabbed him in the ribs. "What are you doing?"

Keeping his eyes locked on the manager's, Kendrick smiled. "Trust me."

My gaze shot back to the manager whose frown had dissipated. His head dropped to the computer screen in an almost mechanical movement. "Oh, yes. There you are." A befuddled expression wrinkled his middle-aged face. "My mistake." He drummed his fingers across the keyboard and glanced up. "All set. Now, what shoe sizes?"

After collecting our shoes we headed for our lane, my head swimming. The way the manager had responded to Kendrick reminded me of my only successful attempt of compulsion on the bouncer outside *Pulse*.

Mom had explained compulsion at the cabin. It was a form of mind control, of distorting someone's perception of reality. She'd even tried to teach us how to use it. But like my lack of natural vampire agility, the ability to compel seemed to escape me as well as Dorian.

"Head's up!" Kendrick's light voice startled me.

My head snapped up. Any thoughts of compulsion shrank as a black bowling ball hurled through the air, flying straight for my head. In a split second my muscles snapped into action. My hands flung up just in time to catch the black boulder. I dropped onto the U-shaped bench bordering lane one, my heart pounding. Having a ball flying through the air at my head had shocked me. And I was surprised my reflexes had reacted fast enough to catch the thing. "I can't believe I caught that."

"I know. You're getting faster," Kendrick said, pulling on his oversized bowling shoes. He stood up, lifting a matching ball to mine from the ball retriever. It was the heaviest available. "Let's bowl."

Kendrick sauntered toward the lane, rolling his arm back before flinging the ball forward. The black ball met the buffed and oiled lane with barely a sound. It spun as it sped forward, colliding with the pins in an explosive crash. Every single pin was knocked over. Kendrick turned with a haughty smile.

"Well done," I congratulated, still yanking on my shoes. Then with my ball in hand, I strode forward, gauging my shot. From our training at the cabin, I knew my strength lay in planning my next move. In a second my attack was set. Stance slightly right of the lane, eyes zoned just left of the ten-pin center. I curved my wrist slightly and lifted the ball to my chin, leading with my right foot. The ball flew from my grasp with the flick of my wrist, grazing the wood with a light thud. I turned to Kendrick with a pleased smile playing across my lips as the ball struck the pins with force. I heard each individual pin fall and hit. Nine of the ten had dropped.

"You missed one," Kendrick gloated.

Unwavering confidence broadened my smile. "Oh, I don't think so." The last standing pin was spinning upright, but it was slowing. It wobbled audibly before it gave way and fell with a *thud*. *Strike!*

After our first game, we decided we'd worked up an appetite and ordered beef nachos. The plate arrived quickly, topped with sour cream and guacamole. As we ate, Kendrick complimented my superior development in reflexes, aim, and control. But I couldn't keep the earlier thoughts of compulsion from my mind.

In a surreal shift, the flashing lights around me faded and I was back in the alley outside the club in Anchorage. Kendrick spoke in a low even voice while forcing Joel's attention. "You were attacked by a rabid dog. *We* saved your life."

The memory faded and my eyes refocused, bringing me back to reality. I looked to Kendrick. "I want you to compel me."

"What?" he spat, dropping the corn chip he was about to eat.

I shrugged. "I'm getting better at the other vamp stuff. So I just thought that maybe we could try again. You can show me instead of telling me how." Kendrick's frozen expression surged an unexpected bout of paranoia through my stomach. "Oh, crap. Have you used it on me before?"

Kendrick's brows knitted, clear hurt saddening his eyes. "Amelia, I would never—"

"Sorry," I said, cutting him off. I felt terrible. How could I have even thought that? I turned on the bench to face him. "Stupid question. I know you wouldn't do that. But now I'm asking you to. Will you show me how?"

Kendrick's expression strained. "Are you sure?"

I nodded again and took his hands in mine. "Definitely. Compel me."

"Alright then," Kendrick said, still looking a tad reluctant. He stared down at our entwined fingers. "As I told you at the cabin, it's all in the eyes. It's the concentration of looking not just *at* a person's eyes, but through them. Like you're glimpsing into the very core of someone's soul." His eyes rose to meet mine. They sparkled like drops of liquid silver swimming in a sea of aqua. He took a deep breath. "Ready?"

At my nod, his irises began to rage. They looked like an impressive electrical storm, liquid silver struck through by blue-sparked lightening. The sight was so enthralling it was impossible to look away.

"Kiss me," his ragged voice whispered while his pupils dilated.

"What? Don't be silly..." I faltered as my expression fell slack. My want and need to refuse him dwindled like a snuffed flame.

"Kiss me," Kendrick repeated. This time his voice was deep and commanding. It sent invisible fingertips dancing across my cheeks and down my neck. "You want to kiss me."

The world around us faded, flashing lights replaced by an endless black abyss. Yet in the darkness, Kendrick's eyes remained. His glossy black pupils grew until they had extinguished his silver irises entirely. Without rational thought, my body leaned forward, closing the gap between us. My lips edged closer and closer, parting to graze his. I could feel the warmth of his breath tickling my lips, and taste the sweetness a single kiss would grant. There was nothing I wanted more than to press my parting lips to his full and waiting ones, eliminating any and all space between us. But a millisecond before I could take what I so inherently needed, something buzzed against my leg, breaking the spell. It was my iPhone, signaling a new text.

My focus returned in a sudden rush, causing my head to swell. Back was the bowling alley with its flashing lights and loud pop music. Surrounding kids were laughing, drinking, and having fun. Kendrick was sitting before me, frozen stiff, his face a mask of shock.

Embarrassment burned my cheeks while uncontrollable anger pounded through me. I jerked away from Kendrick, glaring. "How could you do that?" My shrill tone earned me a number of onlookers who had suddenly ceased bowling. I lowered my voice. "*Why* would you do that?"

Kendrick's expression remained calm as he crossed his arms over his chest. "You asked me to compel you," he spoke with an irritated whisper. "That's *all* I was doing."

The next words spat from my lips dripped acid. "I didn't ask you to do *that*. You could have made me bark like a dog or cluck like a chicken."

Kendrick clenched his jaw. A muscle contracted beneath the smooth, pale skin of his cheeks. "You're so damn blind, Amelia. All this time and you still can't even see what's right in front of you."

"See what?" I demanded. "What are you talking…" my words choked back. A notion that was both crippling and like a physical force pushed me back against the bench. "You *wanted* to kiss me?"

Kendrick unclenched his jaw and reached out, gently folding my hands in his. His face was suddenly filled with a vulnerability I had never seen in him before. "I'm in love with you, Amelia. I always have been."

I tried to speak, to say something, anything in response. But my whole body felt shaken to its core. My breath caught in my throat, and my mouth and tongue were paralyzed.

"Amelia…" Kendrick's eyes were silver-blue again. They strained, as though what he was about to say caused him deep, physical pain. "I know you feel something for me, too. I see it in your eyes."

Nothing in this world could make me deny the strong feelings I had for Kendrick. He was my best friend and the one person who kept me grounded, who had always stood by me. But since finding Ty, I knew that anything I had ever felt for Kendrick—or anyone else for that matter—would always be lukewarm in comparison, a gentle flame rather than a raging inferno. Still, knowing the words I had to say to him filled me with sickening dread. There was the option to lie. But I couldn't lead him on. I wouldn't.

Kendrick yanked his hands free, his face turning to stone as though he had read my internal thoughts.

"Of course I love you," I cried, throwing my arms around him. "Kendrick, you're my best friend. You always will be." I released him, my eyes pleading for understanding. Please don't let what I have to say break us. "But I'm not *in love* with you."

Rejection contorted Kendrick's expression. The thought of breaking my best friend's heart bore into me like tunneling parasites.

"It's because of *him*, isn't it?" The sharp perception in Kendrick's harsh voice felt like a fisted blow to my chest. "Even after everything that dog's done to you?" He sighed, seeing the anguish scrawled across my face. "I'm sorry. I didn't mean to bring it up. It just makes me sick that he could hurt you like that." Our eyes met. His were strained and vulnerable. "Amelia, I know you're still getting over him. But I want you to know that I will always be here. And I would never hurt you like that, not *ever*."

My heart sank to the pit of my stomach. There were still so many secrets I was keeping from my best friend. Lies I had allowed him to believe. But how can I explain it to him now? The forlorn look on his face was already more than I could take. I couldn't hurt him any more than I already was. I couldn't tell him that my feelings for Ty were still as strong as ever. No. Not now.

"It's okay." Kendrick rose to his feet and collected his bowling ball. "You don't have to say anything now." Drawing his shoulders back, he turned and began our second game. The comfortable air we had arrived with was long faded. Over the following hour, the ease of our relationship didn't return.

As we left the bowling alley, quiet tension hung between us. Kendrick left to pull the car around and I thought back, remembering the text that had interrupted his attempted compulsion. I retrieved my iPhone from my jeans. The text was from Ty.

'*CU in UR dreams 2nite.'*

～

I AVOIDED Kendrick for the rest of the evening. His profession of love had utterly surprised me. But that wasn't the only reason I was avoiding him. Tonight I would learn the truth, the whole truth. And if Ty was exonerated, I would have no choice. I would have to reveal everything I had kept from Kendrick. The daunting realization kept my stomach in knots and made it almost impossible for me to keep it together around him. It was the real reason I was avoiding him.

With my brain exhausted from the mental and emotional strain, I fell into a deep sleep. When I awoke, I was on the same bed of ferns from last time. Their fronds scratched through the lace of my black camisole and boxers. Disappointment gripped me as I glanced around. The almost full moon that gleamed through the clearing drew ghostly shadows. Ty was nowhere to be seen.

I called out into the wilderness. "Ty, are you here?" My voice echoed back at me, bouncing off the bordering oak and pine trees. My heart sank.

Then in an instant shift that caused my head to spin, the scenery blurred and reformed. Suddenly, I was no longer sitting at the peak of a mountain. Instead, I was in the depths of a lush, bursting-with-life rainforest. The quiet disarray of sleeping mountains layered with ghostly shadows was now gone. Replacing it was the sound of gushing water and the soft darkness of sun-drawn shade. I gaped around, mystified. A sunlit waterfall was materializing beside me. It streamed over a rocky cliff face to plunge into the swirling river below. Still, Ty was nowhere to be seen. I slumped against the trunk of a mossy evergreen. *Where are you?*

A change in the steady flow of gushing water from behind startled me. I shot to my feet. Ty was emerging from between the fall of water plunging over the cliff. "Sorry I kept you waiting."

With confident steps, he crossed the surface of the swirling river as though it were solid, mirrored glass. What he wore was minimal, just a pair of soggy jeans. They hung low around his taut waist and stuck to his legs. Golden sunlight defined his sculpted chest and abs. He ruffled his thick hair, and as he did it became instantly dry, along with his jeans.

The gentle words of Skillet's song *Don't wake me* lifted on the breeze. The emotion of the song dared me to rush into his arms, but I fought back, digging my nails into the dirt.

"I wanted to tell you everything last night. But I needed to build up the energy." He glanced around at our picturesque surroundings. "Dreamscaping really takes it out of you."

Unable to quell the intrigue that gripped me at witnessing Ty's power in manipulating dreams, I asked, "A dreamscape? So that's what this is?"

I dropped back down against the evergreen. Ty followed, taking up position beside me. Even though he wasn't quite touching me, his skin sent a flux of heat across my arms and legs. It was so warm I could have been right beside an open fire.

"I'm still learning," Ty said, as the song changed to *Yours to hold*. "So, I'll get better eventually. But we don't have much time now."

Am I yours to hold? I wondered. There was nothing I wanted more than to have his arms around me. But I still needed the rest of his vindication. "I'm ready."

Ty nodded, eyes lifting to mine for a split second before looking away. His voice was rough and gravelly. "Like I said last time, Marika is a werewolf. But there is more to being a werewolf than you're aware of." Ty paused and took a deep breath whilst shaking his head. "Lycanthropes are able to transform their appearance to match another person's, creating a temporary doppelganger. Marika used Dorian to keep tabs on us. It was her plan all along to force us apart. She had intended to act during the sleepover. When the opportunity presented itself at the auction, she decided to put her plan into action early. She imprinted your essence, taking on your form. And well...you know the rest." Ty reached out as though he were about to touch me. He froze at the last second, curling his hand into a fist. "If I even thought for a second it wasn't with you—" The desperation rose steadily in his uneven voice and he turned his head away. "Amelia, you have to believe me. I didn't know."

Like a fragmented puzzle, all the pieces fused in my mind. Troy and Marika's argument at the party and her sudden interest in Dorian had been part of the plan. She'd been overly eager at Dorian's sleepover idea, probably because she'd planted the idea herself. At the auction, she'd disappeared after Ty went inside to make the call to his father. After the fact, there had been her guilty pleas for forgiveness from Ty. Then she'd suddenly dumped my unsuspecting brother, no longer needing the ruse. Two things still puzzled me though.

"Then why doesn't she have the same scent as you and Troy? And her eyes..." I trailed off in thought. Her irises had been deep brown at the start. Only they hadn't stayed that way. Before Kendrick and Ty faced off yesterday in the cafeteria, her eyes had been brighter, almost hazel. "She was wearing contacts?"

Ty nodded and cringed, muttering what sounded like a curse and someone's name that I didn't quite catch. "And she's been marked by an alchemist's tattoo. It works like the elixir but is more permanent. It masked her scent and made it indiscernible, even to me. Had I known or even suspected..." Ty broke off again, shaking his head.

In his silence, I remembered the golden filigree of crossed wavy lines backing Marika's neck. A barely audible whisper escaped my lips. "I believe you." Relief cascaded across Ty's face and he blew out a long breath. "How did you find out it was her?"

Ty's eyes darkened, turning stormy as he stared away. "After you ran from the room, I looked back to the girl in your bed. She leaped up and flew to your bedroom window. But imprinting is extremely draining. As she made her escape, I saw her morph from blond and pale to dark and tan." Ty reached out with caution, slowly lowering his hand to rest it on my own. His pained eyes shifted to meet mine. "I was gutted when I realized what had happened. What I had done and what you must have thought." He trailed off, looking away and squeezing his vibrant eyes shut.

"Marika and Troy, they were both in on it." I reached out to graze Ty's cheek. "They know what I am. And they hate the thought of us being together."

Ty hesitantly curled his arms around my body, pulling me against his hot, sculpted chest. The touch of his naked flesh spiked my beating heart. "It doesn't matter how they feel." He pressed his scorching lips to the crown of my head. "They will never interfere again. I'm their alpha and have ordered them to butt out. They *cannot* disobey me."

There was no doubt in my mind that everything Ty had told me was the truth. Still, the revelation wasn't about to make my life any easier. A solid mass had risen up my throat and my stomach turned. I reached for a stray leaf and began tearing small confetti pieces off it. There was nothing I wanted less than to have to ever speak to Marika again. But I needed to confirm the facts before spewing all my secrets out to Dorian and Kendrick. *Kendrick.* Knowing how much hearing the truth would injure him caused my heart to ache. There was already so much friction between us. I could just imagine the backlash my confession would create. With a mental shake, I swallowed my fear, pushing the solid mass back down. "I need to hear it from Marika."

Ty's arms tensed around me, biceps bulging. "Of course. But

don't expect any apologies. She's adamant in her reason for causing all of this." Ty's warmth around me began to fade, and I peered up. "Sorry, I have to go," he whispered, his body turning transparent and sizzling touch fading. He inclined his head, pressing his lips to mine. Around us, the music and surroundings blackened into cold darkness.

CHAPTER 17

*E*ntering the cafeteria after geography the following day, I collected my lunch—a single chocolate bar—then headed for Dorian and Kendrick at our new table. With anxiety making my heart skip, I set the tray down and gave them both a stern frown. "I need to speak with Marika, and I want you *both* to butt out." Dorian turned his attention from a blond across the room, his eyebrows raised in question. "I can't explain now," I said, waving him off. "So don't ask."

"I'll be watching Ty," Kendrick mumbled, shoving away his snowboarding magazine. "He'd better not try anything."

Across the room, Marika sat alongside Troy, her shoulders visibly tense. Guess she knew what was coming.

Ty glanced up at my arrival with a resolute smile, which I returned before looking pointedly at Marika. Her eyes were focused down on the tabletop, unwilling to meet my accusing stare. "Can I have a minute, alone?" Without waiting for a response, I stalked past their table to the glass doors that led outside.

Marika rose, not bothering to tug down her micro-mini, and Troy reared up beside her. She caught his arm. "Don't. I can take care of myself."

Troy nodded, face hardening as Marika turned away. She followed after me, through the doors and past the aluminum benches. A set of curved, concrete stairs led to an isolated courtyard of paved squares. The space housed a single picnic bench and was hedged by thick shrubbery that veiled us from prying eyes. Their branches danced with the force of a flesh-biting breeze.

I perched atop the aluminum bench and waited for the bitch to sit. With slow and obvious reluctance, she lowered onto the edge of the bench. Sitting as far away from me as possible, her body hunched and her head turned.

I placed a rigid had on the table in front of her. "Tell me you did it," I demanded in a low, raking hiss. "Tell me it was *you* who imprinted my appearance to seduce Ty."

Marika peered up through a curtain of wavy black hair, hazel eyes insolent. "It's true. But I will *never* regret what I did. And if you're waiting for an apology, don't hold your breath." Her face brightened for a moment and she tapped her lip. "On second thought, please do."

Her arrogant words boiled my blood, which suddenly felt like liquid lava streaming through my veins. She had disrupted not only my life, but Ty's, and she didn't even regret it, could only make snide comments and aggravating jokes? "I can't believe you," I spat. "What you did was despicable, and disgusting, and…"

"And what you're doing isn't?" Fierceness edged her tone and her eyes rippled gold. "You're not meant to be with him. It's wrong and disgusting. After everything his family…" Her sentence cut off and she narrowed her eyes at me. "It doesn't matter. All that does matter is that Mr. Malau will *never* accept this. None of us will."

Rage bubbled inside my chest, and I had to struggle to hold back the urge to roar in anger. A strong part of me felt like ripping her throat out with my fangs. The rest felt like tearing the flesh from her bones with my bare hands. Neither was a good choice. My lips pursed together. I curled my fingers into fists, nails biting into my palms. In seconds, any and all self-control I had would vanish. With my body beginning to tremble with restraint, I forced myself from the bench. "If you ever come between us again, I will…"

I couldn't bring myself to speak the dark and enticing words, *kill you*. Instead, I shot back up the concrete stairs and into the cafeteria, before I could change my mind. I could feel the weight of Ty's eyes bearing down on me along with Troy's, Vanessa's, Dorian's, and Kendrick's. In my state of rage, I couldn't afford any of them a single glance. She's wrong.

I glared down at the blue-checkered tiles as I passed Ty's table, making my way into the girl's bathroom. My hands curled in a vice grip around the edge of the porcelain sink. A crack sounded with the appearance of thin, hairline fractures. With great effort, I pulled back the gripping urge to crush the porcelain to pieces and peered up.

The mirror spanning the entire blue-tiled wall above a succession of sinks reflected my face. My cheeks were tinted with a blood-colored luster and beads of sweat dotted my brow. I splashed cold water up in an attempt to cool the lava still surging through my veins. As I did, the door behind me swung open. Someone entered noisily, the sound of high heels clipping tiles with each step. Even without her vibrant, red mane reflected within the mirror, the sound was a dead giveaway. Only one girl in the whole student body loved fashion enough to religiously wear stiletto heels to school.

Vanessa paused then placed a hesitant hand along my shoulder. "Ty wanted to know if you're okay. Are you?"

I shuddered and turned, swallowing my hate for Marika. "She

shouldn't have done what she did." I frowned, studying Vanessa's sapphire eyes. They revealed no surprise and no confusion at my statement. "You knew, all along…"

"That they're Lycanthropes?" Vanessa smiled, pixie nose scrunching. "Of course I knew. We all grew up together. I've always known."

I couldn't control the pang of jealousy that invaded my heart. She was closer to Ty than I was, and they all accepted her. Why? What else did she know? I leaned my weight against the sink to block the damage I'd caused. "So, I'm guessing you know why they wanted me and Ty separated?"

Vanessa shrugged, seeming almost disinterested. "'Cause…apart from me, they keep to their own. They don't approve of Ty forging a relationship with a human. I'm the only one they have ever really accepted."

Trying to hide my surprise, I brushed the streaked-wet hair from my face. Human? She didn't know what I was? The thought of her being one of them *had* crossed my mind, but I'd quickly discarded it. She didn't have their matching honey-glazed eyes, tan complexion, black-as-night hair, or over-heated flesh. The only similarity, which she seemed to share with Marika, was her lack of scent. For a split second, I remembered a flash of gold. When she'd been hinting at Ty's hunting expedition during art class, I thought I had imagined it. She's been marked by an alchemist tattoo. It made sense, I supposed. Though I couldn't really figure out why she would have been marked when she clearly didn't seem aware of the monster before her. If any human knew what I was they'd be shit scared. Or running away screaming, I thought. Instead, she seemed comfortable and confident. And she had said the word herself. She thought I was just a human.

With a shrug, I turned away from her. In the mirror my pale

features were returning. "Tell Ty I'm okay, and I'll be in touch, soon."

Vanessa's reflection nodded. Then she turned and exited back through the bathroom door.

After stalling for a few minutes, I left the restroom to brave Dorian and Kendrick. They both sat staring at me with mirrored looks of suspicion. There was no doubt I would have to explain everything to them. But I needed time to get my thoughts together. What could I say to lessen the impact on both of them?

I sank into my seat, ripped open the chocolate bar, and took a big bite. "Don't ask," I mumbled. "I'll explain everything…later."

AFTER MY LAST class of the day, Dorian dragged me by the arm from the main building. Math was the only subject we shared, and he'd waited impatiently throughout the whole class. Now in the parking lot, a light drizzle fell, clouding the air. When we reached our cabriolet he released me. "Okay. I've waited long enough," he said, voice sharp as a tack. "Spill…"

With eyes raking over the parking lot, I slumped against our car. Other students were talking in clustered groups, but Kendrick didn't appear to be anywhere in sight. A breath of relief passed through my lips. Revealing what I knew—along with everything I had kept from Kendrick—to both of them at the same time would be hell. Just telling them would be hard enough without having to endure their matched reactions.

"Fine. But you have to promise to keep an open mind." When Dorian nodded, I drew in a deep breath and blurted out what he needed to hear. "Marika is a werewolf, too. But there's more to being a werewolf than either of us knew. They can transform themselves to resemble other people. It's called imprinting. She..." I broke off, choking on my next words that felt like acid in the back of my throat.

"I already knew that," Dorian said. "Well, the part about her being a werewolf. She might not smell like one, but the heat of her flesh matched what I had encountered when Troy was pummeling my face."

Disbelief stole across my expression. "You knew? And you didn't tell me?" Inside I felt betrayed, though I had no right to be. I had kept Ty's secret from Dorian in the first place. I had been the one to start this deception.

"You already hated her." Dorian shrugged, winking at yet another girl, this one a pretty brunette from math. "I didn't want to add any fuel to the fire." His hand rose to settle on my shoulder. "But what does her being a werewolf have to do with Ty?"

Dorian was far from dim. Of course I would never talk to Marika if it didn't have something to do with Ty. I detested everything about her. A fact Dorian knew all too well.

I looked up to his frowning face. What I was about to reveal would hurt, no matter how good he was at acting like he was over her. But he deserved to know the truth. "Marika was the girl in my bed, with Ty. She transformed herself to look like me. Dorian," I said, hurting to see the expressionless and distant look in his eyes. "Ty didn't know it was her."

Dorian shook his head and pinned his eyes shut. Tension-filled silence radiated from his body. "W-why," he finally spoke in a broken voice. "Why would she do that?" The etched lines across his brow betrayed the pain of what I had revealed. The feelings he still held for that bitch were deep.

I took his hand, squeezing in a show of comfort. "Because she knew I would find them. Dorian, she hates what we are." Her hate-fueled words swirled through my mind. *You're not meant to be with him. It's wrong and disgusting.* I shook off the bubbling rage that threatened to rise. No. She's wrong. "She used you, Dorian. It was her plan all along."

"I guess this means you and Ty will be patching things up," Dorian said, eyes straining. He was clearly trying to bury the heartache he was feeling.

"You're taking that prick back!" Kendrick's venom-filled voice sent a bolt of horror through my bones.

My head snapped up, startled. Kendrick was stalking forward through the dispersing students, scattering now with the onset of heavier rain. Dammit! The sudden pounding force of my heart sent stabbing pain through my ribs. I didn't want this. I didn't want him to find out this way. Yet defensiveness that I couldn't—and didn't want to—control, painted my words black. "You don't understand, Kendrick. It wasn't Ty's fault."

Kendrick's face darkened. He moved forward, droplets of rain falling down his face as he clutched my arm. "That doesn't excuse what he did. I won't let him hurt you again."

Dorian had moved to lean against the side of our rain-slicked car. He seemed oblivious to the deteriorating weather as he stared into the hazy distance.

And I wanted to rush to him, to comfort him, to not be dealing with my best friend's jealousy in the pouring rain. I ripped my arm free from Kendrick's grasp. Anger at his disruption to my plans clouded my judgment. I swiped the rain-soaked hair back from my face and gritted my teeth. "He thought it was me."

"Are you fucking kidding me? What? Was it too dark for him to tell he was about to screw some else? Is that what he told you? Are you seriously that blinded by him?" Kendrick's fingers tensed as though he wanted to strangle someone. "You can't believe this shit, Amelia. You can't forgive him. I won't let you."

Now you're telling me what I can and can't do? My eyes narrowed, turning cold enough to splinter ice. "I already have."

Kendrick's face hardened. The muscles of his jaw and throat bulged. He whirled on the spot and darted back across the puddled asphalt. Spurts of water shot up, drenching the lower half of his black cargo pants. In seconds, he disappeared past the bordering oak trees edging the far side of the parking lot.

My anger dissolved as I stared after him. Gut-wrenching guilt churned my stomach. I went to lunge, to take off after my best friend. A tight hand around my wrist stopped me.

"Let him go," Dorian said. He pushed back the rain-drenched hair from his forehead. "He needs time to process. Believe me, I know."

Defeated, my shoulders slumped. "How'd you become so wise?"

Dorian smiled, a clearly forced expression that didn't lift the dullness from his eyes. "You don't have to be a genius to see that he's in love with you."

"Oh." The guilt within me flared, scorching me from within. This was all my fault. I searched my brother's eyes. "Will you be okay?"

"Of course," Dorian said, walking around to the driver's side door. "Now let's go home. You need to figure out what you're going to say to make Kendrick feel better, before he returns."

A deep groan escaped my throat as I opened the passenger door and fell into the seat. "*Great!*"

I SPRAWLED across my princess-style bed with Lifehouse's album

Smoke and Mirrors playing. Angst sat like a building mountain of stones in the pit of my stomach while I sniffled. In my ear *It is what it is* was playing. The song made me wonder if Kendrick and I could get past this giant wall I'd built between us.

It was almost midnight, and he still hadn't returned home. Of the many calls I'd made to his phone, every one remained unanswered. He hates me. Inside my heart felt hollow. Kendrick knew I was back with Ty. But did he know what Ty was? I groaned and rolled onto my side, burying my head within the throw of purple-clad pillows.

A quiet buzzing, accompanied by the beep of my phone spiked my pulse with nerves. I bolted upright and swung my legs over the edge of the bed. The force sent pillows flying across the moonlit shadows of my room as I snatched my phone.

Please be Kendrick. With my hands trembling, I stared at the text. The message wasn't from my elusive best friend.

'*R we OK? XOXO Ty.*'

Instantly, I felt somehow worse than I already had. I hadn't called Ty yet. It had been a form of penance, a resolve not to allow myself happiness until I had made everything right with Kendrick. Still, although I felt worse, there was an evident skipping of my heart. The feeling doused some of the worry for my best friend. I punched in a quick reply. '*Sorry, I meant to call. But yeah, we're okay.*'

I turned on the black velvet bedside lamp and then pushed aside the thick mauve drapes. Their color matched that of the silk draped around the corner posts of my bed. Then I crouched on the wide base of the windowsill. Outside, the landscape was a ghostly blur under the night's thick fog. The moonlight shining through the fog emphasized twining tendrils of growing mist. A shiver ran like a rippling current down the length of my body. Kendrick, where are you?

My iPhone vibrated against my palm, making me flinch. '*I have 2 see U.*'

It was Ty again. I began to type a rebuttal when a quiet tap stopped me short. Something had hit the glass windowpane right beside me. Swallowing my surprise, I threw open the window. A dark figure was standing by the large oak tree just below my window. The thick, browning foliage partly obscured my sight of him. The dense fog muffled his scent. Still, there was no mistaking who stood down there. His stance, build, and the flash of gold eyes were a dead giveaway.

"What are you doing here?" I whispered.

Ty stepped out from the shadows, the glimmer of a smile lighting his face. "Stand back. I'm coming up."

Words of protest became trapped on my tongue. I watched as he sprang from the soggy ground, grasping the lower trunk of the solid oak. His body tensed, muscles bulging as he swung, launching his body feet-first toward the window. I jumped aside just in time as he flew in, landing as silently as a cat on the sill.

Ty dropped barefoot and dripping wet from his crouched position to stand. All he wore was a pair of board shorts, with steam rising from his bare chest. The sight caused my head to swoon. He stepped forward, drawing me into his strong arms. His hot touch forced my pulse to quicken, while the flare of his scent flooding my lungs left me breathless.

"I had to see you," Ty said, burying his head in the disarray of my tangled hair. "God I've missed you."

"Me too," I whispered, struggling to hold back the urge to extend my fangs. A question rose in my mind, spiked by the potency of his blood. "In the dreams, your scent...?" There the scent of his blood had been detectable, but not nearly as compelling as it was now. "It was weaker."

Ty's arms loosened around me, and I noticed a new scar along his collarbone. I peered up into the mosaic of his sparkling gold, amber, and russet eyes. "Amelia, I control *everything* in a dreamscape. And I didn't want to use your thirst for my blood to draw you back to me. I didn't want to manipulate you into forgiving me."

The memory of Ty with who I now knew had been Marika, forced my eyes to squeeze shut. Bursts of light exploded behind my eyelids. I could still see everything so clearly. Their exploring hands. Their frenzied kisses. Their bodies screaming for one another. Worst of all, I could almost hear their labored breath as their intensity had escalated. He thought it was me, my rational mind reminded. And I believed that. Still, belief didn't stop my heart from aching with the pierce of a tightening line of barbed wire.

Ty's hot hands found my cheeks, tilting my dropped face up to his. "It kills me to see you hurting. I would give *anything* to take it away." His head dipped and his lips trailed over mine. "Amelia, please forgive me. I can't bear to be without you."

"I forgive—" The sudden opening of my bedroom door killed my words.

"Amelia, I'm sorry. I—" Kendrick's words snapped off and he froze in the doorway, dropping the black calla lily he'd been holding. His nostrils flared, picking up Ty's unmasked scent. Disgust twisted his face. "Werewolf!"

Oh shit, oh shit! "Kendrick, please." My voice shook and my limbs trembled. "Just let me explain."

"Get out!" Kendrick hissed through gritted teeth, poison-filled eyes boring into Ty. He shot forward, fingers tensing into clawed weapons. "Are you deaf, or just suicidal? I said, get out!"

A warning rumbled from Ty's chest. He squared his shoulders. "I don't want to hurt you," he spoke slowly, receiving a grunt from

Kendrick in return. "But if you think I'll back down, you're mistaken."

With a physical standoff imminent, I forced my shaking limbs to move and darted between Ty and Kendrick. "Stop it, both of you!"

Kendrick paused, poisoned eyes narrowing at me. I turned to Ty. "I need you to leave." When his mouth opened in protest, I held up a silencing hand. "Ty, please, I need some time with Kendrick, *alone.*"

Ty's expression had hardened, eyes turning as cold as gold chips. Still he nodded, leaning forward to briefly join our lips. The connection forced a hiss to rasp from Kendrick's mouth, but he didn't budge. Then with a single backward glance, Ty dove through my open window and disappeared into the night.

I turned to Kendrick, my heart racing. He had folded his visibly shaking arms into tight bars across his chest, a barrier that separated us. His face was set in a frozen scowl.

"I'm sorry!" My eyes turned glassy and I loathed how helpless I felt. "I wanted to tell you, I tried…"

"*You knew,*" Kendrick cut in, irises blazing silver. "The guilt was written all over your face the first time I encountered *him.* It wasn't because you were worried I'd be against you dating a human. It was because you already knew what he was: our sworn enemy; a disgusting, filthy mutt. You've been lying to me this entire time."

My heart sank to the depth of my stomach. It turned in bile and what felt like teeth lining my churning gut. "I didn't want to lie. It tore me apart to keep this from you."

"All this time…" A dry mirthless laugh rolled from Kendrick's lips as he shook his head. "I thought we were friends. I thought I had earned your trust."

Tears spilled from my eyes and down my cheeks. I clutched Kendrick's crossed forearms in desperation. "Kendrick, I'm sorry. You're my best friend. I love you."

Kendrick's eyes pinned shut. "Don't say that." He yanked his arms free from my grasp, his expression sealed with visible anguish. "It just hurts." He turned with slumped shoulders and began walking away. I started after him. "Don't," he murmured. "I can't be around you right now."

The teeth clamped shut around my heart as I watched him escape out my door. A flood of icy tears streamed down my face.

Kendrick, I'm sorry.

THE RIDE TO school the next morning was excruciating. Kendrick sat in the front passenger seat, staring out the window and refusing to acknowledge me. Dorian as chauffeur, tried to cover the thick tension by blasting rave music. It didn't work.

Soon enough Dorian veered into the student parking lot. Surrounding the rectangular space was a barrier of skeleton oak trees. Their browning leaves had almost entirely dropped with the progression of fall. I groaned. Inside the border the asphalt was filled with arriving students. Great, an audience! And Ty was waiting for me, leaning against his reflective blue WRX with his training bag on the trunk. His hands were shoved into the pockets of his leather bomber jacket and he wore a pair of black shades. With the cloud-masked sky they seemed overkill.

Trying to limit my enthusiasm, I crossed the asphalt. Ty's arms spread wide to draw me in with an intimate embrace. His hot lips found the crown of my hair, his scent ballooning around me. "So, what's with the shades?"

Ty eyed me with bright-gold irises over the rims of his black-framed Oakleys. "Full moon's coming. Which *usually* wouldn't pose a problem, but with your kind around," he said without even a hint

241

of aversion, "controlling our body's metaphysical changes seems a bit more…challenging."

"Oh," I breathed. Guilt at being the reason for Ty needing to disguise his appearance tried to impede on my subconscious. But I had bigger problems to deal with. Dorian and Kendrick were fast closing in.

Dorian glanced up with a forced smile.

But Kendrick completely ignored us, eyes glaring ahead. He brushed past, knocking shoulders with Ty who was forced to take a step back. "You don't deserve her, mutt."

Whispers escalated around us. The angry interaction was hot on every student's lips. I stared after Kendrick as he disappeared into the sea of students entering the main building. My tongue felt like sand in my mouth.

Ty curved his arm around my waist and we began walking in the same direction. "Guess your talk didn't go too well."

My hand rose to my neck, scratching absentmindedly at my flesh. Ty didn't know that Kendrick's anger stemmed from more than just me seeing a werewolf. It was because he was in love with me. My heart was pounding against the clarity in my head. No more lies. I pulled us to a halt and spoke past the tightness clogging up my throat. "He's pissed because of what you are. But that's not all he's pissed at."

"He's in love with you," Ty said abruptly, a troubled smile thinning his lips.

"What?" I frowned, unable to read the rest of his expression hidden behind his dark Oakley lenses. "How do you…?"

"I'm not blind, Amelia. I see it in the way he looks at you, the way he watches you." Ty took a slow breath then exhaled. "The only question is…do you feel the same?"

My pulse thrummed through my ears, beating almost in time

with Ty's. He's nervous, I realized, worried that my heart could already belong to someone else.

I collected Ty's hands and lifted them to the flutter of my heart. "Feel that?" I asked, staring into my likeness reflected in his black lenses. Ty nodded and I smiled. "My heart beats *only* for you."

WHEN I ENTERED the cafeteria at lunch, my stomach was already knotted with dreaded expectation. Our two groups were still divided. With wet hair and smelling of chlorine from swim practice, Dorian sat by Kendrick's side at our new table. Ty sat at our old table with his friends, his training bag at his feet. Kendrick's eyes were set across the room at Ty, glaring with avid loathing. *This'll be fun*, I thought sarcastically, making for Ty's table.

"Hi." Vanessa peered up with a welcoming smile, while Troy and Marika scowled behind sunglass-shielded eyes. She motioned to the spare seat between Ty and her. "Joining us today?"

"Ah, hell no! You have gotta be kidding." Marika pushed her tray of sloppy Joes away with an expression of contempt. She must have been at the animal shelter that morning, because stray hairs marred her busty top. "How am I supposed to hold down my food with a vile leech sitting across the table?"

I placed a hand in front of Marika and leaned down to her level. My voice remained low and threatening. "You managed just fine all last week when you had your tongue down my brother's throat."

Troy stiffened while Marika growled, lips parting to reveal sharpened wolf-like teeth.

But it was Ty who broke the mounting tension, rising to his feet. "Marika, knock it off. I order…"

"Hah," Troy spat, folding his arms across his overinflated chest.

I straightened as his fiery gaze slid from me to Ty. "Ty, you may be our alpha. And you can order us out of your business all you like— even if it does have *everything* to do with us. But you can't force either of us to like your decisions any more than you can force us to like *her*." He slid a pointed finger my way.

Ty went to move at Troy, scarred hands fisted as I darted in front of him. I afforded a quick glance across the room at Kendrick who was watching us with hate-filled eyes. "Ty, it's okay. I wasn't going to stay. I just…"

At my broken-off words, Ty sighed. "It's alright," he said, slow and even. "I get it. You should go to him."

Ty's perception and unselfish gesture warmed my heart. "Thank you," I mouthed. Our lips joined with a touch so brief I regretted pulling back so fast.

Before I could change my mind and decide to brave lunch with the wolves, I turned, heading back to Kendrick and Dorian. Intrigued students craned to see as I walked past, creating a sea of turned heads in my wake. I ignored every one of them. The sight of my best friend's hunched and stiff form made an audience the least of my worries.

When I was only steps from Kendrick, his disgusted stare tore from Ty and propelled straight at me. "Don't sit here on my account. I know you would rather be with *him*," he growled, acid dripping with the words.

Of course I hadn't expected this to be easy. But after coming over here to sort things out, his venom-drenched attitude was seriously starting to piss me off. Growing resentment unfurled like a fast-blooming rose within my chest. Words hissed from my mouth, "What the hell is your problem?"

Kendrick's eyes bore into mine with hate. "You," he said, then pointed at Ty, "and *that*!"

Dorian shot up between us, tight fingers curling around my arm and pushing me back. A low rumble emerged from his throat. "Amelia, this is *not* helping."

All close-proximity chatter had ceased. Now a throng of eyes stared while hushed whispers erupted at the developing commotion.

"Just go, sit with Ty," Dorian implored. "I'll talk to Kendrick. Try to get him to understand."

Every fiber of my being screamed for me to not let this go. Though deep down I knew there was no point. Kendrick clearly couldn't stand to be anywhere near me, and a calm conversation was a fool's hope. "Fine," I mouthed, and then turned to stalk away.

Ty stood awaiting my return as I stomped back toward him. "Is everything okay?"

Troy and Marika simply ignored that fact that I was even present under a warning stare from Vanessa.

Letting irritation and desperation at my best friend's hatred prompt my words, I was about to reply. An audible buzzing against my backside stopped me. It was my iPhone signaling a new text. I freed it from my jeans and peered at the screen. The text was from Kendrick.

'I H8 what UR doing. But I could never H8 U.'

My eyes skittered sideways to rest on Kendrick. He was slouched in his seat and staring blankly. His phone was clutched so tightly in his hand that his knuckles protruded. It was almost surprising that the phone was still in one piece. Claws tore at my heart. He made no move to look up. In fact he was sitting so still, he almost resembled a sorrow-filled statue.

I sighed long and hard, lifting my eyes to Ty. "No, but it will be."

~

I HAD a break from the Kendrick and Ty issue in my afternoon classes, at least until last period. Psychology. A class I shared with both Ty and Kendrick. *Fan-freaking-tastic!*

Armed with the boarding magazine I'd skipped school to buy so I'd have a peace offering, I walked into class. I glanced around the room, my palms sweating. Over the heads of students already occupying their regular desks, one thing was glaringly apparent. Kendrick wasn't here.

With the sounding of the final bell, the teacher entered. I frowned and crossed the room to sit beside Ty. Mr. McKenna called the class to attention and began reading aloud from the textbook.

Ty's warm hand found mine under the desk and squeezed. "Where's Kendrick?"

I peered over my shoulder at the empty desk Kendrick usually occupied. My heart contracted. He's not here because of me. Guilt coupled with defeat intruded on my emotions. "I don't know," I replied, gaining a dirty look from our teacher.

Ty pulled his calloused hand from mine to slip a note across the desk. *I want you to meet my father.*

Shocked, I met his Oakley-shielded eyes, fingers twitching for the chocolate hidden in my jacket. "You can't be serious," I whispered. Nerves swirled like a tornado through my chest. "With everything that's gone wrong, all we need is more drama."

Ty smiled, pearly white teeth gleaming through parted lips. "That's why I want you to meet him now," he stated. "If he finds out any other way, he'll never accept us. But if we're up front…"

Ty's words broke off when Mr. McKenna cleared his throat in our direction. We both glanced down at our textbooks, pretending to follow his reading.

After a few minutes, Ty scribbled into his notebook. I peered over his arm to read the message. *If he can see who you really are, the girl I trust and adore, then maybe…*

"Maybe what?" I hissed.

Ty scribbled a response down before moving his arm to reveal what he'd written. *Maybe we can get past all this drama, and just start being us.* He tipped his head, peering over his glasses with vibrant, hopeful eyes.

Freeing the chocolate bar from my pocket, I took a nervous bite. I looked away, staring blankly out the window at the darkening sky of ash-filled clouds. All this time, Ty had trusted my every instinct and never once condemned me for my choices. Even after Kendrick's reaction and the revelation of his daunting feelings for me, Ty was still standing by me. I had known this day would come, eventually. In the end, if I wanted to have a real future with Ty, our families would have to know the truth. We couldn't hide forever. So, it was my turn to trust Ty.

Swallowing hard, I looked back at him. "Okay."

Ty's expression was a picture of perfect surprise. "Okay? Are you sure?"

I bit my lip. There was nothing I was less sure about. Still there was one thing I knew I would never doubt again: Ty. It was time to put all the faith I had onto him. "I'm sure. Let's do this."

CHAPTER 18

"Where are you off too?" Kendrick's voice cut through the air as I darted to the front door.

Apart from his text, they were the first non-loaded words he'd said to me since the cafeteria scene yesterday. I whirled to catch him resting against the arched entry to the kitchen. Quiet music from the snowboarding app on his iPhone hummed from his cargo pants. He was eyeing me from head to toe. My initial instinct was to lie, to not awaken the hatred I had previously endured in his now level expression. But I couldn't. My lies had already caused too much trouble. I had to be honest, no matter the cost. "I'm going out, with Ty."

Kendrick's jaw clenched. The muscles along his neck corded. "Where?"

"I don't know," I replied honestly. All I did know was that Ty would be waiting down the road to take me out on a date he'd planned solely himself. "Why do you care, anyway?"

Kendrick crossed his arms over his chest. "Because I don't trust him." He sighed then dropped his arms. "I still care about you, Amelia. Just promise me you'll be careful."

I wanted to say, *I don't need to be careful with Ty*, but didn't. Instead, with my heartstrings tugging, I nodded and opened the door to leave.

"By the way," Kendrick called after me, stalling my escape. "You look beautiful."

I squeezed my eyes shut and slammed the door behind me. I hurried down the paved driveway, while gusts of wind blew russet leaves in swirls around me. Thought and emotion rushed through my mind. Kendrick's attitude was shifting; he was making a clear effort, restraining his words and reactions. And I just left him. I sighed again, glaring at my low heels and tugging at the hem my purple A-line dress. I was far from comfortable. It wasn't by any means revealing, but it was still a dress. This time I hadn't been coerced into wearing the outfit by my mom, who was so thrilled Ty and I had patched things up that she extended my Friday night curfew to midnight. No, tonight for probably the first time ever, I actually wanted to look *nice*.

A billowing breeze came off the rolling waves of Rye Beach to my right. Ty's faint scent hung in its swirls. He was already waiting. Right now there wasn't time to get into another argument with Kendrick. I'd fix everything later, I decided, trying without success to push my best friend from my thoughts.

Ty stood just down the road, backed by browning trees that lined one side of the gated residential street. He was leaning against his freshly washed WRX, wearing black jeans and a white stretched shirt. His hands were buried in the pockets of his leather jacket.

As I closed the space between us, my pulse galloped. My arms flung around Ty's neck and I breathed in his mouthwatering scent. Instantly my worries for Kendrick disintegrated. In preparation for tonight, I'd downed a giant glass of blood before leaving the house. It helped dull my thirst for his blood, though not my desire. Ty hugged me back with enthusiasm, lifting my feet off the ground. Yet something felt off. His fingers pressed into my lower back with a force that seemed desperate. Through his locked embrace I noticed stiffness along his arms and chest.

I arched back to glimpse the reserved expression bordering his flat eyes. "What's wrong?"

Ty lowered my feet to the road. His hands remained locked in a clasp behind my back. "There's been a slight change of plans."

"Hmm," I mumbled, pursing my lips. "Why do I get the feeling I'm not going to like these *changes*?"

Ty's flat expression didn't alter. "My dad agreed to meet you. We're having dinner with him…tonight."

Nausea flooded my insides, causing my stomach to twist like a towel being wrung out. I felt like vomiting. "Tonight," I squeaked, wishing I had heard him wrong, but knowing I hadn't. "Like now?"

Ty smiled a tense and totally non-reassuring smile. "It'll be fine. I promise."

TY TURNED off the winding road and drove through a set of spear-pointed wrought-iron gates. My heart sank to the pit of my stomach. An imposing estate rose above the horizon. It was monstrous, rendered slate-gray, and set in multiple levels. Its large, rectangular windows watched me like eyes.

The passenger door opened and I blinked away from the structure. I tried to still the quivering of my hands as I looked to Ty. In seconds I'd have to contend with a doubled onslaught of Ty's potent scent. I groaned, secretly longing for the nasal tube.

Ty held out a hand and smiled down at me. "We don't have to do this. If it's too soon—"

"We're already here," I cut in. I took Ty's hand and allowed him to pull me from the car. With a deep centering breath, I squared my shoulders. I wished I had a secret sipper of blood hidden in this body-hugging dress *and* a full block of chocolate. "Let's just do this —before I change my mind."

As Ty led the way into and then through his house, the melodic playing of a piano rose in the air. All too soon, the hall gave way to an expansive room, fully furnished in leather and beechwood. The left wall was constructed entirely of glass sliding doors that led out to a balcony. Beyond their rails was a spectacular view of the distant mountains. The sun's radiant, crimson orb now dipped below their peaks.

Positioned at the far end of the room was a baby grand piano. A man wearing an ash-colored suit with his back to us was keying the melodic song.

My heart pounded in negation as Ty pulled me toward the man who sat, seemingly unaware of our arrival. The scent of their collective blood soared. "Father, I would like you to meet my girlfriend, Amelia."

Mr. Malau's fingers ceased with a disturbing thud across the keys and he twisted to face us. My eyes widened at the aged, mirror reflection of Ty. He had the same dark tan complexion and reflective, gold eyes below black-as-night hair. Ty's expression the day I had first met him had been open and curious. His father's was nothing like that. His propelled a mixture of suspicious anger and unmasked resentment.

"I guessed as much," Mr. Malau remarked. His gold-pulsing eyes raked over me like I was the vilest thing he had ever seen.

A throat-constricting gulp did nothing to clear their scent or the tingle from my gums. I extended a sweat-dampened hand. "Mr. Malau, thank you for allowing me into your beautiful home."

Ty's father stared down at my outstretched hand as though it were rotting vermin. He sniffed the air, flaring his nostrils. His eyes slid sideways to Ty and his mouth thinned into a tense line. "Dinner is waiting." He rose from the piano bench and walked past us back the way we had entered.

Ty laced his fingers through mine and squeezed as we began to follow. "You're doing great."

Mr. Malau paused inside a squared opening near the center of the hall and pushed a button on the intercom. "Harper, dinner is ready." He then positioned himself at the head of a long, beechwood dining table.

"So, the brat is home early?" Ty pulled out a velvet-cushioned chair for me and took a seat next to his father, picking up the white folded napkin from his plate. Before us was a large platter of spit-roasted pork, surrounded by an array of colorful vegetables. "I thought he wasn't expected until the morning."

Mr. Malau grasped the bottle of red in front of him and popped the cork. It launched from the bottle and flew across the room, connecting with the wall only an inch from an enormous oil painting. Pictured was Mr. Malau, a young boy, who at a second glance I realized was a very young version of Ty, and a woman who was cradling an infant. My eyes narrowed at the face of Ty's mother. She was breathtakingly beautiful with billowing raven hair, delicate tan features, and full rose-red lips. Yet there was something about her appearance that struck me with confusion. Her eyes weren't the gold or even the honey-glazed with bordering green of werewolves. They were blue. Not the silvery-blue of vampires, or even the lackluster blue of most humans. Instead, they were the intense blue of a sun-speckled ocean.

"Well, I would have preferred him to arrive tomorrow." Mr. Malau's stern voice redirected my wandering gaze while snuffing the rising questions in my mind. His expression hardened, shifting to me. "But some things in life *cannot* be controlled."

The sound of footsteps bounding down stairs broke the tension growing in the air. A second later an exuberant boy blew into the room. The moment he caught sight of me he tripped on the contemporary rug that spanned almost the entire floor space of the room. The boy's jaw dropped and his tan skin paled. His deep-brown eyes stared at me in complete horror.

Ty swiftly broke the thickening silence, pointing at the staring boy. "This is my brother, Harper." He then turned his head to scowl his sibling. "Harper, stop staring. It's rude."

"This is Ty's *friend,* Amelia," Mr. Malau explained, his voice drenched with contempt.

Harper broke his stare on me, nervous eyes flicking to his father. "But she's a vampire."

Mr. Malau motioned with an authoritative hand for the young boy to sit. He wordlessly complied, sliding into the spot opposite Ty, close to the safety of his father. "Ty informs me that Amelia and her family are *different*. They *do not* hunt or kill." His skewering eyes turned on me. "You will have to forgive my son. We are not used to encountering *your kind*," he enunciated the words with disdain, "on neutral terms." He poured wine into his crystal glass then handed the bottle to Ty. "An imported French drop."

Ty began topping my glass and I looked at his father questioningly. I desperately wanted a glass to distract my thoughts from their blood, but this wasn't an unsupervised party and neither of us was anywhere near drinking age.

Mr. Malau caught my eye and glowered, his narrowed eyes

boring into mine. "Sorry, Amelia, but we don't stock anything richer *unless* you intend on tapping a vein."

Ty's head snapped up, his hand on mine tightening. "Father!"

The intensity of their scent grew so thick I felt my fangs pricking through my gums. An image—so clear and surreal—of biting Ty in the hot tub, rushed through my mind. Could he know? My stomach lurched, the taste of dead blood licking my throat. The rush of blood through my veins quashed any lingering nerves and gave way to tumbling indignation. In light of my enemy's unbridled resentment, a primal need to defend myself rose. I gritted my teeth, letting my fangs slide free. "I drank a pint of blood before Ty picked me up. But there's always room for more."

Ty coughed beside me, almost choking, while Harper's face faded to gray. Mr. Malau's eyes narrowed. His expression revealed no shock at my outburst, but rather, a basking expectation that I had readily fulfilled.

Regret instantly coursed through me, retracting my fangs. My challenging eyes dropped. I was here to show Ty's father I wasn't a threat, that my family and I were different. Not prove his suspicions right with uncontrollable outbursts. I shrank back in my seat, my thirst for their blood quashed. "I'm sorry, I didn't mean…"

"*She's* the one," Mr. Malau's sharp tone cut through me like a knife. My eyes snapped up to view his glare. He drew in a long breath, sniffing the air. Utter disgust wrinkled his nose and face.

"Father, don't!" Ty pleaded.

"Ahh…" Mr. Malau's lips curved with an amused smile. "She doesn't know."

"Know what?" Harper questioned. His voice was shaky but his color had returned.

"Harper, shut up!" Ty growled. His intense stare didn't shift from his father who had braced himself, hands strained into tense claws that bit into the wooden tabletop. "Don't do this."

Fear and mind-muddling confusion caused my body to tremble. What didn't I know? I looked sideways at Ty, keeping his father in my peripheral vision. "What's going on?"

Ty looked away while a sinister chuckle rumbled from Mr. Malau's chest. "I picked up your scent on him, all those months ago, in Alaska. The smell of monstrous fear and blood-hungry desire."

My insides squeezed and my muscles grew tight. The sound of my voice was a quiet echo. "*Alaska?*"

"You may pretend not to be a killer…" Mr. Malau tilted his head and leaned back in his seat. Smugness careened across his face. "But *I* know the truth. You have tried to kill, to drain a human of their lifeblood. Soon enough you will again."

The breath was knocked from my lungs. Too many memories were flooding my mind. The boy who had appeared in the alley outside *Pulse* had been intent on killing me. My surreal dream had revealed Ty as that very same boy—but when I'd asked, Ty had completely denied having ever been to Alaska. Last, I recalled Ty's words after I had lost control and drank his blood at Troy's party. *I knew what you were from the very first moment I laid eyes on you.* My head was shaking back and forth. My brain throbbed against my skull. No, it can't be.

"I see the realization in your eyes," Mr. Malau stated. "Ty was there that night, and you know it. He was there to kill you."

Ice invaded my chest and tears clouded my eyes. With my heart beating with a rapid ache that stole my breath, I turned my sight to Ty. "*You?*"

Everything was suddenly adding up, holes being filled with a truth I couldn't deny. All this time, Ty's absences, his excuses, the scars… The hunting expeditions had never been for fresh game.

J.L. MYERS

Vanessa had hinted at the truth on a number of occasions. But I had been too blind to see, too caught up to force the truth from him. All this time, Ty had been hunting vampires.

Adrenaline spiked my veins and I kicked my seat back. It toppled to the ground, connecting with the wall behind me with a crack of wood and plaster. Ty jumped to his feet, his face parchment white. "You lied to me!" I tried to scream, but what came out was a croaked whisper.

"Amelia, please," Ty pleaded, stepping forward with raised hands. It almost looked like he expected me to lunge at him like the monster we all knew I was.

I spluttered a cough, clearing my throat. "Don't you dare come near me! I don't know you. I never did." With my muscles bunched, I darted from the room and Ty's house, fleeing my enemies' turf, fleeing Ty. The thought that invaded my mind was far from fleeting. It imprinted across my heart. Ty was my enemy.

WITHOUT MAKING a sound to alert Kendrick, I flew through the foyer of my house and launched upstairs. With my heels clutched in my hands, I slumped against the inside of my bedroom door. Instantly an unmistakable scent alerted my nostrils. My eyes sifted through the darkness of my room to a moonlit figure perched on my windowsill. Ty's chest heaved with ragged breath. The hard lines of his pecs were visible through the thin fabric of his shirt. Frost-chilled air blew through my open window. The force billowed the dark curtains in a ghostly wave around him.

Against the anger still surging through my entire body, my heart fluttered. My skin prickled—at the sight of him or from the icy air, I wasn't sure. With effort I retained the bitter edge to my low tone. "What do you think you're doing here?"

"Amelia, please." Ty pushed off the sill. "You have to hear me out."

"Why," I spat, fighting the temptation to strike out at something. "So you can tell me it wasn't you? That you were never in Anchorage? That you *didn't* intend on killing me?"

"It was me." Ty sighed. He blinked slowly. "I was in the club when you entered. And I saw you let that drunken guy take you out back. I could smell your desire for his blood. I knew you planned to attack him."

In a moment's pause, I recalled what Kendrick had said to me as I'd left for my date. His words had been simple. *Because I don't trust him.* Kendrick's suspicions had been right all along. When I replied after a few long moments, I had intended my tone to sound harsh and sharp. Instead, it emerged toneless and hollow. "Why were you there?"

"My father was tracking a rogue vampire in Anchorage. As long as we're not taking any down without just reason, the Vampire Council doesn't seem to mind. Really, I think they prefer it. Saves them from getting their hands dirty. This one had already killed three people. You must have seen it on the news—all those people *killed by animals?* Anyway, I went with him." Ty glanced out my open window, eyes staring at the bright, moonlit sky. "He sent me to scope out *Pulse*. It's a popular vampire hangout." The distant look in his eyes faded and his focus returned to me. "And that's when I saw you."

I could so clearly remember the night my existence had changed. Mom and Uncle Caius had been oblivious to my growing hunger as I crept down the dark hall. The breaking news playing from the lounge room had been a distraction.

J.L. MYERS

I shook my head and dropped onto the foot of my bed, one arm curling around the corner post. A daunting notion hit me like a jolt of electricity. "You thought *I* was the killer?"

Ty came over and lowered beside me, leaning back against his scarred arms. "It was a possibility. But I had to be sure."

Letting my eyelids droop closed, I could remember that night with startling clarity. The glint of a weapon had caught the moonlight at his side. *"Kill me,"* I'd cried. *"I'm a fucking monster!"*

And the boy had faltered. Ty had faltered, surprised words escaping his lips. *"You* want *to die?"*

The panic I had experienced that night, the desperation of realizing that my mom and uncle's revelation was true, surged through me now, just as gripping. Just as chilling. *I'm a living, breathing monster, a blood-hungry vampire.* I bit my lip, head twisting to face Ty. "Why didn't you?" When he frowned, I said in a fading voice, "Kill me. Why didn't you kill me?"

The muscles along Ty's neck constricted with an audible gulp. "I was going to. I really was."

Alarm shot through my heart, quelled in an instant by his next words.

"But I couldn't. Your reaction to what you did to that guy, the pain and regret that contorted your face... It was like nothing I'd ever seen." He shook his head. "And my father was wrong. Your scent holds no comparison to a true monster's. It's volatile, I won't deny that. Like a warning of an approaching electrical storm. But it's the purest scent I have ever encountered. It's as pure as your very soul."

He took my hands and threaded his rough fingers through mine. "I knew then that you weren't a cold-blooded killer, just a scared and confused girl. Your blatant self-loathing as you begged for death... Your humanity is part of everything you are. It stirred something in me. I didn't care what you'd done, or what you were." His head dipped, lips grazing mine. The intimate touch rippled with a shiver down my entire body. "I wanted to know you, Amelia, to comfort and pull you into my arms. To tell you that everything would be okay."

"But Kendrick appeared," I whispered, made breathless and dizzy by his blood.

"I didn't want to leave." Ty released my hands and folded me in his strong arms. "And I will never leave you, again. I don't care who stands against us."

My hands connected with the hard outline of his chest, fingertips feeling their way over the many scars that marked him there. I clutched his shirt and pulled his body against mine. "No more lies."

Ty smiled, his lips finding mine and parting them gently. His kiss sealed an unspoken promise as I reclined, drawing his body onto mine. His voice emerged with escalating breath, melting away the last of my anger. "Amelia, I couldn't stay away from you even if my life depended on it."

Warmed by his touch, scent, and words, I pulled him closer, my body telling him how much I needed him too. Ty's body pressed harder into mine, hungry and pinning me against the soft mattress. Fire scorched where his calloused hands crept up my thigh and under the hem of my dress. I gasped, raking rigid fingers down over the muscles and scars of his back. When I reached the bottom of his shirt, I tugged. Ty's chest lifted off mine, hungry eyes watching me as I removed the covering. He leaned down, kissing me with a hard ferocity that surprised and excited me. My pulse hammered with anticipation. Then a rumble, halfway between a growl and a moan, vibrated through his chest. Instantly every muscle along his body snapped tight.

"Wait!" he uttered.

I was breathing as hard as Ty as he pulled away. My body screamed against his retraction. "What's wrong?"

Worried Kendrick had entered my eyes darted to my bedroom door. No one was there. With a quick sigh, I frowned and followed Ty's gaze through my open window. The bright, full moon, littered with delicate gray clouds, gleamed down on us.

"I'll shift soon," Ty said, as though it were the most normal statement in the world. He leaned back on his elbow, his slowing breath hot on my skin as he pressed his lips to mine. "We don't have long."

The touch did little to disintegrate my disappointment. "Oh…"

"I'll stay till you're asleep," Ty added.

I looked up and noticed dark circles lining his eyes. He looked incredibly tired. "You don't have to stay…"

Ty smiled. "It's okay." He strung his arm under my neck, guiding my head against his bare chest as he rolled onto his back. The beat of his slowing, steady heart echoed through my ears. "I want to."

With his scent filling my lungs, warmth cascaded throughout my body. The sensation was calming and made me feel safe and totally secure. There was nowhere in the world I would rather have been. *I belong to you*, my internal voice whispered. All I said out loud was, "Good night, Ty."

The mental and physical exertion of the night was creeping up fast. My eyelids blinked with exhausted weight. Sleep claimed me moments later, a nightmare forming within my subconscious mind.

I stood in a forest clearing with Ty before me. His entire body shook. A sickening crack sounded, followed by a low growl. Ty fell to the snow-topped grass on all fours. Another agonizing growl tore from his throat as his back arched up. I went to rush forward, but I couldn't move. An invisible force planted my feet to the ground. I struggled to break the hold. Then my vision shattered.

The sound of continuing cracks transcended into waking reality, ripping me from my nightmare. It was the crunch of bones breaking. My eyes flung open. Clouds fogged up my consciousness, disorientating me. But one thing struck me. Coarse hair scratched at my skin. I wasn't alone. Limbs wrapped around my body, trapping me within the concrete embrace of a fur-covered beast.

A blood-curdling scream bubbled up my throat while my heart jumped to marathon speed. I thrashed, loosening the beast's grip.

Instantly alert, the creature startled.

It leaped away from me, razor claws cutting my flesh. Pain radiated down my arm, while the scent of spilled blood reached my nostrils. I took no notice. My eyes were wide, unwaveringly fixed on the black beast as it flew through the air. It moved at a speed that was mind boggling and landed without a sound in the center of my moonlit room. Its tall ears were perched forward and its canines were covered. The creature looked like a wolf, but unlike any I had ever encountered before. Its solid and muscular body was entirely covered in dense, black hair. With its size, it was more comparable to a bear.

As I stared, frozen not in horror but awakening confusion, the creature moved forward. It covered the space between us in just one bound. I knew I should have backed away or lashed out, but I didn't. There was just *something* about the creature that kept me planted. It was a recognition I couldn't quite grasp.

It slowly reached out with an enormous paw—claws retracted —to graze my arm. I followed its touch to find deep lacerations scoring my flesh. Blood ran in thick rivulets down my arm, collecting at my elbow. Fat drops fell steadily onto my lavender sheets, and what looked to be shredded black denim. Even as I watched, still struggling against the block in my mind, the blood began to clot and dry. The rapid healing process had already begun.

When no more blood oozed from the cuts, my eyes rose to the beast. The gold of its eyes shone with brilliance, holding my stare. Within that mosaic of color, a slow understanding etched through the fog clouding my mind. Realization dawned on me. I wasn't looking at a monster, an intruder or enemy, or even a creature I should fear in any way. I was looking at the boy I was falling for, at his magnificent wolf form. I was looking at Ty.

A sound at the end of the hallway snapped me out of my reverie. Footsteps, and more than one set, were hammering our way. My heart jumped into my throat. "Quick, you have to go!" I cried. When Ty hesitated, I pushed against his shoulders. "Now, they're coming!"

Conflicting emotions showed across Ty's wolf expression before he bounded across the room. His fluid movements blurred with speed as he leaped from my open window. In a panic, I shoved the shredded denim—which I now realized had been Ty's jeans—under the sheets. Then I tugged the quilt up, covering my slashed arm and bloodied purple dress.

A split second later, Kendrick exploded into the room. He was wearing nothing but boxers and a *Red* T-shirt. Dorian was right on his tail. The chandelier flared on, casting away the shadows of my room with glorious light.

"What's wrong?" Kendrick shouted, panicked eyes darting around my room. "Are you okay?"

Closing my eyes, I shook my head and waved a dismissive hand. I almost expected my mom to storm the room next. "I'm fine. I just had a nightmare." Shit! I bit my lip and cursed myself. After resolving not to keep secrets, I was lying again, telling whopping half-truths. But how could I tell them what had happened? That Ty had been here? That he'd changed while asleep, and that I had the marks to prove it? It was an accident. But Kendrick would never understand.

Dorian sucked in a deep breath and rolled his eyes. "Geez, Sis, you scared the shit outta me!"

Beside him, Kendrick raised one brow, regarding me with wary eyes. It was a look I understood well, one that filled me with dread. He's not buying it. He had stormed into the room with as much force and alarm as my brother had, but it was obvious from his reserved expression that he still hadn't entirely forgiven me. Clearer than that was the fact that he didn't trust me, or believe my mounting lies.

"Well," Dorian said, looking from me to Kendrick. "I've got a date tomorrow. So if I'm gonna bring my A game, I need a few more hours sleep."

Ignoring Dorian's innuendo, I broke from Kendrick's watchful gaze. The alarm clock on my bedside table read 12:15AM. That's why she isn't here. Mom was still at her meeting. Mindful of keeping my arm concealed, I looked back to the guys. "Yeah, sure, see you in the morning."

Dorian slipped past Kendrick without further encouragement, leaving my best friend lingering mute by my door. His eyes were still set on me, radiating distrust. I forced a smile, which he didn't return as he strode across the room to my open window. He peered out into the bright night sky, lit by the glowing full moon. Then he tugged the panes shut and secured the latch. My eyes remained fixed on him as he retraced his steps. Fear that he would rush to me and tear back the shielding covers had my pulse throbbing. But he didn't look at me or even utter a single word. Relief washed over me.

But as he was about to close the door behind him, he paused, nose tilting up to test the air. I could smell it now, too. Without the fresh night breeze flowing through my bedroom window, the scent of my own blood lifted in the air. It was still drying on the remains of Ty's jeans and my tainted sheets and dress.

"Whose blood do I smell?" Kendrick swiveled to face me. Worry and anger stained his expression.

My eyes dropped and my head turned, preparing for the backlash that would erupt with my confession. As my lips parted to speak, something caught my eye. It was the glass of blood I had downed before leaving to meet with Ty. It was perched beside the alarm clock and rimmed with half an inch of drying blood. I pointed to the glass, shrugging. "Midnight snack."

Kendrick's eyes narrowed. For a long moment he just stood there, watching me. Each passing second raised the rapid contractions of my heart. Then without speaking he turned, dousing the chandelier before closing the door behind him.

At the sound of his retreating footsteps, I snatched a piece of chocolate from the bedside drawer. I shoved it into my mouth and fell back against the mountain of purple pillows. *Shit. Shit. Shit!* I wanted to slap myself. To be punished for breaking my own resolution. The continued strain between Kendrick and I was wearing thin. And I knew it was all because of me. In the morning, I would fix *everything*.

CHAPTER 19

Sunlight woke me after a night of restless sleep. I slipped into black cotton pants and a long-sleeved purple top. Better Kendrick not see the angry, red welts painted across my arm. I was about to head downstairs when my iPhone buzzed from my bedside. It was Ty. I snatched the phone and raised it to my ear.

"Amelia!" Ty's voice was frantic. I was almost surprised to hear a human voice, rather than the growl of a wolf. "Are you alright?"

"What? Of course I am." I cringed at the memory of last night. He was asking if *I* was alright? Ty was the one who'd transformed. He was the one who'd had every bone in his body broken and reset, and his flesh stretched out to cover his expanding beastly shape. Not me. "Are you?"

His next words escaped in a rush. "I called as soon as I could. I'm so sorry. I didn't want to leave you."

"Ty, where are you?" I knew I had resolved to fix things with Kendrick, but I couldn't leave Ty in such despair. I had to at least prove to him that I was fine. "Can I see you?"

"No!" Alarm rang in Ty's voice. "I mean, it's not safe. I'm not stable." He sighed, a terrible rattling sound. "Tomorrow afternoon. Meet me at Mount Major, below the bluff beside the river."

The same forest Kendrick and I hunted in. My throat felt dry and I swallowed, recalling how hard it had been not to kill my prey. "Okay," I said, blinking away the memory. "I'll see you then."

Pushing my anxiety aside, I hung up and bounded downstairs. Dorian and Kendrick were both in the kitchen, busy stuffing their faces. The space was in disarray. Littering the limestone counter was an omelet-rimmed mixing bowl, a bacon-spattered frying pan, burned toast, and scattered eggshells.

Dorian glanced up at my entrance. Then his eyes slid sideways to Kendrick who had ceased eating to sit motionless and stiff at the breakfast bar.

It's time. With a deep inhale, I planted my hands on my hips and walked over to him. "Kendrick, I need to speak with you, and I'm not taking no for an answer."

Kendrick's eyes flicked to me, his expression provoking. Irritation scratched beneath my skin. The urge to slap that look off his face grated on me, but I thought better of it. Instead, I grabbed his hand, pulling him from the bar and out the terrace doors. He stomped with reluctance and yanked the hood of his boarding jacket over his head as I led the way. Down the stone path to the hedge-bordered alcove, I forced him onto the stone bench. It was the same one Ty and I had sat at before the auction. Memories of that day lifted in my mind. It was the day I had learned how wolf transformations worked. It was the same day Ty had unintentionally shattered my heart.

With great effort, I forced all thoughts of Ty and that day from my mind and focused on Kendrick. He sat at the end of the bench, elbows resting on his knees and resentment pouring from his hunched stance.

I reached forward, placing a gentle hand across his knee. "I know you're still mad at me, and I understand why." Kendrick frowned, lips parting as if he were about to rebut, but then thought better of it. Instead, his head turned, meeting my staid expression. Taking the silence as encouragement to go on, I said, "I should have told you. Not kept all this from you. But with everything between us…I just didn't want to hurt you any more than I already had. I never, *ever*, want to be the cause of your pain."

The slightest warmth returned to my best friend's face. "I know it's not fair that I'm still...*upset*. I don't want to be. But just the thought of you and *him*," he spat the word then hesitated, taking a deep breath. "I can't understand what you see in him. You know it will never work." The anger from his expression had completely subsided. He turned on the bench to face me, drawing his posture straight. A light breeze had picked up, rustling the leaves of the surrounding hedges. "When your mom finds out—and you know eventually she will—she is going to freak. Besides, you could outlive him ten times over."

The sun peeked over the barricading hedges. Water pooled in my eyes from the blinding orb coupled by his stinging words. Like trying to see underwater, my vision turned misty. I turned my head away. Everything he had said was the truth. A normal relationship could never work. How could Ty and I stay together when we're so different?

After meeting Ty's dad, I knew my mom would be just as against our relationship as he had been. Plus with her position on the Portsmouth Vampire Council, I didn't even want to consider the complications. Tightness constricted my throat. *Uncle Caius.* What would he do? Being a royal like Kendrick, and one of the reigning

Pure Bloods, he'd have to be explicitly against our union. Ty and I were supposed to be mortal enemies. And the aging issue was another huge hurdle that we still hadn't covered in realistic detail.

Unable to look Kendrick in the eye, I stared at the lush grass while breathing in its freshly cut scent. A sigh escaped my throat as the weight of the heavy task ahead of me settled in. "I know it isn't going to be easy. But it will work. It has to."

"You're deluding yourself if you think this will last," Kendrick expressed not unkindly. Blinking, I forced my misty eyes up to meet his somber expression. "But what I've said in the past is still true. I love you, Amelia. My feelings for you will *never* change. I will still be here when he's dead and gone."

Every factual word from his mouth caused a maddening anger to well up my throat. The thought of giving Ty up was too agonizing to bear. I freed my hands from Kendrick's and sprang to my feet. "You don't know anything!"

I began to stalk away, but Kendrick clutched my wrist, stopping me. "Amelia, wait," he pleaded. "I'm sorry. I don't want to fight with you."

My anger fizzled at his gentle words. It wasn't him I was angry with. It was the situation. The one *I* had created by allowing myself to fall for a werewolf. "I'm not mad at you." I dropped back down beside him. "I just don't know what to do."

Kendrick smiled and draped his arm around my shoulder, pulling me against him. "I know what might help."

He wanted to help us? For a moment I wondered what his true motives were. A second later I chastised myself for the thought. Kendrick was anything but deceptive. Sure he'd kept things—like being a vampire—from me in the past. But anything he'd ever hidden had been for my protection. I looked up at his hope-filled eyes. "What'd you have in mind?"

"There's an arts and psychic fair in town tomorrow. You could get your fortune read, get some answers."

I recalled the flyer that had been taped to my locker on Tuesday and frowned. "You believe in that crap?"

Kendrick arched a single brow. "Don't you?"

I bit my lip, considering the possibility. This world held monsters who were strong and powerful, with mind-bending capabilities. Anything was possible.

"Either way," Kendrick chimed in, "it can't hurt."

I studied his expression. It was open and honest, and his tone had been level. Any lingering suspicion I felt towards his idea evaporated. I smiled. Our friendship was repairing. Kendrick almost seemed his old self again. The tension-fueled angst that had crippled his expression and body language had now fully dissolved. "You're right. It can't hurt."

KENDRICK EMERGED from the passenger side of my black A5. A hood and cap sheltered his face, and his hands were shoved deep into the pockets of his boarding hoodie. Yesterday we'd spent the night watching a snowboarding documentary followed by the latest season of Supernatural. Now it was early the next morning and we had just arrived at the Arts and Psychic Crafts Fair.

"Can't you feel that?" Kendrick asked while looking over my denim shorts and thin, cardigan-covered purple tank. He glanced up at the sun which had broken through thin, dispersing clouds. Its intensity grew by the second.

I shook my head. "What, the sun?"

"The tingling," he said, picking up the pace through the packed parking lot toward the community hall. "It feels like my skin's crawling."

I frowned. Royal vampires, as far as I knew, weren't affected by the sun's rays like turned vampires were. "But you're a royal. Aren't you immune?"

Kendrick flashed a playful smile, fangs glinting through parted lips. "Yeah, but that doesn't mean I don't still feel uncomfortable. Royals, and well, you and Dorian, can endure sunlight. But it's still not a natural royal trait."

This was news to me. "What do you mean?"

Above the front entrance of the hall was a large awning. Kendrick moved into its shade and slouched against the sheet metal wall. "At the dawn of time," he began in a storyteller's voice, "all vampires were slaves to the sun, forced to rise only in darkness. Then the Dawn of Reckoning came and our ancestors were given a choice. Banishment to hell or align with light. Those that didn't fall were instilled with a conscience and a soul, a linked connection to humanity. They were the first royal vampires, the original Pure Bloods. They were gifted with the ability to withstand sunlight, as a show of good faith." He squinted, glaring at the intensifying sun as if his look alone would snuff out its golden heat. "That's enough history for one day. Let's get inside. It's like an inferno out here."

I followed after Kendrick through the glass doors as he pulled back his hood. *Align with light...* The words held a weight within me that I didn't understand. I was about to question Kendrick further on the subject, when a wall of incense slammed into me, burning my nostrils and causing my lungs to clench. Kendrick's nose wrinkled at the same onslaught, and we both coughed. "*This* is your great idea?"

Kendrick pounded a fist against his chest, clearing his throat. "Superior sense of smell... I guess I didn't think it through."

A chiming sounded, and Kendrick jerked before retrieving his phone from his hoodie. He peered at the screen and grimace. "I have to take this." Then he walked a few steps away, turning his back.

With a shrug, I glanced around, my lungs and nostrils slowly adapting to the onslaught of scents. The hall was flooded with an assembly of slow-moving people. Row upon row of cloth-draped tables filled the space. Each sported a variety of artsy things and cheap jewelry. Some of the stalls even came equipped with hippie-looking tents.

The cluster of people in front of me dispersed, and my eyes fell on a woman. She was positioned at a stand in the front corner of the hall. Heavy wrinkles marked her face and she had crazy gray hair. Her beady, black eyes watched me intently, and a smile thinned her lips.

"Why do you need to know?" Kendrick's elevated voice cut through the blurred sounds of hundreds of flapping mouths.

I broke from the old woman's piercing gaze and turned to watch Kendrick. His back was still turned, shoulders visibly stiff and muscles along his neck taut.

He nodded and slipped the brim of his cap up, scratching his head as if frustrated. Then he pulled it back down into place "Yes, I understand. I believe she is…" He hesitated, head twisting to the side and voice dropping. His next words were lost to the rising chatter of people between us. He hung up and shoved the phone back into his pocket before returning to my side.

"Everything okay?" I asked, curiosity sparking within me.

Kendrick sighed and nodded. The tension that had stiffened his shoulders was gone, yet his face remained detectably strained. "It's just royal stuff. Nothing you need to worry about." He slung an arm around my shoulder. "Now, let's get your fortune read."

After meandering around most of the stalls, we somehow found ourselves back in front of the tent I'd noticed earlier, though the old woman was nowhere in sight.

"This one looks interesting." Kendrick motioned to the black tent with silver-embossed stars decorating its gauzy fabric.

Surprisingly, this was the only tent in the whole room that was decorated with stars. Most of the others had been plain black or white. Only a few had been printed with moons or glitter that resembled the Milky Way. Fronting this tent, much like all the others, was a table. Similar to the others it also housed an assortment of gemstones, polished and smooth. One piece in particular caught my eye. It was positioned right next to a stand of personalized business cards printed with *Madam Rosalie, Fortune Teller Extraordinaire*. The amethyst pendant was tear-shaped and held by a spiral of gold. It was suspended from an adjustable cord necklace. Under the hall's domed lighting, its semi-transparent surface gleamed in an infinite spectrum of purples. It somehow reminded me of the delicate jewelry box Caius had given me. I'd almost forgotten I had the thing. I frowned. The jewelry box had held such a magnetized draw when I'd first seen it. Yet when I'd found it gifted in my room, the draw had been gone. It could have been any other meaningless possession.

The gray-haired woman stepped out from the tent, drawing my eye. Her beady eyes smiled and her voice emerged raspy, almost like I imagined a fairytale witch's would. "Reading for the pretty girl?"

I was still unconvinced on the whole fortune telling gig. But this *was* the reason we'd come here.

"Only thirty dollar," the woman added.

"It's now or never," Kendrick whispered into my ear while nudging my side.

The ancient woman drew open the curtained entrance to the tent with a toothy smile, then stood aside for us to enter. Within the tent's round walls was a small foldout table draped with black cloth. A cane chair sat at either end, and a deck of tarot cards occupied a neat pile in the center, flanked by two lit candles. The scent of vanilla wafted from their flickering flames.

"Sit," the woman demanded, handing me a business card that I shoved into my short's back pocket. "I am Madam Rosalie."

I followed her direction. With only two chairs available, Kendrick waited just inside the entrance.

"Now, take my hands and close your eyes," she instructed. "I must find your center."

I frowned and collected her frail hands. The skin was so thin that blue veins bulged above jutting bones. "Don't you just have to deal some cards out?"

Madam Rosalie exchanged a quick look with Kendrick then closed her eyes. A pasty smile tugged at her dry lips. "You are here about a boy, yes?"

Vague and broad. An easy assumption. I frowned, watching her pinned shut eyes. "Yes…"

"This boy will alter the path of your life," Madam Rosalie said. "Deliver you unto danger."

A sudden ripple of tingles passed through our joined hands and we both gasped at the shock. I went to pull away, but the fortuneteller's hands clung even tighter to mine. "Your future," she said, then paused, eyes moving behind closed eyelids, "is not set. Many hold a hand in your fate, in your imminent death."

Iced fingers crept up my spine and my heart skipped a beat. "My death?"

Madam Rosalie's eyes flew open. The flickering candle flames reflected in her glossy pupils. "It is not set. But you must beware." Her gaze shifted with a sly slide of her eyes to Kendrick, then back to me. "Those you trust most are not always what they seem."

J.L. MYERS

"Amelia, I'm sorry," Kendrick grunted from right behind as his hand found my shoulder.

The shock of his closeness caused an involuntary bolt to strike through my chest. Hadn't he been standing at the entryway?

"I truly thought this was a good idea," he went on. "The last thing I expected was to encounter the biggest whack-job in town."

The fortuneteller's eyes snapped to Kendrick, skewering with vehemence. "Hush boy. I am not done!" I went to pull my hands away, but she clutched my fingers tighter. Her beady, black eyes bore into mine. "Beware the blood that runs in your veins..."

Bone-seeping dread caused my heart to slam against my ribs. *This woman is delusional*, I told myself, though the voice inside my head was anything but convincing. I snatched my hands free and threw the thirty bucks down onto the table, rising with shaking legs. "That's enough!"

Kendrick caught my hand and began pulling me from the tent.

"WAIT!" Madam Rosalie commanded.

The edge to her raspy tone stopped me in my tracks, and I turned, pulling my hand free from Kendrick's.

Madam Rosalie was on her feet and rushing our way. For such a frail-looking woman, she was quick. My eyes lowered. Dangling from her outstretched hand was the purple pendant I had been admiring outside. "You must take this," she insisted. In my brief hesitation, she caught my hand and placed the amethyst against my palm, closing my fingers around it. "It will..."

"We don't want your stupid trinket," Kendrick said, hand hooking around my arm.

He began to pull me back and I frowned at him. "Kendrick, wait." I wasn't sure what prompted me to stop; getting away from this nutbag and her premonitions of death should have been a priority. But there was something compelling about the pendant. It was much more than it being my favorite color. I just couldn't leave without it. I reached into the pocket of my denim shorts and pulled out a few crumbled tens. "How much?"

"My gift," Madam Rosalie said, dipping her head. "But once you put it on, *never* take it off."

I barely had time to utter thanks before Kendrick reclaimed my arm, forcing me back through the curtained entrance. "C'mon, we're leaving."

"The light," Madam Rosalie's escalating voice reached me through the thin material of the tent. "You must accept the light. It is the only way to save him!"

I BOUNDED DOWN AN EMBANKMENT, purple-laced Vans biting into freshly fallen snow. The pendant the creepy fortuneteller had given me only hours ago, bounced against my chest. I wasn't sure why I was wearing it. In this moment I didn't care. The sound of a crackling river reached my ears. I was late. Ty would already be waiting. And there was something I was dying to ask him.

The tree-lined embankment gave way to a small clearing that resembled a winter wonderland. Snowy pine trees bordered one edge of the entirely snow-sheeted clearing. On the opposing side was a fallen, moss-covered tree. It acted as a bridge over the rippling stream. Winter had come early to the forest. Ice-crusts had already begun to form across its banks, budding a foot in on either side of its glassy water.

Ty, as I had already expected, was waiting. Perched in the middle of the fallen log, he was dressed in just a pair of black pants. His face was sullen as he looked up, acutely aware of my approach in that way of his. His snow-drenched hair hung in his eyes.

"Amelia, I'm so sorry. I must have fallen asleep." His complexion paled, and he swallowed, wincing.

I walked the line of the broad log and dropped down beside him. Grief contorted his expression as he reached out to graze my arm with rough fingers. "Please believe me, I never meant to hurt you. Are you really okay?"

With a reassuring smile, I removed my dark, blue-violet cardigan and tied it around my waist. "Of course I'm fine."

The gashes had closed up soon after Ty had fled, and were now faded to pale jagged scars. The sun broke through the thick white clouds for a brief moment. Its rays caught on my arm, causing the marks to glisten in its light.

"I saw the blood…and your face." Ty traced the line of each one with a hot finger, raising goosebumps over my skin. "I didn't want to leave."

"It's just a few scratches…" I ran a gentle hand across his cheek, forcing him to look at me. "I'm fine, really."

Ty nuzzled into my hand, kissing my palm before trailing up my arm to cover the scarred flesh. My heart skipped at his touch, and I curled my fingers tight around his neck, pulling his face up to meet mine. Our noses brushed before I pressed my lips to his, parting his mouth and finding his hot tongue. His scent, taste, and touch mesmerized me, causing my gums to tingle with much more than physical desire. Trying to keep my movement from being abrupt, I edged away. Our chests rose and fell with shallow breath. "See." I peered into his now radiant gold eyes. "I'm fine."

Ty folded me in his arms, and I nestled into him, our bodies molding together perfectly. The slowing beat of his heart echoed through my ears. Ty broke the sweet aura of our silent embrace. "Does Kendrick know what happened the other night?" He peered down at the stream below, eyes distant. "Did he see the marks?"

"No. Well, I don't think so. He was suspicious, but I forced him to talk the next morning. I think he's finally forgiven me. We actually went to that psychic fair in town. It was his idea." I blinked, and the beady eyes of the fortuneteller formed across the back of my eyelids. She was delusional, I thought again. Though hidden deep inside was a growing unease at her chilling fortune. *You must accept the light. It's the only way to save him.* A chill transcended my bones, making me want to tremble. What light? Save who?

Ty's scarred arm squeezed around me, and I realized he was comforting me. My body was actually trembling. "I hope I didn't frighten you too much."

Shaking off the memory of her cryptic fortune, I entwined my fingers in his free hand. "I will admit I was shocked at first. But when I realized it was you..." I trailed off in thought. I wanted to know that side of him too. "I guess I was more curious than anything."

Surprise lifted Ty's brows. "Curious?"

Biting my lip, I swallowed my hesitation. I hoped this question would lead to the outcome I'd prepared for. "How does it work? The transformation, I mean. I know you told me when you change, but I want to know you, Ty. I want to know everything about you."

Ty's eyes darkened as he stared down to the settling stream. Nervous energy brewed within my chest. Had I asked too much?

My thoughts stilled as he began to explain. "Our bones crack and break to be reformed. Our brains shut off some of the pain receptors, so it's not so bad." Guilt turned his face grim. "I just meant to lie beside you for a moment longer. But I was so tired..." He lifted my hand to his lips. "Had you not woken to the sound of my bones cracking, I could have..." His words died on his tongue and desolation rippled across his face.

Touching his cheek, I turned his face to mine. "But you didn't. And I'm fine, remember?"

Ty shook his head. "Will you ever forgive me?"

"Of course…" I paused. Now was the perfect time. "But there is one condition." Ty's now hazel, green-rimmed eyes rose to mine, curiosity questioning within them. "Will you show me?" I asked, then shook my head, hearing the agonizing growl that had plagued him in my dream. "Unless it's too painful, I wouldn't want you to be—"

Ty caught my hand in his, causing my words to break off. "The pain is momentary and dulled, and I would endure much worse, for you."

"But?" I questioned, sensing his hesitation.

"But, I don't know," he said, eyes searching mine. "I wouldn't want to hurt you. We can lose ourselves for a moment. And I never want to risk harming you, not again, not ever."

Ty was still worried about hurting me? The concept was almost comical. I planted my hands on my hips. "I thought we already discussed this. I am *not* human. I am a vampire who's stronger and faster than that. I'll be prepared this time." I searched his strained eyes for understanding but received none. I decided to play dirty and leaned in, running my lips up his neck to his ear. "Pleeeease?"

Ty made a small sound, somewhere between a growl and a groan. "I can't say no when you do that."

A smile tugged at my lips. "So that's a yes?"

Ty rose from the fallen tree and pulled me up beside him, holding me against his warm chest. "If I do this, you have to stand back. You have to promise not to come any closer. No matter how painful it seems."

Excitement and trepidation washed over me as I nodded. "What-ever you want, I'll do it."

Ty led me from the log and into the clearing. He turned to face me, tense fingers curling around my shoulders as he pressed his lips to mine. A reserved smiled thinned his full lips and he backed away, putting a few long strides between us. "Now, don't move."

I nodded and watched, eyes widening as Ty dropped his pants. He flung them aside to stand scarcely dressed in just a pair of boxer briefs. The sight of his perfectly toned and almost naked body sent searing heat up my neck and across my cheeks. Not that you could blame me. Apart from the many scars that marked his tan skin, the guy was practically airbrushed.

Too soon my moment of ogling was overshadowed. Ty's muscles corded, bulging and straining. A split second later his entire body began to quake. A sickening crack sounded, followed by a low, deep growl that rumbled from his perspiring chest. He fell forward on all fours, clawed hands disappearing into the soft snow. Terror stung my heart. What had I done? Another agonizing growl tore from his throat as his back arched up, a bone splitting straight through his skin. That's where the scars came from?

I went to rush forward but stopped. The draw of his spilled blood had my fangs breaking free. And you promised, I reminded myself. Resigned, I kept my feet planted to the ground.

The cracking of bones continued to echo through the silent woods surrounding us. The sound was eerie and totally surreal, forcing a startling realization to tug strings from my memory. It can't be possible. Still I couldn't deny the scene before me, the mirrored reality I was standing in. *I dreamed this.* A sudden heat against my chest drew my attention, and I reached up to find the amethyst pendant. Its polished surface was warm to the touch. I twirled the stone between my fingers, frowning eyes returning to Ty's blurring form.

A distant but clear noise of splintering wood erupted through the trees. A jolt of panic rushed through me.

"Get away from that mongrel!" Kendrick burst from the tree line, brandishing a full-sized tree limb fit with branches and leaves. In a single bound he launched, landing to block me from Ty. His chest heaved with fast breathing and his eyes glared down at me. "Are you trying to get yourself killed?"

Kendrick tracked me? Resentment crawled beneath my skin like live bugs eating living flesh. I slammed my hands against his chest. "Kendrick, get the hell out of my way! You're not supposed to be here."

Confusion creased his brow, while his face burned red. "You want this to happen? You actually want to see what kind of a *monster* he is?"

"He's not a monst—"

Kendrick seized my wrist with his free hand. "I knew it was your blood," he spat. "*He* did this to you!"

I followed his wild stare to the scars marking my flesh. Suffocating dread swept through me. "You don't understand!" I wriggled my wrist free from his painful grasp. "It was an accident."

A snarl emerged behind Kendrick. He spun, turning to face the huge, black wolf. Ty's beastly form towered above us, solid and muscular. A force to be reckoned with. His ears were flattened against his skull and his wolf eyes glowed intensely. They were fixed on Kendrick who shielded me behind him.

"Don't come anywhere near her," Kendrick hissed. His body braced and his arm held up the tree limb like an oversized bat, ready to swing.

The beast barked out a retort and stepped closer. His hackles bristled and his lips curled back to bare jagged, spittle-covered teeth.

Kendrick's muscles twitched, but he stood his ground. "I mean it, mutt. Back off!"

This had already gone on too long. There was no way in hell I was about to let them actually face off. With a swift maneuver, I broke from Kendrick's hold. I jumped over the wooden weapon to land between them. Anger at Kendrick's intrusion rushed like venom through my veins. I shoved a loaded hand at his chest. "Kendrick, I need you to leave. Now."

"What?" Disbelief etched across Kendrick's face. "You want to stay here with that...that abomination!"

"Of course I do. I love him!" My lips snapped shut too late. Kendrick's face dropped and he stumbled as though his legs were threatening to give out. My insides felt like they had torn in two. This wasn't how I had imagined saying those words for the very first time. Not shouted in frustration at Kendrick. And not laced with boiling resentment.

The misery across Kendrick's face quickly shifted to rage. "You'll be sorry." He twisted and took off, abandoning the tree limb with a powerful sweep of his arm. He was gone before his weapon crashed into the tree line, exploding in a spray of unrecognizable pieces.

I slumped, edging into the curve of Ty's coarse-haired shoulder. Beneath my ribs, my heart was pounding. Yet somehow the heat emanating from his huge body calmed the storm within. "I'm sorry Kendrick ruined this for us. I could just throttle him!"

Ty's muzzle nudged my shoulder in a show of support. His teeth were now covered, and his hackles had flattened. I flung my arms around his broad shoulders. As big as he was, I could barely get them halfway around him. I lingered there, wishing I could forget everything that had just happened. But I couldn't. Kendrick's hate-fueled words had begun pulsing through my mind. *You'll be sorry.*

Sudden understanding shook me to my core. I understood without any uncertainty exactly what his threat had meant. My stomach lurched with drowning dread as I shot to my feet. "Shit, shit, shit!" Ty pawed my hand in question. "What he said. He's going to tell my mom. I have to try and stop him!"

Ty stretched on his limbs, ready to take chase. I stilled him with raised palms. "No. Ty, please. It will only make things worse. I have to do this on my own."

With one last panicked glance, I took off after Kendrick, following his trail back through the dense scrub. The sun had long faded, and a fresh blanket of lightly falling snow caught my face and hair as I sped on. The dread in my twisted stomach grew with every leap and bound. I wouldn't make it.

CHAPTER 20

I exploded through the front doors of the house. "Kendrick!" I screamed, making for the stairs. It was way too early for Mom to have left for work, though there was a slim possibility that she could be out shopping with some of her socialite friends. "KENDRICK!"

"We're in here, Amelia." My mom's irate voice flowed through the archway to the kitchen. "And I need to speak with you, now."

Fear-fed adrenaline pumped through my body. I'm too late. Hurt from Kendrick's betrayal choked up my throat. I wished the ground beneath my feet would crack and open, swallowing me whole. Any diversion to keep me from having to face the onslaught, the questions, and the punishment to come would do. But wishing couldn't help me now. I swallowed my fear and dragged my feet into the room.

Mom stood behind the island in the center of the kitchen. Her blouse quivered over her shaking chest while she drummed her French-tipped nails against the limestone counter. Her eyes were frozen on me as I entered. Kendrick was standing to the side, body motionless and eyes strained.

Mom's impetuous tone struck fear through my heart. "Amelia Athobry-Lamont, do you have something you would like to tell me?"

I glared at Kendrick. "What'd you tell her?"

He shoved his hands into the pockets of his hoodie and turned his head away. His lips tightened into a straight line.

"Kendrick, how could you?" I shouted, tears welling up my eyes. "I trusted you!"

"Leave Kendrick out of this," Mom demanded, pointing a thin finger at me. "*You* are the one who's been lying to me for weeks."

Defeat clouded my emotions. I'd lied to everyone. I'd brought all of this on myself. My chest constricted and my boiling anger began to subside. I looked up apologetically. "Mom, I didn't want to keep this from you. But I knew you would overreact like this."

"How did you expect me to react?" Losing her control, Mom's hands clenched into fists and belted down against the benchtop. The force sent hairline fractures straight through the limestone. "When you're seeing that...that filthy mongrel?"

Déjà vu slammed into my chest like a ton of bricks, striking the wind from my lungs. My eyes flickered to the stacked, dirty plates and blood-tinged glasses collecting beside the sink. I've been here before. I've seen this play out. Still, an uncontrollable fury at her insult of Ty ignited within me. "Don't speak about Ty like that. You know nothing of what he is."

Mom shook her head, causing her hair to fall over her face. Still, I couldn't miss the glimmer of guilt in her eyes. "You knew," I accused, freezing her in motion. "You knew werewolves existed. Why didn't you tell us?"

Mom folded her arms over her chest. "What I have or have not told you and your brother is my prerogative, Amelia. I have sacrificed more than you know to give you both as normal an upbringing as possible." Sorrow colored her eyes. "Without your father, I have done the best I could." She placed her hands on her waist. Her nails dug into her blouse, but her face remained soft. "Amelia, you must understand that this cannot continue. Caius *will never* allow it."

I threw my arms onto the benchtop in desperation, clutching my hands together. "Why do you need to tell him? Mom, please. He doesn't have to know!"

Mom shook her head almost regrettably. "I cannot keep this from your uncle. He is the only family we have, and he's always looked out for our best interests. In his position *he* will know how to handle this." She stepped around the island, about to lay a hand on my shoulder when she paused. Her eyes scoured my scarred flesh.

I cursed myself for not being more careful. How could I have run into the house without even the thought of a plan? Or even the sense to cover up the evidence?

"Amelia." Mom sighed and covered the scars with her hand. "Sweetheart, you know this must end. It is not safe for you to associate with one of theirs."

I threw my hands in the air violently, batting my mom's arm away. "Not safe? That's a load of prejudicial bullshit. You don't even know him. And I won't stay away from him. You can't make me!"

I stormed off, glaring at Kendrick as I flew upstairs to my room. Every fiber within me screamed for me to flee, to seek out Ty. But I couldn't. My immature secret-keeping had created this mess I was in. Acting like a child now would only make things worse. Instead, I snatched my iPhone from the back pocket of my jeans and tore off the Three Days Grace cover. Being from Kendrick, it reminded me of him. I let it fall from my hand then smashed it to pieces with the heel of my Vans. Then I stomped to the window ledge and dialed Ty's number.

"Amelia," Ty's frantic voice echoed down the line. For the second time today, I was almost surprised not to hear the growl of a wolf. "What happened?"

Sinking onto the window ledge, I stared out at the snow-blotted sun sinking toward the hazy horizon. I blinked back tears. "It's too late. She knows."

A long exhale sounded through the speaker. "What happens now?"

It felt as though fear were drowning me. I drew my legs up and squeezed my free arm around them. The pitch in my voice rose. "Mom's going to tell my uncle. She's going to let him decide."

"Oh."

Tears glazed my eyes. "I won't let them hurt you."

"You don't need to worry about me," Ty said, sounding strong once more. "Believe me. I can take care of myself."

On the verge of blubbering into the speaker, I rushed my words. "I have to go, 'kay? I'll call later." The urge to pelt my phone at the wall filled me. Somehow I resisted and hung up.

Alone with my insides churning, I waited for the powers that be to decide my fate. What would they do now? Would we move again? Would they go after Ty? But even with all of this to contemplate, a new revelation clogged up my mind. The theory was utterly ridiculous. Still, I couldn't ignore the proof. More than my argument with Mom had been preconceived. Within dreams, I had witnessed things before they'd happened. Some things I'd seen after the fact, but in a new light. There was Ty's transformation in the forest. Then the time I'd dreamed Ty as the boy from the alley. I'd also envisioned my own eerie likeness as the girl Ty had cheated with. Topping it all off was the fight I'd just had with Mom.

My dreams, my nightmares…they come true.

A QUIET TAP at my door tore me from my waking nightmare. The chandelier beamed on, chasing away the darkness of my room. I tugged on my hoodie and zipped it up. Mom had already seen the scars, but reminding her wouldn't help what was about to come.

But it wasn't Mom. Dorian entered and came to my side. He took my hand, pulling me from the windowsill. "The verdict is in."

The dread of what was to come overshadowed my new burdensome revelation of clairvoyant dreams. With my brother's unwavering support, we ventured downstairs and into the dining room.

A mixture of aromas filled the hardwood furnished space. Mom's specialty had been served onto china plates. Duck Margaret, served with snow peas, caramelized carrots, and mashed potatoes. Each table setting was paired with a crystal flute topped with blood. A crystal vase also sat in the middle of the table, filled with fragrant lilies. Mom waited at the head of the table. Kendrick flanked her, hunched over his plate with downcast eyes. Mom watched Dorian with a stern frown as he took the spare seat beside her and opposite Kendrick. I went to take position next to him, thankful for the safe distance he'd put between me and Mom. A movement behind Kendrick's head caught my eye. It took me a second to realize what I was actually looking at. It was my own reflection in the silver-framed mirror mounted to the wall. My hair looked like a warped bird's nest, and my face was even paler than usual. Dark shadows cut my cheeks and lined my eyes. Today's exertion and mounting strain had seriously worn me down. And I was starving, for much more than food. I glanced back at my steaming plate and blood-topped glass. My stomach lurched, too tight with apprehension to eat or drink anything. I quickly sat and pushed my plate back.

After a second, it occurred to me that no one had uttered a single word since my entry. A strong foreboding silence was growing by the second. It tainted the air that had smelled so good only moments ago, making me want to gag.

Finally Mom cleared her throat. "I've spoken to your uncle," she announced without preamble. Her hands folded in front of her. "He is extremely disappointed, though was quite understanding and generous, given the circumstances."

Generous? I narrowed skeptical eyes at her. "What does that mean?"

A satisfied smile lit Mom's face. "Your uncle has a proposition for you. Kendrick has informed us that you've been learning more about our kind from him. Which I believe is good *if* this is something you're interested in." She paused to take a sip from her wine glass. The crimson blood tainted her pale lips. "Until now, I have shielded you and Dorian from all the things I thought you were better off not knowing. I realize now that my protectiveness may have been a detriment."

So far everything sounded okay. Still, a dread-filled sensation welled within my stomach, turning it in knots.

"We think it would be best," Mom went on, "if you got to experience and learn what life as a vampire can offer, in a setting that isn't filled with temptation."

My heart jumped into my throat and my voice emerged shrill. "What the hell does that mean?"

"We have decided you will go back to Alaska for a few months." Mom's expression strained. "You will be staying within the Armaya's walls, inside their castle with your uncle."

I smashed my hands down on the table. The crockery clattered in protest. "You're sending me away? Just like that, we can't even talk about this?" I had expected the outcome would be bad, perhaps changing schools or towns. But not this, not the Armaya, a place Ty could never set foot in.

With authority, Mom crossed her arms over her chest and leaned back in her chair. "There is nothing to talk about, Amelia. The decision has been made, and we will *not* compromise."

"Mom, really?" Dorian interrupted. "That's a bit harsh. Can't—"

"Dorian," Mom snapped with skewering eyes. "You are lucky not to be served the same fate. I know you were involved with that werewolf girl, Marika."

Dorian's eyes narrowed, shifting to Kendrick. Mom's words made it clear. Kendrick had revealed a lot more than my own deceit. He had told her *everything.*

"How could you?" I directed to Kendrick, who had slumped further in his seat. I took a glimmer of pleasure from the utter misery clouding his expression.

"Anyway," Mom continued. Her body language appeared stiff but her expression remained neutral, almost apologetic. "Once you've had time to digest all of this, I think you might actually be a bit excited about the endeavor. You should know that this is quite an exclusive offer, Amelia. Those of the Armaya generally don't grant non-royals residence inside their castle. However, given Caius's position and sway, this time they have made an exception."

Her words caused my anger to spike again, boiling my blood. "*Excited!*" I shrieked. "You think I'm going to be excited that you're sending me away!"

"Given the circumstances," she said, voice and face hardening, "you should appreciate this outcome. It could have been much, *much* worse."

I caught the deadly edge to her voice and realized what she

wasn't saying. Much worse meant certain harm to Ty. I glared at my mom. "When am I leaving?"

With a sigh, Mom's eyes fell and she almost looked sad. "All the flights are set. You and Kendrick will be leaving first thing tomorrow."

I had to travel with that *traitor*? Holding back the urge to smash everything in sight to pieces, I stood up. It was a long shot, but I needed to try. "Mom," I said sullenly, keeping my fingers straight and tense to stop them from curling into fists. "I know your mind's made up. So I won't even try to argue. The only thing I ask is that I can at least say goodbye to Ty, in person."

Mom watched me, a look of sympathy crossing her face. She nodded. "I'll allow it, *but* you've only got one hour, and Dorian will go with you."

It was a small consolation, but at this point I'd take anything I could get. I snatched my case-less iPhone from my pocket. *'Meet me at the lookout.'*

I set a countdown on my iPhone, giving me enough time to get back in the set hour. Then I flung off my hoodie and looked to Dorian. "Ready?"

He smiled and skipped around the table. "Like I said, I'll always back you up."

We escaped out the front doors in true vampire style, muscles lengthening and retracting at a speed that was unimaginable. Trees, gated properties, and parked cars along the beach-line flashed past. Then the suburban roads dispersed and began to wind. I veered off the asphalt, leading the way up through the depths of thick greenery. The tree branches ripped through my tank top and jeans as I pushed on. Unequipped for such speed, my Vans skidded on the snow-littered ground. Above, gunmetal-gray clouds opened up to shower my already snow-drenched hair with glacial rain.

A second later, we burst through the trees to the mouth of the lookout. We skidded to a stop on the gravel road. The rain and snow-slicked surroundings painted everything in glimmering monotones.

Ty sat across the way, a despondent frown lingering across his tight lips. He pulled away from the log railing that framed the glow of a night-lit Portsmouth. A luster of sweat beaded across his heaving naked chest. The sheer sight of him stole my breath.

"Well, go on," Dorian said, giving me a nudge. He turned and began walking back the way we'd come. "I'll walk slowly. You can catch me on the way back."

When he disappeared through the trees, I turned back to Ty. Without command my feet pounded the gravel, sending me flying at Ty until my arms enfolded him in a tight, desperate embrace. His hands pressed into my back and his heart hammered in time against mine. Tears pooled in my eyes and I hugged him tighter, breathing in his scent. I never wanted to let go, never wanted to reveal my punishment for loving such a creature.

But the moment shattered like cracking glass that fell in cutting shards. Ty reached up to loosen my strong hold. He held my hands firm. Foreboding loomed within his beaten expression and radiated from his slumped body. "A decision's been made?"

I slumped in despair. Ty slouched back against the log railing, running a tense hand over his face. Something inside me was being torn apart, flesh and muscle ripping at the sight of his defeated expression. I curled my arms around his body and squeezed. My lips pressed against the bare warmth of his neck. His hammering pulse throbbed against my mouth, his scent hanging on my tongue. The temptation to extend my fangs was there, but I held it back.

Ty's cradling arms released me and he peered into my tear-filled eyes. His hands lifted to cup my face. "Amelia, I need to know. Tell me what happened."

"My mom's sending me away." My eyes fell and tears spilled down my cheeks. I couldn't look him in the eye—the boy I had fallen for so irrefutably. Not when his face mirrored the hurt I was inflicting. "I'll be going to the Armaya, back in Alaska. It was my uncle's idea."

"But you're coming back," his words choked out, "right?"

"It's only for a few months." I tried to sound confident, even though I was seething with dreadful uncertainty. "I'll be back before you know it."

"A few months…" Ty's hand traveled across my back, pulling me against him. "When do you leave?"

"Tomorrow…"

Ty sucked in a sharp breath then became very still. Finally he exhaled. "Oh."

Ice shards invaded my bones, turning my body ridged. My blood ran cold. All this drama was too much to expect him to handle. This was the end of us. My arms fell from around him and I began to step back.

Ty clutched my hips, stopping my retreat. The breath knocked from my lungs as he drew me back against his hot body. His lips connected with mine and my pulse spiked. Fresh tears escaped my eyes as that deep kiss sealed our fate. A goodbye kiss. I began to draw away, my lips lingering for one last taste. *Goodbye, Ty.*

Ty's hands connected with my forearms, halting my retraction. "Don't do that," he breathed against my lips. "Don't say goodbye. This *isn't* goodbye."

My eyes fluttered open, peering into the luminosity of his golden irises. "But I thought…"

"I said I would *never* leave you." Ty dipped his forehead to rest against mine. "Amelia, I meant it. There is nothing in this world that

I want more than you. You are *everything* to me. As long as you still want me, I'm yours, *always*."

Breath escaped my lungs with a sigh of relief and Ty's arms curved back around me. I lingered within his secure arms for a long while. Neither of us spoke as we soaked up the dwindling moments we had left. Long minutes of intimate silence passed almost in the blink of an eye. The moon, not quite as full as Friday, began to rise and the air became damp with frost.

I shifted, feeling the countdown on my iPhone go off. "I have to go. Mom only gave me an hour."

Ty's urgent hands found my cheeks and his lips closed over mine. "I will see you in your dreams."

CHAPTER 21

*M*y tired eyes widened. An enormous castle seemed to have appeared in the blink of an eye. It grew by the second, a formidable structure nestled within a mountainous valley of the Alaska Range. A hard mass crept up my throat. My impenetrable prison.

After three connecting flights, the day had disappeared with the setting sun. Kendrick was sitting hard up against the other side of the limo, not daring to speak. I could still remember our conversation, the only conversation he'd attempted.

When the plane had left the tarmac, lifting into the sky, Kendrick lifted surrendering hands. "Amelia, please. I'm sorry. I overreacted."

Fire had boiled my blood, their flames flaring up my neck and across my face. Mock sarcasm drenched my words. *"Overreacted?"* It'd taken every ounce of my strength to fight the overwhelming urge to explode. Knowing surrounding passengers would stare helped me rein in my outburst. Instead, I snarled through gritted teeth. "I never thought I could hate someone as much as I hate you."

"I thought I was protecting you." Kendrick moved to catch my hand and I recoiled. "Amelia, please believe me. I would *never* hurt you intentionally. I love you."

Love... A cruel laugh cackled from my throat, and the bubbling rage took over. "You know *nothing* about love." Restraining the need to belt Kendrick in the chest, I clenched my hands. My next spoken words were slow and drawn-out. "I will *never* forgive you."

That had been the end of his begging for forgiveness. The remaining flights passed in acidic silence. Through it all, a tiny part of me wanted to forgive him, to let him off the hook. But the part of me that was hurting with the heartbreak of leaving Ty behind just wouldn't allow it.

With the sun's rise, we finally arrived in Anchorage. A suited chauffeur holding a card printed with our names was waiting. He hadn't uttered a word as he collected our luggage and escorted us to the limo. Now almost two hours had passed in complete silence, on a road surrounded by nothing but thick forestry. Just over ten minutes ago, we'd passed through a chain-link gate topped with razor wire. Threatening warning signs had been posted along the electrified fence, which disappeared into thickening trees. There had been two mute guards, who inspected the limo before granting us entry. Still the chauffeur hadn't uttered a single word.

I glanced back out the heavily tinted window as we drove through another guarded entrance. This one was an impenetrable gray stone wall. It was yet another barrier to keep the outside world and Ty away. Cobblestone lanes snaked around the castle. They fronted what appeared to be residential homes and shop fronts. The Armaya was an entire vampire community.

Kendrick exited the limo at once. He shoved his hands into the pockets of his boarding jacket and took off. In seconds he'd disappeared down a cobblestone lane.

An impatient throat clearing drew my eye to the chauffeur. He was now standing at my door, shielded beneath a thick-skinned umbrella. Without a word he turned, climbing the stairs to the castle's thick, iron-braced doors. I hurried after him into a dark foyer lined with pews, then down a corridor lit with wall lanterns.

With a knock at the first door, the chauffeur spoke for the very first time. "Miss Amelia Lamont, Lord Bathory." He pushed open the creaking door and stepped aside. Then he bowed deeply before scurrying up the hall.

A throat clearing drew my eyes up to my uncle. The sight of him spiked my pulse, nerves instantly refocusing all my attention onto him. He was formally dressed in a soot-colored suit and seated behind a leather-swathed desk. A mountain of askew papers surrounded him like a small fortress. The room was dark, shielded by thick drapes. Heavy bags circled his eyes and were emphasized by the poor lighting of a single desk lamp.

Caius pushed one stack of papers to the side and smiled. A relieved sigh escaped my lips as he stood, walking around the desk. His outstretched arms wrapped me in a welcoming hug. "Amelia, my dear, it is truly wonderful to see you."

Considering the circumstances, I had expected him to be at least angry, if not livid. But he wasn't. He seemed genuinely happy to see me.

Caius released me from his welcoming embrace and cleared his throat again. "So, I hear you are involved with a lycanthrope."

Caught off guard, I coughed and averted my eyes. The air suddenly seemed thick and stifling. A rhythmic ticking drew my sight to the swinging pendulum of a grandfather clock. It was positioned between shelving units that bordered almost the entire room. The pendulum barely ticked a quarter as fast as my now racing heart. I knew my uncle was waiting for a response, but any and all words seemed lost to me.

"You are lucky Kendrick came forward when he did," Caius went on. "Had The Council found out, I would not be responsible for their actions."

The grim edge to his tone raked across my skin, while the mere mention of Kendrick's name flooded a fuming anger throughout my body. "What would they have done?"

Caius motioned to the door. "Let us not worry about that now. It is late, and we have mere hours before a new day begins."

I glanced back to the antique, grandfather clock. It was almost 1PM.

"Oh," Caius chuckled. "Lamayli—I mean, your mother—must have forgotten to mention it. As vampires largely reside within the Armaya's walls, we run on a schedule opposite to that of humans. It is our natural way." He held out his elbow for me to take. "Come, I will escort you to your room."

With our arms linked, we cleared the corridor before climbing a stone stairwell. After passing a number of closed doors, Caius paused at one near the end of the corridor. "I have arranged a mentor to school you in vampire history. Your mother expressed your interest to learn. Plus I do believe the knowledge will be invaluable."

He fished into his pocket. Out came an ancient-looking key that he handed over. I kept my lips pinned shut. Any encouraged conversation could bring Ty back into discussion.

"I have afforded you a day's rest. Your tutoring will commence the day after tomorrow." A controlled smile spread over Caius's lips. It was the kind that didn't quite reach his dull, silvery eyes. "This will be your room. I trust it is satisfactory. If you require anything at all, dial one on the landline. Your every need will be taken care of. Now, try to get some rest and I will see you tomorrow."

After a hard twist of the key, I forced the heavy door open. I found the light switch and stared around my new prison. Lanterns matching those in the stairwell flashed on, lighting the space with a yellow glow. Iron-footed, antique furnishings minimally decorated the room. A wall-mounted flat screen was positioned above an age-worn wooden cabinet. It was the only modern touch.

Dragging my feet across the room, I slumped onto the turquoise quilt covering an enormous bed. I sighed and pulled out my iPod to play Three Days Grace. All the flights and time involved had seriously drained my energy. I needed a boost, a boost that sleep alone would not replenish. I grasped the phone from the bedside table and dialed one.

A female voice answered after a single ring. "Service operator, how may I help you?"

I needed blood. That was clear. Only I had no idea how the Armaya operated. "I was um, wondering," I floundered, "if I could get a drink. I'm a little low on…energy."

"Ah, this must be Amelia. Welcome. You'll find a minibar in the cabinet below the television. It's stocked with *refreshments*. Is there anything else I can assist you with?"

I vaulted over to the cabinet, yanking the door open. As promised, inside was a minibar. An assortment of beverages stocked the shelves: water, soda, milk, and glass-bottled blood. "No, that's all I needed. Thanks."

I hung up and downed the contents of an entire bottle. The dead blood was nothing compared to Ty's. Yet somehow it tugged at a memory. The one time I had lost control and drank his delicious blood. My face warmed while my aching heart sank. I hadn't allowed myself to think about him too much. Now I was trapped and alone in this expansive, stone-walled room and I couldn't stop myself. *God, I miss you.*

I crossed the room with a sigh, about to fall back onto the bed when a dark shadow caught the corner of my eye. Across the room was an open door, beyond which appeared to be a bathroom. A gold-framed mirror spanned the entire length of the wall. In its reflection was the shadow I had seen. A wooden door with an iron bordered keyhole. A wardrobe in the bathroom?

With a frown, I bounded into the bathroom. A claw-footed bath sat in the center of the room, which I dodged, before pushing down on the handle. Beyond the door was a bedroom. It was decked out with modern furniture rather than antique pieces. I breathed in sharply. Posters decorated the rocky walls, ranging from the bands Skillet and Threes Days Grace to a bunch of snowboarding ones too. A snowboard fitted with bindings was propped against one wall. A thick boarding jacket was slung over the couch. This was Kendrick's room, the one he must have lived in his entire life.

We're sharing a bathroom? In the background the song *I hate everything about you* came on from my iPod. I slammed the door. Fan-freaking-tastic!

DARKNESS SURROUNDED me as I paced impatiently, waiting for Ty to join my dream. The only light source came from above, where the waning moon propelled a ghostly glow down at me. Then there was a sudden and instantaneous shift. The night turned from dark to light as the sun soared over the rolling horizon of trees. I blinked in amazement. Around me, the sound of soothing water flowed over a tall cliff face. It plunged into the river below, dusting me with a fine spray. Straight overhead, sunbeams cracked light through the thick canopy of trees. Gold laced their leaves and warmed the air around me.

"I'm getting better at this," Ty's voice floated on the air. He materialized right in front of me, wearing a black collared shirt and blue jeans over his hunting boots.

I smiled, and sensing cool fabric against my own flesh, I glanced down. I was no longer wearing the clothes I had fallen asleep in. Instead, I had on satin shorts and a cotton tank top. "You dressed me?"

A mischievous smile lit Ty's tan face and his eyes twinkled. "I told you I can control everything." His arms wrapped around me, lifting me off the ground. "I know it hasn't even been a full day, but God I've missed you."

His closeness washed over me like a rolling tide. The onslaught of his potent scent made my gums prickle. I struggled to hold back the urge to extend my fangs. Thankfully Ty lowered me back to the ground. I stepped back, drawing in a deep, clearing breath.

"What's it like there?" Ty asked, appearing unaware of my strain. "Did your uncle give you a lecture?"

"No," I replied, taking a much needed further step back. "He was quite...*controlled*." I didn't want to reveal my uncle's words or the danger we had escaped. "But," I went on, wanting to change the subject, "we run on an opposite schedule. Sleep during the day, awake at night. So, I guess it's going to be harder to correlate dream-scapes with you awake and at school while I'm sleeping."

Ty smiled, though I could sense tension growing within his masked expression. He moved forward and pulled me against his chest. "We'll make it work, somehow. But we don't have long now. After all the transformations and the full moon, I'm struggling to keep this dream going." His lips grazed mine. "I wish it could be more."

A sense of urgency seized me, causing my pulse to jump at more than his touch and mouth-watering scent. I entwined my fingers in his sleek hair and pulled his face to mine, kissing him with passionate force. Ty gasped with surprise. A second later he recovered, gripping my back and deepening our kiss. His hot body pressed against mine while his scent flooded my lungs. "I want you."

His hot breathy words against my lips sent a shock of intoxicating desire through me. I wanted him too. My hands crept under his shirt, finding the scar-covered muscles there, before pulling it over his head. His perspiring skin slid under my fingertips as they traveled back down the lines of his chest. Electricity shot through my body, tingling with the searing heat of his touch. His hands trailed across my back to my sides, creeping under the thin fabric of my tank top. I sucked in a sharp breath as his fingers caressed the naked flesh of my stomach, slowly rising. Fangs split from my gums, piercing my lower lip. My body screamed, yearning for every part of him. I tore my top off, barely able to think past the lure of his blood while tasting my own. Ty responded at once, reaching up with expert fingers to undo my bra. His lips broke from mine, finding my collarbone as the straps fell down my arms. I shivered at the firm brush of his lips. Then I hastily threw my bra aside before lowering shaking hands to unbuckle his pants. I sank onto the soft grass and gripped both ends of his belt, pulling him down on top of me. A broad smile tugged at Ty's lips as he gazed into my eyes, dipping his head to re-join our lips. His smoldering body molded against mine while he trailed hot kisses down my neck.

It's not real. The damning thought invaded my mind. It cut through the undeniable yearning I felt to give myself to Ty. A shockwave bolted through my body. My hands froze, no longer pulling Ty against me. *This is just a dream.*

Instantly Ty hesitated, lips drawing away from my neck. His intense eyes peered into mine from behind the hair that fell over his face.

"This isn't real," I whispered, struggling for breath.

Dawning realization stole across Ty's features: shock, disappointment, and longing. There even appeared to be a glint of regret. He lifted his body from mine with a shuddering sigh.

My heart squeezed, my body still screaming for his. "*I'm sorry,*" I whispered, arms awkwardly lowering to cover my exposed chest. "Are you mad?"

"What?" Ty seemed genuinely surprised. "No. Of course I'm not." With a sigh, he slung one arm under my legs and the other around my neck. Then he drew me onto his lap. He reached for his discarded shirt and pulled it over my head, covering my bare flesh. "I should be the one who's sorry, and I am. Amelia, I wasn't trying to pressure you." His hot lips met my temple, and his sweet breath ruffled my eyelashes. "I wanted you, so bad. I still do." He sighed again, long and hard. "But not like this. Not in an alternate reality that exists only in our minds and not on any lasting physical plane. I want the real you, flesh and blood. And I would rather wait than rush it like this. I just forgot where we were. Can you forgive me?"

"There's nothing to forgive." A genuine smile brightened my face and I hugged my arms tight around Ty. "And I want that too. More than anything, I just want you."

IN THE MORNING I awoke alone. The heated brush of Ty's lips and hands lingered on my cold skin. A vivid reminder of what we had been about to do ran through my mind. His flesh connecting with mine had shot electricity through my body, awakening my every sense. In the fleeting moments we'd had together, missing him had taken over. I'd wanted nothing more than to be with him, to give myself to him entirely.

But I hadn't. Reality had edged its way in, along with a daunting realization. It was just a dream. The physical interaction would forever remain in our minds. But any remnants of the intimate act would disappear as he did.

Unable to clear the image from my memory, I threw open the thick, maroon drapes. Beyond the row of four narrow, arc-topped windows, the sky was black with night. Not a single star was visible under a cloak of heavy clouds. I glanced at the analog clock beside the phone. It was minutes from midnight. A new vampire day had already begun. One I had slept through almost half of.

With my tutoring not commencing until tomorrow, I forced myself into the bathroom. At the foot of the door to Kendrick's room was a block of chocolate. A Post-it note was attached. *You can't hate me forever.*

Wanna bet? Chocolate had always been my weakness, my kryptonite. But I wasn't ready to make nice. And no amount of chocolate was about to change that. I scrunched up the note and made sure his room was empty. Then I had the quickest shower ever before throwing on jeans and my favorite purple tank. Claustrophobic air was building up around me. It was an inability to breathe properly knowing Ty was so far away. I needed to do something to distract the aching that still gripped my heart. Plus I didn't want to have to deal with Kendrick again. To escape both issues, I left my room. It was time to get acquainted with my new surroundings, my prison.

Getting lost within the Armaya's expansive labyrinth of snaking corridors revealed many locked doors and hardly any people. Finally I stumbled across my uncle's office. Sweat instantly dampened my palms. Talking about Ty with him again was the last thing I wanted to do. Still, avoiding the situation wouldn't fix anything. I had to be accountable. I had to prove that I was mature enough to decide my own fate, my own future.

With a deep breath, I knocked on the door. It creaked open. Inside the lights were on but the room was vacant. Weight lifted from my chest. I turned to leave, but a glimmer caught my eye, something catching the dim lamplight. My eyes fell on the antique grandfather clock. The pendulum that swung behind the glass covering was reflecting more than just the room's light. A rainbow danced over the silvery surface each time it passed a vertical point. Going inside, I knelt and opened the glass door, exposing the pendulum. My hands scrounged below in the darkness of the solid base of the clock. Then I grazed something cold and smooth. It was a glass vial, I realized, topped with a thick, silver liquid. I tilted it back and forth, entranced as it glittered a spectrum of colors.

"Ahem," a voice sounded from behind.

Rising I whirled, my heart suddenly hammering and the vial clutched in my hand.

Uncle Caius stood in the doorway, his expression stern and his arms crossed over his chest. "What are you doing in here?"

Just like a child being reprimanded, I peered down to the Persian rug covering the wooden floor. "Sorry, Uncle Caius. The door was open. I…I…"

Caius stepped forward and seized my hand. "*And this?*"

With a throat-clearing gulp, I forced my eyes up and shrugged. "The light caught my eye. I was just curious."

My uncle's expression softened. He turned my hand and pried open my clutched fingers, removing the vial. Then he walked to his desk, placing it in the top drawer.

Following with caution, I took the seat opposite him. "The vial, what's inside it?" And why did I feel such a strange pull toward to it? I wondered.

Caius waved a dismissive hand. "Merely an herbal remedy, though the main ingredient is quite hard to come by." He clasped his hands in front of him. "Now, how would you like a guided tour around your new home?"

CHAPTER 22

"*A*melia," the guy said with a smile. He rose from his perch on a desk centering the library to extend a welcoming hand. "It's nice to meet you. I'm Marcus Vladimir, your tutor."

The library, as I had discovered yesterday during Caius's guided tour, was more than expansive. It stretched thirty feet high, its walls covered with unending shelves of books. Above, the ceiling was entirely made of curved glass that right now revealed a star-speckled sky.

I frowned at the guy standing before me. With glossy blond hair and not a single age-line marking his pale, angelic face, he looked barely a few years older than me. Too young for what I had expected my tutor to be. Then I remembered the name. He was Kendrick's friend. I huffed at the thought of him. Another note had been left this morning along with a packet of chocolate mint slice cookies—my favorites. At least there was one good thing about being a vampire. We could eat whatever we wanted without effect. Otherwise I would have wondered if he was trying to make me fat.

Marcus's hand was still outstretched, and I was being totally rude, standing in dumb thought. I quickly accepted his waiting hand, which he turned, raising the back of my hand to his lips. At the same moment his teal-flecked, blue eyes froze on my face. Then something totally weird happened. A flaming bolt ignited with his touch, scorching a channel from his connecting lips into my core. Recognition kindled within me. I jerked away with a frown, eyes darting to see if anyone had seen. The librarian was manning the front desk. No one else was visible past the eight-foot, freestanding stacks. We were essentially alone.

I glanced back at Marcus with caution. I was absolutely certain I had never met this guy before this very second. Yet there was something there. It was in the twinkle of his unwavering eyes and the electricity of his touch. A kindled awareness I couldn't quite ignore. A whisper deep within that somehow our souls recognized one another.

Don't be ridiculous. I shook myself and forced my tongue and mouth to move. "It's um, nice to meet you, Marcus." My eyes shifted warily over his casual attire. He wore faded jeans and a snug-fitting, white T-shirt that clung to his toned chest. Then I looked to the stacked books and papers that cluttered the desk behind him. He didn't look anything like a tutor. *Who are you?* I wondered, but only said, "Am I interrupting?"

Marcus shrugged with complete indifference. "Not really. I'm just studying for what will soon become my obligation." When I remained silent, unabashedly studying his face, he continued. "My father, Lord Vladimir, is one of the seven reigning royals. He's nearing the end of his shelf life. When he kicks it, I'll take his position."

Though his lack of emotion struck me, I couldn't forget the

feeling he ignited within me. My lips spoke without permission. "But you're so young."

A fanged smile lit his chiseled face. "Same age as you, I believe."

"You're sixteen!" I almost shouted.

"Just turned seventeen. Unfortunately age does not negate responsibility." Marcus moved around the desk, taking one of two seats. He seemed totally unaffected by my lingering stare. "I'm guessing you know very little of vampire custom. So," he said, patting the seat next to him, "shall we get started?"

Over the next few hours, Marcus skimmed over an endless list of vampire-related topics. There were so many details that by the time we were done, I didn't think my brain could hold another single piece of information. First he touched on vampire aging, which in royals began to slow at around twenty. Next was our need for blood, which increased with age while our desire for human food declined. We could still eat regular food, but its taste would be less appealing. This was not going to be good for my chocolate crutch. After that, he covered the Armaya's rules and regulations, including their reluctance to allow outsiders within their walls. Lastly was a brief mention on compulsion and its rules of use, as well as a little speech on why those rules existed.

"Let's see," Marcus mused, rifling through a stack of books.

My elbow rested on the desk, propping up my head as I watched him. The unwavering feeling of recognition still perplexed me. How could I feel connected to him?

"Ah," Marcus said, pulling a thick book from the stack and placing it in front of me. It was leather-bound and visibly old with a cracked spine and that strong musky scent that came with age-worn pages. "The War of the Races."

A shiver gripped my body and my elbow slid out from under my head, connecting with the stack of books. The force sent them flying off the table and onto the ground. I scrambled to pick them up. "Races?" I croaked out, slamming the last book back onto the desk.

"Vampires and lycanthropes." Marcus looked down at me, the teal of his eyes gleaming. "It was a distant time when the wolves existed to serve us, as our guardians and slaves. Their place was to protect royals against beings stronger and faster than us, beings we have since driven to extinction." He leaned back in his seat and cracked his knuckles. "This story, however, does not begin in war. The actions of a single female lycan, of which there were and are very few, changed the way in which our races coexisted."

A toxic lump had climbed up my throat and I couldn't restrain myself from asking. "Why? What'd she do?"

Marcus regarded me with a speculative expression. "She used the lure of her potent blood to attract the affections of a royal. The royal was a young heir in line for one of the twelve thrones."

Dead blood spiked my throat and my pulse galloped. From the start I'd felt an undeniable draw to Ty's blood. But Marcus's last words rang in my ears. *Twelve thrones?* "I thought you said there were only seven royal seats."

Marcus nodded. "There are now, but centuries ago there were twelve thrones." He shook his head, eyes becoming vacant. "The war changed that. And when their *relationship*," his tongue grated over the word with hatred, "came to light, a deeper betrayal was discovered. The lycan was carrying the royal's own flesh and blood, a hybrid abomination." Marcus crossed his arms over his chest. "After their imprisonment, there were whispers of a revolt amongst the wolves."

I recalled the prison chambers Caius had shown me yesterday and shuddered. The damp stone walls had been strung with hanging shackles. The pungent stink of death and decay had thickened the air. I shook off the memory and looked to Marcus. He seemed to be waiting for my undivided attention. Seething dread coursed through my chest. My brain screamed for me to keep my mouth shut, but I had to know. "What happened to them?"

"An example needed to be made. The wolves needed to be reminded of their place, not be led to question it."

Marcus flicked open the leather-bound book to a page printed with a black-and-white illustration. My throat choked closed and my head spun, threatening to make me faint. The illustration portrayed a man, shackled to a post above a furnace of blazing flames. His face was twisted, mouth gaping and fangs extended in a torturous cry of pain.

"They burned the royal heir alive," Marcus's voice cut through me like a knife. "His lover was forced to watch."

Tears stung my eyes, remembering my mom's outrage and Kendrick's hissed words after discovering me with Ty in the forest. *You want to stay here with that, that abomination!* In his eyes I had betrayed our kind. Betrayed everything he was raised to believe in. I lifted my eyes to Marcus, blinking back tears. "What happened to the werewolf?"

"She was to be executed next," Marcus said with an expression that betrayed no emotion. "But as feared, the guardians did rebel. They rose up, creating a bloodbath—and the woman escaped intact. That fateful day was the beginning of the War of the Races. The day the guardians turned against us and became our sworn enemy."

Marcus reached out, covering the tremble of my hands with his. I didn't pull away, his touch somehow easing the uncontrollable shake. "Do you see why you can't be with him?"

My eyes grew wide. Marcus knew about Ty? I tried to cover my stunned expression while struggling not to hyperventilate. "W-what do you mean?"

Marcus leaned in, his shoulder grazing mine and lips brushing against my ear. "The wolf…it's the reason you're here. Isn't it?"

Instant nausea rippled through my gut. I freed my hands and clutched my tightening stomach, struggling not to gag. Caius would never have revealed such delicate information. There was only one other person here who knew. The ability to control my breathing vanished. I began to hyperventilate. "Kendrick told you?"

"No." Marcus shook his head, looking irritated. "Your reaction to the story said all I needed to know."

The room began to spin and my lungs ached with shallow breath. I'd just endangered Ty.

I wanted to run from the library to call and warn him. But Marcus's hand tightened over mine, keeping me frozen in morbid fear. His eyes rose. "Amelia, I won't tell anyone."

I almost choked in disbelief. Then my suspicious mind kicked into overdrive. What would it cost me for him to keep such delicate information? I was a turned vampire, a nobody. I had nothing of value to offer. "Why? What do you want from me?"

Marcus looked wounded, and I questioned his sincerity. "Amelia, it's not like that." He ran his tongue over his teeth and sighed. "I'll keep your secret for one reason and one reason only."

"And what might that be?"

At my narrowing eyes, a thin smile played across Marcus's pale lips. "Because we share a connection… You felt it too, didn't you?"

Vulnerability scrawled across his face as I stared at him, stunned. He'd felt it? I forced myself to nod. "I did."

Marcus released my hands and clenched his jaw. "Just understand the consequences of affiliating with one of theirs. If The Council finds out…" A muscle in his cheek ticked. "History has a way of repeating itself."

THE SUN BEAMED DOWN, heating what felt like coarse sand beneath me. I arched up into a sitting position, tucking my knees under my chin. The intensity of a midday sun warmed my icy skin, while inside I remained frozen to the bone. The movement of water reached my ears then. It wasn't the plunging of a waterfall or the swirl of a river. Instead, it was the crushing repetition of rolling waves.

Trying to force the blur of sleep and the blinding light from my eyes, I squinted. The surroundings slowly cleared, like a camera lens coming into focus. Everything around me appeared illuminated. Ocean swells and rocky sand dunes all glowed as though they were a reflection of the sun. A dizzy spell rolled through me and forced my head to tip against my knees. Where was I?

A shadow grew in front of me, striking out the warmth of the sun. "Are you okay?"

Forcing my face up with my hands, I met a familiar face. "Ty!" I jumped to my feet and instantly wished I hadn't. Blood rushed to my head and I staggered, threatening to crumble.

Ty caught my arm before I fell, and lowered me back to the blistering sand. Leaning into his body, I rested my head against his chest. "I don't know what's wrong with me." I peered up into his face, which appeared gripped with worry. "I just feel...cold."

The intense sphere behind Ty created a heavenly glow around his tan body. My breath caught in my throat. He was the picture of perfection, an angel cast down from heaven.

Ty wrapped a strong arm around me, rubbing the chilled skin of my bare arm. His voice was soothing. "Tell me about your day."

I thought back, but my brain felt like it was packed with sludge.

All I could see were foggy snippets of events. I rubbed at my temples.

The concern in Ty's voice grew. "You can't remember?"

When I thought harder, my brain throbbed against my skull. "I met a...vampire." The pieces of my memory slipped in and out of focus, a puzzle refusing to come together. I could see the book-lined walls of the library. There I had met a guy for the very first time. *Marcus.* I scanned my memory again, trying to recall the rest of the day. What else happened? When did I go to sleep? The wind was knocked from my lungs as the terrifying story Marcus had told me resurfaced. "The War of the Races," I choked out.

Ty's comforting hand ceased traveling across my arm. "Ah."

Surprise caused me to curve his way. Ty was staring vacantly at the crashing waves on the sandy shore. "You've heard of it?"

Ty nodded, but there was pain in his expression. He was clearly trying to hide it, but I could see that it cut deep. "A war, forged out of love..."

Something triggered within me. His reaction was more than just recalling the bloody tale of how our races had become mortal enemies. It was deeply personal. "Ty, what aren't you telling me?"

Ty's chest rose and fell with a deep sigh. "You're not gonna like this. And I wasn't keeping it from you. We just..." He broke off and shook his head. "The lycan that caused the revolt...she was my grandmother."

My jaw dropped and my mouth felt like it was stuffed with cotton wool. "You're part...*vampire*?"

"Barely..." A thin smile tugged at Ty's lips, returning some of the animation to his expression. "The lycanthrope mutation is more prominent in a hybrid. So each generation has diluted that part of us. Well, so long as we partner another lycan."

I thought of the family portrait in the dining room at Ty's house.

The woman in the picture, his mother, had in almost every way resembled a werewolf. Her hair had been raven black and her skin as tan as Ty's. There had been only one distinct difference: her eyes. They hadn't been reminiscent of lycans or even vampires. They had been a marrying swirl of green, blue, gold, and silver. The varying shades of a sun-speckled ocean.

"The portrait. Your mother was part vampire." Ty nodded, but there was one part of this revelation that didn't quite add up. "Then why is your father so against me, against us?"

"Because..." Ty's gaze returned to the crashing waves. "My mother didn't die of natural causes, or through an unavoidable accident. She was hunted down for being a half-cast, and murdered. Her killers were vampires."

I groaned. "No wonder your father hates me so much. I'm not just his sworn enemy, I..." I broke off at the tightening of my chest. It felt like my ribs were strapped by solid metal plates that were pulling tighter by the second. Ty was part vampire, maybe only a small part, but still what he called a half-cast. Was he already at risk of being hunted like his mother? Was being with me only further endangering him? I understood then why Ty's father feared me— maybe even more than he hated me. I was a risk of history repeating. Marcus had said the words so plainly, but I hadn't understood their magnitude. Now I couldn't ignore it. I curled my arms around Ty, pressing myself against him. "Ty, I would give anything to be with you. But..."

As I tried to rise, to move away, Ty's arms tightened around me. "Amelia, it is not up to you to save me. And I would rather die a thousand deaths than live without you." Skillet's song *Never Surrender* rose in the sea breeze as if to prove the depth of his feelings. "But if you don't feel the same..."

With a quickly raised finger to Ty's lips, I stilled his words. "I do. But I can't risk you, Ty. I won't."

"You're not," Ty said, sounding a little exasperated. "With or without you I'm *already* on the wanted list. I may have so little vampire in me that I don't even require blood for sustenance, but that doesn't matter. I'm stronger than either race, a threat." At my stubborn look, Ty went on. "Look, it wasn't royals who took my mother's life. And the War of the Races was centuries ago. Things have changed a lot since then. The wolves are their own people now. We only inter-fere with vampire business when your elders don't take action. And you're not a royal, Amelia. You may not be entirely free to make your own choices, yet. But they can't harm either of us for being together."

A chill gripped my spine, liquefying my insides. Madam Rosalie's words rang in my ears. *He will alter the path of your life. Deliver you unto danger. You must accept the light. It's the only way to save him.*

Danger, light…what did it all mean? A wave of fear pierced my heart, one that I tried to ignore. She was nuts. It means nothing. My arms coiled around Ty. There was one thing I knew for sure—whether or not my fears were real, I wasn't strong enough to let him go. "I hope you're right."

THE PHONE RANG, tearing me awake. I fumbled in the dark for the receiver and knocked it to the ground. "Shit!" With my eyes refusing to focus against the room's darkness, I searched the ground blindly. Finally my fingers grazed the phone. "Sorry, hello."

"Excuse me, Miss Lamont. Lord Caius Bathory requests your company for dinner," a woman advised before the line went dead.

My vision cleared as I adjusted to the dark shadows of my room. I touched my phone on the bedside table to light up the screen. It was midnight—the day after yesterday. Where had the hours gone? I rubbed at my forehead. Somehow a chunk of time was missing. But as I tried to think back, I couldn't recall anything after my tutoring session with Marcus. Any recollection of going to sleep didn't exist. And I couldn't understand why I had only just woken up now, more than a day since my last memories.

A loud gurgling sounded as my insides squeezed with the nausea of being totally empty. Apparently I was starving. With Uncle Caius waiting, I tried to push my memory concerns to the back of my mind. I threw on the discarded clothes that lay across the foot of my bed. They were the same jeans and T-shirt I had worn two days ago. When I darted into the bathroom to splash cold water on my face, something caught my eye. It was a packet of triple-choc cookies and another note: *I miss you.* Unmoved and starving, I scoffed a few cookies then ran out the door.

Downstairs, the smell of delicious food hung in the air. It made my stomach groan with desperate hunger. With a single knock, I entered Caius's office to see a platter overflowing with colorful food. Caius peered up from behind his desk, dressed formally in a sharp, black suit. He rocked back in his leather-padded chair.

I took the seat opposite my uncle. "Good evening, Uncle Caius."

He smiled, causing the lines of his middle-aged face to crease. "Roast pork, compliments of our chefs."

There were cuts of pink meat, roasted vegetables, and apple-sauce with crackling on the side. The sight made my mouth water. "It looks amazing." I filled my plate with hungry eyes and began eating without pause.

Caius chuckled quietly, and I glanced up to meet his watching gaze. "My dear, you would think we had been starving you."

Self-conscious, I slowed my eating to an acceptable pace. "Sorry," I managed between bites. "I forgot to eat lunch." *And now I'm lying. But how could I explain missing more than a whole day?* Anxiety seized my filling stomach. *Does he know I missed my tutor today?*

Caius motioned to the goblet waiting beside my plate with an instructive nod. It was made from solid brass and encrusted with sparkling, multicolored jewels. "A drink should help wash it all down. Though it is a rare drop, so savor it, my dear."

Overwhelming thirst quelled my anxiety with a deep bodily need that I couldn't ignore. *When did I last drink blood?* I grasped the goblet in both hands, absently noticing the dark blue veins that ran up my arms. A warming against my chest caused me to pause. My eyes glided down to the amethyst pendant. *Why am I still wearing this stupid thing?* Ignoring the warmth, my mouth watered with expectation. I raised the cool edge of the jewel-encrusted cup to my lips, taking a long, slow sip. A rich, metallic taste exploded on my tongue. It coated the walls of my mouth and throat. It felt as though the blood was absorbing straight through the soft flesh of my mouth. With an uncontrollable cough, I slammed the goblet back down on the desk. Ice-cold tingles followed, cascading down my body.

Caius chuckled. "I do forget how rich this blood is." He took a sip from his own goblet. "My senses have grown accustomed to its effects, as yours soon will too." He nodded back to my drink with raised brows.

Obediently, I picked up the cup and took another tiny sip. I braced myself as the same cold metallic taste coated my mouth, and iced tingles gripped my body. My throat constricted as I fought the need to cough. "What kind of blood is that?" I choked out.

Caius paused between mouthfuls, arching one eyebrow. "Ancient vampire blood." When my eyes grew wide, imagining royals slaughtered for their rich blood, Caius laughed. "Amelia, we are not barbarians. Centuries ago, Pure Bloods bottled their own blood and stored it to age like a fine wine. Some of us still do today."

A fragmented memory that I couldn't quite grasp teased the corners of my mind. Ancient vampire blood... My brain began to pulse against my skull. Where have I heard that before? A question formed on my lips. "Why would we drink another vampire's blood?"

Caius relaxed back into his office chair, regarding me with narrowed eyes. "I thought Marcus would have already schooled you in this."

Marcus. My pulse rose. I tugged harder at my memories. Still I couldn't recall a thing Marcus had taught me. I could only remember his face. It had been ageless and still somehow mature beyond his seventeen years. Why couldn't I remember?

"Vampire blood," Caius went on, "especially a Pure Blood's, holds healing properties. It helps rejuvenate, and in centuries past was used to assist the healing of mortally injured guardians."

My stomach turned, threatening to crawl up my throat. Guardians? A rush of words, followed by a gruesome fiery image, spun through my mind. My heartbeat took off. The War of the Races. The werewolf and vampire lovers... In that moment, I recalled the entire grisly tale and my following dreamscape with Ty. How had I forgotten?

"Is everything alright, my dear?" Caius's voice shook me. "Did you not find your tutor lessons informative?" He forked a piece of pumpkin, vibrant blue eyes watching me intently.

I swallowed, pushing down my rising stomach. "I did..." I think. "There's just so much to learn. I guess I'm a bit...overwhelmed."

"Well, you still have many lifetimes ahead of you." He collected a huge, diamond-cut paperweight from his desk, passing it from hand to hand. The solid crystal caught the desk lamp's light, reflecting a flash of brilliant white. "Now, I would like to further discuss the situation that brings you here."

My heart sank and my memory issues became a distant second thought. Shit! I had gotten off light on arriving. Still I knew this had to come up sooner or later.

"Amelia, my dear, you must understand that your affiliation with that creature cannot continue." Caius's tone was level and devoid of the disgust my mom and Kendrick had displayed. "He will die before you've even lived out a tenth of your life."

My lips moved without permission. "I understand that. But I love him."

My uncle's jaw tensed, the vein across his temple throbbing. He took a deep, steadying breath. "I understand how you feel, Amelia. Once upon a time, I too was in love. Though you must understand that love does not come without sacrifices."

"You were in love?" In all my life I'd never seen Caius even look at a woman. Well, apart from Mom. But that was different. "With who? What happened?"

Uncle Caius's eyes dropped. "I would rather not reminisce." He sighed, tilting his face up. "Amelia, please consider this. Saying goodbye to that boy now seems unbearable. But how much more destroying will it be when you lose him, forever? When nature takes its course and he grows frail with age while you do not. Will you be able to stand at his side? When the time comes, will you have the strength to watch him die?"

There was no response I could offer to my uncle's question. He didn't appear to expect one. Unable to eat anymore, I pushed my plate away. The reality of one day having to watch Ty die filled me with uncertainty and dread. My heart squeezed so tight that I struggled to breathe through the pain. How can I watch him die? I rose to my feet, unable to look my uncle in the eye. "I need some time to think."

"Of course." But as I reached the door, Uncle Caius cleared his throat. "One more thing, Amelia." I turned to view my uncle's steady expression, his eyes set on mine. "I understand that your friendship with Kendrick is still strained, though you must realize his actions were out of concern for you. In any case, I know you will mend and strengthen your relationship. You will become even closer than you were before."

Having barely heard my uncle's words, I raced up to my room. I needed to talk to Ty and hear the certainty of his deep voice. My limbs felt weak though, inexplicably unstable. I tripped on the last stone stair to the second floor. But that didn't slow me down. I flew through my room's door and grasped my iPhone from the bedside table. The phone's incessant ringing as I held it pressed against my ear made my heart squeeze tighter. I threw my hand into the bedside drawer and pulled out a choc-mint cookie, chomping into it. Please pick up. Disquiet rose up my throat as I stared out into the darkness beyond the window. A dusting of ice-flakes fell, settling on the outer rail and sill.

A gravelly voice answered. "Amelia?"

Breath escaped my lungs and my tongue tied up with cookie crumbs.

"Do you know it's only five in the morning here?"

"Sorry," I croaked, swallowing to find my voice. Sweat dampened my palms and I swiped them against my jeans. "I forgot. I just...I had to hear your voice."

"Amelia, what's happened?" Worry tainted Ty's words. "Is everything okay?"

"I just..." Unsure of what I actually wanted to say, I closed my eyes. The image of Ty frail and struggling through his last, dying breaths, flashed across my eyelids.

"Amelia," Ty spoke, his voice laced with growing strain. "Tell me what's wrong. You can tell me anything."

With a deep, lung-aching breath, I blurted out the puzzling feelings blurring my emotions. "I just don't know what our future holds."

"Are you having second thoughts already?" Ty joked, though there was an underlying edge to his tone.

"I'm being serious, Ty." My sharp words surprised me, but I couldn't control it. There was just so much standing in our way. "How can we stay together? We're so different."

"Amelia, I don't understand. What we have between us is more than what we are." A ragged breath blew through my ear. "Don't you still feel the same?"

A growing ache to be near Ty surged through me, to see his face and those eyes that glowed with a love I never wanted to live without. In the same moment, growing uncertainty muddled that want. One day I would have to say goodbye, *forever*. I threw the other half of the cookie into my mouth and spoke around it. "I just can't bear to watch you die, to lose you forever."

Ty sighed a long, drawn-out breath. "Amelia, I am not dying. And you could never lose…"

"But one day you will!" I screamed, spitting crumbs. "You'll grow old and frail, and you'll die. How am I supposed to go on after that?"

I fell back against the soft, turquoise pillows on my bed, fighting the urge to hyperventilate. Tears stung my eyes. A pause of silence raised my heartbeat with trepidation.

At last Ty responded. "So, you're afraid you won't love me

when I'm old and gray and you're still young and beautiful?" He sounded wounded at the thought.

Aware that I was hurting him, I pinned my eyes shut. It was undeniable that my feelings for Ty ran much deeper than his physical attributes. I knew his age and appearance would never diminish my love for him. "No, that's not it." Icy tears spilled down my cheeks. My voice rose with frustration. "I just don't know how I can go on without you. How could I live on after that?"

"Amelia, we have decades before we need to worry about that." Ty's now level voice was reassuring. "All that matters now is that you still feel as strongly for me as I do for you. You are the most important person in this world to me. If I have to fight till the day I die to be with you, I will. We can make it through this separation if you just hold on to what we share."

My heart thudded in my chest. Of course I still loved Ty, more than anything. There was nothing I wanted more than to be with him. So why couldn't I rid this growing self-doubt from my mind? "You're right. I know you are." I pulled into a sitting position, pushing stray hairs from my face. "I don't know what came over me."

"Feeling better?" Ty asked.

"Yeah, I think so." I sighed. My heart rate had slowed but the muscle felt raw and battered. I miss you so much. "When can I see you again?"

Silence rang in my ears, seconds dragging on forever until Ty finally spoke. "It's a bit tricky with the opposite schedule and school. It might have to wait until next Friday."

Disappointment crashed over me like an avalanche. Friday. That was a full week away.

"At least you've got Kendrick to keep you company," Ty added.

I let out a harsh little laugh. "Yeah, great!"

"You still haven't forgiven him?" Ty sounded surprised.

Had I? I shook my head, glancing at my bedside table. A mountain of edible gifts was taking up the drawer. "I don't know."

"Well, either way, it's up to you. But I have to get going. I have swim practice this morning, and coach will kill me if I'm late. Just send me a text when you're going to sleep on Friday, and I'll be waiting. And call me anytime, night or day. Promise?"

My heart tightened with longing. A whole week apart. Talking on the phone was nothing more than a poor consolation. "I promise." I hung up the phone and fell back against my bed. *Goodbye, Ty.*

CHAPTER 23

In the morning when I woke up, I remembered where I was and why. I groaned, tiredly pulling myself out of bed. The few months Mom had threatened were growing increasingly unbearable. And knowing I'd have to wait almost a week to see Ty made each minute feel like an extended lifetime. My emotions were running rampant, filling me with doubt that made me question my actions. Were my feelings for Ty still as strong? Was I really doing the right thing by staying with him?

Inside I felt torn in two directions. A new world was opening up before me. A world where I wasn't a monster who should be feared. Here I was just normal. On the other hand, being without Ty instilled a sense of loss in me. At times the grief would swell, and at others it diffused. My brain pulsed against my skull. The hours of sleep hadn't relieved any of my strain. I needed to wake up.

With fatigue ravishing my body, I stumbled into the bathroom. My toe smacked the lifted edge of the tiles and I swore. My head felt heavier with each step, and my eyes burned with exhaustion. I stripped off my tank top and underwear and stepped into the circular, claw-footed bath in the middle of the room. I turned the tap up to what I hoped would be a scalding but awakening temperature.

The water that fell from the showerhead in the ceiling sparkled under the fluorescent lighting. The sight reminded me of Ty's unique golden eyes. The temperature only reminded me of the uninhibited moments I had spent in his heated arms. It didn't awaken my body or mind, and it didn't relieve the aching of my muscles that felt like I'd run a hundred miles, either. In a feeble attempt to clear my sleepy vision, I rubbed at my eyes. Sharp stinging from soap pierced them and I cried out in pain. With irritation growing, I turned off the water and searched blindly with my lids pinned shut for a towel.

A loud click, followed by a door opening, shot my heart into my throat. I froze, naked and dripping wet. My still-burning eyes flung open. The door to Kendrick's room was wide open. Standing in the doorway was Kendrick, gap-jawed and holding a box of Whitman's chocolates. His staring eyes scoured my naked flesh.

Heat flared up my neck. My flesh ignited. "Don't just stand there!" I groped for the towel hanging from the wall and flung it around my body. "Get out!"

Kendrick's face flushed, but he didn't move. Instead, his gaze traveled up and down my towel-wrapped body, eyes sparkling as though my flesh were still exposed. "I-I…"

Why the hell was he still standing there? Incensed, my jaw snapped shut with a growl. I leaped from the bath and shoved my hands into his chest. "I said, get out!"

Surprise stole Kendrick's expression and he stumbled back through the doorway.

I slammed the door shut. Sharp breath controlled the rapid rise and fall of my chest. My eyes flickered to the gold-framed mirror spanning the marble vanity. My face was alight with embarrassment, burning crimson. Kendrick just freaking saw me naked! I forced my breath to slow, causing my lungs to ache in protest. At the same time, an unexpected awareness dawned on me. The livid and consuming hate I'd felt towards him had evaporated. I wasn't pissed with him anymore.

In a hurry, I threw on some clothes and combed through the knots in my long hair. Then I knocked on the adjoining door. "Kendrick, can I come in?" My pulse elevated and I raked my hands through my golden tresses. Nervous energy tightened within my chest. *Why are you being like this? It's just Kendrick.*

"Um," Kendrick's shaky voice echoed through the barrier. "Just a second..."

The sound of rustling reached my ears before the door swung open. Behind Kendrick, his room was still the same, all posters and dark shades. His snow-dusted boarding jacket and gloves were slung over the couch. The chaise by the night-bordered window held up his snowboard. My sight quickly returned to Kendrick. Now that I wasn't staring at him through startled eyes, he appeared dog-tired with puffy crescents lining his eyes. Uneasiness strained his face.

"Amelia, I'm sorry. I honestly didn't realize you were in here. I just came in from hitting a few slopes and didn't hear any water." He shoved his hands into the pockets of his damp cargo pants, ashamed eyes downcast.

A flutter of butterflies swarmed my stomach, his genuine unease stealing my words.

Kendrick frowned, shifting his weight from leg to leg. "I know. You're still pissed at me. You have every right to be."

Although I could hear my best friend speaking, I wasn't listening. My eyes had narrowed at the exposed flesh of his slender chest —visible through the three opened buttons of his V-neck. They glided over his jutting collarbone and the throbbing vein that curved over its ridge, to settle along the side of his neck. My mouth drained of all saliva, dry as though it were packed with sand. I was seriously thirsty.

"Amelia, please." Kendrick's pleading tone drew my eyes from his neck. "You have to believe me. I only told her to protect you. I thought I was doing the right thing."

Told who what? I frowned and reached out to touch his arm. "Kendrick, what in the world are you talking about?"

"Telling your mom about Ty," he said with narrowing eyes. "About him being a werewolf. It's the reason you're here."

Understanding flashed through my mind as I recalled what had somehow vanished from my memory. "Oh, yeah..." I shook off the clouds of confusion. Every detail of that day came back, along with what Kendrick's actions had caused. But the constant anger I had felt towards him no longer raged through my veins—and right now, I didn't even care why my feelings had shifted. Instead, warmth fluttered my heart at knowing I had now forgiven my best friend. "I must still be half asleep." I smiled and threw my arms around him. "And I'm sorry too. I don't want us to fight anymore. I hate it."

Kendrick pulled from my ecstatic embrace. He curled his strong hands over my shoulders while studying my face. "Are you feeling okay?"

I brushed off his arms, still smiling. "Of course..." My eyes flickered back to the vein along his neck. There was an underlying draw to yield to his flesh and blood. I swallowed back the conflicting feelings. "Let's get some breakfast. I'm *starving*."

Caius had shown me the expansive dining hall during his guided tour. Until now I had remained reluctant to eat there. I hadn't wanted to allow myself to get comfortable in this prison of mine, to find commonality with the race I belonged to but so deep-heartedly wished I didn't. But with Kendrick beside me, the reluctance to separate myself seemed to be dissolving. My need and want to refrain from the thing I was and all that came with it, somehow felt less important. *I'm changing*, I thought with a frown.

The hall was light and inviting. Each table was set with gold-plated cutlery, white china, and centerpieces stuffed with black calla lilies. For a moment I wondered if they grew the rare flowers inside the castle's grounds. They could be quite difficult to come by.

Before I could ask Kendrick, my eyes glided up the exposed columns before the far wall. Their patterned edges met the cathedral ceiling and the edge of a perfectly circular hand-painted piece of art. The vivid painting depicted an angel with wings of satin-black, reaching from darkness into light. His face contorted with clear conflict. My eyes remained frozen above as we took up a table centering the expansive hall. "The painting," I spoke to Kendrick. "What does it mean?"

Kendrick followed my line of sight to the artwork above our heads. "It's a depiction of Lucifer," he explained, "and his struggle to join both worlds, to bring light and darkness together as one."

The light… *You must accept the light. It's the only way to save him.* The fortuneteller's chilling words sounded in my ears. They were as clear as if she had whispered them right beside me.

Coils tightened around my throat and I gulped. "Why is it here?"

Kendrick inclined his head toward me, his expression solemn. "As a reminder…" The line he quoted then brought a rippling shiver to my bones. *"Though born through darkness, we must strive for the light, even if it burns us, even if it kills us."* He leaned forward and clutched my hand so hard that his nails dug into my flesh. "Amelia, why are *you* here?"

My eyes grew wide at his brash question. "What do you mean?" I pried my hand away, rubbing at the indents his nails had left. "You know I had no choice."

Kendrick glared away, hands curling into fists above the table. His next words were whispered so quietly that I had to strain to hear them. "You shouldn't be here."

A pang of ice shot through my heart. Kendrick didn't want me here?

The sound of the glass doors to the dining hall swinging open diverted my gaze. Uncle Caius, along with Marcus and a few other vampires, had entered. Caius was deep in conversation with a familiar-looking red-haired woman—the woman from the auction. Marcus was trailing behind the group when he caught sight of me. His hand rose to wave, then at noticing Kendrick, dropped. For a split second his expression appeared to harden. Then the look was gone and he was smiling.

Kendrick stiffened in his chair. He nodded without blinking at Marcus before painting a smile across his lips. "So, I was thinking pancakes and a non-virgin Bloody Mary, *if* you know what I mean. Although on the other hand, the waffles come with chocolate sauce. And I know how you can't resist chocolate."

AFTER BREAKFAST I escaped down to the library, without Kendrick. According to him, he had *boring as hell council work* to get back to. Skillet's song *It's not me it's you* blared through my earbuds. The words made me wonder what I had done to encourage Kendrick's unexpected words. *You shouldn't be here.* I cringed, remembering his agitated tone. Was he over my mood swings? Or just sick of loving someone who kept hurting him?

With my pulsing mind reeling, I walked past the freestanding stacks to the desks centering the library. I desperately needed a distraction, a sense of feeling close to someone, of feeling safe and accepted. Only one guy made me feel that way here, and I hardly even knew him. Marcus.

But he wasn't there. All I found was the desk he usually occupied packed with towering books and tilting manila folders. My eyes scanned past the freestanding stacks. A vacant desk at the back wall housed a desktop computer. No one sat there. Across the room the librarian was reshelving books. She appeared to be the only other person in here.

With a shrug, I sat behind the messy desk and began flicking through a pile of manila folders. Hopefully there'd be something interesting in them to help pass the time, and distract me from thinking about Kendrick. My focus skimmed over much of the handwritten scrawl, not really taking notice, until one folder in particular made me stop and stare. Inside the cover was a name written in block letters. AMELIA LAMONT.

Blood roared through my ears, and my eyes transfixed on the folder. Was Marcus spying on me? Fueled confusion tore into my stomach. Growing suspicion was swiftly creeping over me. What the hell was going on?

Desperate for a rational explanation, I flicked through the loose sheets. My eyes bugged. There were pages upon pages of handwritten notes, detailing events of my life. The night my lust for blood had risen and my victim from *Pulse*. The progress I'd made in hunting at the cabin. The day Kendrick had taught me to refrain from killing wild prey. There was mention of Ty and him being a descendant of the werewolf who caused the revolt. Following that were private moments Kendrick and I had shared, including his attempt to compel me. Then the interaction I'd had with the fortuneteller and Ty's transformation in the forest. Lastly was the decision my mom and uncle had made to transfer me to the Armaya.

The list was extensive. It was almost an entire recap of my life since I discovered the monster within me. Chocolate-drenched waffle remnants crept quickly up my throat. My hands shook as I continued flicking through the pages. Then they froze. A thicker, smaller piece of paper had slid from between the sheets. With my heart slamming against my chest, I picked up the piece of paper. It was a black-and-white photograph of my uncle cradling two infants, one in each arm. A proud smile glowed from his drawn face. At first I thought the photo must have been of Dorian and me. Then my eyes did a double take on noticing a distinct feature. Even in a black-and-white photograph, one thing was unmistakable. Both newborns had pure blond hair. The color matched my own tresses but was a stark contrast to Dorian's almost black locks. With a frown I turned the photo over, hoping for a date or even some names. I froze. The ink on the back revealed something much more crippling, a recipe of malevolent sorts.

Combine Ingredients with Pure Blood.

- *Black Hellebore (slows heart and weakens strength)— Dry and crush entire cutting of plant, including flower.*
- *Hemlock (depletes all muscle function)—Extract liquid from stem of live plant. DO NOT DRY.*
- *Belladonna (induces paralysis)—Crush dried roots into dust.*

The past few days rushed to the forefront of my mind. My missing time, the fatigue, my confusion, and even my sudden forgiveness of Kendrick…was Marcus behind it all? The pendant around my neck blazed with blistering heat. I went to lift it from my flesh, but the picture being suddenly ripped from my grasp stopped me. Marcus threw the photo inside the folder and slammed the cover shut. "What do you think you are doing?"

His wrath-twisted expression threw me, knocking the wind from my lungs. Yet I couldn't ignore what I'd held in my hands. Questions whirled through my mind. "What the hell *is* all this?" I demanded, thrusting the evidence into his face.

Marcus dropped into the seat beside me and snatched my hands. Electricity stung where his flesh connected with mine, and I futilely tried to pull away. "Let me explain." He clung harder to my hands, eyes staring into mine. The silver of his irises came alive, extinguishing the teal flecks of his unusually colored eyes. Then his pupils dilated. "Forget what you saw."

I fought to look away, to break the magnetized draw of his eyes. But I couldn't. He was too powerful. My head dipped, nodding.

"You never saw the folder marked with your name or any of its contents." Marcus's voice was as smooth as silk. It caressed my prickling flesh with each spoken word. "After breakfast you came to the library for our tutoring session, but now you have a splitting headache. You will ask to skip today's lesson so you can return to your room and rest…"

"Amelia, hello?" Marcus's tone, although light, somehow shook me. "Shall we begin?"

Feeling disorientated, I shook my head. In response, my brain ached with the repetitive pulse of pumping blood. Marcus was sitting right beside me, eyeing me as he rifled through a stack of books. "Um, sorry," I said then winced. Each word made the pressure in my head throb harder. "My brain feels like it's trying to crack straight through my skull. I think I need to lie down." I looked up, eyes pleading. "Can we skip our lesson, just for today?"

Marcus smiled. "Do I look like a tyrant?" When I remained silent, for some reason hesitating in answering his obvious joke, he laughed. "I'll take that as a no. And if you're really in that much pain, I demand you skip our lesson and try to sleep it off." He rose to his feet and helped me up. "Go, get some rest. If you're up to it, I will see you tomorrow."

GROWING concern churned up my insides. After resting off the headache that threatened migraine debilitation, I had planned to confront Kendrick. There was no way I'd let his strange behavior during breakfast go without demanding an explanation. But on entering the bathroom, I'd found a note taped to his door.

Catching a few slopes. Don't wait up. K.B.

That had been yesterday. Now the following day was coming to a close, with the sun set to rise in less than an hour. Kendrick still hadn't returned to his room. Apprehension grew within my chest. The amount of chocolate I'd eaten to diffuse my worry was now making me feel sick. *Kendrick, where the hell are you?*

I had gone about my day, getting in a bit of text tennis with Ty before he went to bed and before my own tutoring and meals. Every now and then I had checked back at our rooms. Now I was out of patience. It was time to seek him out.

Fleeing my room, I began searching the endless corridors of the Armaya and every unlocked room along the way. The castle appeared almost abandoned. The few vampires I did encounter— mainly uniformed staff—were rushing about in what I guessed was an effort to avoid the dawning sun. Now I was picking a path through the pews of the blacked-out foyer for the second time. Defeat-tinged exhaustion began to set in. My concern for Kendrick was quickly turning to panic. *Great, now I'm going in circles.*

I made for the corridor that would provide the most direct route back to my room. Please, let Kendrick be there. A crack of light shining through an almost closed door stalled my footfalls. It was coming from my uncle's office. The pendant warmed against my chest. At the same time, two distinct voices traveled on an invisible wave around me: Caius's and Kendrick's.

Relief at finally locating my elusive best friend washed over me. I turned toward the door and was about to push it open when Kendrick's defensive tone rose. My whole body froze.

"I don't understand why this is necessary," he was saying.

"Kendrick." Caius's sharp tone surprised me. "Our actions have not been without just cause. This is for her own good. Do you no longer agree?"

Her own good? With my breath held and lungs aching in protest, I dared to peek through the doorjamb. Uncle Caius sat behind a stack of folders at his desk, hands steepled in front of him.

Kendrick stood facing him. His back was turned to me and his head was shaking back and forth. "This isn't right," he said. "I can't keep deceiving her."

The dim glow from the single desk lamp cast shadows across my uncle's face. He chuckled. It was a dry and almost mocking sound. "And here I thought you loved her, that you would do anything to protect her. Is your conscience so contrite that you would have me send her back now, only to reunite with that fleabag? Does her friendship truly hold that little value to you?"

Tightness constricted my chest. They were talking about me. I backed away from the door, feeling sick to my stomach. Kendrick's voice elevated, sounding defensive. But I wasn't listening. My legs were already forcing me away, up the corridor and stairs. My heart squeezed over and over in my chest. *Our actions,* Caius had said. What the hell had they done?

Kendrick's voice rang in my ears as I flew through my

bedroom door. *I can't keep deceiving her.* Then Caius's words, *does her friendship truly hold that little value to you?* Damning suspicion caused my heart to jump. Our friendship was a lie? I began to pace back and forth. With my Vans wearing shoeprints in the plush carpet, a memory swirled through my mind.

Those you trust most are not always what they seem. The fortuneteller had spoken those words, shifting her beady eyes to Kendrick. And I wrote her off, labeled her as crazy, delusional. I was wrong all along. A new fear gripped my chest. What else had she been right about? My hand rose to the pendant around my neck. *It will...* I had cut off her words before she could finish. It will what? I wondered.

An ethereal voice whispered into my ear. *"Warn you."* It was so soft I questioned if my mind was playing a twisted trick on me.

The sudden slamming of a door caused my entire body to quake. My thoughts evaporated. Heavy falling steps sounded, growing louder and louder. My heart jumped into my throat. Then the bathroom door swung open and Kendrick entered my room.

"Amelia, you're still up." He smiled. "Sorry I haven't been around. After boarding yesterday, council stuff caught up with me. It's so tedious and time consuming. If my mom weren't in Russia, I would have heaps more time. Can you forgive me?"

Watching Kendrick stand there without a shred of guilt, I knew the truth. *An act, it's all an act.*

Kendrick held his arms out to embrace me. I darted back, connecting with the edge of the iron-footed table behind the couch. "Dammit!"

Kendrick's smile vanished. "Amelia, what's wrong?"

My hands were shaking at my sides. I curled them into fists in an attempt to still the uncontrollable movement. It didn't work. The tension gripping my arms only caused my entire body to quiver. "I heard you," I choked out. "I know."

All color drained from Kendrick's face and his expression contorted. He looked like I had just sucker-punched him in the gut. "I..."

"Was it all a lie?" Tears stung my eyes while my insides ignited. "Were we ever really friends?"

"Of course we were. Amelia, we *are*. Everything I feel for you is real. I never lied about that." Kendrick stepped forward and reached out, but I swatted his hand away. His shoulders slumped. "I hate what I did. But I honestly thought we were doing what was best for you."

Lies, all lies. How could I believe anything he said? Pain tore through me. Inside, my heart was breaking. "What did you do?" I hissed through gritted teeth, trying to steady my voice. "And stop stalling."

Kendrick raked tense fingers through his hair. "Amelia, I didn't know before you got back together with Ty. You have to believe me. I thought he was just concerned that there'd be a repeat of your attack in Anchorage. That's the only reason I agreed to it. I was just looking out for you."

"What the hell are you talking about?"

"Your uncle knew Ty and Marika were werewolves when he saw them at the auction."

I frowned, remembering my uncle's reaction to Ty entering the marquee and the separate measures that kept his and Marika's scents hidden. "How could he tell?"

Kendrick shook his head. "Amelia, Caius has been around for over five hundred years. I may only know about werewolves from books and study, but he would have been there for the War of the Races. Scent or not, he could pick them out."

Too much information was spinning through my head. Something just didn't add up. "But if Caius knew at the auction, why didn't he tell my mom then? Why wait to force me to move away?"

Kendrick took a deep breath and lowered onto the floral couch, propping his elbows on his knees. "Your uncle caught up with me at the auction when you went to look for Ty. He didn't tell me what they were. He only said he was concerned that we'd have a repeat of what you did in Anchorage. He planned to talk your mom into moving you to the Armaya before anything could happen. But I pleaded for him not to. I could see the change in you. The happiness that shone from you when you were around Ty." Kendrick choked on his words, shaking his head. "It made me jealous as hell. But I wanted you to be happy. So I told Caius I'd keep an eye on you. Make sure you didn't lose control."

I dropped down beside Kendrick and took his hands in mine. Everything he'd done had come from a good place. "It's okay—"

"There's more," Kendrick said, cutting me off. He squeezed his eyes shut with a slight shake of his head. "After I'd confessed my true feelings to you, and after what he did, I didn't think anything could make you take him back. Then when I realized you had…" His voice lowered almost inaudibly. "I think death would have hurt less." The levelness of his voice returned, but he didn't look at me. "I was insanely jealous. It took all my willpower to keep what Ty was from your uncle. I wanted so badly to tell him, to have him intervene." He lifted glassy eyes to mine. "But I didn't. Instead, I tried to make you see that you weren't meant to be with him." A sigh blew through his lips. "It was foolish. Getting your fortune read was my final attempt to sway you. And it would have worked if that silly old bat had stuck to the story." My eyes had grown wide with surprise, and Kendrick waved me off. "I know. I shouldn't have done that, either. But—"

"You paid her off?" I cut in, suddenly doubting my growing belief in the old woman's crazy words. My hand rose, fingers toying absentmindedly with the smooth amethyst stone.

"No. Well, yes," Kendrick stumbled over his words. "I mean I did pay her. But she was just meant to say the part about Ty bringing danger to your life. The rest was made up bull that she must have come up with on the spot. Although none of it did me any good. Because even after her cryptic fortune, you still went to him. Even with the real threat that being with him put you in. Then you wanted him to change, to be present while it happened."

The vein along Kendrick's neck pulsed with the bunching of his muscles. Yes, he had lied and tried to manipulate my decisions regarding Ty. But who could blame him? Since his arrival I'd put him through so much. Over and over I'd tested his friendship with lies when I should've trusted him. Even though I didn't deserve it, I knew he was still my best friend. My heart clenched. "Kendrick, I'm sorry. I never meant to…"

Kendrick's hand rose, silencing my words. "Let me finish. I need you to know everything." When I nodded, he continued. "I was hurt, but I only told your mom to keep you out of harm's way."

Struggling to keep the defensiveness from my tone, I spoke slowly. "Kendrick, I was never in any danger. I know you saw the scars, but that was an accident. Ty would *never* intentionally hurt me."

"He didn't tell you?" Kendrick's pale face flared red and his jaw clenched. With a growl, his body trembled so violently he seemed almost on the verge of exploding. He brought a loaded fist down onto the antique coffee table, splintering it in two. For a second he frowned, almost looking surprised by his sudden outburst. With a long, controlled breath, he stretched out his long fingers. Then he curled them back into knuckle-whitening fists. "A single bite from a werewolf can kill a vampire."

It felt like a spiked whip had just come down across my back. My entire body shuddered. Ty knew all along. That's why he was so rattled after his claws cut my flesh, why he'd argued against transforming before me in the forest. He knew the danger, and he kept it from me. A storybook of events turned through my mind, all the deceptions, all the lies. Ty had kept so many things from me, secrets he only repented for when I discovered the truth myself. And he had planned to kill me all those months ago outside *Pulse* in Anchorage. I shook my head. So many lies... What was he still keeping from me? And how could I fight to stay with someone who didn't trust me enough to tell me the truth?

I forced my lips to speak, even though my mouth felt bone dry. "I understand why you and Caius did what you did. I won't excuse it, but I do understand." I squeezed my best friend's hand and bit my lip. "Kendrick, I forgive you for everything. I just need some time, alone."

Relief brought the ivory back to Kendrick's face. He cupped my jaw with his hands, bringing his lips down to my cheek. His eyes squeezed shut. "Amelia, I promise I will do *anything* to make this up to you."

CHAPTER 24

"$\mathscr{I}$ got your request to see me," I said to Uncle Caius as I entered his office.

The environment seemed less formal, with his leather-swathed desk clean and tidy for once. The folders and books that usually cluttered the space had been cleared for two goblets. One was empty and one was already filled. Yet somehow under the quiet observation of my uncle's eyes, tension thickened the darkened, lamp-lit room.

The steady ticking of the grandfather clock was quickly over-shadowed by my rising heartbeat. Nerves had my eyes dropping to my purple laces. The lethargy that seemed to build within me by the day grew.

Caius released his steepled fingers and motioned to the chair opposite him. His face appeared drawn with dark shadows. "Amelia, I have not requested your company for small talk." His level tone was filled with the strong authority of a leader. "Please sit."

I complied while Caius poured glass-bottled blood into the

second goblet. "You look as tired as I feel." He slid the blood-topped drink across the desk. "This should help."

My mouth watered with expectation and the pendant warmed. With a frown, I recalled that whispered warning and wondered if I was losing my mind—or if I should listen. I raised the goblet to my lips, taking a slow sip. My worries subsided. This time the feel of the ancient blood coating my mouth and absorbing through my flesh was almost enjoyable.

Caius placed his beverage down after a quick mouthful. Then his head tilted to look me square in the eye. "Have you and Kendrick made amends?"

A dizzy spell blurred my vision, catching me momentarily off guard. I shook off the exhaustion-fueled sensation and probed my brain. Aside from getting my best friend to keep him informed, why would Caius care about the state of my friendship with Kendrick?

After everything that had happened yesterday, we'd spent most of the day together. While watching a full season of *Being Human* and gorging on chocolate, Kendrick had regaled me with stories of the treacherous slopes he'd taken the other day. In no time at all the natural ease of our relationship had returned. I was so relieved. Being at odds with my best friend had hurt me, more than I had been willing to admit. And with my growing insecurities regarding Ty, I knew I needed Kendrick's support.

Caius thinks I'll stay here for Kendrick. Remembering our embarrassing encounter in the bathroom brought heat to my cheeks. God, I could still feel Kendrick's eyes scouring my naked flesh. "Yes we have," was all I managed to croak out.

My uncle smiled and leaned forward in his chair. "I am glad to hear of it. I do hope his company will make your stay here more *tolerable*." He took another draw from his beverage, which I mimicked as he relaxed back into his chair. "And the boy back home. Have you realized what you must do?"

It felt as though the earth had just opened up beneath me, ready to swallow me whole. I coughed, choking on the ancient blood. Since discovering Ty's latest reluctance to divulge life-altering information, I had felt conflicted. Many calls and texts had come through to my iPhone today. I had ignored every single one of them. I couldn't bring myself to talk to Ty. Not yet. Not when my feelings were still so muddled. There were just so many conflicting voices in my mind. I needed to step back and for once think with my head rather than my heart.

"Amelia," Caius's stern voice pulled me back to reality. "I am protecting you from The Council. All they know is that you are here to learn our histories. They would never accept such an indiscretion."

The Council... I remembered the image of the vampire sentenced to death and being burned alive. Just for loving a werewolf. "But I'm not a royal. It's not their place to intervene."

Caius regarded me with saddened eyes. "You may not be my niece by blood, but I am your creator. You are my family. I have already gone against The Council in letting you and Dorian live all those years ago."

My blood turned to ice. Letting us live? I looked to my uncle with wide eyes. "You were going to kill us?"

"No." Uncle Caius rose to stare vacantly out the tint-blackened window behind his desk. Beyond the glass, streetlamps dimmed with the rising hue of dawn over the mountainous horizon. "You do not understand. When I saved you, Dorian, and your mother after the attack, I could not keep it from The Council. Though as you are well aware, my dear, turning children is forbidden. So once your existences were discovered, I was sent to take care of it. The order was to kill you and your brother." He turned back to me with a sigh, grimacing as he shook his head. "Amelia, I could not do it. So I devised a plan to stave off the transformation. It was meant to stop the vampire blood within you and Dorian from taking over."

I remembered Mom and Caius's cryptic words before revealing the reason behind my sudden lust for blood. There had also been Kendrick's reveal after bringing me home from *Pulse*. He'd said Caius had gone against The Council, that he'd defied their laws and his obligation as a royal. "Mom thought it would halt the process forever," I whispered. Her words, *you said this wouldn't happen,* and her desperation were so clear in my mind.

"Yes," Caius said. He reached across the desk, covering my hand with his. "There were never any guarantees. Though you both resisted the change for long enough. You are no longer children, no longer an uncontrollable threat." A smile thinned his lips. "You see, my dear, I risked my reputation and position to give you all life. Now everything you do reflects upon me. The Council considers you and Dorian my responsibility. My warnings are only meant to protect us all. Do you understand, Amelia?" His serious eyes held mine. "You will see, my dear. What you thought you had with that boy will soon enough become a distant memory."

Shell-shocked, I sat there in complete silence as Caius released my hand. He had spoken out of love and concern for me, for all of us. I was risking more than Ty's and my safety. And Caius was covering for me, lying to his counterparts. My heart squeezed with the pressure of a vice beneath my ribs. Uncertainty rode in every beat. How could I stay with Ty? Nausea poisoned my insides. I felt like vomiting. "May I be excused? I need time to think."

I forced my tearing eyes up to my uncle. Instantly I was taken aback. He sat watching me, now reseated in his padded chair. Something was different. His skin gleamed under the desk's poor lighting, his features radiant and youthful. It was a stark contrast to his disheveled appearance when I had first arrived. The ancient vampire blood worked as Caius had stated, rejuvenating and restoring. Still, its effects hadn't seemed to penetrate my body in the slightest. The mental and emotional strain I felt over Ty drained me to my core. No amount of blood could ever relieve that. Only change could.

"Of course," Caius answered with a nod, his expression frozen and hard. "I trust you will make the right decision. But do not take too long. This issue *must* be put to rest, before it is too late."

"WHAT IS THIS PLACE?" I questioned Marcus, frowning at the red neon sign flashing *Bite* above our heads.

On arriving at the library this morning, Marcus had opted for a different lesson, one he stated, *Books could not teach*. Instead, he had toured me around the Armaya's expansive grounds. Victorian streetlamps lit the cobblestone streets. They curved in a labyrinth, fronting stone and mortar residential homes, followed by an entire commercial community. It was surprising to see how populated the streets were. People—all vampires—moved from one boutique store to another. Others kicked back at one of many cafés. It was all so...*human*.

Marcus chuckled, hoisting the strap of his leather messenger bag across his chest. "I figured you'd never have visited a club like this before."

Marcus passed through the thick wooden doors. I followed after him, leaving the well-lit street and star-spangled night sky behind. Inside, I glanced around the darkened space. The club was almost vacant. Only a handful of patrons occupied booths just past the blackened dance floor. Being mid-morning in vampire time, it wasn't surprising. Yet a scent wafting from their tables was clear. It hung thick in the air. Human blood.

Marcus laced his fingers through mine and smiled, distracting me from my thoughts. The movement sent a spark through my hand. It somehow felt alien and natural all at the same time. I didn't pull away. Instead, I allowed him to lead me past the velvet-draped lounges. We stopped at an impressive bar that was entirely made of glass. It was even tinted by the glow of red lights.

The bartender turned from a group of women who caught sight of Marcus. They smiled before wrinkling their noses at me in unmistakable distaste. Each held a cocktail glass tipped with thick blood.

"Marcus, we're free for a date," one of the vampire women toyed. She drew aside the collar of her blouse to expose the supple flesh of her neck. "If you're thirsty…"

I flinched in shock, banging my elbow on the glass bar top. Was that woman actually offering her blood, among other things?

Marcus smirked. "Sorry ladies. I have less *sordid* companionship today."

The woman who had spoken flicked her hair over her shoulders and twitched away. Her entourage scurried after her.

The waiter mumbled to himself and tipped his head. "Lord Marcus Vladimir, the usual?"

Marcus's lips split to reveal sharpened fangs. "I do think you forget your manners, barkeep. This," he said while eyeing me, "is Miss Amelia Lamont."

The bartender's eyes widened and he looked me up and down. Suddenly I was the most interesting thing he had ever seen. He bowed his head and crossed a fist over his chest. "P-please accept my apologies, Lady Lamont. I...I did not realize." He raised his eyes to Marcus. "What may I do to amend my insolence?"

"Penance is not necessary," Marcus said, waving his free hand, though the sharp look in his eyes said otherwise. "But we would appreciate some privacy, in The Pit."

The bartender nodded then cast a glance at a bouncer manning a robed entryway. The mono-muscled man dipped his head. Then he disappeared into the darkness beyond the archway.

"Much appreciated," Marcus directed to the bartender. He squeezed my hand and we walked over.

The entire interaction left me feeling confused, and totally out of place. The manner of respect-tinged fear the bartender had projected was unlike anything I had ever encountered. "He knew who I was?" I whispered. "How?"

We paused before the entryway and Marcus turned to me. He brushed my loose hair behind my ears. "You and your brother, *Dorian*." His voice almost prickled over my brother's name. "You're the only people who were turned as infants and allowed to remain alive. You're an anomaly. An urban legend, most believe. Never meant to be, but now regarded with the status of royalty. You're one of us."

"Oh." From the start, Caius had taken the risk of giving us life when we should have been put down. I shivered at the thought. He'd defied vampire law to save us. Yet my actions were still causing him grief. Here, no matter how ridiculous it seemed to me, I was considered one of them, royalty. And even though I remained attached to Ty, Caius continued to protect me. *Ty...* The thought of him made my heart ached. There were so many issues. He'd called again last night, but I couldn't talk to him. Why? I knew the answer. It was because I wasn't sure anymore, sure about him, sure about us.

"The Pit is ready, my lord."

The bouncer's deep voice caused my body to jolt. Total trepidation overrode my internal torment. *The Pit?*

"You may leave," Marcus said with a nod to the bouncer. He

pulled back the velvet robe and smiled impressively. "After you, Lady Lamont."

With caution, I stepped past the barrier, pausing to let my vision adapt to the darkness. A wide hallway spanned ahead. At its end was a stairwell that led beneath the ground. Marcus's hand found mine, directing me down the blacked-out stairs. "Where are we going?"

A fanged smile tugged at his lips. "You'll see."

The stairs' landing opened onto a circular room. Kerosene wall lanterns offered minimal lighting to the stone-walled and wood-braced chamber. Humidity thickened the air, elevating a scent I couldn't confuse. Human blood. It was the same scent I'd detected upstairs with only one slight difference. This blood, I could tell, was fresh.

My mouth watered and my eyes darted around the room. Partitions were set at intervals, each with two chairs facing toward each other. Chairs that supported slumped over people, humans. Their quiet breathing reached my ears. "T-they're human," I said, my voice shaking. A lump crawled up my throat and I swallowed it back down. "What are they doing here?"

Marcus's fangs glinted through parted, smiling lips. "They're lunch."

I almost choked on his words. Then I reigned in my startled reaction as I remembered something Kendrick had said.

"I'm sick of dead blood." Throughout the parking lot, students had been scurrying to get out of the rain. Kendrick had watched them as though they were cattle. *"But your mom was quite clear on the conditions pertaining to my visit. No human victims."*

Back then my stomach had dropped, churning with predatory instinct and seething disgust. But my fear had been unwarranted, at least when it came to Kendrick. He didn't have to kill to feed. The humans were merely a meal, not a sacrifice. "You don't kill them, do you?"

Marcus laughed. It was a short-lived but amused sound. "No, we don't kill these humans. It's purely their choice to donate."

Despite the humidity, Marcus's words made me shiver. What human would willingly subject themselves to a life like this? Waiting in the pit of a club to be drained day in and day out by monsters?

"I know what you're thinking," Marcus said. "And in answer, in payment for their...*services*, these humans are offered the chance at a longer life as a vampire."

They *wanted* to become vampires? How could anyone if given the choice want to become a bloodthirsty monster? To live in the shadows as only turned vampires could? To never live a normal life and have a family that they could grow old with?

I stared down at my free hand. Blue veins were visible through my pasty and almost transparent flesh. Those veins would darken, becoming more prominent if I refrained from what my body needed most. Blood. "How could anyone want this?"

"Would you trade knowing Kendrick or even me, and the superior world you could live in to be *just human?*" Marcus snapped. He glared over the slumped and almost unmoving forms. "To be a weak, dwindling flame without a cause?"

He gripped my shoulders with tense hands and shook. A sense of déjà vu rose at his personality change, and I flinched. "Marcus..."

His teal-blue eyes were lasers through spikes of blond hair. "Amelia, you belong here, with me, with all of us."

His harshness stunned me, but it also made me think. When I had first discovered the monster lurking beneath my flesh, I would have given anything to be normal, to believe I was *just human*. But so much had happened since then. I wasn't a killer as I had dreaded.

I *could* control it. And within these walls, I was accepted. Not a freak. This was where I belonged. I shook my head. "I wouldn't change a thing."

MARCUS and I walked hand in hand from *Bite*. Fresh, warm blood swarmed my veins, fueling excitement at my accomplishment. There had been no struggle to pull away from the blood donor. I had been in complete control.

Now humming Skillet's song *Awake and alive*, I felt alive in a way I had only experienced twice before. Except this time there was nothing catastrophic to taint the high. Every inch of my skin tingled and my pulse was noticeably elevated. My mind felt sharper, like I was seeing the world through brand new eyes. Even with a thick cloud cover now across the night sky, the lamp-lit streets seemed brighter. I could hear individual footsteps and entire conversations. There was the sound of a door opening and closing with the chime of a bell. They were all things that surrounded us but were out of sight.

"I feel like I could literally run across the country." *Or*, I thought, *nick a motorbike and take off, feeling the wind like fingers through my hair.*

"Well, that's an option," Marcus said. We rounded a bend that opened onto what appeared to be the town's center. "But, I did have something a bit more exciting in mind."

A vast fountain centered the cobblestone path, spouting water from the hands of a winged angel. Cafés lined one side. Most were packed with vampires enjoying what I could tell was re-heated blood. The other side opened onto a park with lush grass spanning out to bordering snow-capped cedars.

I felt like kicking off my Vans to run through the park, feeling the tickle of grass and ice under my bare feet. "More exciting?"

Marcus released my hand and circled the fountain. He lowered himself down onto the curved edge and patted the space beside him. As I sat, he began rummaging through his messenger bag. A moment later, he had retrieved a very old, green, leather-bound book.

A loud groan vibrated up my throat. "Not more study."

"Hardly…" The teal-blue of Marcus's eyes shimmered. He thrust the book into my hands. The title was embossed with gold onto the cover. *Elemental Magic and Compulsion.* "Have you heard of elemental powers?"

When I shook my head, fully intrigued by his words, Marcus continued. "Most Pure Bloods will develop an affinity for one of the four elements, Earth, Air, Fire, and Water. Which means," he said, catching sight of my befuddled expression, "we can harness energy that gives us the aptitude to manipulate the essence of that element."

My frown deepened at Marcus's gibberish-jargon. "Huh?"

"Here." He collected a piece of paper from his bag and scrunched it up before balancing it on his upturned palm. "Watch this."

Marcus's fingers strained, cradling the air around the ball of paper. His eyes focused with intensity. A quiet crackling reached my ears and a plume of smoke lifted from the crumpled paper. Then it instantaneously burst into flames.

My eyes widened as flames swallowed the ball, dying only after the paper had turned to ash in the middle of Marcus's palm. I grabbed for his fingers, staring, studying. There was no scorched flesh or bleeding. No indication the flames had penetrated even a single layer of his skin in any way. "That's amazing!"

Marcus shrugged. "*That* was a party trick."

He flicked open the book in front of me to an illustration inside the cover. Four quarters split the page with an eye joining them in the center. Each quarter displayed a different image, a portrayal of one of the four elements. The first showed three hurricanes dancing in curves around each other and decimating everything they touched. The second was a surging wall of water that rose in a wave to crush anything in its path. In the third, fire raged even below a thick blanket of rainfall. The last had rampant growing vines that looked like they wanted to crawl off the page.

My awestruck gaze returned to the eye connecting the four elements. "What's that?"

"The *Fifth* Element." Marcus eyed me while brushing the ash from his hands. "As with the other elements, only royals can harness its power, the affinity for spirit."

A sudden fear I didn't understand caused my heart to patter and my hands to shake. "Spirit?"

"The rarest of abilities," Marcus said, flicking to another illustration. This one had ghostly shadows quaking across the page. Their mouths gaped, and their arms reached as though they were trying to escape the yellowing parchment.

Ice-cold fingers gripped my spine, causing my entire body to shudder. I had a sudden urge to slam the book shut and throw it into the fountain, drowning it.

Marcus's eyes remained set on the illustration. "Those gifted possess the aptitude to see and speak with the dead. A rare few hold the ability to create a blood bond with another vampire. Even rarer than that is an ability called The Sight, allowing the gifted to glimpse into the past, present, and future."

The Sight? Memories slipped in and out of focus, causing my brain to push against my skull. It almost felt like a warning to stop probing into my subconscious. Why does that feel so familiar? I raised my eyes to Marcus. He was now watching me with a look of contemplation. "You said only Pure Bloods, royals, can possess these gifts?"

"Yes." Marcus narrowed his eyes. "Why do you ask?"

Why *did* I ask him that? It was like the words had been spoken to me, like they weren't of my own volition. My brain pulsed again, jagged pain rippling through my skull. I bit my lip to stop myself from crying out and shrugged. "No reason. Just curious, I guess."

NAUSEA CRIPPLED me as I climbed the stairs to my room. My legs suddenly weighed as much as solid concrete pillars. I clutched the wooden railing and took a deep breath. Then I forced my pin-tingling limbs to move. An uneasy sensation tightened within my stomach. I wasn't alone. My eyes darted back down the stone stair-well. Shadows seemed to move with the flicker of wall lanterns. But there wasn't anyone there. Like Dorian would say, *you're just being paranoid.*

I pressed on. Then as I reached the top of the stairs a dizzy spell seized me. My limbs quaked and I fell. The wooden railing collected my ribs. I spat profanity through my lips while I struggled to regain my composure. Weight made my head feel heavy and haze littered my mind. I sucked in a number of deep breaths. *What the hell is wrong with me?*

Slowly some of the feeling returned to my legs. I pushed off the wall, praying I'd make it to my room without collapsing. Prayers were useless, I realized. Just as I reached and unlocked my door, my vision blurred. My knees buckled. And then I was falling. My trem-bling legs refused to respond to basic motor instructions.

A millisecond before I hit the ground, a set of strong arms caught my weight. They lifted and cradled my body against a hard chest. "Amelia," a familiar voice spoke. "What happened? Are you okay?"

I peered up into Kendrick's concerned eyes. He was frowning intensely. Where had he come from? Inside I felt cold, a shell of death. Like a living, breathing creature that had lost almost all animation. "I think I'm just tired," I downplayed, not wanting to worry him. "You can put me down now."

Kendrick ignored my request with a doubtful grunt and carried me to my bed. "Just tired?"

The day's events ran through my mind like watching a movie reel. Marcus had escorted me to *Bite*. There, the bartender had reacted on discovering who I was. The pit had followed, where I'd taken a woman's delicious blood. Was I forgetting something? There seemed to be fragments of my time with Marcus that wouldn't reassemble.

I glanced at the antique clock on my bedside. It was after 6AM, the end of a vampire day. But I had checked the time when leaving Marcus and it had only been 4AM. What had I done after? Where had I been, and with who? My brain throbbed against my prodding, feeling far from *awake and alive* like before. My brow creased. "I um, think so."

Kendrick supported my weight with one arm and pulled the sequined quilt back. He was still frowning when he placed me down against the pillows. "You look like you haven't slept in a week."

"Thanks." Still feeling confused and disorientated, I rubbed at my forehead. "I think I just need a good night's rest." Too dizzy and weak to undress, I pulled the covers over my fully clothed body. There was no way in hell I was about to ask for Kendrick's help. My cheeks blushed. He had already seen me naked once, which was more than enough.

Seeming to read my thoughts, Kendrick pulled back the

turquoise quilt, exposing my feet. "At least let me take off your shoes." He removed my Vans then stood back, examining me. "You're really pale." With a click of his tongue, he darted around the floral couch to rifle through the minibar. A second later he returned with a bottle of blood. "Here, drink this."

I pursed my lips. Although I knew I needed the blood, something had changed. This substitute wouldn't even come close to the fresh source I'd tapped at *Bite*. Not that I was about to make live drinking a normal thing. Resigned, I took the bottle from Kendrick and chugged the contents. A loud burp bubbled up my throat. "Oops, I uh, guess I needed that."

Looking less worried, Kendrick leaned in to kiss the crown of my hair. "Now, go to sleep." With a tense smile, he edged away and strode toward the bathroom. With one last hesitant look, he doused the lanterns then exited through the door to his room.

CHAPTER 25

*T*he sound of birdsong whistling from surrounding trees drew me awake. Beside me, a clear river swirled while the warm afternoon sun beat down against my icy skin. The sound and sight of babbling water over the rocky riverbed relaxed my mind. A steady breeze blew, carrying with it dry russet leaves and the scent of a warm summer's day.

"I thought you weren't coming." Ty's sudden voice startled me. He jumped down from the branch of a large oak tree to stand before me. All he wore was a pair of black corduroy shorts. His scarred chest was bare and his lips were parted with anticipation. Sexuality oozed from every muscled inch of him.

It had completely slipped my mind that today was Friday, the day Ty had promised to visit my dreams. In fact the thought of Ty —bar his incessant phone calls and texts, none of which I'd answered—had been voided memory. The remainder of the week had flown by with all my spare time occupied. Kendrick and I had hung out watching my favorite TV shows in between his snowboarding excursions. Marcus had continued to reveal this whole new world to me during his lessons. Everything now seemed so much clearer. This world was where I belonged, and I wanted to remain part of it.

"Sorry," I replied with hesitation. "I guess I forgot to text you."

Ty stepped forward, arms raised to embrace me. "Are you okay? You don't look so good."

My mind felt hazy as I straightened from the damp grass, absently noticing what looked like fresh scars across his torso. There was something important that I needed to do. With a little prodding, the haze fogging up my brain shifted and I remembered. I couldn't keep ignoring Ty's calls and texts. I couldn't keep putting the inevitable off. And I couldn't continue to act like nothing had changed when it had. Everything had. I had.

Ty's arms circled around me and mine shot up, fingers curling around his biceps in negation. I pushed him back, catching him by surprise. Hurt flashed across his face. "Amelia, what's wrong?" Confusion coupled the hurt in his eyes as I stood there, shaking my head. His voice rose with worry. "Seriously. Are you sick or something? Talk to me!"

It was time. I knew exactly what I had to do. "Ty, I need to talk to you," I began, struggling to piece together all the conflict still clouding my thoughts. "It's about us. I won't be returning to Rye. I plan to stay here at the Armaya."

Ty's eyes widened. He lunged forward, grasping my hand. "What do you mean? What about us!"

Unable to look into his pleading eyes, my head turned away. I wriggled my hand free. "There *is* no us." The lack of emotion in my sharp tone surprised not only Ty. Why was I being so cruel?

Ty raked his fingers through his hair. Desperation colored his tone. "Amelia, what's happened? Why are you doing this?"

"It's just not going to work." My heart constricted with pain that almost brought me to my knees. My hand braced against the oak tree. I shook off the sensation then cracked my neck to the side. "*We can't work.*"

"It can, we can," Ty pleaded. Sweat beaded across his creased brow. "You know we can get through anything. We just have to stick together." Dejection painted his expression, riddled by the pure grief I was causing. He moved within a split second, crushing me against his bare chest. His lips covered mine. "Amelia, I love you."

Breath squeezed from my lungs. His proximity and touch still affected me, more than I cared to admit. Part of me still yearned for him. But a stronger part just didn't care anymore. Sudden irritation flared at his refusal to accept the inevitable. It sent a sparking wave of fury outward from my core. I drove my hands into his chest and he stumbled. Without instruction my lips spat, "Well, I don't love you!"

The breeze suddenly intensified, whipping as if it were an extension of my hostility. My hair whipped behind my shoulders.

Seething rage suddenly twisted Ty's expression. "What the hell is that?" The ferocity within his eyes prickled my skin. He was glaring straight at my neck.

My hand rose to find two fleshy bumps. *Bite marks?* I combed through my memories. My brain pulsed against my efforts but offered no answer. A gentle hum of panic climbed up my throat. "I-I don't know."

"So that's what this is about?" The disgust that drenched Ty's tone and expression struck a dagger through my heart. "There's someone else."

Disbelief widened my eyes. Of course there wasn't anyone else. I had agonized over leaving Ty. I'd been riddled with guilt and despair ever since deciding. I had never wanted for a second to be apart from him. But everything had changed. I had changed. I belonged here.

Ty lashed out, striking the oak with a cracking blow. A deep split shot up from its center. "It's him, isn't it?" he accused, his disgusted stare propelling back at me.

There was no doubt he was referring to Kendrick. "You're joking, right?" How could he even think that? I laughed and pulled my hair forward to cover the marks. "Don't be ridiculous."

"How'd it happen, then?" Ty's hands were balled into ready fists. His body began to tremble. "Just happen to fall and land in someone's mouth?"

A recollection flitted to the surface. It was earlier in the week. The day I had felt so inexplicably weak and exhausted. The day I had almost crumpled to the floor when returning to my room. Except nothing had happened. I was certain of it. Kendrick had only helped me to bed, nothing else. Racking my brain, I tried to recall where I had been earlier that day. The memories seemed to slip away, fragmented pieces that refused to bond. "I-I can't remember."

Ty threw his trembling arms over his chest. "Well, that's convenient. Isn't it?"

I exhaled, frustration outweighing any panic I'd felt. "Whatever. It still doesn't change the facts. We can't be together. We never should have deluded ourselves in the first place."

"I won't accept this," Ty growled. His voice dropped to an unstable whisper. "I can't."

I knew what I had to say, the only words that would force his acceptance. My throat choked up and a single tear rolled down my cheek. "Ty, you have to. I don't want you anymore."

A glazed look stole across Ty's eyes and his body shimmered. He was becoming transparent before my very eyes. "Fine..." His mouthed word echoed through the trees. Then he disappeared and empty darkness swallowed me whole.

I woke to my stomach doing backflips. I rushed to the bathroom and shoved my head into the deep, round sink. Just in time. A split second later I was coughing up disgusting yellow bile. Something I ate? Not that I could recall eating dinner the night before. In fact I couldn't recall eating dinner all week. The heaviness of a cinder block weighed down my head, and my heart ached with a sting of claws piercing through the muscle. I squinted. The fluorescents were too bright, gleaming against the pearl-white, floor-to-ceiling tiles. There was something very, very wrong.

While struggling to hold back the urge to heave, I swiped my mouth across the back of my hand. Then I splashed cold water over my face. When it seemed to be helping, I dared to stand upright. Blinking back pins that probed my eyes, I saw my reflection in the gold-framed mirror. The whites of my eyes were bloodshot, with heavy bags circling underneath. My flesh appeared grayish. My cheeks were gaunt. I looked like death warmed up. Like a corpse.

A blaring from across my room sounded, causing my heart to leap into my throat. It was my iPhone belting out a line from a Skillet song. I bolted back through my room, snatching my phone from the bedside. Dizziness swelled up my head and I fell back onto the bed's turquoise quilt.

"Amelia, it's Dorian." There was a distinct edge to his voice.

Guilt surged through me. "Oh, hey…" I hadn't spoken to my brother since leaving Rye. I hadn't even tried to call. Time here just seemed to slip away. But that was no excuse. "Sorry, I meant to call. Is everything alright?"

"Uh, not really..." He sighed. "What happened between you and Ty?"

The mention of Ty's name struck fresh pain through my heart. I bolted upright. My brain pulsed against the dizziness of my abrupt movement. I clutched the paint-chipped edge of the bedside table to keep from falling. I remembered breaking up with Ty and things getting heated, but I couldn't recall what we'd been arguing about. Was I forgetting something? "Dorian, it was just time to move on. I have no future with him."

"This doesn't sound like you, Sis. I know how much you were into him. You've never been like that about anyone. Not even Kendrick."

My fingers tensed around the phone and I had to struggle not to crush it to pieces. Like Dorian had a right to judge. Besides, I couldn't understand why he cared. He'd never approved of Ty anyway. Before Marika, he'd been the biggest chauvinist I knew. Always making girls fall in love with him, only to get bored and break their hearts a week in. "Feelings change, Dorian. You know that better than anyone."

"But you're not like me. What you had with Ty was different. Even I can admit that." Dorian sighed. "He also said you're staying there. Is that true?"

Dammit! This wasn't how he was supposed to find out. I snatched a chocolate cookie from the bedside drawer and began nibbling nervously at its edges. "Dorian, I'm sorry. I was going to tell you." The only response I got was my own chewing. "Dorian?"

"Yeah, I'm here." An uneven breath blew through my ear. "I guess I just didn't believe it. But I am glad you're finally finding acceptance. Peace in being a vampire. It's a good thing, really."

"So you're not mad?"

Dorian chuckled. "No. Besides, now I have a good reason to get out of this small town and visit."

Relief curved my lips. "I'd like that."

During our belated catch-up, Dorian bragged about finally being able to compel someone. Not that he would say who. Which left me to assume it was the latest girl he was into. At least he was over Marika. After that I gave him a rundown of the Armaya and anything else I could think of. An hour later we said goodbye, promising to make more of an effort to keep in touch.

No longer feeling sick, I showered and chucked on some fresh clothes. Then I headed for the door adjoining Kendrick's room. Today was the first day of the rest of my life, and I couldn't think of anyone I'd rather spend my day with.

After knocking repeatedly, Kendrick drew open the door. His brow was furrowed, his expression distracted.

"Wanna hang out?" I asked, certain that with Marcus's laid-back attitude he wouldn't mind me skipping one day of tutoring.

Kendrick pursed his lips, not meeting my eyes. "I can't. My schedule's packed today… Rain check?"

"Oh. Okay." I couldn't hide my disappointment. A need to reveal my decision to remain at the Armaya surged within me, but now didn't seem like the time. "What about tomorrow?"

Kendrick frowned, clearly distracted, but nodded. "Definitely."

I LEFT Kendrick to his 'busy schedule' and ventured down to the library after a quick bite to eat. The weight of my head seemed to be lifting. I was slowly waking up. My stomach, now satisfied with a meal and a full pint of blood, no longer swelled with nausea.

Once inside the library, I headed behind the freestanding stacks to the small desktop computer. Now certain my future was here, I wanted to learn as much as possible about what it meant to be a vampire. Plus knowing how this new world operated wouldn't hurt.

Where to start? I drummed my fingers across the computer keyboard while ignoring the impulse to look up Ducati pictures. That's not why I was sitting here.

A whispered, raspy voice reached my ears. *Compulsion.*

Startled, I turned to glimpse the librarian. She was reshelving books from a packed wooden trolley all the way across the room. There were a few other people reading around the central desks. The sound of their turning pages was crystal clear. But not one of them was looking my way. I frowned. Imagining things? It was the only rational explanation. Only the raspy voice and the word it had spoken was still fresh in my mind. *Compulsion.*

With a shrug I keyed the word into the computer's search engine. A page of results flashed up on the screen. The category was listed under *abilities*, with call numbers ranging from 2100 to 2189. I committed the numbers to memory. Then feeling an instinctual pull to follow, I headed for the wall shelves labeled 'A.'

The bottom of the first row began at 1000 with the next spanning up from 3040. My gaze slid up the wall-lined shelves that ended just below the thirty-foot, glass-domed ceiling. *Going up...* With another shrug I clutched the wheel-footed ladder, minding the jagged splinter protruding from the wooden frame. Then I began climbing. *1500, 1700, 1900...*

Finally two shelves from the ceiling I located 2100. Not knowing what I was really looking for, I pulled out the first hard-cover. *Compulsion Effects.* I skimmed through, reading at a pace that surprised me. *Few vampires are able to use the full force of compulsion on humans and vampires alike. Royals namely reserve the ability.* I flicked ahead, reading faster than I ever imagined possible.

Vampire speed and sight, I mused. Why had I been so against all this?

When I reached a chapter titled, *Compulsion and Side Effects,* my skimming slowed and my brow knitted. *Memory loss, erratic behavior, dizzy spells.* The list of side effects went on and in-depth details to each followed. Something pulled within me, an alarm telling me this information was significant. It all just seemed too *familiar.* Lately my recall of events, even mundane things like eating meals, seemed a thickening fog. And how many dizzy spells had there been? *I was just hungry, malnourished, low on blood*, I assured myself. But a simmering paranoia was beginning to set in, coiling through my gut.

Deciding I needed to look further into the subject, if only to ease my mind, I shoved the book under my arm. *Keep looking...* The raspy voice was so soft that I questioned whether I had heard anything at all. Still, I gave in, reaching for the next book. As I went to pluck it from the shelf, something caught my eye. Wedged behind the book was a thin, age-worn hardcover with faded silver etching on the front. I pulled it from the shelf and flipped it open. *1729.* Calligraphic writing was printed inside the cover. *Diary of Uriel Aswind.* There were only a handful of blank pages and jagged paper edges where diary entries had been torn out. With a shrug, I was about to close the diary when an internal nudge caused me to pause. An overwhelming sense to view the inside back cover washed over me. I flicked through the remaining pages. There were no ink marks to indicate an entry. But the cover was not totally unmarked. Indents from a heavy-penned hand scarred the page, revealing a single gripping message.

We are neither alone nor safe. The damned intend to steal our souls.

Fear swooned within my chest and my heart began to pound

against my ribs. I turned back to the inside cover, viewing the last person to check out the book. Marcus Vladimir. My brow creased and an unsettling sensation tugged at me from within. Had he ripped out the pages? Or had he been looking for something that was already gone?

A sinister suspicion warned that the message was important, that I needed to remember the words that were written there. Balancing on the balls of my feet, thirty feet up, I released the ladder to pull my iPhone from the back pocket of my jeans. For a second I frowned at its lack of case, which I'd crushed in a fit of rage. At least that's all I had broken. Then I typed the words into a Post-it app. Find Kendrick. The words pulsed in my mind, compelling and unavoidable.

I shoved the phone back into my pocket and plunged down the ladder, so fast I was almost free falling. When my feet touched the ground, striking pain shot up my hand and arm. A low curse blew from my lips. The jagged splinter of three inches that was jutting out from the wooden rail was fully embedded in my palm. I winced and slowly lifted my hand from the spike. It made a terrible flesh-tearing sound.

"Off so soon?"

The familiar, husky voice caused the hairs on my neck to stand. I spun, shoving the compulsion book onto the shelf behind me. I flexed my injured hand, watching the blood loss slow as the skin closed over. Marcus was perched atop our usual study desk. *How long had he been there? Had he been watching me?* I tried and failed to push my growing mistrust of him from my mind. Now that I thought about it, there was so much fog surrounding the time I had spent with Marcus. Was I just being paranoid?

"Um," I forced my mouth to speak. "I didn't realize what time it was." If my suspicions held any weight, I had to act as though everything was normal. I had to feel out any anomalies with a prepared and conscious mind. "So, what are you teaching me today?"

AFTER SPENDING the entire day with Marcus, I ventured back up to my room. My plan had been to figure out what, if anything, Marcus had been up to. But the entire day felt fresh in my mind, no haze, no memory lapses, and no confusion. I'd even told him of my decision to remain at the Armaya. The entire interaction left me feeling silly for my paranoia. Marcus was my friend, and in this new world that was now my home, I needed a friend. One who had time both to school and spend time with me. One who made me feel normal and accepted, no matter what. And the connection I felt to him, though inexplicable, had returned. All of this only further instilled my sense of belonging, making it clear that this *was* where I was meant to be.

As I reached my room, key in hand, I froze. The door was slightly ajar. Housekeeping? Frowning, I pushed the door open and peered into the shadows of my room. "Hello?"

No answer. My chest tightened with fresh paranoia. *Pull yourself together.* I flicked on the lanterns and scanned the room. My bed was made, and the towel I had flung across its foot this morning was gone, replaced by a fresh one. The air escaped my lungs with a sigh of relief. It was just housekeeping.

I dumped the compulsion book on the replacement coffee table before dropping onto the faded floral couch. I'd planned to look further into the book but my eyes warmed, fuzzing with tiredness. I glanced over my shoulder to the antique clock ticking by the bedside. 5:30AM. In vampire terms it was late, past dinner and time to go to bed.

But I'd left Marcus over an hour ago. I had asked him for the time and had even glimpsed the hands of his silver-faced Rolex to confirm it. *Where have I been?*

My body slumped, exhaustion catching up with me as I pushed into my memories. Suddenly my head felt heavy, unable to think coherently. Something else was bothering me too. After eating a light lunch with Marcus, I should've been starving by now. But my stomach felt full and content. When did I eat, and with who?

Too lethargic, my mind refused to search for an answer. I slumped further into the hard-cushioned couch.

Sleep was ready to claim me. There was no holding it back. My eyelids slowly dropped and my mind blanked, giving way to unconscious sleep.

An almost inaudible sound tore me back to waking—the sound of footsteps. My heart leaped beneath my ribs and I bolted upright. "Who's there?"

Silence. A dim glow caught the corner of my eye. It was the amethyst pendant. When had I taken it off? I snatched the stone from coffee table, but my fingers instantly released. The pendant fell to the ground, and the smell of burned flesh reached my nostrils. The surface of the stone was boiling. It had literally singed my fingers.

Another sound drew my eyes to the bathroom. Darkness emanated from the partially open door. I clambered from the couch. "Hello?"

Within the blackness, I could almost detect the ominous outline of a figure, a person. My heart jumped into my throat. Adrenaline turned every one of my muscles taut. There was no turning back. I kicked the bathroom door in and launched. My body connected with the figure, and we crashed to the ground.

"Ouch!" it yelped as we skidded with a thump into the vanity.

The assailant's voice was deep and unmistakable. "Kendrick?"

"Yeah, who'd you think it was?" He sounded a little annoyed. "Will you get off me?"

Warmth invaded my body. I was still lying on top of him, my chest pressed against his and our faces less than an inch apart. "Oh, sorry..." In an awkward movement I drew away, rising to my feet and turning on the fluorescents. I extended a hand to pull Kendrick up. "What are you doing in here, anyway?"

"I was coming to say goodnight to you." Kendrick crossed his arms over his *Kutless* T-shirt. "What's with the attack greeting?"

Relief cured my embarrassment and my fear. It was just Kendrick. "I thought I saw…" I shook my head. "Never mind…"

Kendrick smiled, a somewhat strained and forced expression. Then he turned to leave.

A memory rose to the surface of my mind. There was something I needed to ask him. "Wait!"

His shoulders tensed and he turned back to me. "What?"

"The d-damned," I stammered, struck by his hard expression and tone. "What are the damned?"

Kendrick sucked in a breath, eyes narrowing. "Where did you hear that?"

I pulled my naked iPhone from my back pocket and handed it over with the Post-it app open. "I came across an old diary in the library. These words were pressed into the back cover."

Kendrick pinched his chin in thought. "The diary, it was from the 1700's, right?" I nodded. "Well, I don't know too much. But I've learned some of the history, which tells of a war between our kind and the damned. In the end we triumphed, hunting them to extinction."

"Extinct? So, they're all gone?"

"Of course," Kendrick insisted. "Now go to sleep. You look like crap." He left without another word, switching the fluorescents off before disappearing into his room.

Standing in darkness I found the pendant on the floor and fastened it around my neck. Then I frowned. Something was wrong. Kendrick and I had a close friendship, one I thought we had completely repaired. But this morning and again just now he'd seemed different, somehow cold. *Am I imagining things?* I wasn't sure. With the weight of my other concerns creeping to the surface, the lethargy I had felt before was quickly returning. In the morning, I thought to myself. I'll figure it all out in the morning.

CHAPTER 26

I relaxed across from my uncle, sipping from a blood-filled goblet. As usual, his desk was askew with a messy pile of folders that sat beneath the diamond-cut paperweight. I began nibbling at my second choc-mint cookie. Caius had sourced them, knowing they were my favorites. Apparently tonight marked a special occasion.

For a second I wondered if he knew of my decision to stay. Then my thoughts returned to where they had been set most of the day. Kendrick. Despite his promise to hang out today, his distant behavior had increased. It had gotten so bad that I was questioning his constant excuses. It felt as though he was continually making an effort to avoid me. Had I done something?

"Marcus has informed me," Caius's voice pulled me from my troubling thoughts. "That you have decided to stay, to forge a new life within our walls."

So that was the reason for the cookies. A broad smile spread across my lips. "Yes. I hope that's okay." There were still so many things I was confused about, but one thing I knew with total clarity. *I belong here.*

"I would love nothing more."

Uncle Caius was smiling, but something felt off. *Paranoid much?* I shook off the feeling and sipped from my goblet. The cold liquid coated my mouth, absorbing straight through my flesh. This time I savored the sensation. Caius had been right. My senses had become accustomed to the ancient blood, so much so that I barely felt the urge to cough.

"And if you become interested in a court-appointed job," Uncle Caius added. "I am sure I can put in a good word. There will be many important sub positions available once you mature."

I was about to reply, thanking him for his generous offer, when my vision shattered. The amethyst pendant against my chest warmed. Then the ground beneath me seemed to open up, swallowing me in darkness.

My eyes rolled back in my head. Then without warning it was suddenly light again. Starbursts pierced my eyes and I blinked rapidly, clearing my vision. I was no longer within the comfort of my uncle's office. Instead, I stood between two freestanding bookshelves in the library. My skin prickled, feeling alien and cold. How had I gotten here? Was I missing time again? Was this even real, or just another dream?

The sound of a wall-mounted clock above my head chimed with the repetitive signal of a new hour. I took no notice, my sight set on a gap created between musty books.

Pressure constricted my throat. Kendrick stood beyond the barricade. He wasn't alone.

Marcus paced in front of him, dressed in all black with the sleeve of his collared shirt rolled up. "It's happening tonight." He stopped pacing to stand before Kendrick, placing both hands on my best friend's shoulders. There was a deep gash across Marcus's wrist with a smudge of blood drying around it. "Kendrick, you will not interfere."

Kendrick's eyes glazed over and his face became expressionless. He nodded almost robotically.

"Now, take this to Amelia," Marcus directed, handing Kendrick a glass topped with blood.

Fear stole my pulse, my legs felt weak. Something within me clicked as I somehow recalled what had become less important in my mind. All my confusion, missing time, lethargy and dizzy spells... It was Marcus all along. And now he was using my best friend through compulsion. Why? What was he planning? And what did it have to do with me?

My jaw dropped. I wanted to scream, to break Marcus's hold on my best friend. But all that emerged was white noise, a high-pitched squealing sound that barely registered on an audible level.

Marcus drew back his shoulders, eyes darting about the dark and seemingly empty library, before regaining their hold on my best friend. "Make her drink all of it. Force it down her throat, if you must." His silver-raging eyes, now entirely extinguished of teal flecks, bore into Kendrick's. "And I need you to compel her to remember. Remember *everything* she has been made to forget."

Kendrick's voice emerged mechanical, emotionless. "I will make her drink the blood. I will compel her to remember."

Barely a second later, the tension returned to his face. He shook his head, disorientated, the haze clearing from his eyes. "Sorry, what was I saying?"

With a last stitch of desperation, I went to dart around the book-shelves. But I couldn't move. My mouth opened to scream. And it was like a living nightmare. Not a single sound came out.

Then the library melted. It pulsed right before my eyes like a hospital patient being shocked by high voltage. The jolt rippled through me with the force of being slammed against a brick wall. I gasped for air, lungs squeezing. I felt like I was being strangled.

"Amelia!" My uncle's worry-struck voice reached my ears. "Are you alright?" It almost sounded like he was calling out from a distance. Only that couldn't be the case. Because his broad hands were curled around my shoulders and shaking my body. "Amelia, answer me!"

The strength of his shaking caused my head to rattle. My brain felt waterlogged, not quite conscious yet. I forced my tongue and mouth to move through the numbness. "Yes. I'm okay. Just stop shaking me."

Uncle Caius did as I asked and I opened my eyes to view his stricken face. His eyes widened for a split second, looking surprised. Then his chest rose and fell with a deep breath, calculated concern changing his expression. "Amelia, you scared me half to death. What happened?"

Shock vaulted through me as my brain finally caught up. I was back in my uncle's office, able to smell the remaining choc-mint cookies on his desk. What I had just witnessed hadn't been missing time or even a dream. It had been real. What the hell?

Marcus. My heart sank. Inside I felt hollow. The connection I'd experienced between us had been a warning. One I had foolishly ignored. It can't be true. Yet something I had realized many times before, and somehow forgotten, dawned on me. A pressing weight against my stomach made me want to gag. My dreams come true. And now I knew the truth. Marcus was plotting against me and using my best friend like a stringed puppet to act out his plans. I ran over the time frame of my previous telling dreams. Other than the distortion of already played-out events, I dreamed everything before it came to be.

Urgency struck me, an electric thunderbolt that seared from the inside out. What time had it been in my vision? When would this happen? I recalled the chiming clock but knew I hadn't seen the face of it. Then it hit me. The chimes, there had been six of them. 6AM, the perfect time with no one awake to overhear them. My eyes darted sideways to the ticking grandfather clock against the wall of Caius's office. 5:55AM. If the time was correct, I didn't have more than five minutes. But I had to try. I had to get to Kendrick before Marcus did.

"Amelia?" Caius tilted my head up with the palm of his hand.

He was still waiting for me to answer his question, but I couldn't tell him. What was there even to tell? I had no proof, nothing to back up my fears. And I had no time. I shook my head. "I thought I had gotten used to the ancient blood," I lied. "I guess I took too big a gulp. I was just so thirsty." In truth, the last part wasn't a lie. A thirst, similar to the night I had learned monsters existed, gripped me. All moisture was stripped from my throat. "I'm really tired, though. Do you mind if I go to bed?"

Caius rose from his crouched position beside me, looking wary. "You do look worse for wear. May I escort you?"

Taking my uncle's outstretched hand for leverage, I rose to my feet. "No, thank you. I'll be fine."

Caius, though clearly doubtful, nodded. "Very well..." He wrapped me in gentle arms then walked me out the door to the hall. With a short pause and a tip of his head, he said, "Sleep well, my dear," and closed the door behind him.

There wasn't a second to waste. So where was Kendrick? Already in the library, or up in his room readying for bed? Dawn was close to breaking. So his room was the most logical place. But what if Marcus had already lured him down there? Indecision crippled me. The clock was ticking. I had to make a choice.

Library.

In a flash, I had cleared the corridors and burst through the door to the library. Everything was dark and silent. No footsteps across the carpet. No whispered voices, and no Marcus or Kendrick. My eyes flew up to the wall-mounted clock. 6:05AM. Was I wrong altogether? Had my dream even played out yet, or was it still to come? There was no way to know. Not until I found Kendrick.

I bolted up to my room and flew through the door. I was heading straight for the door joining Kendrick's room when something jarred me to a standstill. I wasn't alone.

Kendrick stood stiffly before my bed. The bedside lamp backlighting his figure emphasized his expressionless face with hard shadows. Blood raced through my veins. My heart hammered within my chest. Kendrick's surprise appearance, or even the puzzlement of his blank expression, wasn't the cause for my body's fear-driven reaction. What he held in his hand was.

"Kendrick." Taking a cautious step forward, I eyed the blood-filled glass in his hands. "What are you doing in here?"

Kendrick's face remained frozen, his dead eyes staring through me. "This is for you," he said, holding out the glass.

Terror gripped my heart, sending tingling waves outward to encapsulate every inch of my body. I fought the need to shudder. "Kendrick, this isn't you. I saw it. I know Marcus is compelling you." I dared a further step forward, pleading with my eyes. "Kendrick, please. I know you're in there, and I need you to fight back. I know you can."

A glimmer of conflicting emotions flashed through my best friend's eyes. His hand holding the glass dropped an inch. Then it rose again, higher, extending toward me. The pain riddling his expression made it look like he was being torn apart from the inside out. "You have to drink this. All of it."

My feet were moving, backing up to the door. Marcus's compulsion was too strong. I couldn't get through to him. As I closed in on the open doorway, I turned, ready to bolt. Before I could get one foot over the threshold, the door slammed in my face.

There was a click as a key locked the door. Kendrick's hand, now free of the blood-filled glass, splayed against the wood. His chest pressed against my back. "You will drink."

Goosebumps cascaded down my body at the brush of his breath against my neck. My eyes darted sideways. The bathroom door was open. But I'd never make it. I needed leverage. "Okay, I'll drink it. All of it."

Kendrick's pressing weight against my back eased. It was the opportunity I needed.

I whirled and drove my fists into his gut. He flew back through the air, and I made my attempt, racing into the shadow-cloaked bathroom. I cried out in frustration. The door to Kendrick's room was locked. I was cornered.

And then he was on me. Fingers threaded through my hair, dragging me back across the tiles. With arms and legs flailing, I struck out futilely. Now anticipating my resistance, he blocked each attempt.

Suddenly my feet left the ground as Kendrick threw me onto my bed. He landed in a split second to pin my chest down with his knees. I struck out, aiming for his face with clawed fingers. But Kendrick was fast, too fast. His hands caught my wrists, pinning them above my head. My legs thrashed. Still it was no use.

Kendrick lowered his face to mine, now restraining my wrists with just one hand. His other hand moved to clutch my cheeks. "Stop fighting me." The silver flecks of his irises exploded and his pupils dilated. "Stop resisting."

My body ceased thrashing, turning limp and heavy. Move,

dammit! I screamed internally. Still it was no use. My muscles and limbs were too weak.

Kendrick released my cheeks and leaned forward, collecting the almost full glass from my bedside. His eyes didn't break focus. "Now, open your mouth."

The blood's aroma was peppery and metallic. It made my mouth water. "Don't do this," I begged before my jaw fell open. Icy tears trickled down my face.

Kendrick didn't flinch. He lowered the glass to my parted lips, filling my mouth. "Swallow." My throat complied without my permission. Then the shell of my best friend repeated the process until every last drop was gone. Kendrick's last compelled words were whispered. "Remember all you have been made to forget." He pulled away from my chest, rising to his feet.

Rage swirled through my entire body. I knew none of this was Kendrick's doing, his fault. Still a part of me wanted to launch at him. To inflict pain for the humiliation he'd just subjected me to. But my limbs felt like they were filling with cement, my eyes struggling to stay open. *Remember all you have been made to forget.* The words burned, like a fiery pen branding them across the inside of my skull. The solid brick wall I felt around my memories—a wall I hadn't even realized existed—glowed and pulsed. Veins of hairline fractures split out across the barrier. Marcus had accomplished his goal. What would happen now? My stomach knitted with a churning horror of the unknown. "Kendrick, please," I choked, struggling to speak through the numbness that was fast swelling across my tongue and down my throat. "Please don't leave me."

Kendrick didn't reply. He didn't even look at me. Instead, he doused my bedside lamp and turned away with a nod as if he'd been released after completing his tasks. No longer able to hold themselves open, my eyelids drooped. I could hear my best friend's softening footsteps depart, the pitch changing as he entered the bathroom. Then there was a clatter of metal on metal. A bolt unlocked, and then the door to his room opened and closed.

I was alone.

The words embedded in my head pulsed again, forcing bricks to fall and crumble. A flood of images knocked the breath from my lungs. They were fragmented and splintered, barely intelligible and struggling to reform. With the last of my dwindling strength, I rolled onto my side with a groan, curling my body in on itself. My breath had slowed, continuing to decrease as my pulse waned. Then with the last moments of consciousness, one memory slipped into sharp focus. A folder with my name printed inside the cover, and a concoction of ingredients. I wanted to gasp but couldn't. Those ingredients would slow the heart and deteriorate muscle function, rendering a person into a state of paralysis.

Combine with Pure Blood.

I remembered then the gash and dried blood across Marcus's wrist. His blood, Pure Blood, mixed with poison. Terror clawed through my heart and I became very still. Consciousness was slipping away. I couldn't hold it off any longer. I couldn't do anything to stop this. Everything faded, and then there was nothing but silence.

TANGLED sheets clung to my body, restraining my movements as I dreamed of a cold, dark place. A throat-constricting smell of decomposing flesh hung thick in the air, threatening my gag reflex. Only one exit was visible, a solid wooden and iron-braced door. A door that sat closed. I tried to move, to pull myself up from the moist stone ground, but stalled. The clang of metal on metal raked through my ears. Weight was pulling at my wrists.

Alarm bit into me. I was shackled, and I knew exactly why.
Marcus.

Any thoughts of looking for an escape, or a way to unbind my
shackles forfeited as my vision blurred. I was being torn back to
reality. "No, no, no!" I knew what was coming, and I wasn't ready. I
didn't have a plan.

The stone and shackles faded as consciousness gripped me, and
the amethyst pendant warmed against my chest. I wasn't alone.
Broad hands were curled around my shoulders and shaking me. The
room was black. My eyes refused to adjust. But it could only be one
person. Marcus. He was already here to claim me.

Anger struck through me. There was no way in hell I was giving
in without a fight. Still blinded and with my body barely responsive,
it took all of my strength to strike out. My arm flailed, fingers
connecting with the bedside lamp before hurling it back at him. A
sound of cracking porcelain erupted with what I hoped was a clean
hit to the skull.

"Amelia, stop!"

The strong nurturing voice shook me. It was a voice I couldn't
confuse. The last voice I'd expected to hear. My eyes widened in the
dark, finally adjusting. Shattered porcelain littered the carpeted
ground at my uncle's feet. He was standing at my bedside and
rubbing at his forehead. Blood beaded from the gash my retaliation
had created, slowing as the wound began to heal.

"Uncle Caius?" My voice sounded hollow. "But I thought...
What are you doing here?"

"There is no time," Caius said, tugging on my arm. "You must
come with me."

As he pulled me from the sheets that were still coiled around my
body, I staggered, falling. The poison Kendrick had forced on me

under Marcus's order still had a hold. It weakened every one of my muscles, slowing my motor functions.

Caius reacted instantly, his arm curling around my waist and hoisting me up against his side. "Easy there." His next words were mumbled, so quiet I questioned if I had heard them right. "Why are you so weak?"

I frowned as we moved across my room and out to the hallway. My mind felt sluggish, reeling with unending images that made absolutely no sense. "What's going on?" I asked, ignoring Uncle Caius's question. Why was he in my room? "Where are we going?"

Caius kept his narrowed eyes focused ahead, leading us down the shadow-cast stairwell. "There has been a security breach. You are in grave danger."

He knows about Marcus? A glimmer of relief washed over me, but it was short lived. *Kendrick.* Marcus had been using him, and I didn't know if he was still part of this. What if he was still in harm's way? "Kendrick," I said as we moved down the strangely unlit hall, nearing my uncle's office. "We need to go back for him. He could be in danger, too."

Caius's supporting arm tightened for a split second, then relaxed. "He's not in any danger," he mumbled, jerking me into his office before releasing my weight. "The entire castle has been evacuated."

Evacuated? Uncle Caius's suddenly absent support along with his words stunned me. My legs buckled and I tripped, catching my Vans on the Persian rug. It was by pure miracle that I managed to catch myself on the seat before his desk. My limbs quaked at the sudden burst of energy, aching in protest.

As I turned into a sitting position, a glimmer of brass caught the desk lamp's light. There was something beneath the corner of the rug my shoes had lifted. Not that I was really looking or paying any real attention. Confusion-fueled questions stole my train of thought, distorting my vision while forming on my lips.

As I was about to speak, airing the confusion, I froze. A cluster of lost memories had hit me like glass shards slamming into sharp focus. The meals and hours I had somehow forgotten had been spent in this very office. Each evening I'd sat opposite my uncle while chatting and indulging in mouth-watering dinners and decadent chocolate desserts. *Remember all you have been made to forget.* Kendrick had compelled me under Marcus's command. Because I'd been compelled to forget. Now it was like two people's voices were fighting in my head. Disjointed images swirled through my mind, but there were so many I couldn't make sense of them. Was there more I was supposed to remember?

The pendant pulsed with rapid heat, like a beacon warning. My revelation became a second thought. Marcus was closing in on us.

My head whipped around to Caius, who was rifling one-handed through the top drawer of his desk. His other hand clutched the diamond paperweight. Good, a weapon. He was thinking ahead. The rapid movement caused my vision to blur and I struggled to rise from the seat. It took all the strength my arms and legs could muster to brace against the arm rail. "We have to get out of here!"

Apart from the door we had entered through, there was only a double-paned window to escape out of. Although with my lack of motor function, leaping to safety from two stories up wasn't the greatest option. If we didn't leave now, we'd be cornered.

"Now!" I said. My hand strained uselessly to tear the arm of the chair free for a makeshift weapon. "I think he's coming."

"*He?*" Uncle Caius sounded surprised. He moved around the desk with something gleaming silver clutched in his hand.

The pendant pulsed again. It was so hot it sizzled against my chest. The smell of burned flesh invaded my nostrils. Disquiet seized my slow-beating heart as it ached to drum. My eyes darted back to the open door. The lamp doused and a gust of wind blew past me in the same instant. A starburst of pain erupted from my temple and my limbs gave out. My body crumpled in a heap as unconsciousness claimed me.

CHAPTER 27

$\mathcal{I}$ stirred with a groan, surrounded by darkness. The stink of decomposing flesh hung thick in the air. It made me want to gag. Heaviness weighed down my limbs. My jeans and tank top clung to my body, dripping with rank, foul-smelling water. Agonizing pulses shot through my head in rhythm with the slow beat of my heart. It felt as though I'd been slugged with a sledge-hammer. Where was I? What happened? Frustrated, I tried to move, to pull from the moist stone ground, but stalled. The clang of metal on metal raked through my ears. Horrific reality dawned on me, knocking the breath from my lungs. I was awake in my living night-mare. We hadn't escaped, and now Marcus had me. But where was Uncle Caius?

Desperation began to set in and I tugged at my restraints. It was pointless. The poison was still surging through my veins, weakening every one of my muscles. With every ounce of strength I could gather, I shuffled my heavy body back until I hit the wall. Labored breath rasped through my lips and sweat budded across my forehead. Then a click sounded with the illumination of a dim bulb. Expecting to find Marcus, my eyes darted about the claustrophobic cell. A single bare bulb, swaying on a cable from the mold-caked ceiling, offered a small cone of visibility. In its light I could see a single closed door and my chains. I gulped. They ran along the ground, rising up to where they were bolted to the wall. I was trapped.

A footstep sounded, followed by another and another as a tall man stepped into the light. My heart skipped a beat and my eyes grew wide. "Caius?" Had he intercepted Marcus? Was he here to save me? Words tumbled from my mouth in a barely audible babble. "You're okay? He didn't hurt you?" My eyes scoured over my uncle. His ash-gray suit was stained and speckled by damp patches. Dried blood flaked from his wrinkled forehead—the only remnants of my wrongful attack. Apart from that, he appeared completely unharmed. "What happened? Where are we?" I tried to raise my cuffed wrists, but they barely budged. "Can you break these?"

Caius made no attempt to answer my questions. He just stood there, his face shadowed and lined in an unreadable expression. A deep unsettling twisted through my gut. The throbbing pain inside my skull sent a shockwave down my spine, causing me to wince. Where was Marcus?

"Best we get this done," Caius said with a smile. His lips parted just enough to reveal the point of extended fangs. "Before anyone notices you missing."

The hair across the back of my neck prickled. "What are you talking about? Get what done?"

Caius shook his head. "I guess there is no harm in revealing the truth to you now... It is not like you will live to *tell* anyone."

Ice grew within my chest, snaking out in tendrils that brought a traveling shiver to my entire body. Won't live? I shook my head. I'd heard him wrong, I must have. But Caius's face—lit by a grim frown—did not placate the nervous tension growing inside of me. The black of his pupils shimmered. His expression looked so alien compared to the uncle I had grown up with, the one I trusted and loved. Any hint of caring was lost behind predatory eyes. Fear coiled through my heart with shell-shocked understanding. My trust had been horribly misplaced. "*You...*" My blood ran cold and I choked on my next words. "*You* did this?"

I shifted, cowering. Something pressed against my backside. I didn't take notice. My eyes were already scanning for a weapon, an escape, anything to release me from these chains. There was a burlap sack crumbled on the ground, well out of reach. There was only one door, wooden and iron-braced. And just as in my dream, it was shut. Was it locked? It didn't really matter. Not yet. Not while chains imprisoned me.

Despair gripped my heart. Another set of shackles hung from the opposing wall. Apart from that, the room was empty. Just me and the man I had loved as my uncle.

Caius stepped forward, clasping his hands before him. "This day has been a long time coming. I have waited patiently all these years for you to come of age, so to speak. You see, my dear…"

The use of his loving name for me brought bile to the back of my throat. I fought the urge to cough and groaned, struggling to pull my knees up to my chest. Absently I noticed how damp and stained my purple-laced Vans were. I'd never wear those again…if I lived. And there it was again, the feel of something digging into my backside. What am I sitting on? Then it dawned on me. A lifeline!

"I had to wait for your blood to complete the transformation." Caius turned and began pacing. His eyes became distant while he continued his story.

It was the distraction I needed. Focused only on the task and knowing it was my only chance, I made my move. The lack of function in my limbs made my arms tremble with strain. I reached behind my back and winced. The chains rattled like an alarm going off.

But my uncle was lost in thought, recalling events that seemed to bring him satisfaction. "...to turn into a fully-fledged vampire, before I could put my plan into action," he was saying.

Then my fingers grazed the smooth rectangular disc hidden inside the damp back pocket of my jeans. My iPhone! The reprieve I experienced was short lived. Getting hold of the phone unnoticed had been my first goal, but what now? Kendrick might be the only person I could still trust, my last hope *if* he was free of compulsion. I needed to send out an SOS. The dank space reminded me of the cells Caius had shown me during his guided tour. Except there was a distinct difference. Those chambers had solid steel doors, not iron-braced wooden ones. And the cries of imprisoned beings had filled the air there. Not here. The air was deathly quiet. Defeat dampened my mind and soul. I had no idea where I was. Don't give up, my internal voice challenged. If you do, you're dead. With renewed desperation I tried to spot any clue that could reveal my location.

Caius's direct tone drew my eye. "The stories you were told of how you were saved and created are not entirely accurate." He was staring down at me with a look of anticipation. "Your mother had to be on the brink of death before I could infect her."

Infect her? I remembered Mom's explanation of how we were all turned. She had been heavily pregnant when the rogue vampire attacked, and our father had died protecting us. She would have died too, *if not for Caius,* she had said. *He gave us new life when the only alternative was death.*

The truth of our past hit me like a blast of icy water. "There was no rogue vampire," my voice quavered. The hand that shielded my iPhone behind my back began to shake violently. "It was you."

Caius nodded with eyes almost solemn. "Though this is not how I had planned for all of this to play out. You see, my dear, taking your life had not always been my intention." For a moment he appeared angry. Then his expression seemed to drop with a look of regret. "If you had only remained compliant and non-rebellious, a seed I could mold as my own to continue my legacy, well, then this would not have been an inevitability. I gave you many last chances, but in the end you acted too late. You are not the asset I once saw you as. You are a liability." The regret striking his expression shifted with sound resolution. "In any case, it was the only way."

Anger spiked my blood as I glared. The monster in front of me had orchestrated the attack on my family. The man I had accepted as my uncle had been the one to turn us all. He had damned us to life as vampires, and he had murdered my father. And we had all trusted him, seen him as our savior. My blood boiled, ice instantly turning to fire.

"Oh, don't look so appalled, Amelia," Caius spoke as though I were an unruly child. "You should be thanking me. Your mother was never part of my plan. I could have let her bleed out. Yet I didn't. I showed her mercy and allowed her to live, allowed *you* to have a mother to grow up with."

Insolence blemished my tone. "You want me to thank you?" Tearing my eyes away, I fought the urge to crush my iPhone in my still obscured hand. iPhone! Caius's revelation had shaken me and rewritten the past. It had distracted me when I needed to figure out where I was. "Where the hell are we?"

Caius shrugged. "Does it matter?"

Of course he wouldn't tell me. Why would he? I shook my head, thinking back to the last moments I could remember before waking in this dank cell. Caius's office. He had lured me down there with lies and pretense. Why had he taken me there? For the life of me I couldn't remember leaving, just wanting to, expecting Marcus to blaze into the room at any second. Everything, from the stacked piles of papers littering Caius's desk, to the bookshelves and grandfather clock, had all appeared as usual. There hadn't been a single thing out of place. I probed harder into my memories which were still swarming with too many images to comprehend. Then I saw it. On entering Caius's office I'd fallen without the support of his arm, tripping on the rug before his desk. A split-second glance I had disregarded at the time glowed behind my eyes. The desk lamp's light had caught on something brass which had shone beneath the edge of the lifted rug. A latch... We never even left his office. We moved below it. I wasn't at all certain that my hunch was right, but it was all I had to go on.

I forced my gaze up to Caius who was watching me with narrowed eyes. "You said it was the only way?" I hoped encouraging him to talk would distract him enough for me to send out my SOS. "The only way to what?"

Caius bent down, causing me to flinch. The dim light created a glow around him but left his face hardened by shadows. With a single finger he forced my chin up. My skin crawled, disgusted by his touch, and I tried to jerk back. "It was the only way to create a vampire whose blood would hold the key," he said, then paused. His eyes became thoughtful as though he were choosing his next words carefully. "...to immortality."

Immortality? The word rippled through my entire body, shocking, intriguing, and utterly *what the hell?* The elixir Caius had given us had done a lot more than hold off our transformation into vampires. It had started the groundwork for Caius's plan. With a throat-squeezing gulp, I forced my wide eyes up. "Does that mean…"

Caius's sharp laugh stole my words. "That *you* are immortal? That you could live forever? Perhaps…" He shook his head, rising from his crouched position, and turned away with a sigh. "But now we will never know."

With the split-second opportunity, I began keying a text. My hands shook and I winced at the clang of my chains. '*Mortal danger. Trapped below…*'

Caius turned back at the noise of my restraints. His eyes zeroed in on the iPhone in my hands. Then he lunged forward. My thumb hit the send button just as he snatched the phone from my grasp.

"Stupid girl," Caius spat. "What have you done?" He glanced down, thumb traveling over the face of the phone. Fangs glinted through his split lips with an amused smile. A look of intention shimmered through his eyes. "He will never find you," he said. Then with a belting force, he hurled my phone at the stone wall. It connected with a crunch and burst into shattered pieces.

An acidic lump crawled up my throat and I swallowed, feeling like I was drowning. The text was too vague and unfinished. Caius was right. Kendrick would never find me. "What are you going to do to me?"

Ignoring my question, Caius knelt and dug into the burlap sack. "Enough stalling…"

He pulled a glass jar from the bag and flipped the latched lid open. It was filled with a thick, dark-red liquid. Blood. It wasn't human. It was something else, something peppery and metallic, a royal's pure blood. For a moment I wondered if it was Marcus's. It was a strong possibility, but I still didn't understand what his part in all this had been. Why had Marcus helped Caius? What was he getting out of this? Inside I felt hollow and betrayed. Even more than that, I felt pissed. Pissed at my own naive trust of a guy I hardly knew, and of the uncle I had always loved.

Caius smeared blood in a wide circle before me and began painting a symbol into its center. It was a sort of jagged bolt with a line through the middle.

A knot of cold unfurled within my chest. I needed to know what Marcus's involvement had been in all of this, and why. I needed to understand. But fear of what was to come formed a question on my lips. "What are you going to do to me?"

Caius smeared his blood-caked hands across his gray pants, moving toward me. Then with little effort he cradled my body, lifting me off the dank ground. I tried to struggle against his grasp, but he was so strong, and my body was still so weak. The chains clanked, dragging along the stone ground, long enough to reach the spot where Caius paused. He lowered my body to the middle of the blood-painted circle. His hungry eyes traveled from my face and down my neck. "I am going to…"

A crash beyond the solid door caused me to jump. Caius's words died on his tongue.

Kendrick was my first thought. Only it couldn't be him. If he had even received my text, he could never have found me in this expansive castle. He didn't know who had trapped me. He had nothing. No clues to go on.

"Looks like we have a visitor," Caius said. He didn't look at all surprised, only expectant and in total control.

The cold knot within my chest grew, sending ice shards through my bones. *Marcus.*

Caius moved, stepping back into the shadows and leaving a clear path between me and the doorway. What was he doing? Had I been wrong, again? Was Marcus the one calling the shots?

I heard sloshing and splashes, then footsteps drawing nearer and nearer. My slow-beating heart, still restrained by poison, sank with total despair. There was one set of footsteps, one person approaching.

The latch bolted to the door lifted with a creak and the solid door flung open. My breath caught in my throat as someone leaped into the light, arms outstretched toward me. No, no, no!

"Amelia!" Kendrick cried. His hair was plastered with sweat to his forehead and his soggy jeans clung to his shins. His panicked eyes registered only me.

Caius moved from the shadows in a blur of ashen gray, porcelain, and red to collide with Kendrick's side. My best friend stumbled, the wind crushed from his lungs. He never reached the ground. Caius already had him by the throat and was driving him back against the wall. A *thwack* sounded with the connection. Kendrick's eyes grew wide, glimpsing his attacker.

It was the only hesitation Caius needed. He lifted Kendrick off the ground, eyes locking on his prey. "Do not move, or speak." The intensity of his silvery eyes was like an impressive electrical storm, alive and commanding.

Torment contorted Kendrick's face, but he didn't move or speak. Deathly shivers cascaded down my spine. I wanted to scream, to cry out. But I couldn't. Fear drained my mouth of all moisture, leaving it as dry as sandpaper.

Caius slowly lowered my best friend's feet to the ground, and released his clenched fingers from around his throat. "It did not have to end this way," he said with a shake of his head. "But now that you are here…" With a pin-centered spin Caius turned. A smug smile curved his thin lips. "It may intrigue you to know, my dear, that Kendrick has been helping me all this time, reporting back to me with your developmental progress." His chuckle was dry and goosebump raising. "It was his interference alone that brought you to me."

The last part I already knew from Kendrick's confession. Still my eyes shifted to my best friend, desperate for him to negate the other allegation. His face was set in a torturous grimace. But he couldn't respond. As I watched him, clouds shifted from my mind. I remembered the strange call Kendrick had received at the psychic and arts fair back home. He had been talking to Caius. More lies... A tiny part of me wanted to hate Kendrick, to blame him for everything. But I couldn't. He was my best friend and I loved him. I would *always* love him, no matter what he did to me, knowingly or not. And really, no matter what Caius claimed, it was my own actions that had delivered me into harm's way, no one else's.

"Without Kendrick, this would not have been possible," Caius remarked with satisfaction. "He has been a useful minion." His last words were mumbled, low and emotionless. "Up until now…"

"No!" I choked out, coughing. "C-Caius, please. Do whatever you w-want to me." I spluttered again, my throat clenching in retaliation. "I won't f-fight it. J-just don't hurt Kendrick."

"Brave words, my dear." A proud smile lit Caius's age-wrinkled face and he stepped forward. "But you are not in any position to bargain." He knelt, touching my cheek with bony fingers. "Now, it is time."

My skin crawled at his touch, tiny bugs pinching my flesh. Knowing compliance wouldn't save Kendrick's life, I tried to jerk away, tugging weakly at my restraints.

Caius sighed. "You may as well stop struggling. It will do you no good."

Fear seeped from my extremities to my core. Inside my head a word resurfaced. *Remember.* It pulsed against the walls around my memories, chipping away at the solid bricks. "What the hell are you going to do to me?" I demanded again.

Razor-sharp fangs protruded from between Caius's smiling lips.

"I am going to drain every drop of your delicious blood until the point your heart stops beating and you die." His deadly tone raked over me while his face beamed with ambition. "Your life's flame will not extinguish without meaning. Your gift of eternal life will grant me the stepping stone I require to save—" At his broken-off words he shook his head. "The reason matters not."

For a split second the image of Madame Rosalie invaded my vision, along with her chilling words. *"Beware the blood that runs in your veins."*

The crazy old woman had been right about everything. And I had been totally skeptical and dismissive, ignoring her warnings of my demise. My death... It was inevitable now. Beware the blood that runs in your veins. It had been tainted since my first breath. Now, according to Caius and after everything he had done, it might bestow immortality? Though it seemed immortal blood would not save me from death. Caius had made that abundantly clear.

"Though, I will miss feeding from you." Caius licked his lips. "Testing your blood these last few weeks has been quite enjoyable."

The remaining bricks blocking my memories suddenly crumbled with Caius's words. Everything that had eluded my mind suddenly flooded back, like shattered glass reforming into one crystalline piece. Within the reflected projection, a series of events I had somehow forgotten rose. The evenings I had only vaguely glimpsed earlier were now crystal clear. Caius had sat across his desk from me, using the compulsion of his eyes to distort reality. Some nights he'd made me believe we'd enjoyed harmless meals, while others he'd erased the whole encounter. But nothing about those nights had been harmless. My stomach swelled. The images were so violating that I had to fight the urge to retch. Each night Caius had rendered me into a comatose state. He'd pulled back the cascade of my hair to press his open lips to my neck. Then his fangs had broken my skin.

Pain I couldn't consciously respond to had followed, searing through me as he drank my blood.

I lifted a muscle-aching hand to my neck, causing my chains to rattle. New images were unfolding. They now rotated like they were spinning on the glass faces of a revolving door. My dreamscape with Ty, the last time I'd seen or even talked to him. He had noticed the bite marks then, and I had shrugged off his finding. I'd been so totally caught up with the only task I had to accomplish, that I'd forgotten so easily—because I'd been compelled to. Now I remembered everything. I said I didn't want him anymore, and that I wanted to stay at the Armaya. And, oh my God, how could I? I said that I didn't love him. Pain pulsed through my heart. It felt like a dagger was slicing into the slow-beating muscle, then ripping down until it hit my guts. I doubled over, cracking my head against the stone floor. Fresh throbbing pain had my brain pulsing against my skull. I glared up at Caius kneeling over me and tried to scream. My weakening voice choked on a sob. "Y-you and Marcus, you were b-both compelling me."

Caius's smile broadened. "Well, to be honest, my dear, you made it more than easy."

My tearing eyes shifted to Kendrick. He was still standing motionless, pinned against the stone wall by an invisible force. A pained expression was plastered across his face, and his fingers twitched beside his frozen body.

Caius fished into the pocket of his stained pants, retrieving a small, glass vial. "Now, open your mouth."

It was the same vial I had discovered, hidden within the base of the grandfather clock in Caius's office. The silver liquid inside caught the dim light from the naked bulb. It glistened almost magically, a rainbow spectrum of colors. Except the vial—unlike the day I had uncovered it—was almost empty. The same magnetism I had felt when I'd first discovered the vial called to me now. It beckoned me as though its contents somehow *belonged* to me, were somehow a part of me. The eerie sensation was alluring and familiar, like I had experienced it before ever discovering the vial. But where and when my faulty memory couldn't recall.

"That's not an herbal remedy, is it?" My eyes were scanning the room again, searching futilely for anything. There had to be a weapon or a way to break the restraints, something to save my life, or at least Kendrick's. There was the empty jar that had been filled with blood and the fragmented remains of my iPhone. Both were well out of reach. There was nothing else.

Caius was tipping the vial, forcing the liquid to flow back and forth as he watched. He seemed entranced by its beauty. "No. This is…" He hesitated for the briefest moment. "Ancient vampire blood. It will complete the conversion of your own blood." Anticipation brightened his wrinkle-rimmed eyes and his tongue slid over his gleaming fangs. "Without this, your death would be no more than a satisfying meal." He turned the cap, removing it from the vial. Then he grasped my cheeks, tilting my face up. "Drink!"

My lips pinned shut for a split second, then released, hurling spit directly into my enemy's face. "Fuck you!"

Caius flinched away, wiping the spit from his face with his sleeve. A roar reverberated from his chest, "insolent child!" And he spun, violently throwing a clenched fist across my cheek.

A crack sounded with a shot of pain through my jaw. I crumpled with a thud to the mold-caked ground. My jaw hung, aching and almost swaying. It was broken, the bone cracked through and dislocated.

Kendrick growled and his trembling fingers tensed. They were trying to curl into fists. Still he couldn't move.

Now weight pressed against my chest. Caius's knees pinned me to the ground. He struck out, grasping my cheeks to forcefully pry my hanging jaw wide open. My eyes glazed as pain-spiked tears blurred my vision. A second later, a few drops of liquid fell into my mouth. Instantaneously the taste of ice-cold metal exploded on my tongue. It soaked through my flesh like pure acid. Tingles traversed through my body, and my throat constricted. Every one of my muscles ached with bone-deep fatigue.

I knew I had experienced this same sensation before. With my resurfaced memories, I knew it had been almost every night. The blood Caius had supplied in his office had provided a similar sensation, absorbing through my flesh. But its potency had been watered down. Regular blood spiked with this silver liquid he claimed to be ancient vampire blood. He'd been drugging me the whole time. All the pieces were coming together. Everything he'd done had been for this moment. So I could come to this point...and die.

Caius cradled my limp body and knelt within the painted circle. My mind screamed for me to move. To fight the monster who trapped me with his arms. But my body remained paralyzed, a prisoner of flesh and bone. Inside I was striking out with limbs, nails, and teeth. But any connection to actual movement was lost. Marcus's poison still had a debilitating grip on me, and Caius's drugging only complemented my total immobilization.

Caius tilted my head and brushed back my hair, exposing my neck. Kendrick's breathing became louder and desperate. Fear snaked through my soul. He was next in line to die, and it was my fault. I had been the one to lead him here. "Kendrick," I cried. "I'm so s-sorry. P-please forgive me."

Caius closed the distance between my neck and his parted mouth. He hovered momentarily, taking a deep breath. The sound of Kendrick's raspy breath was interrupted with the last words I would ever hear. "Enjoy the show."

I heard the smack of his tongue across his lips. Then his mouth closed over my neck. Horror seeped through my veins, and an everlasting moment seemed to pass before his fangs tore through my flesh. A fleeting gasp escaped my lips, while an inextinguishable fire bloomed from the punctures. It swarmed over my skin, striking inward with cutting pain that was so real I almost thought I was being stabbed. Vampire bites were meant to elicit a sensation of ecstasy. Except not when the victim was a vampire too. We weren't made to feed off each other. The pain continued to radiate throughout my entire body as his arms constricted, clutching my paralyzed form tighter and tighter with every sickening gulp. Now I knew first-hand how Elena had felt on The Vampire Diaries when Klaus had ripped into her neck, killing her. Only this wasn't a TV show. This was real life. My life.

When the searing pain within my body began to dull, my internal screams to fight faded. Without the current of blood filling my veins, violent shivers took hold of me. My body was giving up.

With shallow contractions, my slow-beating heart faltered. My mind wavered as my body began to fail. The crushing pain of imminent death faded. As my eyes fluttered shut, a fleeting memory of the boy I loved floated across the backs of my eyelids. Lush greenery filled with the sound of singing birds surrounded me. The warm afternoon sun broke like lace through the treetops. Instantly I knew what I was seeing, and where I was. This was the memory of my last dreamscape with Ty.

He materialized before me. Dejection painted his expression, riddled by the grief I had caused. He moved within a split second to crush me against his bare chest. His lips covered mine. Then he spoke the words I had heard for the very first time. "Amelia, I love you."

Breath escaped my lungs now, just at it had then at his proximity and touch. A part of me had still wanted and yearned for every part of him, and still did now. But my lips had spat without permission as I pushed him away. "Well I don't love you!"

Ice-cold tears escaped my eyes. Now he would never know the truth. Never know that my feelings for him were still as irrefutable and irrevocable as ever. Never know that I would give anything just to be in his arms and feel the warmth of his lips one last time. The knowledge was more excruciating than knowing my fate, more excruciating than the returning physical pain. Now he would never know the truth. The memory faded, dissipating like a cloud of smoke. A final whisper blew through my lips. "Ty, I love you."

Déjà vu slapped me like another concrete blow from my uncle's hand. The night I'd learned I was a vampire, I had woken from a nightmare. All those months ago in Anchorage I'd seen this very cell and the monster who would take my life. The second I'd woken it had been gone. But now I couldn't forget it. The monster was not some faceless creature. It was my very own uncle. Grasping at the remaining fragments of the nightmare, I gasped. There'd been more to that nightmare than the monster. The boy I loved, the very same boy I'd dreamt about before I had ever even met him…was Ty.

The room began to blur and spin. Knowledge couldn't save me now, nothing could. Unable to blink, my eyes stared up at the dusty light bulb. Blood loss pressed in on me. I was so deathly cold. The edge of my vision turned black, light being eaten away by a stain that looked like blotted ink. Then empty darkness took hold.

This is it. I'm dying.

CHAPTER 28

An eternity passed in this dark void as death clawed at me, trying to claim my soul. The beat of my heart faded. It became so weak, so slow, it was almost non-existent. The point of no return was closing in. Then something changed. The taste of fresh blood hit my tongue. It dripped steadily into my mouth and down my throat, spreading and absorbing gradually throughout my entire body. The ice shards freezing my insides began to thaw as I slowly came awake. Involuntary twitches undulated from my head down to my toes. The rich, peppery blood hypnotized me. Before, the dying thrum of my heart had been ready to quit. Now it grew in strength and speed.

Without any form of rational thought, but through primal necessity alone, my body responded. The monster inside of me awakened. My arms reached up, gripping tight to the lean torso of a male. His arms held me, and now mine prevented his escape. With my eyelids too heavy to lift, I pressed my lips to his neck. Then with a crack, my jaw fused back together. I sank my fangs into his bleeding flesh.

The muscles along his broad shoulders and neck bunched with a throaty gasp. But he didn't struggle. He didn't even attempt to pull away.

A greater surge of blood now flooded my mouth. Each mouthful further returned life to my deprived body. And I needed more. With my body still repairing from its comatose state, I craved every single mouth-watering drop. Warm tingles kindled my heart, spreading like wildfire to encase my entire body. The sensation didn't stop there. Instead, it continued to grow. Snaking from my own flesh, the warmth swallowed the person my arms still restrained.

Without warning, a sonic boom exploded with a glorious blinding light, splitting from our connected bodies. Even through my dropped eyelids, a piercing sting attacked my eyes. A sudden pulse shot through my brain. It felt as though the organ was somehow expanding, almost doubling in size. Yet it was still crammed within the solid plates of my skull.

I will give my life for you. The deep voice shrouded with grief rose in my mind. It wasn't my own. It was Kendrick's. *I will die for you.*

The life of his blood was still streaming from his neck and into my mouth. His arms loosened around me. Then they fell slack, hitting the stone floor with a thud.

I'm killing him.

The realization rattled me to my very core. I broke my fangs' hold on his neck abruptly and pushed off his lap. My eyes flung open. My heart, now coursing with pure, fresh blood, *Kendrick's blood*, hammered against my ribs. Kendrick was slumped before me, motionless. Blood-tinged tears streamed down my face. "What have I *freaking done?*" I scrambled ahead and violently shook my best friend's shoulders. "Kendrick! Kendrick!" He didn't respond. "Dammit, don't die on me."

A sudden electric jolt knocked my hands from Kendrick's shoulders as images swarmed my mind. I was pinned against the mold-caked wall of the cell, surrounded by the scent of death and decay. My wide eyes stared in horror. Caius held a girl in his arms, his fangs embedded in her neck and draining her of blood.

Was she another victim? Had Caius done this before?

There was something eerily familiar about the girl. She had porcelain-perfect vampire skin and golden-blond hair that splayed around her shoulders, hanging matted with dirt down to her waist. The girl wore damp jeans, a tank top, and...*my* ruined Vans. Oh shit! The girl was me.

Pinned against the wall and watching the horror unfold, I struggled. I couldn't move. But I could hear. *Do not move or speak.* The compelling words repeated on a constant loop, clouding my head. No. Not my head...*his*.

Move! Kendrick's internal voice screamed.

It was impossible, but somehow I knew exactly what was happening. I was reliving my own murder through my best friend's eyes. I was seeing everything he had seen and feeling every crippling emotion he had felt.

Stop him! Desperation stole his breath, while his wide eyes remained locked on me. Within Caius's arms I had stopped moving, stopped trembling. My arms now hung lifelessly and my head rolled back. *I'm too late.* Kendrick's complete desolation tore into my heart. *She's dead.*

Before him, Caius had ripped his fangs from my neck. Slowly he lowered my limp body back to the blood-painted circle. Then he pushed back the matted hair from my face and sighed.

Still locked inside Kendrick's mind and body, I knew what would come next. Caius was going to kill my best friend. Fear coiled within my subconscious mind. But Kendrick wasn't scared. He didn't fear losing his own life, not anymore, not after failing to save mine. I could feel his emotional state as though it were my very own. He wouldn't fight to survive, to live on, not when the girl he had loved and still did so purely had ceased to exist. He wanted to die.

Caius's compelling eyes, deep-set within his face, now appeared youthful and radiant, thoroughly rejuvenated by my lifeblood. They locked on Kendrick. "*You* killed Amelia in a jealous fit of rage. If you could not have her, no one would." A look of sadness, perhaps even regret plagued his eyes. "You will forget I was here and everything I did. The use of your limbs and vocal cords will return after I depart. After that, you will remain within the catacombs until the guards discover your treachery. You will confess to murdering of my niece in cold blood."

Kendrick's mind glazed with thick clouds. Before him, Caius returned the empty jar of blood to the burlap sack. Next he smudged the blood-painted symbol around my dead body. Then he pulled a slightly crumpled black calla lily from his breast pocket. He laid the flower over my chest. He released the shackles from my wrists with a sigh. Then he folded my arms, placing my hands over the stem of the flower. For a long moment he just stared down at me, kneeling at my side. His back was turned to Kendrick and his slumped shoulders almost seemed to tremble. Finally he rose with a swiped hand across his face. Affording Kendrick no notice, he disappeared, striding into the darkness beyond the gaping door.

Once Caius's retreating footsteps had faded, feeling began to return to Kendrick's body, tingling back to life with penetrating pins and needles. His eyes were set on my crumpled and lifeless form, mortified. Guilt loomed within his chest, escalating to swallow every inch of him. "Now no one will have her."

Still watching through his eyes, our shared vision blurred with his heartbreaking tears as he staggered forward. After being frozen for so long, the sudden movement made his legs quake and buckle. He stumbled to his knees. His jeans tore on the uneven ground, but he didn't even notice. Instead, he hastily drew me into his arms. "I killed her!"

In his shaking arms, I could feel how cold my flesh was. How stiff and rigid my limbs were becoming with the lack of circulating blood. With the palm of his hand he smudged muddied water from my face. Then his eyes strained. Peering down at my lifeless expression he half marveled at how I could still be so breathtakingly beautiful. How death had not yet stolen the shimmer of my graying complexion under the cell's faint light. *It can't be too late*, he wished, so badly wanting it to be true.

But my lips were blue and parted, without the breath of life passing through them. In his arms I was motionless. He had loved me his entire life. I could feel it somehow. But there was nothing he could do. And even though he knew that he was unable to let go.

Kendrick reached up, placing two extended fingers along the carotid artery along my neck. "Please let there be a pulse," he prayed. Still there was none. Anger began to pollute his crippling guilt. He shook my limp form. "Amelia, please. I'm sorry. I'm sorry. I never meant to... You can't be dead."

He elevated my chest, pressing his ear against my ice-cold flesh. There was no sound. No heartbeat. No rise and fall that would indicate shallow breath. Fresh tears flooded his stinging eyes, spilling down his cheeks and onto my chest.

Thud...

The faintest beat emanated from beneath my ribs. A sudden surge of hope-tainted urgency took over, giving Kendrick renewed strength. He lowered my inert body, resting my cheek against his shoulder. Then using the nail of his extended finger, he sliced open his neck. Trapped inside Kendrick's body, I felt the sting. It made me want to flinch. But I couldn't move. I had no power. I wasn't really there.

The deep incision along Kendrick's neck now seeped with a steady flow of crimson. "Amelia, please come back to me," he said, kissing my forehead. He clutched my head and pressed my gaping mouth over the wound. "Grant me absolution. Take *my* life as your own."

A gravel-throated groan tore me from Kendrick's memories, slamming me back into my own body. The dank and foul-smelling cell rose up around me.

Kendrick shifted, slowly lifting his drooped head. "You're alive?" A mixture of emotions swarmed his face, and I gasped. Somehow deep within my core I could feel every one of them. There was relief and elation at saving me. Sadness and regret at his part in all of this. Most of all there was guilt.

I knew where the guilt came from. The experience I had just lived—which must have been another dream—had revealed the cause. Kendrick believed *he* had attacked me. That he had tried to kill me in a jealous rage. Still, beyond his guilt, I couldn't forget that he'd been willing to die to save me. The fact that I hadn't killed him now surged jittery warmth within me. I threw my arms around his slouched body. "You freaking idiot, I could have killed you!"

Kendrick stiffened in my arms, self-loathing devouring his heart. *And I would have let you.* His voice, so unwavering, so true, wasn't vocalized. It was internal, filled with heavy-hearted conviction.

Even without the weight of his guilt, I felt the undying truth within his words. If giving his life could bring me back, he would do it a thousand times over. Still the notion of feeling Kendrick's emotions, of hearing his heartfelt thoughts, was unbelievable. I'm delirious, I told myself. But my conclusion was contradicted by the growing weight of my best friend's guilt drowning us both. The pressure against my lungs was making it hard to breathe. "You didn't kill me!" I blurted, needing to somehow relieve the sensation. "It was Caius!"

Kendrick's brows creased and he looked away, disbelieving. Crippled by his self-loathing, I instinctively knew what I had to do. I seized his forearms and shook them, forcing his eyes to meet mine. *Please remember…*

Instantly, Kendrick's eyes grew distant, empty. Then I felt it, a prodding inside my head like actual fingers poking into my brain. It almost felt like being on an operating table and waking in the middle of brain surgery. It was dizzying, exhausting, and entirely foreign. Yet somehow I understood what was happening. Kendrick was skimming through my memories. First he relived the torture of my death, then the compulsion Caius had used against him.

Focus returned to Kendrick's eyes. The guilt that clung to his heart and soul relinquished its grip. Inexplicably, I knew that he now knew the truth. That he remembered everything that had happened. With the relief that lightened my entire body, I knew he believed it too. Caius's compulsion had been broken.

Abruptly the openness into his thoughts, emotions, and memories rippled with a concept I didn't understand. *How is that possible?* I wondered.

Kendrick smiled and cupped my hands with his. "I never thought…" He bit his lip and stared into my eyes. "When I offered my life, my blood to bring you back, the act…*bound us*."

Bound? The word seemed too plain, too ordinary to explain the out-of-body experience of sensing Kendrick's thoughts and emotions, just as he could mine. *Blood Bound?* "How?"

"It doesn't make any sense." Kendrick shook his head, causing light from the naked bulb to cast highlights through his hair. "Only spirit users, royals by birth, can create bonds in this realm and the next."

"So you're..." I began but stalled at an internal jab from Kendrick.

No, you are, he responded wordlessly.

Fragments of something Marcus had said pulsed across my mind as another one of my lost memories reformed. With it I could almost hear the trickle of the angel fountain and smell the ash-turned paper still cupped in his palm. Speak with the dead. Create a blood bond. Glimpse past, present and future events. They were all abilities solely reserved for a vampire linked to spirit.

I gulped, craving chocolate to calm my rising nerves. *I'm* gifted by spirit? No, hell no! It was impossible, wasn't it? I was a turned vampire. Not a naturally born one. I definitely wasn't a Pure Blood. But so much of my past now seemed a contradiction. My lack of any reaction to the sun, superior even to a royal's natural resistance, was abnormal. And the story of how we were turned had been rewritten with Caius's own admission. Can I really believe any of what that monster revealed?

"I don't know," Kendrick spoke, answering my unvoiced question. *But we'll figure it out. Together, we'll uncover exactly who or what you really are.*

Leaning into Kendrick, I thanked him in silence. I was about to say *let's get the hell outta here before the guards come*, but stalled. The amethyst pendant was flaring against my chest. A second later the splash of running feet through pooled water sounded. Someone was bounding straight for the gaping door.

"The guards!" Kendrick jumped to his feet, blocking my body from the approaching threat. He swayed on his heels. The sacrifice of his blood had left him weak, but not me.

With Kendrick's blood feeding my pounding heart, I felt

stronger than ever before. I snatched a set of chains and sprang up beside Kendrick. My free arm linked through his, steadying him. My shoulders squared. There was no freaking way I was about to let anyone determine our fate again. Today we would fight. And with conviction that reinforced me, I knew *somehow* we would win.

But the person who materialized through the iron-braced door was not a guard. It was Marcus. His speedy entrance created a gust of wind. Caught in its path the naked bulb swung on its suspended wire. Rising shadows curled where its golden light evaded. My racing heart jumped into my throat. Caius knows I'm alive. He sent Marcus to finish the job.

Marcus had pulled to an abrupt halt, barely a few feet before us. His face was flustered as his teal-flecked eyes scoured over us. What I thought was a look of disappointment tinged by resentment shifted the determination from his expression. "You," he hissed, glaring at Kendrick. "*You* saved her?"

"No thanks to you," Kendrick spat.

My best friend was breathing hard and fighting to stay upright. Recollections of the dream I now knew had been a vision because of The Sight, buzzed through his mind. He saw and now knew what Marcus had compelled him to do. Every detail of his harsh violation in forcing me to drink Marcus's poisoned blood returned. Damning weight tugged at his soul, transcending through the bond. His guilt consumed us both.

It wasn't your fault, I reassured wordlessly. *None of this was. It was his.* I shot an icy stare at Marcus. He stood stationary, livid eyes filled with uncertainty as he stared from me to Kendrick. I choked on a sob. *Marcus.* Even now I could feel the connection to him, the inner part of me that recognized his essence.

"No." Marcus shook his head. "It wasn't meant to happen this way." He threw a quick glance over his shoulder down the dark corridor beyond the door. Then he reached out to take my hand. "We have to go."

I inched away from him, staring at his outstretched hand as though it were flesh-eating poison. My hand tightened on the chains. Yet against my better judgment, the irrational and stupid part of me ached to take his hand. Just to feel the electricity that fired when we touched.

But Kendrick swatted his hand away with a threatening growl. "She's not going anywhere with you!" His voice was so level, so strong and protective that it made me want to bawl. Inside his body was trembling, barely holding onto consciousness. But on the outside he was a pillar of strength. He'd die before he let any harm ever come to me again. "Make another move, and I will *kill* you."

Marcus's hands curled into fists. "I'm not going to harm her," he grated. "Amelia…" His eyes shifted to mine, straining. "I would *never* hurt you. Deep inside you know that. I was coming to…" He began pacing and I cringed, reminded of Caius. "It was supposed to be me. *I* was meant to save you."

Kendrick's fury grew, flames licking at his insides. But I faltered. My connection to Marcus made me want to question what I knew and believed. Were my suspicions wrong?

Kendrick however, had no such reservations and hurled himself at Marcus. "Liar!"

Marcus ducked, dodging Kendrick's advancing fist. His hand easily collected Kendrick's wrist, then twisted his arm behind his back. With his face lit by hardened rage, he drove my best friend against the stone wall.

"Stop!" I screamed. Kendrick's connection to the wall hit me as if I'd been the one thrown against it. Oxygen belted from my lungs. I gasped for breath, staggering and dizzy. "Marcus, don't hurt him, *please*."

Marcus's hardened expression froze, seeing the unmasked pain he had just caused me. His extended arm against the back of Kendrick's neck softened instantly, but his iron crowbar strength didn't let go. It kept Kendrick pinned without causing further pain. "It happened. Didn't it?"

Kendrick was struggling to free himself, seething with the need to attack again. But he couldn't muster enough strength to escape Marcus's restraining arm.

I too felt the urge to retaliate, to rake Marcus over with the chains I held. But I didn't. Instead, I lowered the ready chains, strung tight between both hands. "What are you talking about?" I demanded. "What happened?"

A strangled smile fell from Marcus's face and his eyes grew stormy. "Your soul, it's bound to Kendrick's."

"How do you know that?" Kendrick's voice mirrored my own.

Marcus released my best friend and shoved him back toward me. "'Cause it was supposed to be me! *I* was supposed to resurrect you. *I* was supposed to bring you back to life."

Don't believe a word he says, Kendrick's deep voice echoed inside my head.

The words Marcus had spoken to Kendrick in my vision blew through my ears. *It's happening tonight.* He had known all along what Caius had planned to do to me. He had helped him. Why would he want to save me? My voice emerged hollow. "But you poisoned me."

Marcus crossed his arms over his double-breasted pea coat. "I did it to save your life."

I laughed, mimicking Kendrick. Yet the part deep within me that recognized Marcus wanted to believe him.

"Amelia, no!" Kendrick tugged on my arm. Then my brain tingled with an almost prickling sensation of something, no someone, sifting through my thoughts. Through the eerie link of our bond, Kendrick could hear my conflicting thoughts. He could also feel the unexplainable connection I felt to Marcus.

I sent a wordless message to Kendrick, lacing my fingers through his. *Let's see where he's going with this.* Squaring my shoulders with mock strength, I looked pointedly to Marcus. My free hand clutched the chains to my waist. "Explain yourself."

Marcus grimaced, eyes set on our entwined fingers. But then he nodded. "Everything I did was to protect you: the compulsion, erasing your memories. You needed to be unaware so that Caius's plans remained unchanged. So that I would know when he would come for you."

Kendrick's grip on my hand tightened as words traveled from his mind to mine. *Lies, all lies. Don't believe him.*

"So, you poisoned me because Caius compelled you?" I was desperate to exonerate Marcus. Desperate to believe he hadn't acted of his own free will.

"No." Marcus shook his head. "That was all me. Caius didn't know."

"See," Kendrick hissed while my heart squeezed. "He doesn't even deny it."

"Of course I don't!" Marcus ruffled his straight blond hair. "Poisoning Amelia was the only way to save her life." He stepped forward, and a low snarl reverberated from Kendrick's throat. "Amelia, I needed your body and heart to replicate death. As your blood levels became dangerously low, the poison would slow the beat of your heart. Caius would mistake its lack of beat for death. Don't you see? The poison saved you. It foiled Caius's plan to become immortal."

Marcus took my hand. I half expected Kendrick to lunge again, to tear him away from me. But he didn't. He was just as frozen by

Marcus's admission as I was. Through our bond I could recall the closeness of their friendship. How Kendrick had looked up to Marcus. How he had confided his feelings and worries for me. And Marcus had always been there to listen and make helpful and unbiased suggestions.

"You were going to be the one to bring me back to life." My tone was hollow as I pieced the puzzle of everything together. Realization etched through mine and Kendrick's minds simultaneously. "You knew I possessed a link to spirit?"

"*You,*" Kendrick coughed, staring at Marcus. "*You* intended to bond with Amelia? To be bound to her in life and eventually in death—for all eternity?"

"What?" Kendrick's thoughts were rushing through my head, too fast, too muddled to make sense of.

Marcus released my hand and turned to the doorway with a shoulder-lifting sigh. "Even in death, a spirit blood bond cannot be severed."

CHAPTER 29

*A*s Marcus turned away I heard a clatter. Something rolled across the uneven stone floor. He moved in a flash, swooping before reaching the doorway. "We have to go, now. I intercepted the guards on my way down and compelled them away. Caius was already gone, but it won't be too long before he realizes something's gone astray."

After a fleeting look at the dank chamber that could have been my final resting place, we rushed after Marcus. Our shoes splashed through an inch of foul-smelling water in the shadow-darkened tunnel. It was so rank I had to fight the urge to gag. That smell was never coming out of my Vans.

After a string of labyrinth twists and turns, Marcus disappeared into a dark recess in the tunnel. It was one of many recesses we had already passed. A loud protesting creak of weakened metal echoed past us. Marcus had begun climbing a rickety, spiraling staircase. Kendrick's hand found mine and he pulled me onward. The rusted stairs protested louder with high-pitched squeals. I cringed. Good luck sneaking out of this place unseen or unheard.

Before I could dwell on the complication, trepidation channeled through my heart, elevating its beat to marathon speed. The feeling wasn't my own, but Kendrick's, except not for this moment. I could see through his eyes and feel the fear that stole his breath on receiving my dire text. He had raced downstairs after searching my room and burst into Caius's office.

For a moment, I wondered if he'd somehow figured out that Caius had been behind my disappearance. But no. He'd instinctively gone there hoping Caius would be able to help find me. Of course he'd found no one. We had already disappeared below.

Defeated, Kendrick had turned to leave. If finding me meant searching the entire castle and its surrounding grounds, he'd do it. But then he paused. The room's light had caught on something that reflected a pure-white flash of light. He spun back, eyes dropping to the source of light and finding the diamond-cut paperweight. Its tip was smeared with blood. More blood spattered the wooden floorboards, disappearing beneath the edge of the Persian rug.

My breath had turned sharp and shallow and I fought to steady it. Kendrick's hand tightened over mine. He was about to ask what was wrong, but then he knew, feeling his way through my thoughts. My free hand rose to the bruised spot on my temple. I remembered the moment pain had pierced my skull, rendering me unconscious.

A stream of light from above forced my attention from Kendrick's memories, slamming me back into the present. Marcus had edged open the trap door and was now scanning through the crack. Nervous sweat dampened my palms.

"It's clear." Marcus flicked us a backward glance before throwing open the hinged door.

I sucked in a breath as we stepped up and into the center of

Caius's office. The room was, as Marcus had declared, 'clear.' Not a single object seemed out of place. The leather-topped desk was its usual mess of skewed papers and folders. The blood that had dripped from my head and patterned the wooden floor had been wiped clean. The diamond paperweight had also been repositioned atop the desk. It was now free of any damning remnants of my spilled blood.

"What now?" I asked. In all truth, I wanted nothing more than to escape the Armaya and its surrounding grounds for good. But I couldn't. We couldn't. Not yet.

"You think we can find a clue?" Kendrick asked, retracing his steps back to me from the door. From the uncomfortable prickle in my head, I could tell he'd read my thoughts. Now he understood my hesitation.

"A clue for what?" Marcus glanced from Kendrick to me. "You know there really isn't any time."

Your gift of eternal life will grant me the stepping stone I require to save—

Caius had said the words when he thought I'd never live to contemplate them. Now I couldn't ignore the threat. There was a hidden meaning behind Caius's cut-off admission. It was clear that taking my life was just the beginning. But what would taking my life help him save? Would immortality ensure his ability to rule forever? That is the ultimate desire of an evil mastermind, isn't it? Power, eternal life…

"Caius is planning something." I moved behind the desk and began rifling through the stack of papers. "Immortality was just the beginning."

"Planning what?" Marcus eyed me then shifted his weight, glancing at the door to the hallway.

"I don't know, exactly." I shoved the remaining folders from the desk, frustrated at only finding minute records from boring council meetings.

Kendrick had begun sifting through one of the mahogany bookshelves. "And we need to figure out," he said, throwing me a quick glance, "how your blood could grant Caius immortality." His next words were mute, for my recognition only. Kendrick may have accepted Marcus's explanation, but he still had reservations about his motives in all of this. *How it's possible that you possess The Sight?*

There was a mental prompt to keep my mouth zipped on revealing my ability. I was about to question it when Marcus dug into his pocket. He pulled out a folded piece of paper and handed it to me. "These are the only immortals I've ever heard of."

Kendrick, intrigued and suspicious, moved from the bookcase to stare over my shoulder. The parchment paper was thin and delicate, inscribed with a scrawl of handwritten cursive. It wasn't addressed or signed.

The damned are evolving, and I fear we may lose control.

"Where did you get this?" Kendrick narrowed his eyes at Marcus accusingly. "I thought the damned were hunted to extinction."

Marcus mocked insult. "I found it during one of my snoops. It was jammed behind the top drawer in Caius's desk. And," he added, "I too believed the damned were extinct."

Acid crept up my throat. Just the word *damned* brought pulsing coldness to my heart that threatened to spread like poison throughout my entire body. I swallowed as a memory rose to the surface. "The diary of *Uriel Aswind*..." I turned to Marcus, disbelieving. "You were the last person to check it out from the library."

"*You* ripped out the pages?" Kendrick accused Marcus, recalling my memories just as I did.

Marcus's looked incensed. "You still don't trust me? Even

after everything I've done for you." When Kendrick and I remained silent, he moved to me. His fingers curled around my hand that clutched the note. A slight spark of electricity tickled my skin. "This note is not the first time I have heard current mention of the damned." He released my hand. "You tend to pick up things when someone believes they can to compel you to forget. And you are right. Caius *is* planning something, but apart from being linked to the damned in some way, I have no idea what that something is."

"Then we have to go to The Council," I blurted, tension rising up my neck. "Tell them what Caius did to me, and show them the note."

"No!" Marcus and Kendrick barked in unison.

Marcus motioned to the door, mumbling at Kendrick, "You explain it to her."

Kendrick tilted his head and grasped me by the elbow, forcing me from the room. The hallway was still strangely unlit, and bar the three of us with our quick, sloshing footsteps, it appeared vacated.

"Explain what?" I demanded, irritated by their childlike treatment of me. This situation had as much to do with me as it did either of them, if not more. Shouldn't I have a say?

They'll never believe us, Kendrick's thoughts merged inside my head. *We have no proof.*

"We have the note," I corrected as we climbed the stairs. With my free arm, I drew back my long matted hair from my neck. "And we have these." I knew the bite marks had already closed up, but through Kendrick's quick glance, I could see white scarring as well as drying, smudged blood. The proof of my punctured flesh was there. "My blood must have marked the ground in that cell, a cell that Caius has access to. Plus there are three of us against one. They'll have to believe us."

We entered my room after Marcus who was now on his phone,

barking commands into the speaker. "Have my car fueled and ready in two minutes."

"Look, Amelia." Kendrick gripped my upper arms with curled fingers. "I want to tell them. You know I do. But the note wasn't addressed to Caius. It's not irrefutable proof. Besides, those tunnels and cells are the catacombs, old ruins of torture chambers and guardian quarters. Abandoned ever since the War of the Races. There are at least a dozen secret entries to the tunnels." He sighed and released my arms. "At most, all we have is hearsay. It's our word against one of the most revered reigning Pure Bloods. No one will ever believe us."

With a deep sigh, I shrugged. The argument was over, and I knew I'd lost. "So what now?"

Marcus returned to our sides and hung up his phone. His lips thinned with a smile. "It time you both went home."

Back upstairs we changed our soiled clothes and quickly packed our belongings. I chucked out my ruined Vans with a sigh. Better them than me. Then I joined Kendrick in chugging down a few bottles of blood. It still wasn't enough, but right now it'd have to do.

Marcus took my bag and warily escorted us from the castle to a shiny, black Rolls Royce. A motorbike would have been a cooler getaway, but I wasn't about to argue and slow us down. I just wanted to get moving, the sooner the better.

It was still daylight. The brilliant globe was high in the sky, casting warm radiance over the horizon's rolling mountains. In vampire terms it was night, the light hours that all vampires apart from me avoided.

Marcus moved to the driver's side window, speaking to the chauffeur under his breath. Kendrick, now wearing beige cargo pants and a polo shirt, jumped into the back seat and scooted into the tinted windows' cover. For just a few seconds before his retreat, I experienced something for the very first time. Through the other-worldly bond we shared, I actually felt what it was like to have the sunlight kissing a vampire's naked flesh. It was warmer than I had expected. A growing heat that sent crawling tingles up my arms and across my face. It was a little uncomfortable. Still, compared to the agony of being drained alive, it was tolerable. Like an almost welcome sensation that showed me what it was like to be ordinary, as ordinary as any vampire could be. Sweat began to bead along my brow and above my upper lip. It was another reminder that I was still alive.

A gripping hand caught my wrist and hauled me into the back seat. *You will never be ordinary.* Kendrick smiled, lacing his fingers through mine. *To me, you are and always will be, extraordinary.*

"Ahem," Marcus interrupted, poking his head through the open back door. He removed his pea coat and hurled it at me. "Use it as a pillow, if you want."

A frozen wince was painted across his face. I wondered if the sun across the exposed flesh between his hairline and collared shirt caused the expression. But he didn't flinch, rush his words, or try in any way to evade the light.

"My driver will deliver you both to Anchorage International. Your tickets home will be waiting." On seeing my confused frown Marcus waved me off. "Don't worry. I compelled him. He won't remember whom he's transporting. He won't even remember leav—"

"No, not that," I cut him off. "Aren't you coming?"

Marcus shook his head. His hair caught the sunlight and gleamed like spun white gold. "No. Caius doesn't know I had anything to do with you surviving, or your escape." A resigned smile tugged at his lips, revealing pearly white teeth. "Besides, my life is here. And you'll both need someone to keep an eye on Caius. I can give you a heads up if he decides to come after you."

"But—" I began to argue but stopped. Kendrick's clasp on my hand had tightened.

"Marcus is right," Kendrick said. But I questioned his motives, feeling a slither of jealousy for the connection I felt to Marcus.

A long, drawn-out sigh blew from my lips. Kendrick's ulterior motives aside, I ached not to leave Marcus. I wanted to figure out and understand this connection we shared, but I couldn't deny logic. This decision was best for all of us. My hand broke Kendrick's hold and I threw my arms around Marcus's neck. A ripple of possessiveness surged through me, Kendrick's. I ignored the irritation and squeezed my arms around Marcus tighter. "Thank you, for everything."

Before I was ready to let go, Marcus wriggled out of my grasp. He reached into the inside pocket of his discarded pea coat across the back seat. Then he hesitated. "Now, remember. Everything I did was to help you." He pulled out a manila folder that had been folded in half and handed it over.

An amalgamation of events filtered to the surface of my mind. Without opening the front cover, I knew exactly what lay heavy in my hands. It was the same manila folder I had found in the library over a week ago. The inside pages held more than the concoction to poison me. They contained detailed events of my life.

"You compelled me to forget." The words I spoke held no accusation, just the strain of confusion.

A tense smile thinned Marcus's pale lips. "I know. But I hope it will help you discover who you are and the secrets of your past."

With a frown Marcus straightened, swung the car door shut, and tapped on the roof. Instantly the Rolls took off, tires skidding over the cobblestone lane. The castle's great walls and reaching towers shrank, disappearing into the distance. The weight of what felt like a pressing bolder against my chest began to lift. I hated the thought of leaving Marcus behind. Still the guys had been right. It was safer for Marcus to stay. The double-edged sword was that we needed him to be our eyes and ears, our warning of approaching threat.

I shrugged into Marcus's pea coat and settled into the comfortable leather back seat of the Rolls-Royce. Lush green and snow-topped rolling mountains passed by. A running stream snaked in and out of the mountainous terrain. Sometimes it disappeared completely. Then minutes later it would reappear, running almost adjacent to the beaten, gravel road. Able to almost breathe normally again, I knew our lives had changed. Our future and innocence would never be the same. I had been weak and unaware, an easy pick. Never again.

"So, are you going to open that?" Kendrick asked, disrupting my resolution. He was staring intensely at the manila folder that sat heavy in my hands.

The memory of its contents burned into my mind. Kendrick of course knew with my own recollection what I had originally discovered inside the cover. Most of the contents had been recapped events detailing my life. Then there was the photo of Caius cradling two infants. And lastly the recipe Marcus had used to poison me. Through our blood's bond, I could feel a stream of anticipation coiling through Kendrick's chest. He was dying to lay his eyes on the information. To see if it could shed any light on why Caius believed my blood would make him immortal. To know how the affinity for spirit could reside within my body and soul.

But I couldn't bear to open the cover, not yet. Resolution or not, it was all too much. After everything that had happened and after almost dying, it was a miracle that I wasn't stark-raving mad. The fact that I was maintaining an exterior air of control was amazing.

But that was the outside. Inside I felt raw to the bone, filled with self-doubt. A gripping pain stung my heart. It had been growing ever since my awakening. I had tried to ignore it, to push it aside, to only focus on our escape. But the thought of Ty had never fully left my mind. A choking sob constricted my throat.

Kendrick hauled me against his side, rubbing a broad hand up and down my arm. "We'll worry about it later. There's no rush." He reached into his pocket and handed me his iPhone.

"What's this for?" I asked, already knowing the answer.

Kendrick shrugged and turned his head. He peered blankly out the window at the thickening green and white rush of snow-veiled forestry. "So you can call him."

Needing to hear Ty's voice almost more than I needed to breathe, I snatched the phone and dialed his number. With every passing ring my heart dropped. Then the ringing stopped and everything fell silent.

After the longest moment of heart-racing suspense, Ty's hesitant voice finally answered, "Hello?"

"Ty, it's me. It's Amelia."

A long exhale sounded, followed by a moment of nerve-racking silence. "What do you want?"

My pierced heart sank to the depths of my twisting stomach. In our last conversation I had declared that I didn't want or love him anymore. I had metaphorically ripped out his beating heart with sharp-nailed fingers. He may have been concerned enough to call Dorian afterward, but his anger over what I had put him through was unmistakable. "I have so much to tell you." My vision blurred. "And I need you to know...*I'm sorry.*"

Next to me, Kendrick's inner angst reared its ugly head. He could hear every heartfelt thought I wanted to blurt out and feel every intense emotion I was experiencing. The desperate need to reaffirm my undying love for Ty was clear as day. And the total fear that stole my breath at possibly having lost him forever confirmed it all.

"You're telling me this, why?" Ty's voice was utterly emotionless.

Every part of me ached to put his mind at ease. But I knew I couldn't. Not now. Not like this. And especially not with Kendrick right beside me, filling my head with his not-so-latent jealousy. I choked on my words. "We're coming home."

"I thought your home was there."

"No! That place will *never* be my home." My free hand curled around my disheveled hair and tugged. Without chocolate I needed to do something to distract me from bursting into tears. "Ty, I made a mistake."

"What does that mean?" Still his voice held no emotion.

"The dream…I didn't mean what I said, none of it. I still…" The words, *I love you,* died on my tongue as I fought back a blubbering sob. I cleared my throat and blinked my vision clear. "I can't explain now, but I will, as soon as we're back."

I hung up the phone and dropped my head into my hands. How did everything become such a mess? To my surprise, Kendrick didn't bother to answer my unasked question. Instead, he simply placed a broad hand over my back. This was hard for him, I realized. Of course it was. Kendrick wanted nothing more than to comfort me, but my tormented feelings for Ty crippled him. No matter what I did, said, or thought, I would hurt him. There was no way to hide my feelings for Ty from him. There was no way to downplay them to ease his suffering. Now and forever, he would know exactly what my heart held.

I slumped into the leather seat and opened the cover of the

manila folder. For my sake and for his, I needed to contemplate something other than Ty.

Kendrick stiffened beside me, staring at the black-and-white photo atop a bunch of papers. The photo was set in a room surrounded by stone walls and rustic, antique furnishings. A wall lantern burned behind Caius's head. Kendrick sent me a mentally confirming nudge. The photo had been taken at the Armaya, inside my former uncle's private quarters. "Marcus had this?"

"Yeah," I said, voice hesitant. "Why?"

Kendrick plucked the photo from my lap and raised it to his eyes, studying. "That's you in Caius's left arm, isn't it?" I nodded. "And in his right arm..."

Anxiety sent blood rushing to my extremities, leaving my head airy and light. "Oh my God, that's Marcus?"

Feeling lightheaded, I swayed. Kendrick steadied my body before I could slump into unconsciousness. He propped me back against the car seat, hearing the drowning suspicion fogging up my mind.

"You don't really think that, do you?"

I bit my lip and nodded. "Why else would Caius have had that photo taken?" Ice crystallized beneath my skin. "It's a memento, the beginning of this experiment. And Marcus is a part of it." I remembered with fond horror the electric connection I felt toward Marcus. This was the explanation I'd been looking for. "I don't think I'm the only one with immortal blood. I think Caius poisoned Marcus too."

CHAPTER 30

"Oh my God!" Mom exclaimed as we entered the front door. She rushed to squash me in her arms. "You're okay?" Her hands gripped my shoulders, holding me at arms-length. Her tear-reddened eyes studied me head to toe. "I can't believe it. I was so worried. And Caius, he's been beside himself."

What the hell did that bastard tell her? I felt like screaming as Mom switched back and forth between hugging and studying me as if looking for an injury.

At her words, Kendrick's expression had turned indignant. He shrugged with a deep sigh then looked sideways at Dorian. *He's not doing so well.*

Dorian's face was a ghastly shade of gray. He stood leaning into the foyer's glass-topped table. It was a sturdy piece of furniture, which was good. It appeared to be the only thing holding him upright.

After a quick call, he'd eagerly volunteered to pick us up from the airport after dropping off his latest squeeze. On his arrival he'd been full of questions. But that didn't last. As Kendrick and I unveiled Caius's plan to take my life, he'd quickly turned to shell-shocked silence. He managed to utter at some point that he believed us but hadn't spoken a single word since. He hadn't even waited to cool our car's turbo down when we'd arrived home.

"Caius called only an hour ago," Mom went on, oblivious to Dorian's detached expression. "He's had the entire community on high alert, searching tirelessly since morning for you both. After the security breach, and when he couldn't find either of you..." Her voice dropped to a choking whisper. "He feared the worst."

Security breach? Caius had used the same excuse to lure me down to his office. Yet I knew through Kendrick's trained thoughts, that there had never been an actual security breach. Well, none that had raised any alarm before we escaped. Back then Caius's plan had been to shift the blame of my death onto my best friend. But when he couldn't find us...

He created a cover-up. Kendrick sent his silent message through our bond. *The perfect diversion to clear him of ANY wrongdoing.*

Caius's arrogance lit a fury within me that spread to encapsulate every inch of my flesh. I had to grate my teeth to keep my mouth from shouting, *that son of a bitch!* Instead, I curled my hands into fists behind my back while struggling to keep my rising voice level. "He said we could be dead?"

Mom's chin trembled with the promise of fresh tears. "But you're not. You're both okay." She fished with shaking hands into her pantsuit pocket and pulled out her cell phone. Clearly she'd already been dressed for work prior to Caius's panicked call. "I must call your uncle. Tell him you're both okay."

"Wait!" I shouted.

My eyes flicked to Kendrick who dipped his head in support.

"Ms. Lamont, we have something important we need to tell you first."

"I'm sorry, Kendrick, but whatever you have to say can wait." Mom's fingers were already keying that monster's number. "Caius is wrecked with fear for you both. He has to know you're safe."

The phone had begun ringing. Before Mom could raise it to her ear, Dorian shot forward, stilling her hand with his. She looked up, startled.

Dorian's eyes trained on hers, trapping her wide-eyed gaze. "Mom, please. Give us a minute. You need to hear what we have to say."

Mom's expression fell slack for a brief moment. Excited hope swelled inside me. My brother, sneaky, shifty, but talented Dorian, was compelling her, another vampire.

"Hello? Hello? Lamayli, is that you?" The phone in Mom's hand had stopped ringing, and Caius's voice was bellowing through the speaker.

Instantly, the cloud of Dorian's compulsion shattered, and the muddled expression returned to Mom's face. She yanked her hand free and raised the phone to her ear while mouthing with stiff lips, "In a minute." She turned and glided into the lounge room, which was darkening with the approach of dusk. "Caius, sorry, I'm here..."

"Shit," Dorian swore. "That usually works."

I raised a questioning eyebrow. *"Usually?"* So Mom had been Dorian's compulsion guinea pig, not some girl. I wasn't sure which was worse.

Despite the situation, Dorian smiled. "Yeah. Mom thinks it was her idea to let any girl I want stay over. Even on weekdays. She thinks she's letting me be a normal teenage boy."

"You can successfully compel her?" Kendrick questioned.

There was a hidden suspicion behind his question. The ability to compel turned vamps and humans was second nature to royals, a birthright. It wasn't like that for turned vamps like us. Our ability to compel humans was a learned and practiced one. It generally didn't fare well on other non-born vamps.

"Caius must have done something to you too," I said, looking at Dorian. "It's the only thing that can explain the greater powers we're developing."

"So, mind control and visions," Dorian said, looking excited rather than disturbed. "I can't say I'm complaining."

I glared at him. "This is *not* great news. It's not a time for cele-brating. He did this to us!" The memories of every time Caius had drawn back my hair and embedded his fangs in my neck slipped through my mind like flour grating through a sieve. I gulped at the spike of vomit rearing up my throat. "And now he's covering his tracks." I nodded towards the lounge. Inside Mom stood pacing before the cushioned bay window. Her closed shoes were wearing tracks in the mink-white carpet. "What if she doesn't believe us?"

"She will," Kendrick said. His hand found my shoulder with a squeezed. "But you don't want to tell her about The Sight." Before I could ask why, a buzzing sounded. With a deep frown, Kendrick shrugged and pulled his iPhone from his pocket. He held it out so we could all view the text on the screen. The number was blocked. But you didn't need to be a genius to figure out who had sent it.

'Keep your secrets, lest the innocent pay for your stolen time.'

"What's going on?" Dorian demanded.

I gulped, raising my eyes to him and lowering my voice. "If we out Caius, he'll kill our mom."

"Yes," Mom said, no longer pacing before the window, but gliding our way. "It was a complete misunderstanding. And thank you, Caius, for being so tolerant. I am sure they didn't intend to cause such a commotion."

"Already forgotten," Caius replied, loud enough for us all to hear clearly. His genuinely relieved and totally understanding voice made me want to scream. "And, Lamayli, I love you."

Rose dyed Mom's cheeks with a sudden flush. Her eyes darted away from us. "Me too." She hung up and quickly replaced the phone in her pocket. Then she turned her attention back to the three of us. "Now, what was it you wanted to tell me?" She glanced out through the long window framing the front door. The sun had dipped below the horizon, leaving a wash of fast-darkening tangerine bruising the sky. She looked back at us. "After all this confusion I'm already late for my meeting with The Council. With a breach in security at the Armaya, it'll be utter chaos."

She can never know what happened, Kendrick's voice rose in my mind.

"It, um… We needed…"

Kendrick, thank God, jumped in with the most rationally expected response. "What Amelia is trying to say is, we're sorry. We freaked when the alarms went off and ran. We should have called."

"Yes, you should have." Mom planted her hands on her hips. "But there's nothing we can do about that now." Her face and voice softened. "I'm just so relieved you're all okay, and I'm so glad you're home."

"Are you going to send me back there?" I asked suddenly. Fresh fear since we had walked through the door had taken hold of me. Now it had a hold of my entire body. Still, regardless of her response, nothing she could say or do could ever make me go back to that place. Or the monster I'd loved as my uncle.

Mom shook her head. "No. Absolutely not. At the moment it's far too dangerous." She plucked her cherry-red briefcase from the foyer table and opened the front door. "Though Amelia, we still have serious matters to discuss."

There was no doubt she was talking about Ty. Although whether we had anything at all to discuss, I didn't know. Not yet. Not when I hadn't even had a chance to see or speak with him. Mom glanced down at her Cartier watch and stepped with a rush out the front door. "But right now I'm out of time. This will have to wait until the morning."

I STARED after Dorian as he walked from my bedroom down the dark hallway. His hunched shadow created by propelled starlight through the adjacent windows lurked across the wall.

Kendrick and I had answered my brother's many questions after Mom's departure. By the end of it he appeared utterly fatigued. He excused himself and promised he'd be okay. Worried for him, I question whether we should have burdened him with any of what had happened. Had telling him only endangered his life too? Or had it prepared him for everything that was sure to come?

I sighed and stepped back into my room. My familiar band posters taking up the walls and splashes of varying purples were a comfort. After everything that had happened, this house and room surprisingly felt like home.

Before Dorian left, Kendrick had also explained why no one could know about my visions. Apart from it being a super rare spirit ability, there hadn't been a Pure Blood with this power in centuries. And I wasn't even a Pure Blood. Kendrick wasn't sure what The Council would do, or what they might expect of me if they discovered the truth. Would being honest put me at risk?

Even with all of this to mull over—*fan-freaking-tastic*—there was something I desperately needed to do.

Kendrick handed me his iPhone, though I could tell that every part of him wished he hadn't.

"Thanks," I said, forging a tense smile. Then I typed what I hoped would begin the repair of Ty's and my decimated relationship.

'We R back. Plz meet me. B W8ing at Mt Major in the clearing below the bluff.'

I stared at the screen for a moment, recalling our call to Marcus. We'd told him that Caius had done something to him too, had altered him in some way. Marcus had guessed his resistance to compulsion could be a side effect. Still, even with the possibility, nothing I'd said had swayed him to leave that place. He was beyond adamant. He would stay as long as there were questions surrounding Caius that we needed answers too.

In the end, I traded one problem for another and handed the iPhone back to Kendrick. He sighed. "This is a bad idea, you know."

In his mind I could read every rational reason against me going to see Ty. I could also feel his struggle as he tried to keep his thoughts to himself. "I'm sorry." I curled my arms around his waist and pressed my face against his chest while holding him tight. "And you know I love you. But after everything that's happened, I won't have anyone dictate my future. Life is too short."

"I know," Kendrick said as he wriggled from my hug. He'd considered arguing me out of leaving, but just as quickly had discarded the idea. He knew that nothing he could say would change my mind. Instead, he crossed the lit space of my bedroom and threw open the high-arched window. "Don't forget. I'll be watching."

The statement was as much a mention of the unavoidable as it was a warning. Kendrick would be keeping an eye on Ty and everything he did. Suppressing a groan, I crossed my room. My hands buried in the pockets of Marcus's pea coat that I was still wearing.

"Don't remind me." As I said the words my fingers connected with something small, cold, and cylinder-shaped.

"What is it?" Kendrick asked.

Already knowing, I pulled it from the pocket. In my hand lay the vial that had held the silvery substance Caius had forced me to swallow. The same one he'd claimed to contain ancient vampire blood. According to him, it was a necessary step to complete the conversion within my blood. The key needed to steal my so-called *immortality*. There was barely a residual drop coating the inner walls of the tube. There was also a card, business sized, that I had pulled from the pocket along with the vial. The front was printed with a name and title. Simon Beatty, Specialist Blood Analyst. On the back was a single handwritten note:

Amelia,
For the answers you need, he's a trusted friend.
Faithfully, Marcus.

"That's why he gave me his jacket?"

"I guess so," Kendrick said. His hand found my shoulder and his eyes lit up with a surge of anticipation. "You know what this means?"

I looked up at him with a frown, ready to demand the answer. Except the time for surprise and secrets was long gone. I knew exactly what he was going to say. "This is just the beginning, a starting point, and our first—real—clue."

I stood pacing in front of a solid red maple beside a frozen river. It was the very same river Ty had transformed before. A browning hole was growing in the crushed snow beneath my crappy, airport-bought shoes. Just looking at them had me missing my Vans. Ten minutes had passed with no sign of Ty. After a mental check in with Kendrick, I knew there hadn't been a reply to my text either. Despair pressed in on me. The night's temperature had plummeted as I'd sprinted to reach my destination. Mist now rose all around. I shivered. Not from the cold, but out of despair unfurling into desolation. He wasn't coming.

"Amelia?" The unmistakable voice rose behind me.

I whirled and almost lost traction in the mud. "Crappy shoes," I muttered as my eyes fell on the source of the voice. Beyond the hazy tree line Ty was materializing through the mist. The sheer sight of his naked, scarred chest heaving and speckled with sweat made my breath catch. It was almost impossible to believe that only days ago I had broken his heart. That I had declared I didn't want him anymore. That I'd decided with all certainty that my irrefutable feelings for him had faded to nothingness. How wrong I'd been. The sight of him now proved that more than ever. My pulse galloped while flames scoured my face red and engulfed every inch of my flesh.

Ty's approach stalled before he reached me. He shoved his hands into the pockets of his black shorts and kicked at the snow with his hunting boots. "On the phone, you said you were sorry."

Being closer to him brought his features under sharp inspection. His usually perfect facade wasn't so seamless after all. Dark crescents circled his eyes, his hair was unkempt and rough, black stubble shadowed his angular face. Did he look so wrecked because of me?

Ty's expression remained a mask of indifference. Though a glint of what I thought could be hope betrayed his eyes. "What were you sorry for?"

I chanced a step forward, fearing Ty's retraction. He stood his ground, face now straining as though my closer proximity pained him.

Start at the beginning, a little voice that was Kendrick's whispered as if he were standing right beside me.

Warmth ballooned from my heart. "Okay." I nodded, lifting my eyes to Ty's. "When I said I wanted a future at court, it was only what I thought I wanted. I..."

"So you're not staying there?" Ty interrupted. "You're back for good?" When I nodded, wondering how to deliver the rest of what I had to tell him, he laughed. "Great! So you threw me away because of a split-second decision. 'Cause you *thought* you wanted a future at that damn place."

"No, wait! You don't understand!"

Ty's jaw clenched and he turned to stalk away. "Thanks for calling me all the way out here to *rub it in!*"

His angry words bit into my chest. This was my only chance to explain, and I was fucking it up. I needed to stop him. I needed to somehow make him understand. There were only two options available. Let him go. Or fight. I made my choice. The only choice I could make. When it came to Ty I would always choose to fight.

I sprang from the snow-littered ground, twisting in the air to land facing Ty. He jerked to a stop and my palms shot up. They imprisoned his face and forced his angry, gold-rippling eyes to meet mine. "I was compelled! I never wanted to leave you. All I ever wanted was you." My words washed away some of the anger from Ty's eyes. My hands dropped from his face. "Ty, please, I'll tell you everything. If you'll just let me."

Ty nodded but appeared unable or unwilling to speak. So I took the opportunity and began the long tale leading up to my bloody demise. I began with Caius's play for immortality, and everything he had done to achieve it. Then I laid out Marcus's poisoning and compulsion, and why it was necessary. Lastly was Kendrick's blood offering, the step that had resurrected me. Though I kept withdrawn the connection I felt for Marcus. There was no logical way to explain that. And I left out any mention of what Kendrick's blood offering had ignited between us, the everlasting blood bond created by my connection to spirit.

When I had said all I could, I glanced up. Ty's face was fuming like a volcano on the verge of eruption. "He *bit* you?" His voice was somewhere between a rasp and the most dangerous, bone-chilling snarl I had ever heard. "Drank your blood? Killed you…" His hands began to tremble, straining into elongating claws. I heard a crack and then a roar as his fingers bent and broke. "I'll kill him!"

Ty's body began to quake with drowning rage. I knew what would come next. The beast was rearing to break free, to seek its vengeance.

Amelia, stop him! Kendrick's voice rushed in my head.

But fear kept me frozen.

Now! Kendrick shouted. *He's too enraged. He can't control himself. Amelia, his bite WILL kill you. And if he goes after Caius, Ty will be dead, too.*

Mobility rushed back to my limbs. I moved like lightning, restraining Ty's arms. "Ty stop! Caius will kill you. He's too strong. And I can't lose you. Not again."

The severity of my words barely registered. The trembling continued throughout Ty's entire body, becoming more violent by the second. The crack of new bones breaking erupted like a nail gun firing constant rounds. Time was running out. I knew what I had to do, the only thing that could calm the beast.

"Amelia, NO!" Kendrick's voice screamed. *"It's too late. Run!"*

But I was already moving. My arms coiled around Ty's waist,

forcing his quaking body against mine. "Ty, I love you!" My lips connected with his, forcing them apart.

For a moment Ty struggled against me, shaking so violently it was hard to keep hold of him. Then I felt a sudden change, quick as a gust of wind. Ty's resistance stalled and his strong hands flew to my cheeks. Our kiss deepened with desperate ferocity as his tongue found mine. The cracking of his bones ceased with a single, full-body convulsion. With a rough scrape of his hands, he released my face to slide them forcefully down my back. They found my hips and his grip tightened before he slammed my pelvis against his. "Say it again."

Finding words between our connected lips and ragged breath, I uttered, "I love you, Ty. I will *always* love you."

The unabated emotion I felt for Ty was suddenly tainted by sickening revulsion. I broke from Ty's lips and flung my arms across my chest, backing away. *Not my freaking feelings.* The emotion was so embedded through me, it was hard to split the two apart. Almost impossible to convince myself that Kendrick's revulsion was not my own.

I looked up. Ty was breathing hard, his face a puzzle of hurt and confusion. "I'm sorry. I didn't mean... It's just..." *How can I tell you that my mind and soul belong to someone else? How could you ever still want me after knowing that?*

"Amelia, what's going on?" Ty demanded. The crippling tremors had released his body, but a light tremble was still visible.

Still I couldn't force my lips to reveal what I knew I needed to say. Not yet. Not when we had barely reunited. Not when I had just tasted the sweetness of his full lips and felt the hard touch of his calloused hands. After everything I had been through, I deserved a moment of blissful happiness, just a few seconds of delusional perfection. There was nothing wrong with that, was there? I wasn't sure. But I needed this almost as much as I needed to breathe. I needed to show Ty how much I wanted and needed him, and how irrefutably I loved him. There was no way to know how he would react to what I would eventually have to reveal. This shared, intimate moment could be our very last. That knowledge alone sent a flood of agitation pumping adrenaline through my core.

I pushed past Kendrick's emotions and darted forward, pressing my body hard-up against Ty's. My free hand caught the back his neck, forcing his lips to meet mine. For the purest moment, Ty kissed me back, lips and body hungry for more. His hands pressed into my back, trapping me against him. Then the revulsion I had so desperately pushed to the back of my mind resurfaced, twisting into total desolation. I knew my time had run out. Even more than that, I realized something with complete and horrific comprehension. Everything I was doing was directly affecting my best friend. He was aware of every single thing I was thinking and feeling. And worst of all, everything I was doing with Ty. In his mind it was like he was himself, pressed against Ty's bare chest while kissing and touching him. In this moment he felt physically sick.

I pulled from Ty for the second time and gripped his forearms. Silently I sent an apology to my best friend. Then I took in a few deep breaths, buying time while an owl hooted from a nearby tree. In the gloom of a cloud-blotted sky, Ty's expression looked more severe, lacking warm emotion. He struggled for level breath. Panicky jitters rose up from my gut, and I gulped. "There's something else you need to know. But you have to promise me you won't run off to kill anyone." It may be Kendrick that I was bound to, but without Caius the bond would never have been created. "Not even Caius."

Ty's hard breathing had begun to slow. He sighed, a long and rattling sound. "I'm not going to like this, am I?"

At the shake of my head, Ty took my hand and led me to the fallen log over the frozen river. He pulled me down next to him. "Okay. I'm as ready as I'll ever be. Let me have it."

I entwined my fingers through his and bit my lip. "I wish I didn't have to tell you this. I wish it wouldn't change us." *Or the way you feel about me*, I thought silently. "But you deserve to know everything." With a long, drawn-out breath in and out, I began. "When Kendrick saved my life, it bound our minds and souls…"

When I had finished talking, Ty sat staring up at the starless, black sky. His expression was set with ground-shattering understanding. For every second he remained mute, a deeper, burdening anxiety filled me. This was more information than any one person should have to endure. More than I could ever expect him to accept. I was bound to Kendrick for all eternity. This was the end of us.

Finally, Ty tilted his head back down. I breathed out, realizing I had been holding my breath the entire time. His eyes didn't meet mine. Instead, they looked down to our entwined fingers. "So, when you kissed me, he felt it? He knew what was happening?"

Surprised that his response wasn't the instant death of our turbulent relationship, I nodded without speaking.

"And you feel his thoughts? You know everything he's thinking too?" I nodded again. "So you know how much he loves you? How much he wants you?"

I wanted to shake my head in denial. But I couldn't lie, not about this. Through the eerie nature of our bond, I could access every conflicted and pure feeling Kendrick held for me. There was no doubt he truly loved me.

Ty glanced up with strained eyes, awaiting my response. I swallowed past the acid rising up my throat. "Yes, I know."

Ty turned his head away and shook his hand free from mine. "And how do you feel about him?"

"I love him too," I whispered. Ty stiffened, fingers pressing into his scarred thighs while hope from Kendrick twined through our bond. My next words rushed. "But not in the way you think. He's my best friend and I would die for him. We will always be connected. And I know my feelings for him will never change."

Ty twisted his head back to me, expression riddled with uncertainty. I collected his hand and clutched it to my heart. "Ty, I'm in love with *you*. Not him."

Deep down Kendrick had known what my heart held. Still, utter misery scarred him, scorching a channel through my core. It was all I could do to keep breathing, to push the pressing weight of Kendrick's emotions down.

"Ty, I know this is too much to accept. I'll totally understand if…"

"No." Ty's quiet but determined voice cut me off. His free hand cupped my neck and he pressed his hot lips to mine. "Don't act like this is the end, like it breaks us. It doesn't. *Nothing* ever could." He peered deep into my eyes, thumb grazing away a single fallen tear. "I love you, Amelia. As long as there is still breath in my body, I will *always* love you."

THANK YOU FOR READING!

Dear Reader,

Thank you for reading *What Lies Inside (Blood Bound Series Book 1)*. If you enjoyed this book please turn to the last page an select a star rating, or if you have a moment to spare, you can leave a review. It doesn't have to be long—one or two sentences would be amazing. The more reviews a book has the more Amazon is willing to put it in front of potential readers. As an indie author, I don't have a big publishing company promoting my work, so every little bit helps and I'd love for my audience to be a part of it. I read every one of my reviews and completely appreciate the thoughts and opinions of all my readers.

http://bit.ly/reviewwli

Thank you, J.L. Myers

**Continue reading for a sneak peek at the Blood Bound Series
Book 2, *Made By Design*.**

AMELIA'S STORY CONTINUES IN...

Made By Design - Blood Bound #2

My eyelids fluttered as my vision cleared. Through the disappearing haze I could see a row of thrones illuminated by the dancing candlelight of a chandelier. The reigning royals occupied them, cloaks draped over formal attire. Muted whispers rose behind me, the sound coming from countless people. Yet there was no scent of human blood. An audience of vampires...

I shot a glance down and my heart stopped. *Elevated on a dais?* I was kneeling, dressed in a white bodice and thin billowy skirt that pooled over my legs.

Approaching footsteps across planked wood drew my sight up.

Panic sliced through my chest, liquefying my insides. Caius stood before me. In one hand he held a scarlet-painted sword, the tip biting the wooden floor like a pointed cane.

What he held in his other hand would have made my mouth water in any other circumstance. It was a gold chalice coated with jewels…and filled with the peppery, metallic aroma of a vampire's Pure Blood.

Caius smiled and held out the chalice. "Take it, Amelia."

Instinctively I went to bolt, to escape whatever heinous act he was about to pull on me. Only my body refused to move. I wasn't in control.

As I fought harder my hands rose against my will. A moment later the chalice was in my grasp.

Stop, I screamed internally, unable to force my lips to move. But it was no use. Inch by slow inch the chalice lifted until its cold edge grazed my lower lip.

There was an instantaneous hush around me and I wavered. Had my scream gotten through? Was I resisting Caius's poison?

The sudden slice of metal cutting air broke the silence. Gasps erupted as Caius's sword arched towards my heart. His eyes gleamed, incredulous and crazed.

"Traitor!"

Get your copy now: http://bit.ly/mbdbb2

CONNECT WITH J.L. MYERS

If you want to stay updated about my latest book releases and get freebies or exclusive review offers, join my VIP list!
Visit : www.jlmyers.com and enter your email address. You can unsubscribe at any time and your email will be kept 100% private.

Come check out my author page on Facebook. I'd love to hear from you:
https://www.facebook.com/author.jlmyers

Come say hi on twitter or Connect with me on Goodreads!
https://twitter.com/authorjlmyers
https://www.goodreads.com/author/show/7178370.J_L_Myers

Don't miss my new releases. Follow me on Amazon & Bookbub
https://www.amazon.com/J.L.-Myers/e/B00DK4P0EO/
https://www.bookbub.com/authors/j-l-myers

ABOUT THE AUTHOR

Jessica L Myers' vivid imagination and quiet demeanor as a child led her to the imaginary worlds of books. Even at a young age, her love for the supernatural was prevalent, with her first loved books being R.L. Stine's *Goosebumps* series. Following that she took an interest in other non-fantasy fiction, including Virginia C. Andrews series *Flowers in the Attic*.

In her teen years, Jessica spent many school hours writing poetry and dark short stories and took up sketching some of the terrifying things that came from the graphic night terrors she'd grown up with.

As an adult and after meeting the love of her life, Jessica got married and started a small construction business with her husband. With the birth of her son, Jessica suffered PPD and found escape in her books and their fantasy landscapes. It was during this time that her need to write flourished. In 2009 the decision was made and the first words to her YA novel *What Lies Inside* were written.

When Jessica isn't immersed in writing about extraordinary characters with dangerous and deadly obstacles to overcome, she likes to spend time with her two kids and husband, curl up with a good book, or watch anything and everything supernatural.

Contact J.L. directly:
www.jlmyers.com

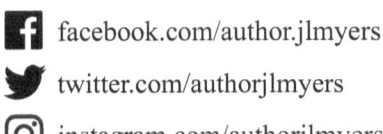

facebook.com/author.jlmyers

twitter.com/authorjlmyers

instagram.com/authorjlmyers

ACKNOWLEDGMENTS

〜

If not for the endless support and encouragement of my family and friends, this book mightn't have spun full-circle to meet its culmination. Thank you all so much for keeping me sane while stoking the kindled fire that was originally lit in my belly.

Special thanks to my husband for offering inspiration and problem-solving ideas when I ran into any inescapable dead-ends. Your support and advice mean the world to me, even when it was to take a step back and have a break once in a while.

www.ingramcontent.com/pod-product-compliance
Lightning Source LLC
Chambersburg PA
CBHW051537250626
47157CB00001B/81